THE LEGEND THAT WAS
EARTH

JAMES P. HOGAN

THE LEGEND THAT WAS EARTH

A Baen Books Original

Baen Publishing Enterprises
P.O. Box 1403
Riverdale, NY 10471
www.baen.com

ISBN: 0-671-31840-3

Cover art by Dru Blair

First paperback printing, October 2001

Library of Congress Cataloging-in-Publication Number: 00-042926

Distributed by Simon & Schuster
1230 Avenue of the Americas
New York, NY 10020

Typeset by Brilliant Press
Printed in the United States of America

Dedication

To Irish cousins;

Willie and Pat; Sister Eucharia and Mary;
Eileen.

And the fond memory of Rita.

Acknowledgments

The help and advice of the following is gratefully acknowledged:

Betsey Wilcox, USAF, for help with military logistics and organization; Robert De Kinder, for information on munitions and obscurants; Steve Dinowitz, for his fascinating insights to Relativity alternatives; Charles Ginenthal, for new ways of thinking about cosmology; Tina & Gordon Grant, for help with local geography in California; Rainer Brockerhoff in Brazil, for advice on local customs and language usage; Preston Richey, for sharing some of his perceptions of China; Sandra T. Hogan (not related), Queensland, Australia, for a wealth of information on local scenery and geography.

PROLOGUE

Sunday was cloudy but warm in Washington, D.C. The crowd below the Capitol steps, extending westward along the Mall, numbered over ten thousand and was still growing. Although many were colorfully arrayed in summer garb with a sprinkling of coats and jackets, its mood was ugly. Banners displayed above the forest of raised arms, fists punching skyward in unison, proclaimed contingents from individual states. The most highly represented were those like California, Texas, Illinois, heavily dependent on advanced-technology industries. Other banners being waved in the foreground before the news cameras panning over the scene protested: ALIEN PAYOFFS MEAN EARTH LAYOFFS; another: NO TO FARDEN SELLOUT; and: DEMAND TRADE CONTROL. To one side near the front, a black female agitator in red leather and braids was leading a group chanting militantly: *"Fuck you!/Where's ours too?"* Riot police looked on from the sides, with vehicles and reserves being held back on Canal Street and Louisiana Avenue.

From the podium at the top of the steps, flanked by grim-faced figures in suits and a few military uniforms behind a cordon of police armed with shields and batons, the speaker who had been repeatedly interrupted leaned toward the microphone again.

"Will you people hear me out? . . . Is a little bit of common decency and courtesy too much to ask? . . . What I'm saying is that things are not the way you think. The contraction of some businesses and industries is natural and inevitable when two diverse cultures come into contact. It spells even greater opportunities opening up in other areas—areas where the things we're better at will be uniquely favored."

Somebody with a bullhorn replied from among the crowd. *"That's bullshit."*

The voice of the police commissioner in charge of crowd control came over loudspeakers set up on pylons: *"THIS IS THE LAST TIME. THERE WILL BE NO FURTHER WARNINGS."*

The speaker resumed. *"To suggest that our economy is being sold off piecemeal is an emotionally motivated misrepresentation of the facts. The facts are—"*

"Tell it to the Bolivians," the bullhorn responded.

Somebody at the front, a TV camera trained directly on him, raised both arms wide to draw attention and shouted, "Why won't Farden come out and speak for himself? We know he's in there. What's he afraid of?"

"Senator Farden is—"

"Selling us out," the bullhorn completed. A roar went up to endorse the judgment. The speaker at the podium looked in the direction of the senior police and Internal Security Service officers watching and

shook his head helplessly. The commissioner nodded to an aide, who gave orders into a hand phone. From among the police massed on the lawns bordering Independence Avenue came a helmeted snatch squad in gas masks. Flailing batons and using their shields as battering rams, they plowed through the crowd toward the spot where surveillance cameras had located the bullhorn. Some of the crowd closed protectively around the target, while others assailed the snatch team with bottles and other missiles. Reinforcements moved in; figures began falling, others retreating, and within seconds mêlées were breaking out across the entire scene. An angry surge pressed back the cordon guarding the Capitol steps. Above, the police helicopter that had been circling came in lower. The commissioner signaled, and security agents began herding the speaker and entourage back toward the doors into the building. Armored cars with mesh-protected windows nosed out from the side streets. Through the rising clamor, the flat *plops* sounded of gas grenades bursting where the clashes were fiercest, followed by figures falling back, coughing and retching amid clouds of white vapor.

Senator Joel Farden from Virginia watched darkly from a window in one of the rooms of the Capitol. He had said there was no point trying to reason with a crowd in that mood. People with no concepts beyond immediate gratification or waiting passively for a better investment to pay off would never be possessors of anything worthwhile to bargain with. Therefore, inevitably, they were the first to lose out in any reshuffle. There was nothing anyone could do; it was the way things were and had always been. The exploitation they complained about was in their genes, just as it was in those of others to come out on top. Trying to deny what everyone had to know deep down was obvious could only result in the denial and rage that they were seeing. Now the mess would take years, probably, to work itself out. Then somebody else with delusions would start demanding fairness for all, and the pattern would go on as it always had. Unless those with the power to do so changed the system. Orderliness and discipline. The Hyadeans had the right idea.

Below the window, knots of demonstrators broke through the police cordon and started scrambling up the steps toward the building. A squad that had been kept in the rear moved forward, equipped with back-mounted devices connected to nozzles. They resembled flame throwers but fired a white stream that turned into an expanding foam engulfing the oncoming rioters. In moments, the foam congealed into an elastic, adhesive mass, inside which the forms of victims could be seen struggling ineffectually. Those immediately behind fell back, while howls of outrage came from farther back. On both sides of the Mall violence intensified as groups trying to flee the area ran into police reserves moving in. An intense, low-pitched drone that seemed to fill the air came from outside, rattling the window, vibrating the structure of the building, and churning Farden's stomach even at that distance, making him feel mildly dizzy and nauseated. Across the Mall, figures were screaming and clutching their ears, others doubling over and vomiting. A hand gripped his shoulder. He turned. It was Purlow, the ISS security agent assigned for Farden's personal protection.

"I'm sorry, Senator, but speeches are over for today. The whole situation's deteriorating. We're getting you and the general out early. The flyer is waiting now. This way please, sir."

Farden hesitated briefly, then nodded. He followed

Purlow back through the suite of rooms, across a marbled hall, and down a stairway to one of the entrances on the far side of the building. A secretary was waiting with his briefcase and topcoat among the group of officials, uniformed officers, and several Hyadeans in the vestibule. Farden took them from her just as Lieutenant General Meakes appeared with his own small personal retinue. Meakes was another figure that the agitators had demonized and the mobs loved to hate. Farden had never really seen the connection, since Meakes didn't have a financial angle, stayed out of politics, and had always confined himself to Army matters. But since when had truth or concern about character defamation troubled political terrorists when they saw an opportunity?

Edmund Kovansky, from the White House staff, seemed to be organizing things. "You were right, Joel," he said as Farden approached. "This was ill-conceived from the start. I guess we'll be having a moratorium and plan-of-action meeting out at Overly later." Farden would be going back to Overly Park, the Maryland estate where he was staying while visiting Washington. It was owned by a financier called Eric York, who was part of Farden's social and business circle. There was little gratification in being told that just at this moment. Not bothering to reply, Farden stepped forward in the direction of the doorway, following Meakes and another officer who it seemed would be traveling with him. Kovansky caught him with a gesture indicating two of the Hyadeans. "And there's a last-minute addition," Kovansky said. "These two want to go with you, if that's okay. They have business with Eric."

Farden paused long enough to return a shrug. "Sure. Why not?" It was their flyer, after all.

Surrounded by a security escort, the party left the

building and walked briskly across the open area of grass and trees separating the Capitol from the Supreme Court and Library of Congress, which had been blocked off by police barricades. The Hyadean flyer was waiting among an assortment of official vehicles and several black-painted ISS helicopters. Dull silver, about the size of a typical hotel courtesy bus, it had the form of a flattened ellipsoid blending into stub wings toward the stern, with a tail fin and several streamlined nacelles and bulges. There were no crew stations, operation being fully automatic, and no nozzles or visible propulsion unit. Farden climbed the steps unfolding down over the port wing root and entered behind Meakes and the other officer, with the two Hyadeans following. The interior was typically Hyadean: stark and utilitarian, with seats and decor of uniform gray making some concession to comfort, but beyond that not a hint of pattern, contrast, or ornamentation to relieve the drabness. Hyadean minds just didn't work that way.

The occupants settled themselves in; moments later, the door closed soundlessly, and the vehicle lifted off. One of the Hyadeans said something, and two of the cabin's upper wall panels became transparent to admit a tinted view of the cloud bank enlarging and taking on detail as the flyer climbed; at the same time, a screen at the forward end activated to present a downward-looking view of the turmoil among the crowds along the east end of the Mall and the surrounding streets.

Farden studied the two aliens in a detached kind of way as they peered at the screen—they had been around long enough, and he had seen enough of them by now, not to be unduly curious. They were tall and blockish in build, with square-cut features like the heroes of old-time comic strips, giving their faces a squashed look, and skin color ranging from purple to light blue-gray. Their generally humanoid form had caused consternation among scientific ranks when they first came to Earth, because according to the then prevailing theories such similarity resulting from separate evolutionary processes unfolding in isolation shouldn't have been possible. The matter had been one of indifference to Farden, who had never paid much attention to scientific theories anyway, and as far as he knew it still wasn't settled. Their hair came in all manner of hues, the two present on this occasion having glossy black showing blue highlights in one case, and a dull coppery red in the other, both trimmed in the standard Hyadean manner. And both wore the familiar tunic-like garb, plain in color, one drab green, the other brown, purely functional, devoid of decoration or appeal to aesthetic styling.

They exchanged utterances in their own language. Then the black-haired one spoke down toward his breast pocket. A voice replied in Hyadean, but including recognizably the words "very long." Hyadeans carried a kind of pocket Artificial Intelligence that acted as a secretary and librarian, and could help them with language translation and other matters. Terrans called the device a "veebee," standing for voxbox. The Hyadean explained to the three Terrans:

"My companion is not here, at Earth, for very long. The ways are new and strange. At Chryse, people acting like that would be . . ." He consulted his veebee again. "Unthinkable." Chryse was the Hyadeans' home world, a planet of the hitherto unnamed star Amaris, in the vicinity of the constellations Hyades and the Pleiades, in the sign of Taurus.

"That word tends to suggest disapproval," Meakes commented. "That he doesn't agree."

The Hyadean who had spoken conversed briefly with the red-headed one. "He does not approve. He asks how leaders can function."

"Tell him we agree on that," Farden said, at the same time praying inwardly that this stunted attempt at conversation wouldn't endure all through the flight.

"One reason we are here is that we educate . . ." (the veebee interjected something) "to educate Earth in organizing a system that will avoid such things. That way means wealth and peace for all. As is true for Hyadean worlds."

Meakes nodded. "I'll say amen to that."

"Excuse me. I am not familiar with 'amen' in this context," the veebee's voice said from the black-haired Hyadean's breast pocket.

"It means . . . True? Truly?" Meakes looked at Farden and the other Army officer inquiringly. They returned shrugs. "Anyhow, I agree with that too," he said.

"Thanks. Noted," the veebee acknowledged.

The black-haired Hyadean waved to indicate the interior of the vehicle. "And we will make Terrans into better scientists, so maybe one day you build craft like these too." What most people considered "tact" wasn't exactly the aliens' strongest point. When they felt superior or considered themselves to be at an advantage in some respect, they made sure to let everyone know. Farden nodded noncommittally. The exchange continued bravely for a minute or so more and then died, and the occupants lapsed into talk in lowered tones with their own kind.

Farden leaned back against the rubbery headrest and thought over what his position would be later at the meeting Kovansky had alluded to, in the light of the day's events. At least the seats were of alien proportions, which was an improvement over a lot of traveling accommodations that he had endured. Another reason for preferring to use Hyadean vessels whenever possible was that the on-board defenses were fast and accurate enough to stop any Terran-produced missile before it got closer than ten miles, or a ground-launched shot from immediately below within a second of firing. With political terrorists in the U.S. taking on the regular military now, and acquiring all kinds of weapons, one couldn't take too many precautions. . . .

Unfortunately, the bolt of plasma fired from below when the flyer was twelve miles north of the city came from a weapon that wasn't Terran, and the radars on Hyadean vessels fitted for Earth duty were designed only to look for missiles. It hit the flyer dead center, vaporizing it instantly.

CHAPTER ONE

Roland Cade stood on the boat dock at the rear of his
waterfront villa on an inlet at Newport Beach, taking a
moment off from the preparations inside the house to
enjoy the cool air and admire the embers of a flaming
California sunset. Lights were beginning to show from
the other homes across the narrow waterway and among
the moored boats, reflecting off the barely rippling surface. A mild breeze brought the aroma of steaks being
barbecued somewhere. On the inland side, clouds of star-
lings were rising and wheeling in their last sortie of the
day. For some people, life was good.

Warren Edmonds, the skipper of Cade's ninety-
foot motor yacht *Sassy Lady*, appeared on the
foredeck and came down to join Cade on the dock.
He was wirily muscular, with lean features that a
shock of black hair receding at the temples seemed
to throw into hard-lined relief. Edmonds had

managed boats large and small, corporate and private, from Seattle to San Diego. He ran a number of enterprises of his own—some of which were quasi-legal at best—which Cade didn't ask about, hence working for Cade suited him. And Cade's numerous legal contacts and acquaintances who owed him favors could be useful at times.

"Everything set and standing by, if we decide to go," he told Cade. Given the balmy condition of the evening, Cade was considering moving the party out onto the water later if the general mood so inclined.

"Did Henry bring out the extra case of Chardonnay?"

"Yes, it's in the cooler."

"No sudden changes expected in the weather?"

"I checked about fifteen minutes ago. It's gonna be calm like this all night, somewhere in the low sixties. Maybe a little cloud tomorrow. Nothing that'll change your day."

Cade showed his palms. "The gods are smiling, Warren."

"I guess we must have done something right lately," Edmonds sighed in a way that said he couldn't think what, but to make the best of it. "Did their flight get out on time—with all the trouble in Washington earlier?"

"The Web said it did when Luke checked, just before he left to go meet them. I don't think Andrews was affected. Vrel would have let us know by now if there were any changes. . . ." Cade looked back as Henry's voice called from the house to see if he was out there. "Uh-uh. You can't hide anywhere. It sounds as if all's in order out here. Carry on, Chief."

"You bet."

Cade walked back along the short path past shrubbery and flowers losing their colors in the fading light.

The white-haired figure of Henry, the house steward, wearing a maroon jacket and tie, was peering from the doorway of the glass-shuttered patio. "Norman Schnyder and his associate are here—Anita Lloyd. Julia and Neville are talking to them now. Also, the catering people have started setting up." That was in case Cade wanted to check anything personally before it got too late to change. Henry had been with Cade long enough to know his ways.

They crossed the patio and passed through a sun lounge with cane furniture and potted plants to the central area of the house, where staff from the catering company handling the buffet were arranging tablecloths and unpacking dishes. While Henry bustled off to attend to something else, Cade ran an eye over the linen, satisfying himself that it was properly pleated and pressed, examined the china and silverware for quality, and looked inside the ice chest containing the marinated crab claws and Oysters Rockefeller to verify that the serving shells were real and not ceramic. Finding nothing amiss, he contented himself with straightening the slightly crooked bow tie of one of the servers, winked at him with a mild "Tch, tch," and went through to the sitting area of paneling and leather upholstery surrounding the bar. Neville Baxter, a businessman from New Zealand, who had arrived early, stopping by at the party to say his farewells before going back in the next few days, was sprawled in one of the easy chairs, a foot crossed over the other knee. He was florid-faced, beefy, and jovial, tonight sporting a lightweight cream jacket and scarlet crimson shirt, open-necked with a riotous silk cravat at the neck. Norman Schnyder and Anita sat nursing drinks on the couch opposite him. Julia must have gone off somewhere to attend to some detail—ever the conscientious hostess.

"Here's the man!" Baxter said, waving across as Cade came in.

Cade helped himself to a Jamesons Irish from the bar and joined them. "Hi, Anita . . . Norman. So how are things? I don't detect any signs of incipient poverty."

"Norman showed up in that new Lamborghini I'm told he's been talking about for a hundred years," Baxter told Cade. "It makes me feel really glad that I don't pay any of that firm's bills."

"Got to be able to catch the ambulances," Schnyder said, sipping his drink. He looked suave and opulent, with hair showing silver at the sides of his tanned face, a dark suit with narrow pinstripe, and expensively glittering tie clip and links. Anita Lloyd, in her early thirties, with auburn hair styled into chic, forward-sweeping points, wearing a sleeveless navy dress with elbow-length satin gloves, had just banked her first million the last time Cade talked to her. They were senior partner and associate respectively of an LA law firm that had been seeing some good years. Henry always got his terms precisely right.

Anita eyed Cade's five-eleven frame in white dinner jacket with black tie. He kept athletically trim at thirty-six, and had wavy brown hair combed back at the sides above an angular face with narrow nose, easy-smiling mouth, and eyes that never quite lost a puckish glint. "You seem to be bearing the burdens of life pretty well yourself, Roland," she remarked.

"Which just goes to show the wisdom of pure thoughts, clean living, and faith in the Lord."

"But be sure to keep a good lawyer in your back pocket all the same," Schnyder said.

"You mean like something to break the glass, in case of an emergency?" Cade quipped, making a toasting gesture.

"Don't joke. You never know. We had a bar in town sued the other week for serving a guy who had a liver condition and *knew* he couldn't take it. Would you believe that? I mean, what are they supposed to do—check everybody's medical records now?"

Julia appeared in the archway to the front part of the house, calling something back to Henry about a rose tree by the front door. She saw Cade, picked up a glass of champagne that she had left on a side table, and came over, perching herself on a couch-arm next to where he was standing and resting her free hand lightly on his shoulder. Julia was Cade's business partner and significant other in life, having moved in to share the house a little over a year before. She was tall, lithe, and red-haired, with a feline elegance of movement that exuded sexuality. Tonight she had enhanced the effect with an ankle-length dress of body-clinging moiré that altered in the light between bottle-green and sage-yellow, set off by an emerald bracelet and earrings. Her former husband ran a couple of night clubs that the right people in southern California frequented, which meant that she knew a lot of names that were worth knowing, making her a natural for Cade to get attached to. Knowing the right people was what Cade's business was all about.

She tasted her drink and ran a questioning eye over the company. "So, what problems of the world are we putting right tonight?"

"Have you seen Norman's new wheels yet?" Anita asked.

"Yes. And I feel sick. Why do you think I'm wearing green?" Julia nudged Cade pointedly. "I want one."

"Sounds like I'd better check with Simon and see what our money's in," Cade replied.

"Well, I hope you don't have too much of it in computers or electronics—or anything high-tech, by the sound of it," Baxter said. "Norman was saying just before you came in that the bottom's falling out across the board. The Hyadeans are going to be flooding the market here with better stuff at prices you can't even think about."

Schnyder was already nodding. "Their production is all run by AIs—totally automatic. Matching what we use here costs them practically nothing. It's like beads. A lot of industries are in trouble."

Cade tried not to let things like that affect him. It was the way life was. Things changed; you couldn't stop them. If you were smart you adapted and let yourself go with the flow. It wasn't his place to protect those who chose to stay in places where they were going to lose out. "There's a lot of opposition out there," he said. "That has to have some moderating effect, surely. The government isn't going to just let it happen."

Schnyder shook his head. "Forget it, Roland. The bills will go through. Too much of Congress is in for a piece of the action. We're talking big bucks here. They're not going to lose out."

Cade and Julia looked at each other, and both made a face. "So what should we be buying into?" Julia asked, looking back.

"You really wanna know?" Schnyder invited.

"Sure. That's why I asked."

"Navajo blankets and sand paintings. Porcelains and sculptures. Hand-built cabinets and carvings—like from that little firm in Santa Monica that they did the show on last week. Did you see it?"

"No, I don't think so."

"Native talents," Anita said. "The Hyadeans don't have anything to compare."

"Is it really the way some people say?" Julia sounded incredulous.

"We've got someone coming here tonight who's been saying the same thing," Cade told the group. "Damien Philps—an export dealer in that kind of thing to Chryse and the other Hyadean worlds for a few years now. Says it's going to grow like crazy."

"Then you should listen to him," Schnyder urged. "It's getting to be a rage with them. You wouldn't believe the prices I've heard for some of the things that went there."

"Want to buy into some totem poles?" Cade asked Julia. He looked away as Henry appeared once more from the depths of the house. "Yes, Henry?"

"Luke just called. He's at LAX now, with Dee. The aircraft has been cleared for landing. With traffic as it is, he says they'll be here in about an hour."

"Tell the caterers to start setting out the food in thirty minutes," Cade instructed. "But let's have a few appetizers out here in the meantime."

CHAPTER TWO

"Side-panel to view mode," Vrel told the veebee, which he had laid on the tray at the front of his seat's armrest along with the screenpad he had been using during the flight. The veebee passed the order on to the control system of the Hyadean staff transport descending over the Terran city of Los Angeles, and the part of the wall alongside became transparent. Vrel rested his chin on a hand and stared out at the carpet of horizon-to-horizon lights. Of the dozen-odd other Hyadeans around him in the cabin, some were talking in murmurs, others wrapped in their own thoughts. Krossig, the anthropologist, was reading. Orzin had dozed through the flight, after a busy schedule in Washington as an official observer assessing Terran reactions to further moves in Hyadean–U.S. cooperation. Hyadean policy was to concentrate on the United States as the focus of Terran political and economic influence.

As with all the cities he had seen here, the conception and layout showed little regard for efficiency or logic, although Terrans were not incapable of such qualities when it suited them. The failure to strike a better balance between building out and building up multiplied travel distances enormously. Trusting to manually controlled vehicles in this kind of traffic density brought appalling problems that the Terrans didn't deny, yet they made no serious attempt to do anything about them. Vrel sometimes thought that the chaotic daily sorties along the Interstates might provide some kind of ritual combat that their adversity-conditioned psyches needed. And they had no concept of segregating north-south traffic flows from east-west on different levels with connecting ramps, with the result that everything was squeezed onto a two-dimensional grid where all movement one way had to be stopped for half the time at every intersection. He wondered what they'd have thought of a computer chip designed that way, with all the wires on one plane, and switches to allow current through a crossover one way or the other at any time only.

But things like electronics and optronics weren't really Vrel's line. A political economist and social commentator, he had first come to Earth almost six (Terran) years ago now, with several trips back and forth to Chryse in the interim. And even after that time, he still found himself more than occasionally bewildered by this intoxicating world with its wild extremes of ecology and climate: plunging chasms and slabs of crust thrown up into snow-topped mountains, and stupefying proliferation of every form of life imaginable to the Hyadean mind—and then some. And to crown all of it, this volatile, quarrelsome race of pinks and yellows and browns and black, short and slender in form, yet curiously appropriate as the culminating expression of the unruliness and vivacity that characterized the whole planet.

At first, Vrel had been bemused by the diversity of governing systems: money-based, land-based, hereditary, military, planned and chaotic, popular choice or authoritarian; by the clashes of ideologies and traditions, spawning creeds and sects of every description, and mixtures of all of them which not even the Terrans seemed to understand. That was the usual Hyadean reaction. It was as if the only discernible universal attribute was the determination not to let anything be universal, leaving such authorities as existed virtually powerless to channel collective energies into achieving the kind of planetary efficiency that could have yielded ten times the productivity with a tenth the effort and spared all the grief and chaos entirely. Weren't the events that had occurred today in Washington illustration enough?

A year ago, Vrel would have thought so unhesitatingly. Now, after spending the last six months at the Hyadean West Coast Trade and Cultural Mission in Los Angeles, he was no longer so sure. Earth was an exotic planet, its surface fresh and young, sculpted only recently by catastrophic forces that affect planetary systems from time to time, and which Terran scientists, for the most part—until the arrival of the Hyadeans—had ignored or failed to understand. This made Earth unlike any of the other worlds to which the Hyadeans had so far spread, including Chryse, whose surfaces were old, shaped over eons by processes of erosion and leveling that rendered them by comparison weary-looking and drab.

The Terrans too were products of those same upheavals which not long ago had reformed, revitalized, and enriched their planet. Vrel was finding that their capacity for seeking fulfillment and finding "meaning" to their existence in ways that went beyond the obvious aim of attaining tangible benefits—which in the early days had been so baffling—now intrigued him. Could their astonishing intuitiveness and creativity, which both enabled them to soar into realms of fancy that no Hyadean mind would conceive, and at the same time wrought havoc with their sciences, represent a state of being that was "closer" to the origins of the forces that drove life, just as they themselves were closer to the creative impetus that triggered the last epoch of their evolution? If so, then maybe there were things the Hyadeans might stand to learn from Earth before they got too zealous about importing their own ideas and social system. Things the Hyadeans themselves had once possessed and forgotten, perhaps?

The veebee beeped to attract attention, then announced, "Incoming call. From Luke, who will be meeting the flight. He says to tell you Dee is with him."

"Put it through." Vrel smiled as he picked up the screenpad. Luke's face appeared: elongated Terran features, black hair, and the tuft of "beard" that some Terrans cultivated—Hyadeans didn't have facial hair. "Hello, Luke," Vrel acknowledged in English. He had been working at it assiduously through his stay and was as proficient as any Hyadean. "And Dee's there?" The image shifted for a moment to show Dee waving, then returned to Luke. Vrel thought of Luke as Roland Cade's second-in-command as well as being a personal friend of Cade and Julia—usually around to make sure things got done, generally a part of the house and business. On Chryse, senior political and military figures relied on somebody like that, who was more than just an assigned administrator, to manage the detailed aspects of their lives and channel the right information to them.

"We're out on the field and will pick you up right off the plane," Luke said. "There's a car from the mission here too. I guess somebody there has decided to pass on the party and made their own arrangements."

The others in the cabin had been alerted by the cabin indicators to prepare for landing and were collecting their belongings together. Krossig would be going back to the house, naturally. So would Erya, the female involved with education, who was on her way back to Chryse and would be joining one of the orbiting Hyadean ships via the spaceport in Brazil. She was the type who could overcome Hyadean reserve sufficiently to enjoy a little unofficial entertainment Earth-style before returning to her familiar world, where everything had to be as stipulated and directed. Shayle, on the other hand, returning to her administrative post in the South American enclave, was always officious and disapproving of the irregular. She would shun any suggestion of letting standards slip and go back to the mission. Orzin, a figure of some authority, maintained an outwardly correct manner, but Vrel had seen hints that it concealed a different self that wasn't above a little off-limits relaxation when the occasion permitted. The rest of the group were either returning from Washington to their posts in South America or going on to Chryse. Vrel didn't know them well enough to guess who would be going where. Given Orzin's lead, most of them might opt for Cade's party, if for no greater reason than curiosity. Three sitting together, upright and proper, would no doubt be going back to the mission with Shayle. Somehow, Vrel couldn't imagine Terrans making such an issue out of an invitation to attend a party. Maybe he was starting to think a little bit like one.

The transport landed, and the Hyadeans disembarked via a covered escalator brought up to the door. Shayle and the three that Vrel had picked out departed at once in a Terran automobile, registering disapproval by declining to say a word. Luke and Dee were standing in front of a limousine-quality minibus. Vrel introduced the remaining Hyadeans except Krossig, whom they already knew because he worked with Vrel in LA. Dee had shoulder-length blond hair, fringed at the front, and was wearing a light wrap over a stretchy orange dress. She slipped an arm through Vrel's as they began walking around the bus. He had to suppress an impulse to flinch at the public display, reminding himself that he was back among Terrans now. A week of conforming to Hyadean protocols had reawakened his social reflexes. One of the arrivals nudged a companion and raised his eyebrows, not a little enviously. Terran women had a reputation among Hyadeans for being sensuous. Vrel pretended not to notice, resisting the conflicting urge to put on a little showiness. Opportunistic exhibitions of good fortune or superiority were considered bad manners here.

"Good flight?" Dee asked him.

"Just fine."

"I was a bit worried . . . with all that trouble on the news this afternoon."

"It was ugly. But we weren't really involved. How's Roland?"

"Oh, he never changes. Going with the flow."

That was a new one. Vrel checked with his veebee. It returned the best it could come up with. "He's on the river?" Vrel repeated, looking puzzled.

Dee laughed. "It means living life as it comes. Not fighting it. Making the best of whatever comes along."

"That sounds like Roland," Vrel agreed.

"One day you'll learn how not to rely on a computer all the time and develop your instincts instead," Dee told him. They climbed into the minibus. There were all-round leather seats, a screen, and a bar. Background music was playing of a kind that Vrel had learned to identify as strings. Classical Terran music had a big following among Hyadeans.

"Who was the composer of this piece?" Vrel asked the veebee in Hyadean.

"Antonio Vivaldi. 1678 to 1741. Born in Venice, Italy."

"And did you get the thing about the river. . . . What was it again?"

"Going with the flow."

"Oh, right. It means . . ." Vrel frowned and thought back. "Not fighting life. Taking things as they come. Is that right?"

"Close enough," the veebee replied.

CHAPTER THREE

Other Hyadeans had arrived direct from the Trade and Cultural Mission by the time Luke and Dee returned with the party from the airport. A number of unattached Terran women, all of them attractive, stylish, sophisticated, and sociable, had also begun arriving.

To most Terrans, Hyadeans came across as rather conformist and image-conscious. From what they were told or saw on Hyadean productions carried by Terran media, life on Chryse and its colonized worlds seemed overstructured and regimented. An example was the rigidity of rules governing dealings between the sexes, which by most Terran standards came across as stiff and prudish. Partly in consequence, Hyadeans found Earth a mysterious, exciting place, where sensual indulgence and freedom of expression which at best would have been frowned upon back home were regarded as normal. Biological nature being apparently much the same in at least the nearby regions of the galaxy, it followed that more than a few Hyadeans would develop a taste for, or curiosity to sample, at least, a little of the risqué that Earth's cultural phantasmagoria had to offer.

Of course, it wouldn't do for visiting officials and other prominent individuals to be seen actively pursuing or even expressing interest in such diversions. But if the price was right, most things could be arranged with discretion. That was where people like Roland Cade came in. Cade was a "fixer." He knew the right people. If a Hyadean wanted to send a small package of coffee, spices, perfumes, a selection of alcoholic bracers, perhaps, to impress the folks back home, where such things tended to be illegal or restricted, Cade had a contact who did business with the Hyadean in charge of loading the surface lifters going up from their spaceport at Xuchimbo in western Brazil. Or if one was tempted to get away from routine for an evening to eat a dinner Terran-style with fresh animal meat (practically unheard of) cooked in unimaginable sauces, washed down with delicious fermented plant juices, while listening to the music they composed spontaneously, and afterward maybe get to dance with a Terran girl (body contact!)—Cade could set something up in places from California to New York, or beyond that refer you to somebody in Russia, Algeria, Britain, or Japan. For a particular kind of souvenir of one's stay on Earth, or for importing high-demand Terran creations, or to find an outlet on Earth for spare Hyadean production capacity that could be made profitable, Cade had the contacts. And naturally, everyone paid for the favor. Sometimes Cade thought that it was impossible for a Hyadean and a Terran to meet without money falling out of the sky for him somewhere. Indeed, it seemed that for him the phrase had come true literally.

He stood with Michael Blair on one side of the buffet area in the center of the house, catching strands of conversations. The Hyadeans who were new to this had at first stood together, males and females alike in their plain, tunic-like suits, sipping fruit juices and surreptitiously popping the pills they were told they needed to guard against untamed Terran germs and food prepared by suspect methods—the Hyadean authorities were tyrannical over health care. Now, at last, they were livening up: sampling the seafood dishes, sipping from the glasses that the wine steward had been told to move liberally, and beginning to mingle. There was a hot food table with roasts of beef, pork, and ham for the more daring. Julia was doing her usual great job as hostess, prying the more stodgy out of chairs and corners where they had taken refuge, steering together the right introductions, and igniting conversations with the élan of an arsonist loose in an oil refinery. The two lawyers and a couple of Hyadeans were talking to George Jansing, who was making a fortune contracting Terran software design skills to the Hyadeans—and also taking the opportunity to show off some Hyadean that he had learned. With them was Clara Norburn, tall, lean, raven-haired, from the state governor's office, her sights firmly set on the opportunities for social and professional advancement that political visibility offered. "I'd like to redirect more of California's technical talent in that direction," Cade heard her telling them. "It sounds really profitable."

"Five times what you'd get from the home market," Jansing said.

"It's this human thing that you call flair," one of the Hyadeans explained. "Our machine designs do the job and are solid. But they are never what you'd describe as brilliant. I have examined some of the tricks and shortcuts that Terran programmers come up with. They astound me."

Dee and Vrel's precedent had encouraged several of the other Hyadeans to try nervous lines with the Terran girls—becoming less nervous as the girls and the wine steward assiduously plied their respective trades.

"I have a wife back on Chryse," a Hyadean told a brunette in purple and pink. "But she doesn't really . . ." He questioned a veebee in his pocket. "Understand me."

"Gee," the brunette said to her companion. "Now there's one I haven't heard before."

"You see, Roland—the same genes everywhere," Blair said to Cade. Blair was some kind of scientist involved with behavior and biology, formerly with the University of California. Nowadays, he conducted private research, a lot of it at the Hyadean mission, trying to learn more of the aliens' sciences, since just about everything he had believed before they showed up had turned out to be wrong. He had been explaining to Cade that the reason why human and Hyadean forms were so alike, confounding traditional ideas of evolution, was that the genetic programs that directed the building of life forms didn't originate on planets at all, but arrived there as space-borne microbes. Planets were simply assembly stations where cues provided by the local environments triggered the programs to express themselves differently. So, similar environments would produce similar collections of shapes and forms. Earth's was more diverse, hence richer in diversity, that was all.

"So where do these programs get written in the first place?" Cade asked.

"They don't know."

"Do they have any theories about it?"

"Not really. They've never really thought about it."

Cade turned his head incredulously. "You're kidding!" Although no scientist, he assumed that would be the obvious question.

Blair motioned with his glass. He looked the academic, with graying hair brushed to the side and parted, metal-framed spectacles, and a rubbery, expressive face that made a joke of any attempt to conceal his mood. As a concession to the occasion he had donned a dark jacket with tie and slacks. But he could have added an evening shave while he was at it. "That's the amazing thing. Their minds just aren't like that. They don't make big theories that try to explain everything. They just look at the evidence that's there and stick to that."

"So is that how come they got here, but we didn't get there?" Cade queried.

"Maybe that's what it needs—just accepting the facts and not trying to go beyond them. They don't have religion either. That's another thing about us that fascinates them. Krossig says Hyadeans could never have come up with anything like that. But they see a lot of what we think is science as being not very different. We get wrapped up in our own inventions and then convince ourselves that what we see is really out there."

Neville Baxter sauntered by, telling a joke to a petite blonde in blue who was clinging to his arm and looking appreciative. ". . . and God said, 'It doesn't cost anything. It's free.' So Moses said, 'I'll take ten!' " He nudged Cade in passing, as if to say, *See, even fuddy-duddy, middle-age-spreading New Zealanders can make out okay too.*

The group that included Norman Schnyder had got

onto the subject of Terran industries folding because of cheap Hyadean imports, and the increasingly militant political opposition movement. "I've never understood why we need those markets," one of the Hyadeans commented, maybe trying to be diplomatic.

"Oh, I'd have thought it's obvious," Schnyder said. "To earn currency here that can be reinvested in land. That's where the big payoffs are going to be. Industrial trading is just the key to the door."

"Isn't that what the guerrilla war in South America is all about . . . ?" Anita Lloyd began, then faltered as she realized it wasn't a good topic to bring up in polite Terran-Hyadean company. Cade rescued her by stepping closer and moving things along.

"You're bound to have clashes when different kinds of people meet, and there's change. But it always works out better for everyone in the long run. The hotheads will get hurt, but they bring it on themselves. There's nothing you can do." He smiled as Julia came over with a fresh drink for him, and slid an arm around her waist. "The woman I used to be married to was a hothead like that," he told the group. "Not accepting change; thinking she could stop it. Well, she's not here anymore, and all of us are. That should say something." He wasn't quite sure himself what it should say, he realized; but it sounded good.

Damien Philps, the arts and crafts dealer that Cade had mentioned to Schnyder earlier, was listening to Erya, the Hyadean educationist who was on her way back to Chryse, marveling at the powers of human creativity. Vrel and Dee were with them along with Wyvex, a colleague of Vrel's from the mission, who was currently collecting information on Terran art forms to satisfy the interest being generated back home. He was tall, even for a Hyadean, and had dark rust hair with orange streaks, cropped fairly short to a central point. Hair styling was one of the few modes of personal expression that Hyadeans seemed to permit themselves—maybe as a consequence of the wide natural variations of colors and textures. Although attired in the unvarying Hyadean gray tunic, he had made the virtually unheard-of concession of adorning it with a badge sewn on the breast pocket, showing a colorful Navajo design, proclaiming his newfound specialty on Earth. Apparently, it had never occurred to Hyadeans to ornament clothing and other objects for no other reason than pure aesthetics. The practice had begun catching on lately on Chryse, putting research like Wyvex's in great demand.

"Erya has discovered Terran classical composers," Vrel told Cade. "She's started learning the violin and wants to set up a music school on Chryse when she gets back. Do you know any teachers who'd be interested in emigrating?"

"I'm sure I could find a few," Cade answered.

"*Ode* is causing a sensation there," Erya said.

"So I heard." *Ode to Joy* was an exported Warner movie about the life of Beethoven. Cade thought for a moment. "How soon will you be going back?" he asked Erya.

"I'll be in LA for a week. Then flying down to Brazil a day before launch. Why?"

Cade's eyes twinkled, as if he were stretching out something suspenseful. "How would you like one of the actual violins used in the movie as a present to take with you?" he asked. He knew someone in Hollywood who he figured could probably swing it.

Erya stared at him disbelievingly, and then, evidently not knowing what to say, asked her veebee for a suitable expression. "You're kidding!" she told him finally.

Cade shrugged, not letting his amusement show.

"I won't stake my life on it, but I'll see what I can do. We might be able to surprise you." Hyadeans found it hard to conceive of a simple favor. Everything they did seemed to be determined by some kind of intricate cost-benefit analysis that computed tangible gain. Their actions tended to be totally pragmatic, directed toward measurable "efficiency" with little feeling for any deeper value system. Maybe that was why they found Earth so incomprehensible and mysterious.

Wyvex spoke, looking at Erya. "There is a Hyadean called Tevlak, down in South America—in Bolivia, I think. He's very much involved in promoting Terran art back on Chryse. You ought to meet him before you go back—or at least talk to him if your schedule doesn't allow it."

"I'd like to," Erya said.

"I'll try to arrange it."

At that moment, Luke appeared with Henry in the archway from the front part of the house and signaled for Cade's attention. Cade excused himself and went over. Luke drew him through, away from all the attention. "We've got police at the door, and a Lieutenant Rossi from the ISS," he murmured.

Cade frowned. "What's it about?"

"Something to do with that aircar that was shot down near Washington this afternoon," Luke said. Cade sighed and went with them to the front door. Two men in suits were waiting, with figures in police uniforms standing behind and in the driveway. The smaller of the two introduced himself as Rossi. He had fair, sleeked-back hair, a thin line of a mustache, and that cold-eyed, dispassionate look that seemed to go with factotums of enforcement bureaucracies everywhere.

"As you probably know, Mr. Cade, four individuals

were assassinated in an incident that took place in Washington today, including two Hyadeans. We have reason to believe that the deaths of the Hyadeans were not planned. However, it's still an embarrassment to the administration. As a precaution, it has been decided to keep prominent Hyadeans under extended security protection for the time being. A guard has been placed at their mission building in Lakewood. Our instructions are to escort your Hyadean guests back when they are finished here. I apologize for any inconvenience."

Cade snorted. "We were thinking of maybe moving things out on the water," he commented, mostly to test how serious this was.

Rossi shook his head. "Under the circumstances, we don't think that would be advisable, Mr. Cade."

Cade nodded. Whatever the form of the words, the tone left no doubt. He turned his head to address Henry. "I guess you'd better go and tell Warren he can stand the crew down."

People who were smart didn't mess with these guys. There were too many ways they could make life miserable. And apart from the occasional intrusion like this, life wasn't that bad. So go with the flow, Cade told himself. What else could anyone do?

CHAPTER FOUR

More than twelve years had passed since the first recon-
naissance squadron of five Hyadean ships was detected
coming in fast from the outer Solar System. In a matter
of days they had arrived. There were no claims of mysterious objects seen by questionable people, or allegations
of strange happenings in unlikely places as had been
depicted in generations of fictional imaginings. These
aliens were here, and all the world knew it. A week later,
they commenced descents to the surface.

The first landings were in parts of South America,
western China and Tibet, and northeast Australia. The
selected areas were similar in being sparsely settled,
rugged, and having climate that varied with terrain
ranging from dense forest to bare mountains. Since
the aliens appeared to be shunning population centers, and their motives were obscure, official contacts
were initiated by Terrans.

The effect on the nations and peoples of Earth was, understandably, stupefying. Some of the first organized representations to descend on the alien bases after the nervous military withdrew to a watchful distance and governments had presented diplomatic calling cards were by the scientists. Some of their most cherished beliefs were already in ruins, after all, and their questions came in torrents.

How was travel over such distances possible in the time the aliens said, given the limitations imposed by the laws of physics? Well, it turned out, the "laws" were wrong. Getting around inside the galaxy fast wasn't a huge problem. And while distances beyond that were certainly vaster, and the Hyadeans had not as yet contemplated travel between galaxies, the distances to them weren't as immense as Terran astronomers believed. The red shift had been misinterpreted.

Okay, even if the supposed restrictions were wrong, how do you get the power, when even nuclear fusion would be impractical for the superluminal velocities that the Hyadeans said they achieved? Raw fusion only tapped into one percent of the mass equivalent, the Hyadeans replied. Nuclear processes could be catalyzed to be far more efficient, in a way comparable to chemical processes. And there were other forces beyond those, anyway. The phenomena hinting of them were there all the time, but Terran scientists too concerned with protecting their theories had ignored or denied them when they wouldn't fit. For the same kind of reason, the theory that life originated on planets was wrong, that it evolved through natural selection was wrong, and the theory of planets and stars forming out of rotating gaseous nebulas was wrong. What about the theory of the Big Bang and the origin of it all? the Terran scientists asked. The Hyadeans didn't know. They hadn't really thought

*about it. Looking at the claims the Terrans presented,
they couldn't say they were all that convinced.*

So much for all of that.

The aliens had little concern for big pictures, grand
designs, or greater schemes of things that went beyond
advancing their immediate interests. They discovered
that humans, often to their own detriment, possessed
unique imaginative powers, unlike anything the
Hyadean culture had known. At the same time, Earth
was fragmented into a patchwork of adversely disposed political units with constantly changing patterns
of alliances and rivalries, whose leaders could surely
benefit from Hyadean notions of efficiency and order.
Hence, a Hyadean market existed for Terran creativity;
those who commanded Terran resources had a need.
In other words, grounds existed for trade.

In the main, the Hyadeans became natural allies
of Western governments and financial interests faced
with declining home markets and attracted by the
prospect of establishing profitable links to the alien
economic system. The supportive nations, including
principally the United States, Western Europe, and
much of South America, organized formally into a
Global Economic Coalition, which became known
popularly as the "Globalists." On the other hand, a
group of reactionary nations, led by China and the
southeastern Asian region, desiring to preserve a
position of growing economic strength, and supported
by the Arab states and much of central Asia in a
tradition of resisting external influences, established
themselves as the Alliance of Autonomous Nation
States, or AANS. Largely because of their exposed
geographic positions, Japan and Australasia maintained positions of uneasy nonalignment. The
Hyadeans abandoned their stations in China and Asia
to concentrate in an enclave straddling the border

regions of western Brazil, Bolivia, and Peru, retaining the Australian base as a scientific field research station and outpost. As the Western regimes became more openly committed to policies that seemed designed to promote the advancement and enrichment of a favored few, opposition movements the world over multiplied.

CHAPTER FIVE

Two days after the reception at Cade's house, Neville Baxter stopped by on his way to LAX airport before returning to New Zealand. He imported agricultural machinery and was experimenting with installing Hyadean AIs for greater autonomy of operation. Cade and Julia ate a salad lunch with him in the sun lounge overlooking the rear of the house. It was a fine day with blue skies, and the glass shutters were open, letting in air from over the water. The boat dock was empty, Warren having taken the *Sassy Lady* out to check some new navigation equipment. Baxter had appeared in a light tan traveling jacket with plaid shirt, and a straw hat crowning his ruddy countenance. As usual, he was in a jovial mood.

". . . so this Maori chief is sitting there while the tourists are taking his picture—old as the hills, wrinkles and white hair—and he says, 'It's going to be a cold winter.' One of the women says, 'It's amazing! How do you people *know* these things?' The chief points across the street. 'White man stacking wood.' "

Cade smiled, leaned back in his chair at the glass-topped cane table they were using, and dabbed his mouth with his napkin before taking a sip of wine. "That's good, Neville. I'll try and remember it. We'll have to find an excuse to come out and visit you some day."

"Do that!" Baxter enthused. "We'll give you a great time. Balance the books for the way you've taken care of me here."

"What time's your flight?" Julia asked.

"Not till three. But I want to stop by the mission and say so long to Vrel and the guys. Dee too, if she's there. If not, say it for me when you see her, will you, Julia?"

"Of course."

Baxter shook his head. "Dee . . . there's one thing. How long has she been going with Vrel now? At least since the last time I was over. It was a pretty rare thing then—with aliens, I mean. She's just . . . you know, does her own thing, and to hell with what anyone thinks."

"That's Dee," Julia agreed.

"My kind of person," Baxter said. "I think it's starting to rub off on Vrel too." He halved an artichoke heart with the side of his fork. "You're doing a great job, stripping the uptightness off these aliens, Roland. Do them good."

Cade held up a hand. "This isn't a social adjustment center. I'm just an opportunist taking what comes, same as you. Same as practically everyone you saw here the other night."

Baxter became more serious. "What drives them? Have you figured it out yet, Roland? It's not just wealth or money. They're all filthy rich by our standards. But they never let up."

"You should have talked more to Mike Blair," Cade answered. "He spends most of his time with them and knows a lot more than I do. . . . But from what I can make out, it isn't so much that what you've got says who you are, as who you are decides what you get. Except 'get' doesn't mean just owning things—as you just said, all of them practically own everything anyway. It involves things like privileges you're entitled to, what positions you qualify for, the recognition you can expect. . . ."

"Sort of like a social rank," Julia put in. "But more complicated. Think of it as a combined credit rating and grade-point average based on just about everything you do. They need computers to figure it out. It translates as 'entitlement.' "

"No wonder they come across like robots off an assembly line," Baxter remarked.

"Oh, be kind, Neville," Julia chided. "You just said yourself that a lot of them are loosening up."

"But not the other way around." Baxter motioned appealingly with his fork. "Does anyone really think they could import their system here? Who'd want it?"

Cade made a face. "I'd say it would suit a lot of people that I can think of just fine," he replied.

Baxter left twenty minutes later. Cade saw him to the front door. As the cab was pulling away, a maroon Chevrolet carrying two people entered the driveway and came up to the house. Even before the driver got out, Cade recognized the fair, sleeked-back hair of Lieutenant Rossi from the Internal Security Service. The passenger was a woman in a blue-gray, two-piece business suit, hair tied high on her head, carrying a black document case. Cade waited at the door as they came up the steps.

"Mr. Cade. I hope I haven't caught you at a bad time," Rossi opened. "This is a colleague of mine, Investigator Wylie. We'd like to ask you a few questions."

"Ms. Wylie," Cade acknowledged, then looked back at Rossi. "What now?" He had a policy of never inviting government into his life, and if they invited themselves, to offer as little encouragement as possible.

Rossi looked past him through the doorway. "Er, could we go inside?"

"Okay." Cade held the door while they entered, closed it, and led the way back through to the sun lounge. Julia was just finishing her meal. Rossi caught Cade's eye pointedly. "Oh, that's okay," Cade said. "We don't have any secrets. Julia, these are Lieutenant Rossi and Investigator Wylie from the ISS. Apparently, they have some questions."

"For *you*, Mr. Cade. I'd rather it were in private, if you don't mind." Rossi's tone left no doubt that whether Cade minded or not had nothing to do with it.

"I was in the middle of something, anyway," Julia said, getting up. "I'll catch you later." She left with a quick nod to the two visitors. Cade indicated a couple chairs, which they accepted. He settled himself in a wicker seat facing them.

"Well?" he invited.

Rossi began, "I assume you're aware of the assassination of Senator Joel Farden from Virginia, General Meakes of the Army, and also two Hyadeans, that happened two days ago in Washington?"

"You already asked me that the last time you were here. When you poured ice water on my party."

"I explained then that it was orders, and we regretted the inconvenience," Rossi said. Cade let it go with a nod. Rossi resumed, "Since then, information has come into our possession that establishes a probable connection with the affiliation of political subversives who call themselves 'CounterAction.' You've heard of them, I trust?" Rossi leaned back, waiting for a reaction. Beside him, Wylie had taken some papers from the document case lying opened on her knee.

"Just what you see and hear. It isn't something I make a lot of time for." CounterAction was the illegal militant wing of the protest movement known as "Sovereignty," which had grown in North America over recent years out of various groups opposing what they saw as the Globalist sellout to Hyadean economic imperialism. Sovereignty had organized the rally in Washington the previous Sunday. After other incidents that had been reported over the preceding months, Cade wasn't surprised to learn that CounterAction might be behind this latest act.

"It's pretty widely assumed—and *we* know for *certain*—that the activities of CounterAction in this country are supported clandestinely by the AANS," Rossi said. Cade made a conciliatory gesture which again admitted to knowing nothing beyond what the media said. Rossi gave him a further moment, as if hoping that Cade might help a little more by not making him spell everything out. Cade waited invitingly. Rossi sighed.

"Up until now, AANS support for illegal groups operating in this country has been in the form of money, training, and the infiltration of weapons. We believe that the incident last Sunday might mark a new phase of escalation. You see, as is normal for Hyadean flying vehicles sent here, the aircar carrying the four victims was equipped with an automatic counter-missile system capable of stopping anything produced by the technology of this planet." Rossi showed a hand briefly. "But the assassins didn't use technology from this planet. They used a Hyadean directed-plasma weapon, which the defense system wasn't designed to deal with because up until now only the Hyadeans had it. But one went missing somewhere, and it found its way into this country. We're pretty sure that the people it found its way to were CounterAction. Can you see the implications, Mr. Cade, if the route by which weapons like that can enter this country isn't uncovered and stopped?"

That much was clear enough. But how did it affect Cade? He replied in the only way he could. "Well, yes, I take your point, Lieutenant. So . . . ?"

Rossi took a couple of sheets of paper from the ones Wylie had extracted and glanced at the top one. "You were married at one time, I believe."

"That's right."

"Your wife's name was Marie Ellen, formerly Hedlaw?"

"Yes." Cade had no idea where this could be going.

"Do you still have some means of contacting her, Mr. Cade? Do you know where she is now?"

Cade could only show both palms and shake his head. "No. That was three years ago now. The last I heard she was supposed to have gone to China." He stared from Rossi to Wylie and shook his head again, this time nonplussed. "Look, can I ask what this is about?"

Rossi seemed to hear, but pressed on with his own line. "Can I ask why you split up?" he said.

Cade had half felt this coming. "It was fun in the early days—you know, a wild kind of fling. But when that wore off, really we had nothing in common. She was an idealist with strong politics—serious ideas about what was wrong with the world and how to fix it. . . . I guess I'm just the opposite: I let the world be and ride with the tide."

"So there's no way you might still be in touch with her?" Rossi tried again.

"I already said, no. And even if I could, I'm not sure I'd want to. Life is good and comfortable. Why should I want to get mixed up in whatever you're talking about? I don't know anything about Hyadean weapons." He cocked an eye pointedly. "Anyhow, you still haven't told me what you're talking about."

Rossi stared at him for a few moments longer, as if perhaps giving him a chance to change his mind if there was anything to reconsider. Then he said, "Your ex-wife's views and her going to China were not a coincidence. We think she's back in the U.S. now, with one of the cells that CounterAction is organized into. We think that cell might be the one that the Hyadean plasma weapon found its way to."

Cade sat back slowly, massaging his brow. Now it all made sense. They were following up any lead, and the ex-husband would be an obvious name to put on the list. But still, what they were saying didn't feel right. Yes, he and Marie had had their differences, which at times had erupted into rows of her venting exasperation with what she saw as lack of principle on the one hand, and his protesting the wasting of life on what struck him as futile posturing on the other. And yes, he could see her agitating for what she believed in, or even wielding a gun if need be when passions ran high. But premeditated assassination in cold blood? . . . That didn't sound like her style. Rossi had evidently been prepared and was letting him think it over.

"You said on Sunday that you didn't think the two Hyadeans were planned as part of it," Cade said at last.

"They were hitching a ride at the last moment. The targets were Farden and Meakes."

"So what was so terrible about those two? Why should CounterAction have singled them out?" Cade wanted to know if they were guilty of anything which by any stretch of the imagination he could see Marie reacting to so drastically. Rossi looked at his colleague and nodded for her to take it. Wylie handed Cade a pamphlet from the document case. It showed a picture of Joel Farden over the caption WHO'S SELLING BOLIVIA? and below, a page of angry denunciation. Large banner type above showed the piece to be a product of SOVEREIGNTY.

"Farden was pushing Congressional bills to open up big sales of Hyadean services and products," she answered. "Their minerals extraction program in Bolivia owes a lot to his pushing." Cade knew a bit about that from his various contacts. The Hyadeans were constructing huge facilities to mine and process minerals from the Bolivian central Altiplano region, which was rich in deposits but underdeveloped due to capital shortage. Their advanced technologies could cut out traditional Terran industries with prices that couldn't be beat.

"A pretty good way to open up resources that it seems no one figured out how to touch before now," Cade commented. "And sure, the people who did figure it will come out okay. Why would they bother if there was nothing in it for them? You have to have movers."

Wylie waved the pamphlet she was holding and nodded. "But you can see how it can be turned into a propaganda piece for stirring up lots of people looking for something to blame their problems on. Some of them get mad enough . . ." She left it unfinished.

Cade nodded. Yes, he could see how somebody like Farden could be made into a hate figure. "How about Meakes?" he asked.

"Even simpler," Wylie replied. "He wanted to revamp our defense capability by incorporating Hyadean weapons and methods. We'd be talking near-invincibility here. You can imagine how the AANS would feel about that. So it was turned around into a story that he was going to put our defense under Hyadean control."

Cade could see how that would work too. But he still couldn't see Marie getting involved in murder over it—simply *because* she had strong principles. Or could she have changed that much in three years? Who knew what she had been exposed to in China? Why get mixed up in it? He showed his hands in a way that said he understood but really couldn't help.

He thought that should have ended it, but the two ISS agents continued to regard him skeptically. Cade could tell when people didn't believe him. They went over some further details, but he still had the same feeling when Rossi and Wylie finally left twenty minutes later.

What they suspected only hit him later. It was that his and Marie's splitting up might have been just a cover, and he was still in contact, acting as an information source for Sovereignty, for which his Hyadean and other contacts would make him uniquely valuable.

And if they believed that she was with the cell of CounterAction responsible for the assassinations, then Cade would be their prime hope for uncovering a lead back to it. There was no way he was going to keep them out of his life this time, he realized bleakly.

CHAPTER SIX

The movie showing at the theater in downtown Baltimore involved an egg-shaped planet whose ends formed immense "mountains" projecting beyond the atmosphere and providing habitats for a range of progressively more bizarre life forms able to exist virtually to the fringes of space. Space adventure had become popular in recent years—the Terran-made varieties, at least. Adaptations of Hyadean imports had been tried in earlier years, but with limited success, mainly due to curiosity which soon passed. The Hyadean themes were invariably exercises in social role modeling more than entertainment, with character stereotypes reflecting approved attitudes and behavior. Terran movies, by contrast, were a sensation back on the alien home worlds.

Reyvek had come here to lose himself in the anonymity for a last hour before committing himself and to reflect one last time on his decision; and also as a precaution. Although there was no particular reason why he should be an object of attention on a routine day off-duty, he had changed seats twice, the second time to put him within a couple of rows of the exit at the rear. Nobody slipped into nearby seats in the minutes following; none of the faces profiled in the flickering light from the screen showed undue interest in him. He checked his watch, waited for a moment when the action quickened to an attention-grabbing high point, then quickly got up and left. Nobody came after him; nobody was watching from across the foyer. Carrying a red plastic bag as he had been directed, he went out onto the street and turned right. It was already dark. His pocket phone beeped when he was halfway along the block. He drew it out and held it to his face. "Yes?"

"Is everything clear?" The voice, a man's, was electronically disguised and sounded tinny.

"As far as I can tell."

"Cross over the street now and take the next left." Presumably, Reyvek was being observed from somewhere. He passed a couple of run-down stores, the front of a boarded-up office building, and the weed-fringed parking lot of a hotel. When he was opposite the entrance, the voice in the phone said, "Enter the hotel that you're outside now. Go to the desk, and ask for an envelope left for your name." The caller hung up. Reyvek did as instructed, was asked for ID, and received an envelope containing a magnetically coded key for Room 843. He took an elevator to the eighth floor and found the room empty except for a set of clothes laid out on the bed, including shoes, wristwatch, replacement phone, and pocket compad; even a new billfold, key ring, and pen. There was also an envelope containing another coded room key. The voice called again while he was examining the items. "Strip completely, and leave everything that you brought with you there in the room. You can take currency, keys, documents, and other paper items that you wish to keep."

"What about this ring that I carry?" Reyvek queried. His mouth was dry, making him sound scratchy. His nervousness was showing. "It's not cheap, and I'm kind of fond of it."

"How long have you owned it?" the voice asked.

"Fifteen, twenty years, maybe. A gift from times that were better. Kind of sentimental."

"That will be acceptable."

Fifteen minutes later, wearing his new outfit, Reyvek reentered the elevator and got out on the second floor, leaving the building via stairs and a side exit. A taxi was waiting. If the contact really was what he had been given to understand, CounterAction certainly didn't believe in taking chances, Reyvek reflected as they pulled away. Or maybe they knew more about ways of keeping tabs on their people than even he did. The thought reinforced his resolve further.

The room in the second hotel was also deserted. Besides the usual bed, side tables, TV, and wall unit, it had a recliner in one corner. Set up in front of it was a TV camera on a folding stand, connected to a laptop operating via a satellite modem. Reyvek sat down facing the camera and smoothed his clothing while he composed himself. Then the tinny voice spoke again, this time from the laptop speakers. "We regret having to take these measures. The risks associated with this kind of contact are extreme—as someone like you will be all too aware."

"I understand."

"So you are Wayne Reyvek, captain in the uniformed division of the Internal Security Service."

"That's correct."

"And you say you want to change sides: to place your services at the disposal of this organization."

"Right, I want out."

"And how would you describe your motivation, Captain Reyvek?"

"Disillusionment."

"Could you be more specific?"

Reyvek had expected the question, of course. He sighed and raised his hands briefly. "Maybe I'm some kind of old-fashioned idealist that doesn't belong anymore. Remember that phrase they used to teach the kids in school: 'Protect and Serve'? Well, that what I used to think this work would be all about. And for a while, I guess, that's the way it used to be, more or less: defending what was best for this country; for Americans." Reyvek shook his head. "But that's all changing. Americans are the victims of what's going on now. The interests that we're really defending are the aliens'. " He paused to make sure this was the kind of response that was wanted.

"Can you elaborate?" the voice invited.

Again, an open-handed gesture. "The whole Security Service is coming under alien influence—instilled with *their* ideas of what's effective. Those aren't our values, human values. You saw what happened in Washington the other day—people screaming, throwing up in the street like dogs; stuck in goo they have to be dissolved out of. Just ordinary people protesting about losing their jobs, watching their towns fall apart, while a few guys are making millions. They didn't deserve being treated like that. . . . And it's going to get worse. Right now, the training programs are being rewritten to include indoctrination for firing on U.S. citizens. That isn't right. They're gearing up for war here in the cities. It'll get the same as it is down south. I've had combat experience in Brazil. The public isn't being told what's happening in places like that. I've had enough. I'm with you guys, okay?"

A series of probing questions followed. The voice, and the people that Reyvek presumed to be with him, were cautious—wary of this being a plant. Reyvek had anticipated it. Infiltration was one of the classic weapons against subversives. "I have information to give you that will prove I'm genuine," he said.

"What kind of information?" the voice asked.

"Proof that Farden, Meakes, and the two Hyadeans weren't killed by CounterAction, the way the country is being told." That would get their interest, he had decided. If the assassination hadn't been the work of their own organization, the people Reyvek was talking to would presumably be aware of the fact.

There was a pause. Then the voice asked, "Does that mean you know who *was* responsible?"

"It was carried out by an operative of the ISS," Reyvek replied. "The order came from an unofficial source connected to the administration. I have the names. I can document the origin of the weapon that was used. It wasn't smuggled into the country by CounterAction via China—as you or your people know already. I've mailed it all to a box in the city. You can have the address, number, and key."

Again there was a pause, longer this time, as if those at the far end of the link were conferring, or perhaps communicating with others elsewhere. At last the voice spoke again.

"A good move, Captain Reyvek. The matter will have to be conveyed higher within our own command structure before I can give you a response. We had considered asking if you would be willing to remain with the ISS as an internal source for us. But the information you have indicated promises to be of such value as to rule out the risk of letting you go back. We'll move you to a safe house tonight. You'll be comfortable there until word comes back down. From now on you will be referred to as 'Otter.' "

Reyvek felt satisfied that he had achieved enough for this first contact. However, he had another important piece of information to impart. A particular cell within CounterAction's Southeastern Sector was being blamed for the Farden-Meakes incident—operating from Charlotte, North Carolina, which was close enough to Washington to have plausibly been assigned the mission. To make things look authentic, security and police units around the country had been fed details to be checked for the official record. The reason that cell had been chosen was that a captive who belonged to it briefly had revealed a lot under interrogation. The ISS knew the names of some of its other members, its drop boxes, the locations of its supposedly "safe" houses. In short, it was blown and readily targetable. After a delay to give the appearance of leads being uncovered and followed up, the cell would be taken out by a kill team. Retribution for the Farden-Mcakes incident would thus have been seen to be dispensed; witnesses who might one day have contested the official version of the story would be silenced permanently; the file would then be closed.

The other message Reyvek had to deliver was for the cell that was referred to within CounterAction as "Scorpion" to disperse fast.

CHAPTER SEVEN

The Hyadean West Coast Trade and Cultural Mission on Carson Street in Lakewood occupied a four-story office block of gray and white panels alternating with glass, and a roof crammed with strange antennas and other structures. Formerly, the building housed an assortment of small businesses. It stood back from the highway behind palm-tree-lined lawns and a visitors' parking area, with access drives on either side and a larger parking area at the rear. The idea had been to establish an informal alien presence without visible barriers isolating it, that would eventually blend in as part of the local scene. Of course, such openness would have been intolerable to the security authorities, had it been genuine. The fences bounding the area were more than they appeared to be, and the building itself had quietly acquired various refinements that the original architects had never contemplated.

It was a week after the reception at Cade's house: the day Erya was due to leave Los Angeles for the Hyadean space port at Xuchimbo in western Brazil. Cade and Luke arrived at the mission around midmorning in the silver-gray BMW, Luke driving. Luke had been with Cade for five years now. He was a rugged-faced forty with a full head of black hair and a beard that he kept meticulously trimmed. He spoke little, was totally dependable, and was not above overlooking a few legal or quasi-moral niceties when the occasion required. Formerly with the Navy, Luke had done Warren Edmonds a favor by introducing him to Cade's employ at a time when Warren's risk-taking with frowned-upon enterprises would otherwise have made his demise only a matter of time.

The security people had relaxed from their tension following the Washington incident, and the temporary police check at the gate had been removed. A number of Hyadean personal flyers and freight lifters were visible to the rear of the building, standing among the regular Terran ground vehicles. A dispensation for operating them had been given when it became clear that the sophisticated Hyadean flight-control AIs presented no hazard to air traffic in the area.

Luke parked in the visitors' area at the front and released the trunk lid using a button below the dash. Cade got out, went back around to retrieve the black, vinyl-finished violin case that they had brought, and rejoined Luke in front of the car. They began walking toward the main entrance of the building.

"I feel like something out of an old gangster movie going in to rob the place," Cade remarked, touting the violin case. "All it needs is the fedoras." Luke grunted.

Inside was a reception counter attended by a Terran woman, with several Hyadeans in an open office area behind. A short passage flanked by display cases of Hyadean gadgetry and pictures showing scenes from Chryse led from the entrance foyer to a door opening to the interior. Two Hyadeans in dark blue garb and gray caps were stationed by the arch framing the near end.

Cade greeted the receptionist with a grin. She had been expecting them. "Hi, Mimi. How's the world been treating you lately?"

"Good morning, Roland. You're looking dapper. You want an update on my life?"

"Just the wicked and exciting parts."

"Yeah, right. . . . Hi, Luke. Still managing to keep him out of trouble?"

"It's tough at times," Luke acknowledged.

Mimi glanced at the violin case that Cade was holding. "What's this? Have you come to give us a recital?"

"A going-away present for Erya."

"Oh, that's right. She's into that, isn't she? How thoughtful!"

"What else did you expect?"

"Please permit inspection of the article." The voice came from a Hyadean AI in the form of a purple, dome-topped cube, dotted with lenses, sitting on the counter by Mimi's elbow. Cade hoisted the case up onto the counter, opened it, and stood back while one of the guards lifted out the instrument to examine it curiously, then poked here and there along the lining of the case and lid. Either he was a new arrival or his English wasn't up to par yet.

"That looks like a quality piece of work," Mimi commented.

"Not exactly special," Cade said. "It was used in that movie about Beethoven that came out a while back—the one with David Quine."

"Yes, I saw it. He was perfect for the part. I loved the bit where he marches through the town waving the cane with the silver knob on the end."

"It's a rage back home there. Erya will get a kick out of it."

The guard replaced the violin and closed the lid of the case. *"Thank you. You are free to proceed,"* the AI announced. *"Hec Vrel has been advised that you are here."*

Cade led the way through, Luke following. There was no call for any ID check. Cade had always thought there was something unnatural about that arch. Probably they had been scanned, sniffed, sensed, and verified before even entering the passage. The door at the end opened automatically and they passed through, into the office section.

The inside had been opened out from the original configuration of suites into larger, interconnecting work areas. Hyadeans tended to shun individual responsibility, Cade had found, making their decisions through committee or relying on the authority of precedent. Perhaps the open layout was preferred for obtaining group consensus and approval. The surroundings were an unimaginatively utilitarian repetition of cream-painted walls and gray or brown furnishings and other equipment, suggesting more the clerical underworld of a low-budget socialist state than the local showcase of a world that could have bought the United States. Screens were everywhere, some showing faces, others graphics mixed with captions in strange scripts and symbols. One type presented its images in relief, looking like windows with solid scenes beyond. Cade remembered Mike Blair telling of his shock at first being confronted by Hyadeans nonchalantly talking to their home worlds with turnaround delay close to instantaneous. The equipment in the mission building communicated electronically with some kind of gravity-wave converters in Earth orbit, which could send signals somewhere around ten billion times faster. The orbiting converters relayed to more powerful devices that the Hyadeans had placed at the edge of the Solar System, which in turn beamed to the home planet. None of this had been especially bothersome to Cade, who had grown up taking instant around-the-world communication for granted; Blair, on the other hand, was a scientist in whose scheme of things it wasn't supposed to have been possible, and he had taken weeks to adjust to it. Sometimes, Cade concluded, there were advantages in not being too scientific.

Cade and Luke threaded their way among the desks and consoles, where Hyadeans sat staring at screens, sometimes murmuring exchanges with them. Just about everything the Hyadeans made was controlled by a built-in AI of greater or lesser capacity, and voice was their normal way of interacting. Another thing that always intrigued Cade were their reconfigurable pages—sheets of flexible plastic, no thicker than regular paper, upon which characters were generated electronically to produce whatever was desired. A stack of them bound like a book could thus become any book or document at all, selected from a library stored in the spine or loaded externally. Mike Blair had calculated that the spine held the equivalent of half the Library of Congress.

Some of the Hyadeans nodded in recognition, though without displays of overt familiarity—as a rule they were more stiff and formal by day. A number of Terrans worked there too in such roles as advisors and translators—the pay the Hyadeans could offer was impossible to turn down. Whether because they had never become comfortable with the practice, or because the Hyadean translation programs couldn't capture the subtleties of natural language sufficiently for fluency, they prefered using conventional touchpad and wireless mouse rather than voice when operating equipment.

The brave attempts at color and decoration that Cade noticed here and there were doubtless due to the Terrans too. A noticeable exception was anything of floral design, which the Hyadeans wouldn't permit, even to the extent of prohibiting it from acceptable office dress. Seemingly, their managerial caste had some hangup about displays of sexual organs, whatever the species.

Vrel was waiting at the far end, his mouth stretched into the faint smile that was the most a Hyadean would allow while on duty. However, he had followed Wyvex's example in relieving the drabness of the standard tunic with a colorful patch on the breast pocket—a fractal pattern this time. Vrel's hair seemed almost to glow in a strange mix of electric blue and violet hues that coordinated well with the paler blue of his skin. He had been among the original group to set up the mission six years previously, and had first met Cade then, already expanding his business circles to make Hyadean acquaintances.

"Hello, Roland . . . Luke," he greeted. "Exactly on time. I'm surprised. The traffic is supposed to be bad this morning."

"Luke has his own routes," Cade answered. Vrel was picking up Terran ways. In some places, conversation opened with the weather or inquiries about one's health. In Los Angeles it was the traffic. Cade gestured at the patch on Vrel's pocket. "What's this riot of abandonment? You'll be showing up in beach shirts next."

"I kind of like it. It amazes me that Hyadeans never thought to put pictures on things. Besides, I couldn't let Wyvex get all the attention."

The complex Hyadean system of social ordering, which Cade had given up trying to understand, exploited competitiveness and was what made them so conscientious about having to conform. By their standards Vrel's gesture would constitute a blaze of individuality bordering on irresponsible. The interesting thing was that Vrel seemed to be enjoying it. "Is Wyvex here?" Cade asked.

"No. Damien Philps took him up to San Francisco to tour some galleries. His friend Tevlak in Bolivia is talking about opening up outlets on Chryse. I was talking to Tevlak about it earlier."

Erya appeared in an entrance behind Vrel and came forward to greet Cade and Luke. "Mr. Cade and Mr. Luke. Mimi said you wanted to see me."

"We couldn't let you go back without saying goodbye," Cade said.

"How thoughtful." Only then did Erya's gaze drift down to the case that Cade was holding. She looked at it uncomprehendingly as Cade, grinning, lifted it onto a nearby worktop and opened the lid. Erya's jaw dropped incredulously.

"From the movie, like I said," Cade told her. "I couldn't get the first violin, as I'd hoped. But this is the next best."

Erya was speechless for several seconds. "You remembered! . . . But I don't understand. I'm just about to go back. There's no possible return. Why would you choose . . ." She consulted her veebee for an appropriate phrase. "Negative payoff."

Even Vrel, who should have known better by now, seemed taken aback. Cade shook his head, doing his best not to let his bemusement show. It was this strange Hyadean calculus of short-term returns again. They couldn't comprehend giving for its own sake. "Don't let worrying about it spoil your trip," he said. "It'll do more good on Chryse than it would have done if it stayed where I found it. You're still on Earth now. Just accept it as a Terran way of saying we're friends. Maybe one day it'll become your way too."

While Erya was making a round of the offices to show Cade's gift before she left for the airport, Michael Blair yawned and stretched in one of the rooms upstairs as he rested his eyes after two hours of concentration at a display screen showing Hyadean text and mathematical representations. Learning the language was part of the program he had set himself for understanding the Hyadean sciences. It no longer awed him to think that some of the sources that he accessed, and individuals that he was growing accustomed to interacting with, were located on strange worlds that existed light-years away.

The ironic conclusion he had come to was that, contrary to everything that anyone raised in the self-congratulatory Terran tradition would have believed, the very unimaginativeness that Terrans found incomprehensible was what had enabled the Hyadeans to make breakthroughs that left Earth's scientific community dazed and incredulous. Truth was, the insights he had vowed to share were turning out to be not really that exciting after all. It was the flights of imaginative fancy dreamed up by generations of Terran scientists that were exciting; the only problem was, overwhelmingly, they had this tendency to be wrong.

The Hyadeans ploddingly followed wherever the facts led, without subscribing to elaborate theoretical constructs that emotional investment would cause

them to defend tenaciously instead of testing
impartially. True enough, the textbook accounts and
rhetoric bandied around on Earth praised the scientific method as an ideal; and academia could always
count on a staunch cadre of apologists to exalt it into
reality. But the basic human drives were emotional,
not objective, resulting in commitment to protecting
ideas that were comfortingly familiar instead of openness to the research that might threaten them. Most
of what Earth took such pride in as "science" was as
much a product of human inventiveness as its other
arts and fables.

By contrast, the Hyadean attempts to understand
the universe were closer to what would have been
described on Earth as engineering. What didn't work
was abandoned without compunction, and what did
was accepted at face value without need of credentials to fit with prevailing theory. The resulting
scheme of things was messy, incoherent, and to
Terran eyes, crying out to be organized under grand
unifying principles postulating answers to questions
the Hyadeans had never asked. But so what? At the
end of it all the fact remained that they were here,
while we hadn't gotten there. That had to say
something.

Krossig, the Hyadean anthropologist who was here
to study humans, came in and began rummaging for
something among the shelves on the far wall. As Blair
watched him across the desktop, he reflected on the
irony that the Hyadean inclination not to question
was also what made them so susceptible to their own
social conditioning propaganda, and hence ideal
subjects for a conformist society. His brow creased
at the seeming paradox. Wasn't readiness to question
supposed to be the hallmark of what science was all
about? If the Hyadeans didn't question, how could

they have made such superb scientific accomplishments? He sat back in his chair and mulled over the problem.

Questioning led to good science when what was being questioned was a belief system that had become dogma. Since the Hyadeans didn't create dogmas, they could get by without need to question them. Accepting uncritically worked when the facts were allowed to speak for themselves. It also produced rigidly structured social orders.

CHAPTER EIGHT

Hyadeans had never fallen into the Terran habit of creating false gods that would reveal the ultimate truths of the Universe. One of the most recent creations to be elevated to the status of infallible deity was mathematics. The Hyadeans took advantage of the fortuitous fact that some mathematical procedures approximated real-world processes sufficiently closely over a limited range to be useful, and looking no further than that, found an invaluable servant. Terrans turned things upside down by persuading themselves that their manipulations of formal systems of symbols defined "laws" that reality was somehow obliged to imitate. In doing so they subjected themselves to a tyrannical master.

Relativity theory had pursued mathematical elegance by seeking to extend to electromagnetism the familiar principles of Galilean relativity, whereby the equations describing mechanical motion came out the same regardless of whose moving reference frame measurements were made from. A consistent solution required that the velocity of light be the same for all observers, which became one of the theory's postulates. Peculiar distortions of space and time were necessary to maintain a velocity as constant, and the various relativistic transformations followed. These also enabled the famous experiment by Michelson and Morley in 1886, and its variants repeated to greater accuracies ever since, which failed to find an ether "wind" due to the Earth's motion around the Sun, as demonstrating that there was no ether—no "preferred" reference frame in which "true" laws of physics operated.

The Hyadeans went out into space—which required, after all, solid engineering more than esoteric theories—and discovered that the sought-after medium was simply the locally dominant electromagnetic field. Since in the vicinity of Earth this traveled with the Earth around the Sun, the Terran physicists had, in effect, been trying to measure the airspeed of their plane with their instruments anchored solidly inside the cabin.

In the Hyadean scheme of things the Galilean transformations remained valid; yet experiments performed on the surfaces of planets yielded the same results that appeared to support relativity. The reason was that the electric field surrounding a photon experienced an aerodynamic-like distortion when moving through a gravity field, which affected the propagation velocity. Since local gravity varied from place to place, the speed of light changed in different parts of the cosmos, upsetting all manner of long-cherished Terran calculations and models.

This distortion was responsible for the phenomenon measured as inertial mass, which explained why mass increased with velocity. Increase in mass resulted in *the slowing down of a moving system's clock rates. Hence, "time" didn't dilate in the way relativity maintained—for example to extend the lifetimes of incoming muons created in the upper atmosphere. The "clocks" of particles moving through the Earth's gravity field ran slower than laboratory clocks at rest in it. Hence, the Twin Paradox didn't arise, and space and time remained what common sense had always said.*

The associated energy dynamics restricted velocities in situations where the gravitational field of the body being accelerated was small compared to the field through which the acceleration was taking place. This had been observed in experiments performed on Earth using nuclear particles, and been misread as a universal limit. But that was merely a locally valid approximation. Away from large gravitating masses, hyperlight velocities could be achieved with surprisingly little outlay of energy, and that was why the Hyadeans were able to measure their interstellar journeys in weeks and months.

The gravitational effect itself emerged as a residue of the electrical asymmetry arising from the distortion of hadrons within nuclei by intense internal field stresses. Disturbances superposed on it propagated at close to ten billion times the speed of light, which afforded the basis for Hyadean long-range communications.

Evidence hinting at such possibilities had been available on Earth all along, filed in the reports of unfashionable experiments and cited by critics of the orthodoxy. But the mainstream had always ignored it, or found ways to explain it away.

Because it didn't fit with the theory.

CHAPTER NINE

In New York, the sun was shining from a clear sky, reflecting as a subdued orb from the tinted windows of the skyscraper at the end of Manhattan island housing the offices of the Global-Interplanetary Export-Import Bank. The board room on the floor below the penthouse commanded a clear view over Battery Park, past Governors Island and the upper bay all the way to the Narrows, with the Jersey City docks fading in haze across the mouth of the Hudson to the right, behind the Statue of Liberty.

Casper Toddrel appended his signature on all six copies of the Deed Transfer Agreement, handing each to the financial secretary to be witnessed and dated. These were followed by a ten-page Disclosure Affidavit, Financial Underwriter's Statement, and Supplementary Articles of Contract. The documents were passed along the table to the signatory for the three representatives from the Brazilian Land Commission, and finally to the head of the Hyadean delegation at the far end. These were top-level Hyadeans, the real movers—taking in the U.S. and parts of Western Europe in what came close to a state visit. They sat aloofly in a group, with fans directing scented air streams on the table in front of them—as if not really comfortable at being this close to sweaty, smelly Terrans. Toddrel would have welcomed a greater display of togetherness, but he wasn't troubled all that much. By his estimation, when the various transactions, payments, share allocations, and commissions were completed, his net personal worth would have increased by somewhere in the order of a cool half-billion dollars.

Toddrel was a medium-set man in his midfifties, with black curls of hair fringing a smooth head, and dark, moody eyes adding depth to a face controlled and inexpressive about the mouth and jaw but otherwise untroubled. He believed in being thorough in all that he did, expected the same from the people he paid, and accepted his secure and comfortable existence as no more than the due return for hard work, innate intelligence, and summoning the will to get things right. He was tired of hearing about the self-inflicted problems of people who never had developed a worthwhile thought in their lives, refused to make decisions, did nothing with opportunity when it came, and then complained that they'd never been given a chance. Professionally, if not entirely socially, he had to admit he had a grudging admiration for Hyadeans. They did what was necessary to get the results they wanted.

Murmurs and chattering broke out around the room when the formalities were over. People began rising. Everyone looked pleased. Toddrel returned the pen to the holder on the table in front of him and stood up, pausing to exchange a few words with some of the other directors. He declined an invitation from the Hyadeans to lunch, on the grounds that he was flying to Europe later that day and had matters to attend to, and left before getting involved in anything further. Ibsan, his former SEAL/Secret Service body-guard, joined him in the anteroom outside, and they walked together to the elevators. Toddrel's limo was drawn up in the basement motor lobby when they emerged. Ibsan opened the door for Toddrel, then got in up front to ride with the chauffeur. Drisson was waiting in the rear compartment as arranged. Toddrel leaned forward in the seat next to him to pour a Scotch and water from the decanters beside the entertainment unit. Overtly, Kurt Drisson was a colonel in the Internal Security Service. Covertly, he coordinated operations related to higher policy, of a kind that it was preferred not to have recorded in official orders.

"So, what have we got?" Toddrel asked as the limo began moving out though armored doors, then up a ramp into the downtown streets.

"Not good," Drisson replied. "Reyvek has vanished without trace. Given the last two evaluation profiles we have on him, the indicated conclusion is that he's defected. Since he was involved with Echelon logistics, I'd guess he took that information as collateral. We have to assume that we're compromised."

Toddrel exhaled heavily. "Echelon" was the code designation for the operation to eliminate Farden and Meakes. Toddrel had made arrangements for the meeting at Overly Park ensuring that the two of them would fly together. The last-minute addition of the two Hyadeans had been an unexpected complication, with unthinkable repercussions now if the story got out. The ruin of Toddrel and his accomplices would be the least of it, with a good chance of a life sentence as a gesture toward making interplanetary amends.

"If they had the profiles, why was he allowed to continue on-duty?" he fumed. "Why wasn't he suspended? What's the point of having profiles if nobody's going to act on what they say?"

Drisson made a vaguely placatory gesture. "It's like a lot of things. Sometimes it takes hindsight to make the right interpretation." He waited, as if giving Toddrel time to vent further before being more receptive. Toddrel gulped irascibly from his glass, savored the taste for a moment, then looked out the window. They were en route for the Waldorf, where Toddrel was staying. In one of the side streets, police were keeping an eye on a speaker addressing a ragged-looking gathering from a platform.

"So what do we do?" Toddrel asked, turning back.

Drisson rubbed his chin, indicating that there was no obvious easy option. "The plan was to sanitize the situation by putting it on Scorpion's account and then taking them out," he said.

Toddrel nodded impatiently. Scorpion was the compromised CounterAction cell being set up to take the official rap. "I know what we planned, Kurt. I'm asking what we *do*."

"Obviously, we have to eliminate Reyvek. But the only way we'll find him now is through someone on the inside. So the proposal is this. We put a hold on taking out Scorpion. Instead, we infiltrate somebody into it to find Reyvek."

"Is that likely?" Toddrel queried. "Isn't CounterAction supposed to be highly compartmentalized?"

"I think there's a good chance. With Reyvek being

involved in the operation Scorpion is supposed to have carried out, there are good reasons why they might end up meeting. The operative takes out Reyvek. When that part's done, we send in the cleaning team as scheduled. End of problem."

"You make it sound like just part of a regular day's work to put somebody inside CounterAction," Toddrel commented.

"Normally it would be a tough thing to do on demand," Drisson agreed. "But in the case of Scorpion, we might have a break. One of the cell members that we've identified is the former wife of a wheeler-dealer on the West Coast who sets up business deals with Hyadeans. Our people visited him a few days ago on a routine check. He says he doesn't have contact with her anymore, but they weren't convinced. This guy knows everybody and has wires into everything." Drisson shrugged. "If we can get him to locate his ex for us, we've got a conduit through to Scorpion."

"And what makes you think he's likely to do that?" Toddrel asked.

Drisson looked across the seat and smiled enigmatically. "Ways and means," he replied.

CHAPTER TEN

North Carolina state troopers had set up a checkpoint on the road out of Greenville, a mile before the junction where Kestrel and Len in the battered farm pickup, and Olsen driving the truck laden with fifty-gallon drums of timber preservative, would go separate ways. Kestrel and Len would trace a route through the minor roads crossing the Great Smoky range; Olsen would keep to the interstates, following I-85 south to skirt Atlanta, then taking I-75 to meet up with them again in Chattanooga that night.

The Scorpion cell in Charlotte had been disbanded suddenly on terse instructions from above. Other members were dispersing to destinations known only to themselves and whoever gave the orders; the names Kestrel had known them by had been retired. On joining the Chattanooga cell, she would no doubt cease being "Kestrel" anymore, too. At first,

CounterAction had given her the pseudonym Kay, but she rejected it. Care was needed in making sure that code words bore no accidental similarities or connections to the things they were supposed to disguise. Lives had been lost through such coincidences. "Kay" would have been too suggestive of her real name: Cade. Marie Cade.

A couple of jeeps manned by armed National Guard and mounting machine guns were positioned at the sides of the roadblock, ready to go. A sergeant came up to the driver's window, while two troopers went back to probe among the bales of roofing shingles that the pickup was carrying. Len presented a wallet containing the vehicle documentation and his ID, then followed with Marie's, made out in the name of Jenny Lawson, as she passed it across. The sergeant perused them casually, recited the names aloud into a compad and waited a moment for the screen's response.

"Where are you heading?" he inquired, running an eye over the interior of the cab.

"Up to Hiawasee. Stuff for a cabin being remodeled along by the lake there," Len replied. He looked the part: unshaven for two days, with a crumpled tweed hat, plaid shirt and padded work vest, a carpenter's tool belt over blue jeans. His voice was gruff and neutral.

"That wouldn't seem to me too much like a lady's kind of work," the sergeant commented, looking at Marie.

"What century are you from? I'll hammer 'em as good as anyone," she answered defiantly.

"Would you have such a thing as a bill of sale for this material?" the sergeant asked. Len produced one from Lowes in Spartanburg, where they had loaded the prom guns. The sergeant glanced back toward the rear of the pickup, where the troopers had been scanning the load with a hand-held spectral analyzer, explosives sniffer, and a metal sensor. "On your way," he told them, waving. Len eased the pickup away amid rattles and grinding of gears, taking care not to seem too hasty. Marie kept her eyes ahead until they were a good hundred yards clear, then exhaled shakily. In the side mirror, she could see Olsen's truck standing in line behind a couple of cars.

It had been intended that the load would attract attention. The prom guns were inside the double-walled back of the cab and the hidden compartment beneath the bed at the rear, between the chassis girders—both metal-enclosed, opaque to the regular search instruments. The guns Olsen was carrying were inside the false-bottom drums—although a spot check and sampling would have drawn the wood preservative they were supposed to be filled with from an internal chamber.

Interesting weapons, prom guns. They had disappeared from Hyadean stocks in South America, and the only details Marie knew were that they had come into the U.S. via Morocco and the Caribbean. "Prom" was a contraction of "programmable munitions." The gun was the size of an assault rifle and launched a stream of self-propelled projectiles containing lateral-thrusting charges carried in a counter-spinning ring, which could be fired to alter the trajectory in flight. Quite complex control patterns could be programmed into the launcher, enabling targets dug in under cover, hidden around corners, or concealed by obstacles to be hit. A skilled user could seek out a target blocked by combinations of them. Marie had tested and practiced with them in remote parts of the mountains east of Charlotte.

"I don't believe what this country has turned into,"

Len growled as the pickup ground and shuddered to gain speed. "Roadblocks; people being pulled out of bed in the middle of the night. Things never used to be that way. Yet the media talk about it as if it's normal. People forget. It's alien ways. They're turning us into a colony in our own country."

"That's what we're fighting," Marie reminded him unnecessarily. The hills back from the highway looked green and peaceful. Water behind the trees reflected patches of sky. Marie felt weary of it all: combat training and sabotage; constantly having to be ready to move; always being haunted by the specter of capture, interrogation, and everything that went with it. Why couldn't she just live a safe and familiar day-to-day life somewhere, enjoying little things like friends stopping by to visit, or being alone with her thoughts on a hill after a walk up through a forest?

All that the people needed to take their country back was solidarity and awareness. Even with all their technology and alien backing, the powers that were robbing them of their livelihoods and turning them into property like some modern version of a feudal order could never prevail against a determined majority. But the majority were uninformed and unorganized. What did it take to wake them up to what was going on? Why did Marie care? She could go back to China, find a niche there, and probably never have to worry about being directly affected to any serious degree again. So why had she come back?

For the same reason she had left the comforts and security of her former life in California, she supposed. The restlessness that compelled her to contribute even a token to putting something right with the world. How anyone could remain complacent when there was so much going wrong with it, she was unable to comprehend. How could she once have dreamed of making a life with Roland? Because he was Roland. She still thought of him, even though all that had been a different universe, a million years ago. That was the stupid thing.

"Do you know there was a time when you could drive from anyplace to anyplace anytime you felt like it?" Len said. "Didn't have sensors under the road reading who was leaving the state. Didn't need no ID with a tax compliance sticker to get gas."

"Anywhere? Like New York to California?"

"Yep, if the fancy took you. Just get up and go."

"It sounds unreal." Marie was distant, still partly lost in her own musings.

"People don't remember," Len said again. "Everything's rules and restrictions. We're being turned into an alien military base, that's what it is."

Marie used to wonder why, if their world was so disciplined and orderly, governed under a single ruling system, the Hyadeans possessed a military establishment at all. Their answer was that they needed to protect themselves against a rival power known as the Querl, who inhabited a group of worlds loosely strung across the same star systems. The Querl were of the same race as the Hyadeans, having split off as a rebellious faction and left to found a culture based on their own political and economic principles. According to the Chryseans—which was the correct name for the Hyadeans of the home planet and its subject worlds—these principles were unsound and illogical, resulting in chaotic rule by ill-defined authorities, with consequent depletion and degradation of the Querl planets. The Chryseans would educate Earth and provide guidance to prevent similar things from happening here. And the institutions that were ultimately in control of things—in the West, anyway—were lending themselves readily to bringing their own houses into line. A compliant media establishment spread the word and the imagery, and for years the people, by and large, had been buying the line and not seeing the regimentation, exploitation, and the slow erosion of what had once been their rights. But now they were feeling the effects, and that was changing. Recruitment for Sovereignty was on the increase, and support was quietly spreading across a wide but largely invisible infrastructure of American life that didn't have access to the interplanetary financial markets and saw little prospect of benefiting significantly from the proceeds. As resistance grew, the classical escalating pattern would develop of what one side saw as protest and suppression being viewed by the powers in control as provocation and response. The times would get ugly before they could improve. CounterAction was preparing.

Mario didn't see herself as a subversive fighting against America. By all the principles she had been told about and grown up believing in, she was fighting *for* what America was once supposed to have stood for.

CHAPTER ELEVEN

The message on Cade's laptop offered a flat introduction fee plus a 2.5 percent commission on net proceeds if Cade could put the sender's brokering agency in touch with a Hyadean concern interested in buying Terran graphical programming services. There was a big demand for Terran software skills on Chryse and its associated worlds. Most programming there was performed by various kinds of AI, with results that were solid, reliable, acceptable ... and utterly without trace of any insight or creative flare that went an iota beyond meeting the minimum specification. The efforts of Hyadean manual programmers fared about the same: in Mike Blair's phrase, which was his favorite appellation for just about everything they did, "dull and plodding." Terran programmers, by contrast, could come up with ways of doing things that Hyadean minds were incapable of mimicking. More often than not they worked for companies whose existence was threatened by Hyadean competition.

But it wasn't a time to be thinking too much about things like that when Julia was sitting at the vanity in her underwear and a negligee, combing out her hair and attending to the feminine bedtime ritual of removing makeup and applying lotion and perfume. Cade stared at her for a while from the bed, watching the tossing waves of her red hair and the lithe, feline motions of her back. Sometimes, he reflected, it seemed as if life treated him too well.

He initiated shutdown, set the computer aside on the night stand, and stretched back comfortably to rest against the headboard, his hands clasped behind his head. Julia caught the movement in the mirror. "So, are you going to fix them up with the same contact that Vrel gave you last time?" she asked over her shoulder.

"Maybe better than that. I was thinking we could use Sigliari. It might lead to a whole bunch of direct lines in there." Sigliari was a promoter from San Diego who had visited Chryse recently and was actively soliciting business there. Who knew what possibilities a lead like that into the home planet might open up?

"Sounds like a cool idea," Julia agreed.

Cade shrugged. "Who knows? I might even work a trip there myself one of these days."

"Even cooler. Does that mean I'm invited?"

"Just try staying behind. Can you see me having fun running wild and free with nothing but Hyadean women around? You're essential baggage—also wanted on the voyage."

"Women here don't seem to have a problem with Hyadean guys," Julia commented. "You've only got to look at Dee and Vrel."

"Which only goes to show how less discerning women are," Cade replied. He realized that didn't sound very good. "Not that there's anything wrong with Vrel. I mean, he's a great friend. It's just . . ." He threw out a hand helplessly. There was no gracious continuation. He had painted himself into a corner. Julia rose, came over to the bed, and disposed of the few garments she was still wearing. Cade let his gaze wander over her, and in moments all thoughts of his impasse had fled. She slid in beside him, entwining bodies, and drew close.

"Then think about a Terran woman for the time being," she murmured.

They made love skillfully, satisfyingly, with the ease and confidence that come when time has bred a familiarity that goes beyond just good companionship and has banished uncertainties. The physical gratification that they shared at night was the ideal complement to the professional intimacy that they shared during the day. At times, Cade was tempted to bring up the possibility of marrying again; but then, he would ask himself, why risk messing with a good relationship?

Afterward, they lay contentedly, Julia resting her face on his shoulder, her finger tracing idle designs on his chest. "You make me feel like a woman," she told him.

"What did you expect? Orangutan? Wildebeest? Sumatran two-horned rhinoceros?"

"Oh, don't be so unromantic. You know what I mean."

Cade grinned and slid an arm around her shoulder. "Of course I do. Life just gets better, doesn't it?"

A few seconds of silence passed, as if Julia were pondering something. "Wasn't it ever good before?" she asked finally.

"It depends when did you mean? Any time in particular?"

"Oh . . . when you were with Marie, for instance. Was it good like this then?"

"It had its ups and downs, I guess." Cade was surprised. "What made you bring that up?"

"I'm not sure. . . . Maybe when those two ISS people came here, asking about her."

Cade shook his head. "Like I told them, that was all over years ago. The last I heard, she was in China."

"They seemed to think she's come back," Julia reminded him. She seemed to let the subject rest there, then added lightly, "Do you ever hear from her?"

"What? Hell, no. Why should I?" Cade turned his head. "Don't tell me you're getting jealous."

"I was just curious," Julia replied.

The next morning, Mike Blair called to inform Cade that he was going to Australia. Krossig, the Hyadean anthropologist at the LA mission, would be leaving almost at once to join the Hyadean scientific field station still being operated there. He and Blair had gotten to know each other in the course of Blair's long periods of ensconcing himself at the mission, which had resulted in an invitation for Blair to go too as Krossig's Terran scientific understudy and consultant.

"It sounds good, Mike," Cade told him. He had taken the call in the gym behind the garage at the side of the house, where he had been working out with Luke. "So when is this likely to happen?"

"Once these guys make their minds up, they don't fool around. It could be a matter of weeks."

"What's the political situation like there?" Cade asked. He was always curious about backgrounds that could affect business.

"With a pure scientific research station, it's okay. The government's trying to keep the contact but stay out of any main currents. The Hyadeans have had a presence there since the first landings. It's probably good diplomacy to just go along with them."

Cade nodded. "It sounds like we're going to need another party to send you guys off, then."

"Well, I wouldn't say no to that."

Luke came through on his way to the shower room, clad in a blue track suit with a towel tucked around the neck, his face still red and perspiring. "It's Mike," Cade told him, gesturing with the compad. "Krossig's transferring to that place they've got in Australia, and Mike will be going too."

"Great," Luke acknowledged.

Cade thought for a moment. "What do you think Hyadeans might say to a day out fishing, Terran style, instead of another party?" he asked Blair on the screen.

"Vrel would like it for sure. Probably Krossig too. . . . I don't think he's ever tried anything like that. Sounds like a good idea."

Cade looked back up at Luke. "Talk to Warren when we're done, would you? Tell him to get the boat set up for a day out. We'll make it a smaller thing this time, just family—something different for them to talk about when they go back to Chryse."

Julia brought up the subject of Marie again that evening, while she and Cade were driving to a dinner party in San Clemente. It struck Cade as unusual. Julia was of a practical disposition and had always tended to leave what was over in the past, where it belonged. What kind of a person had Marie been? Intense, Cade said. A human perpetual-motion machine. One of those women who would never have a weight problem because she burned everything off with nervous energy, regardless of what or how much she ate. So how would he describe their relationship? Julia wanted to know. Cade took one hand off the wheel to make a side-to-side motion in the air. "Mercurial," he told her.

"How did it end?"

"She could never really get comfortable with being comfortable. Know what I mean? When life took swings for the better, she seemed to get more guilty about it—as if it wasn't right for her life to be coming together while so many other people's were messed up. She always had this idealistic streak about helping to make the world a better place. . . . I guess when it became obvious that I wasn't going to change, she decided to move on to find somewhere she could do something about it." They drove in silence, while Julia either contemplated her next question or digested the information. Cade turned his head to glance at her. "What is this? You've never gone into any of this before, and you never do anything without a reason. So what's the reason?"

Julia remained quiet for an unnaturally long time. Finally, she answered, "An old college friend of mine tracked me down recently—through Dee. Let's say her name's Rebecca. She's in some kind of trouble with the authorities and needs help getting out of the country."

Cade whistled silently. "As bad as that? What kind of trouble are we talking about?"

"I didn't ask. But you know what it's like trying to get through the regular exits. Everywhere's watched. They've got everything about you in the computers."

"Have you decided to start a new line—people smuggling?" Cade asked. Even now he was unable to refrain from a mildly teasing note.

"She was a close friend, the kind you'd like to do something for." Julia paused again, then drew a long breath as if committing herself finally. "Look, I was asking about Marie to see if there was a chance you might still be on speaking terms. If she is back in the country as those ISS people said, what might the possibility be of contacting her? Doesn't that organization that they said she's with have ways of getting people out—to Asia or somewhere maybe? They're supposed to have a whole underground organization for moving contraband and people, right?"

Cade glanced at her in mock apprehension. "What are you trying to get me into here? Look, I sympathize with your friend. But even supposing I wanted to get involved, I don't have any idea where Marie is now. I've only got those two spooks' word that she's even back from China."

Julia, however, was evidently not ready to leave it there. "Come on, you're the Mr. Fixit with connections everywhere, aren't you?" she said. "I know how you work, Roland. Are you really telling me that with all the friends you and she made over the years, you couldn't find a way of getting a message through to her if you really needed to?" She reached out and laid a hand on his knee. "Rebecca *was* a close friend. And it does sound as if she's in a lot of trouble."

Cade took his eyes off the road to look across the car for a second. Julia was serious, he could see. "So where is she right now?" he asked.

"In a hotel downtown. I guess one of those non-descript places where invisible people go. Dee didn't give me any details."

Cade shook his head. "That's no good. You'd better bring her to the house while we figure something out. At least it'll be more comfortable. Can you arrange it with Dee?"

Julia hesitated, as if giving him time to reconsider. "Does that mean we're going to help her?" she asked.

Cade stared at the highway ahead, wondering what options he had let himself in for now. "Let's see what she has to say first," he replied.

After they got back home, Julia went out again and returned a couple of hours later with Rebecca. She was mousy haired and plain, a little on the plump side, not given to talk; or perhaps it was the strain of the last couple of days and whatever experiences had preceded them. Henry took her bags and showed her to one of the guest rooms. Later, she reappeared for a late supper of chicken pieces and fries in the kitchen. Cade and Julia joined her just for coffee, since they had eaten earlier. By then, Rebecca had pulled herself more together.

Her story was that she and another woman had coauthored a hard-hitting piece in an underground political newsletter that circulated in print and on the net, detailing dubious and in some cases flatly unlawful electoral machinations that had accompanied the installation of the current administration in Washington, which if proved would make it illicit, and not the result of a constitutionally correct, democratic process. The governor of California, William Jeye, had picked it up in a speech to the Constitutional Club of San Francisco, and the result had been consternation in the Western media, condemnation from the East, and public outcries everywhere. The other author had been arrested. Another woman, who lived on the next street to Rebecca in a house with the same number, was picked up by the ISS at the same time but released twenty-four hours later with an admission of mistaken identity. Rebecca had packed a bag and gone into hiding; she

wouldn't even say where in the country she had
arrived from.

"I know I come across like a wimp," she said. "But
I can hold my own with anyone when it comes to
words. Julia will tell you that. She knew me at college."

"She used to tie us all in knots debating," Julia
confirmed.

Rebecca shook her head and drew in a sharp, shaky
breath that came close to a shudder. "But I'm not
good when it comes to physical things. You know, the
things you hear about: interrogation drugs; all the
intimidation; worse. . . . I couldn't go out on the street,
knowing they might pick me up anytime. Haven't
really been able to sleep since it happened. . . . I have
to get out of here."

"Out of the country completely?" Cade said. "It's
really that bad?"

"She's right," Julia told him. "They won't quit
now—not after the fuss that this is causing." The news
that evening had brought reports of demonstrations
in several cities, with more use of Hyadean sonic
disruptors on the crowds, as had been seen in Washington, along with water cannon. In Kentucky, a group
armed with shoulder-launched missiles and assault
weapons, believed to be CounterAction, had attacked
an ISS depot, declaring it to be an arm of the occu-
pational forces of an illegal regime installed to
advance alien interests.

"So how did you find Dee?" Cade asked Rebecca.
"Did you know her at sometime too?" It seemed an
unlikely coincidence. Julia had met Dee only after
getting to know Cade and joining his circle of friends.

Rebecca shook her head. "When I started asking
around the people we used to know way back, one
of them put me on to Brad." She looked at Julia. "He

used to be your husband, right? Owns a couple of clubs." Julia nodded. Rebecca went on, "Brad put me on to Dee and said I should try through her."

Julia cupped both hands around her coffee mug and drank from it, then gave Cade a searching look. He stared across the table at Rebecca. Despite what she had said earlier about her verbal skills, her voice tonight had been little more than a whisper. She seemed all done in.

Just one more thing crossed Cade's mind. "Do you still have your phone with you?" he asked. "And in your bags is there a laptop, compad, anything like that?" Virtually all electronic devices of any value, as well as things like automobiles and appliances, contained GPS chips able to fix their location on the Earth's surface to within a few yards. In the case of loss or theft, dialing a specified number would cause them to return details of where they were. Rumor had it that government agencies had special numbers too, that would override the normal enabling functions. Cade had never been able to determine whether it was true or not.

Rebecca shook her head. "I threw the phone away. There isn't anything else." Cade nodded, satisfied.

"Well, there's not a lot else we can do tonight," he said. "Why don't we all get some rest? Tomorrow we've got a boat trip organized with some friends. Why don't you come along? A little bit of sun and ocean might make you feel like a new person."

"Maybe," Rebecca answered. She didn't sound enthralled by the idea.

After Rebecca had left them, Cade and Julia went through to the bar for a nightcap. "If you do manage to pull something, I assume it will cost us," Julia said.

Cade pulled a face. "I'm not sure. Rebecca sounds like a pretty good ally on their side. They might be happy just to get her over there." This didn't seem a time to let something like that get in the way. It wasn't as if they were hard up, just at the moment. He downed a mouthful of his drink. "We can worry about that side of it later."

"I can make the necessary arrangements . . . if that helps," Julia said.

Cade looked at her. He knew Julia had assets of her own that he had never made it his business to pry into. "It's really that important to you?" he said.

Julia nodded. "Yes," she told him. "It is."

Later, after Julia had retired ahead of him, Cade sat brooding in his study for a long time. He checked the clock, made several calls, and sent out a few carefully worded messages into the net.

CHAPTER TWELVE

A few miles north of Catalina Island, the *Sassy Lady* trailed a foamy wake across a placid sea rolling gently under a cloudless sky. Cade, in a straw hat and swim trunks, leaned over from a sun lounge on the boat deck aft of the wheelhouse, helped himself to another beer from the ice chest, and passed one to Blair. Vrel and Krossig declined, nursing their previous ones, still somewhat wary of this dubious Terran habit. Julia and Dee were sunning themselves on the bow, while Luke kept Warren company in the wheelhouse, and others were in the main cabin below. A crewman was preparing rods and tackle on the fishing platform at the stern. Rebecca had stayed behind, preferring to remain within the security of the house. Blair was still enthusing about his forthcoming move to Australia. He had some things to finish up in Los Angeles, and would be following on a month or so after Krossig.

"Just think, they're giving me a position to study Hyadean science officially," he told Cade. "I'll be getting paid for it."

"But don't our own people have jobs like that here?" Cade said. "I thought half of Washington was into it."

Blair shook his head. "I'm talking about understanding the *real* science, the attitude of mind that lets them get it right. The government collaborations focus too much on short-term applications—better ways to make weapons and profits. I got offers there a couple of times but it wasn't what I wanted."

Cade really didn't know one way or the other. He nodded, sipped his beer, and left it at that.

"We got a message from Erya, on her way to Chryse," Krossig told Cade. "She says you've shown her a new way of seeing things. She hopes she'll be able to spread it on Chryse."

"Sounds as if the place could do with it," Blair commented.

"I just received a gift too," Vrel told them. He had acquired an outrageously gaudy pair of beach shorts and was sprawled on a blanket spread out over the deck. The Chrysean sun, Amaris, shone more brightly and slightly more toward the violet. Hyadeans had no problem with the solar intensity on Earth and soaked up all they could get. Blair had speculated to Cade that maybe that was why they chose mountainous areas. Vrel made the announcement sound like a special event.

"What was that?" Cade asked him.

"From Neville Baxter—at the party. It's a Maori sculpture, a kind of figurine. Very attractive. I'll show it to you next time you're at the mission. Dee says it's probably worth quite a lot."

"That sounds like Neville," Cade agreed.

"He also says I have to visit him in New Zealand. Apparently, it's important to see that all the world isn't like America. What does he mean by that?"

"A kind of private joke that we have between countries," Cade said. Vrel nodded vaguely but didn't really seem to understand.

"Well, I'm looking forward to seeing the East," Krossig said. "I might even get a chance to visit other areas . . . even the Himalayas, maybe." He leaned back against the sun lounge he was on and tossed out an arm in a sweeping gesture. "Have you any idea how unique this planet of yours is? These huge mountain ranges; chasms like the Yangtze gorges. The whole surface is young, sculpted only yesterday. That's why life here is so colorful and varied. It's life that has been renewed and reinvigorated. The worlds we know are old and tired—endless expanses of monotonous plains and eroded hills, silted rivers, insipid swamplands. Worlds in their old age, awaiting rejuvenation."

"Have those planets been around all that much longer, then?" Cade asked.

"No. They've just been wearing down for longer," Krossig said.

"They haven't had the disruptions that Earth has gone through," Blair put in. "Not anytime lately, anyhow. Our conventional notion of slow, gradual change over huge time-spans got it wrong. Changes happen quickly and violently."

Cade knew that Blair could go on for hours if he was allowed to warm to a theme. He looked over at Vrel. "I don't know about quick and violent changes to planets, but I've seen plenty of them in people. This is starting to sound more like your field." Vrel was the political economist.

Vrel raised the can he was holding, twirled it around and contemplated it for a few seconds, then seemed to change his mind and lowered it again. "Hm. There's something paradoxical here," he said. "Terrans believed in gradualism, but their whole history is violent and catastrophic. Hyadeans accept upheaval as the natural way of change, but we deplore it and try to eliminate it from our affairs. That's what's at the bottom of our problems with the Querl—why we and they are in armed opposition."

"How's that?" Blair asked. The reasons for the standoff and occasional conflict between the Hyadean and the Querl worlds was something that Cade had long wanted to understand better too.

"Well, we are taught that their system reflects values that are incompatible with ours," Vrel said. "They take pride in what we consider to be social ills in need of correction. They could never conform to the system of approvals and entitlements that our social structure is built on."

"So does that make them a threat that you have to defend against?" Cade asked.

"We've always been told that they are," Vrel replied.

Krossig conceded the field to politics and elaborated. "Their system can't work. Our economists have proved it. Because it's based on conflicts and rivalries that consume nonproductive effort, it must devour resources faster than it can replenish them. As the situation becomes more critical, the conflicts will increase, making the imbalance worse. Eventually, the only solution left to them will be to try and take from us—provided we let them. If we make that impossible by maintaining sufficient military strength, the outcome, eventually, must be the Querl's downfall."

Cade drank again and stared at him. It was too pat, like a memorized line that had been drummed in through life. Typically Hyadean. He shifted his gaze to Vrel, whose response had been less automatic. Twice, Vrel had qualified his statements by cautioning that they were what Hyadeans were "taught" or had been "told." Those were surprising words to hear coming from a Hyadean. "I assume the Querl must know the Chrysean position," he said. "So how do they see it?"

"They don't see themselves as disorderly or unruly, but simply as pursuing their ideals of independence and freedom," Vrel replied. He thought for a moment, and then smiled uncomfortably. "And we're supposed to be here to save Earth from going the same way. Yet it seems that those same things are also regarded as ideals by most humans." He looked from one to another of the others helplessly. "Another paradox. There's something wrong somewhere, isn't there? But I can't put my finger on what it is."

Warren came out from the wheelhouse at that point to announce that they had reached the fishing grounds and were slowing down to begin casting, and Vrel's question never did get answered. Later, when Cade and Blair were leaning on the rail together, watching the waves, Blair remarked that it was the first time he had ever heard a Chrysean questioning the home world's system.

"I know," Cade replied. "Interesting, isn't it? Maybe this crazy world of ours is starting to rub off on them more than we think." He lifted his head to follow a group of porpoises as they broke surface to frolic a hundred feet or so from the boat. "And then again . . . maybe it was just the beer."

CHAPTER THIRTEEN

It was strange that the theory Earth's scientific establishment finally put together for shaping the evolution of the cosmos should be based on gravity, when the electromagnetic force was ten thousand billion, billion, billion, billion times stronger, and 99 percent of observable matter existed in the form of electrically charged plasma that responded to it. More so when galaxies, certain binary stars, and other objects were found not to move in the ways that purely gravitational models said they should, and various forms of "dark matter" and other unobservables had to be invented to explain why.

The Hyadean universe, by contrast, was electrical. Matter was fundamentally an electrical phenomenon. The basic force was electrical, and gravity a byproduct. The cosmos, its galaxies, stars, and other constituents, hadn't condensed gravitationally out of gas, dust, and spinning nebulas produced from the debris of some primordial Big Bang. Such an explosion would have resulted simply in permanent dispersion of energy and whatever particles formed out of it. Again, the Terrans' grand theory had gotten things backward. Cosmic objects, from dust clouds and planets to neutron stars and quasars weren't the results of condensation and collapse from rarefied clouds of matter, but of the progressive breaking down from superdense concentrations of it. Electrical interactions operating on a titanic scale spun these objects to instability, causing them to throw off parts of themselves which then repeated the process, engendering a succession of bodies of progressively diminishing mass, rotation, and magnetic energy. Depending on the mass of the original fragmenting singularity, the products could be quasars, which in turn gave rise to radio galaxies, and from them, spiral galaxies; globular halos of younger stars around galaxies; or supernovas evolving into pulsars or white dwarves. Gravity only had any significant effect as a comparatively feeble cleaning-up process in the latter phases.

Fragments that didn't make it as stars cooled to form the gas giants, which when meeting and entering into capture with a star or another gas giant threw off what became minor planets, their satellites, comets, and the other debris that formed planetary systems. These were the times when space became an electrically active medium, transmitting forces that disrupted orbits to bring about the encounters that renewed and revitalized worlds. During the quiescent periods between, the interplanetary plasma would organize into an insulating configuration in which gravity was allowed to predominate. Local observations conducted during a few centuries of such a quiet period had led Earth's astronomers to overgeneralize such conditions as representing the permanent situation.

However, many surface characteristics of bodies in the Solar System were impossible to reconcile with the conventional picture of nothing having essentially changed for billions of years.

Furthermore, the farthest, hence oldest, objects visible in the cosmos—such as quasars—were the most massive and energetic: precisely the opposite of what gradual condensation from initially rarefied matter would predict. And the detection of vast structures of galaxy-cluster "walls" and voids at the largest scales of observation indicated processes having been operating in the universe for far longer than the fifteen billion years that the Big Bang model allowed since its inception.

But things like that didn't fit with the theory.

CHAPTER FOURTEEN

Cade hadn't put a lot of trust in the messages he sent out electronically via the net. They had been worded cryptically, with obscure references that only the recipients would recognize. A friend who worked on communications had told him that most computers these days were required to carry chips that tagged messages with invisible codes enabling senders to be traced. As was his custom, he'd had more faith in word of mouth.

He had no idea how to go about finding a channel to contact Marie directly. People who knew about such things told him if she were indeed back in the U.S. and was working with CounterAction, she would be using a different name and operating in an environment carefully structured such that she *couldn't* be located. However, Cade knew a minister in San Pedro by the name of Udovich, a staunch Republican disapproving of Ellis's Washington regime, who ran a church and a shelter for evicted families by day, and at other times disappeared on long camping and hiking trips up into the Sierra. One of the people that Cade talked to whispered that Udovich was involved with some kind of conduit that routed arms in via Mexico to paramilitary groups up in the mountains. Californian laws would have made this impossible in earlier years. But by this time, even law enforcement agencies were rebelling against the Washington line and turning blind eyes. Many took it as seeds of revolution in the wind. That suggested Udovich could have connections with Sovereignty, and through them access into the higher levels of their militant arm, CounterAction, somewhere. If so, Cade reasoned, they ought to have a way of getting a message through to Marie, even if it meant going all the way back up the tree and then down again via China. Around noon on the day following the boat trip, he drove up to San Pedro and talked with Udovich over iced teas at a sidewalk table outside a sports bar called O'Reilly's, down by the bay.

After opening small talk, Cade mentioned casually that ministers were traditionally respected for keeping confidences, and therefore often trusted to convey sensitive communications. Smiling out at the ocean, Udovich agreed that this was often so. Cade hazarded the guess that a man of Udovich's convictions probably wouldn't be overenamored by the current policies being enacted in Washington. Dreadful, Udovich agreed. Professional middle-class Americans being sold out like cheap labor. Cade regarded the minister long and hard, stroking his chin as if the thought had just occurred to him for the first time, and remarked that Udovich didn't strike him as the kind of person who would sit back and watch it happen. If there were people organizing in opposition, he'd want to get involved. Well, certainly anyone with principles and a conscience would want to do something, Udovich told the ocean, giving away nothing.

His oblique references not having been rebuffed, Cade interlaced his fingers, leaned closer across the table, and came to the point. "I want to contact somebody who I believe might be with one of the underground political groups in this country. I've reason to think you might have connections who might pass a message in the right direction. Can you help?"

Udovich's pink, moonlike, bespectacled features— surely the most incongruous image for the kind of thing Cade was asking—didn't register surprise. He had clearly been expecting something like this. His manner, however, shed its protective cover of vague geniality and became businesslike. "Who is this person?" he murmured.

"My former wife, who went to China. I've heard that she's back now, with CounterAction. I have someone who needs to leave the country invisibly. CounterAction are supposed to have ways."

"What kind of problem prevents this person from buying a ticket and getting on a plane?" Udovich asked.

"Giving the wrong people a bad press can get you into bad favor these days," Cade answered. "If the people who don't like what you say have the power to take you off the streets, things can get awkward."

"Why should I or anyone else care? Why risk it?"

"Because it's the same cause." Cade shrugged. "And in any case, you run a ministry. Protecting your flock depends on donations. You know a little bit about me. I can arrange generous contributions from the most unlikely quarters. I'm sure it all helps."

Udovich considered the proposition for a while, crunching on an ice cube from his tea. "Supposing

I *were* able to pass this request on to where you ask, why wouldn't that be enough?' he queried at last. "Why does it need to find this ex of yours specifically?"

"It wouldn't if whoever makes the decicions were happy to take my word for it," Cade agreed. "But why should they? She and I might have had our differences, but she'd vouch that I can be trusted to play straight. I'm not political. I deal in people. Reputation is my work." He smiled faintly and gestured across the table. "A bit like you, I guess."

Udovich nodded slowly and seemed satisfied. "I'd need her name and a little about when you were together," he said. "And something that would convince her this has come from you."

Cade supplied the minimum details that seemed necessary. Udovich committed them to memory. The second part was tougher. "Tell her . . . there's some red coal," he said finally. Udovich nodded and didn't ask. In their more romantic days, one of the things Cade and Marie had liked doing together was solving cryptic crossword puzzles. It was an anagrammatic play on his name: ROL*and* CADE; take the conjunction out, and the remaining letters rearranged into *red coal*. With a bit of playing around, Marie would get it.

"No guarantees, but we'll see," Udovich pronounced. He finished his tea and stood up. "Well, I must get back to tending my flock." He looked back over his shoulder as he was about to leave. "We must watch out for the wolves, you see." He walked away, leaving Cade to take it whichever way he pleased.

Late that afternoon, Dee and Vrel stopped by the house to collect a share of the previous day's fish catch, which Henry had cleaned, gutted, and set aside in the refrigerator for them. Julia was in the guest suite keeping Rebecca company, since she preferred to stay out of sight of visitors. Cade entertained Vrel and Dee to drinks in the lounge area around the bar.

"Getting daring these days, aren't we, Vrel?" he quipped as Vrel mixed himself a gin and tonic—with a generous measure of tonic. "Taking fish back to eat at the mission, now, and halfway toward becoming an alcoholic."

"I think I'm just beginning to realize how insipid our food is," Vrel said, making a face.

"I hope you're remembering to take those pills they give you. Wouldn't want you going down with any of these terrible Terran germs."

"I know you used to take them once," Dee said. "But I don't remember seeing them for ages."

Vrel made an indifferent shrug. "Maybe, getting to know Earthpeople better has made me start to think that maybe Hyadeans can be a little . . ." He groped for the word, then muttered something to his veebee.

"*Neurotic,*" it supplied.

"Neurotic," Vrel repeated.

Dee laughed delightedly and squeezed his arm in a way that said she liked him better like this. Vrel grinned.

"How is he going to fit in again when he goes home?" Cade asked her.

Dee pouted. "*Roland!* Don't talk about him going home." She looked at Vrel. "That's not going to be for a long time yet, is it?"

Vrel's face became more serious. "I don't know. I suppose a lot depends on what happens here. Two Hyadeans from the mission were harassed and jeered at in a mall near Lakewood yesterday. The police escorted them back. They've put extra security around the mission again."

"Oh. . . . That's a shame," Cade said. The outbreaks of protest and violence across the country were causing anti-Hyadean reactions in places. ISS agents landing in a helicopter assault had wiped out what was said to be the base of the group that had mounted the attack in Kentucky, and security units across the nation were cracking down with arrests of suspected CounterAction supporters. Cade had always tried to steer clear of such things. Yet now, he reflected, his action in harboring Rebecca was probably enough to get him on a wanted list already. He hoped Udovich wasn't being affected. If pressures developed that prevented him from following through, Cade could find himself saddled with having a fugitive from the federal government in the house indefinitely.

He sighed and tasted his drink wearily. One mention of Marie, and life was getting complicated again. Even at this distance—whatever distance; he didn't even know where she was—and after so long, it seemed her nature was still that of catastrophic upheaval, disrupting what had started to become his predictable, gravitationally stable universe.

CHAPTER FIFTEEN

Two days passed by. Independent sources on the net circulated critical accounts of "search and intern" sweeps being carried out by airborne security forces landed in remote parts of Appalachia, Colorado, and Utah. The media billed the actions as counterterrorist, directed at the groups who had begun a campaign of political assassination, which the authorities would not tolerate. A number of helicopters were alleged to have been brought down by missiles. An ISS spokesman called for Hyadean defensive equipment to be fitted to government-operated air vehicles as a precaution.

Then, Cade received a phone call one morning when he was with Julia and their accountant, who had stopped by to review some figures. A smoothly articulated masculine voice asked him what the color of coal was. "My kind is red," Cade replied.

"Then I gather I'm speaking to the right person."

Cade asked the accountant to excuse him but this was private and important, and took the phone through to his study. He closed the door and indicated it was okay to go ahead.

"I have a message from Mole Woman. It says you could always be depended on for surprises," the caller informed him.

Despite everything, Cade couldn't contain a smile. This was his proof of validity. "Mole Woman" was one of the names that he used to call Marie in their lighter moments—from the comic-book Catwoman, a joke at the way Marie had of burrowing into the bedclothes on cold mornings to leave just her nose showing.

"It must be my nature," Cade affirmed. "Okay. What do we have?"

"I understand you have a job applicant seeking an overseas position," the voice informed him.

"Looking for less stress and pressure. An escape from the rat race," Cade confirmed.

"The positions we offer normally pay around twenty thousand. Was that the kind of figure your client has in mind?"

It was double talk, spelling out what the service would *cost*. "We could settle for that, yes," Cade agreed.

"Fine. Of course, we would need to arrange an appropriate interview. Where does the applicant currently reside?"

"I guess you could say on the West Coast."

"Hm. . . . These things are usually managed by our Eastern region. However, if that should be impracticable, it would probably be possible to arrange a preliminary meeting with a local branch representative."

Cade chewed on his lip while he thought about

it. The reference to the East probably meant that CounterAction's route for spiriting people out of the country led in that direction, maybe through the Caribbean to Africa, and then Asia via the Middle East. He didn't want to get any more involved here, in his own backyard, he decided. Midnight callers and furtive meetings around the locality would be the last thing he needed. Better to get Rebecca there as quickly as possible. And if something came of it, she would already be partly on her way.

"I'd prefer that the regional office handle it, if they're the proper people," he said.

"You will be contacted in due course." The caller hung up.

That same evening, a fax came through in Cade's study of a promotional brochure from a hotel called the Metro in downtown Atlanta. Typed across the bottom were terse instructions for the "applicant" to be outside the main doors of the ground-level motor lobby at a given date and time, holding an Atlanta city guide book for recognition.

The date stipulated allowed four days, presumably making allowance for a journey by road. Luke advised against it on the grounds that, with all the trouble in the news, spot checks of travelers on major highways, railroads, and public buses were likely to have been intensified. And besides, he didn't think Rebecca was up to the stresses of a protracted trip. But Cade had never contemplated such alternatives in the first place. What was the point of doing favors for wealthy friends, he asked, if you couldn't ask one back now and again for yourself?

There was one Lou Zinner, based most of the time in Las Vegas, who had interests in casinos and the entertainment world, and fingers in various associated sleazy dealings. It was Lou, for example, who provided the available girls for Cade's Hyadean parties and boat trips. He remained at a distance behind Cade's more respectable front and didn't deal with the Hyadeans directly. Lou also happened to own an executive jet, which he used for attending business meetings, visiting "family," and flying a seemingly inexhaustible supply of mistresses, young admirers, and hopeful starlets to be entertained in exotic places. Lou was always happy to hear from Cade because high-ranking Hyadeans taking time off talked in big bucks. Hence, he was a hundred percent receptive when Cade called and said he wanted the loan of Lou's plane and its pilot for a day.

The craggy, balding head guffawed heartily on the screen in Cade's study. "What's going on, Rolie? Don't tell me. You're expanding the operation. The boat's too tame for 'em now. You've got aliens that wanna join the twenty thousand club, right?"

"Wrong. No, nothing like that. I need to make a rush delivery across the country. It'll be back the same night."

"Okay, then I'm not askin'. So what's the cut?"

Cade thought for a second. "Maybe I'll be able to get you some high rollers out there yet. You know how those ones that come across from Washington are loaded."

"I'll settle for that. Okay, Rolie, you've got it. Just try to send it back in one piece, willya? I've got it booked for the weekend after."

That solved the immediate problem. But Luke thought that if they were going to have an entire aircraft at their disposal, they could make better use of it. "Just to take one person to Atlanta?" he said to Cade when Cade gave him the news. "Why on her own? What happens if something screws up—say nobody shows, and she finds herself stuck there? We couldn't just leave her like that. One of us ought to go too. I say we keep a good eye on her until we know she's in the right hands."

Cade agreed. "In that case I'll go," he said. "This isn't really your affair. I got us into it." Luke shrugged and nodded in a way that said it was fine by him.

Julia, however, was perturbed when they updated her on their thoughts. "Why risk getting mixed up with CounterAction people directly?" she objected. "If you're seen or identified with them, it could start trouble that will never go away. We've had the ISS here already. You know what's going on all over the country. We don't need to get mixed up in all that."

It seemed a strange turn of attitude after the things Cade had heard. "Because she's an old friend, remember?" he replied. "Look, I'm not planning on getting mixed up with anybody. All I'm doing is taking her as far as a hotel lobby. I don't even need to wait there with her—just close enough to see she gets picked up. That's it. Then I'm on my way back."

Eventually, Julia relented, but she still didn't seem happy about it.

Accordingly, Cade and Rebecca made their preparations the evening before the appointed day. Lou Zinner's jet appeared at the John Wayne/Orange County airport early the next morning as arranged, and they took off on time. En route, the plane was challenged by two Air Force jets that radioed for identification and a mission statement. Fortunately, the pilot had filed a flight plan, stated as serving the private business needs of a Nevada-registered VIP. The plane landed at Hartsfield International Airport, Atlanta, a little over four hours after leaving California.

CHAPTER SIXTEEN

Frank Pacelli had worked night shift stocking supermarket shelves, sold kitchen ware, and part-timed at a gas station to pay his way through college, and emerged with a degree in chemistry and metallurgical engineering. He had worked first with a couple of mining corporations in Minnesota and Colorado, later at a smelting and rolling plant in Korea, done well, and come back to a position as process designer with a company in Minneapolis. Then the Hyadeans began flooding the world markets with bulk minerals extracted from places like Bolivia by methods no Terran industry could compete with; the company folded, and now Frank drove a taxicab. He got pretty mad when he heard about some of the dealings that went on in Washington and the kind of money some people were reputed to make out of them. But with three children of high-school age to think about, he couldn't afford to risk getting directly involved in the more militant protest organizations that everyone pretended not to know about. But sympathizing with them was another thing. Much passed his eyes that he didn't see, came to his ears that he didn't hear, and he helped the cause when he could.

He turned off Peachtree Street into the motor lobby of the Metro hotel at the time he had been given, and slowed to scan the few figures outside the main entrance. The pudgy woman in the light blue coat and yellow hat, holding a city guide prominently in one hand had to be the person he was to meet. She had a suitcase and a large traveling bag beside her and seemed to be waiting, looking around anxiously. Pacelli eased the cab forward, steering in toward the curb in front of her.

Then it struck him that a tallish man in a gray jacket, standing a few yards away by the doors, was watching her. The conviction solidified when the man's head turned to follow the cab as it closed in. An alarm sounding in his head, Pacelli shifted his foot back to the gas pedal and sped up again, passing the woman just as she was beginning to step forward. He caught a glimpse of her mouth dropping open before he turned away to leave again through the lobby's exit way. He stopped in a parking strip halfway around the block and pressed the "redial" button of his phone to call the number already entered.

"Yes?" The voice that had given him his instructions answered.

"This is Collector. The party's there, a woman. But there's a guy there too, who looks like he's watching her. It didn't feel right, so I thought I'd better check."

"Good thinking. Where are you now?"

"Just around the block."

"Wait."

Pacelli drummed his fingers on the wheel

nervously. He was just driving a cab, sent to pick someone up from a hotel. They couldn't nail anyone for that, right? He wasn't sure. From the things he heard, who knew what they could do these days?

The city of Chattanooga lay just under a hundred miles north of Atlanta in southeastern Tennessee, on the Tennessee River near the Georgia-Alabama line. Three large mountain masses overlooked it, each one of strategic importance and the scene of a major battle in the Civil War.

Marie and Len had arrived after an erratic tour through the Great Smoky range to find Olsen safely there too, several hours ahead of them. That had been over a week ago now. Their new temporary hideout until they were regrouped consisted of a double-width mobile home situated among trees on hilly ground to the north side of the city, between Signal Mountain and the river. Sharing the quarters with them were two other CounterAction people known only as "Vera" and "Bert," both seemingly proficient, with another man that they referred to as "Otter." Marie could tell that Otter was not from the organization. She got the feeling that he was in transit and temporary hiding, in the process of being moved to somewhere more permanent.

That Otter should in this way meet former members of the Scorpion cell that had been hurriedly disbanded was not accidental. Scorpion had been identified by the authorities, blamed for the assassinations that were partly the cause of the current unrest, and targeted for elimination. Otter apparently knew who *had* been responsible: an officer of the security forces themselves, acting on orders from a source close to the administration. Otter could name the officer and give the source of the Hyadean weapon that was used, which had come from a cache stolen in South America, later recovered but never acknowledged officially. It seemed that Otter was being taken to report his information to higher echelons of CounterAction, but the current disruptions and hasty relocations going on everywhere were slowing things down. Whoever was giving the orders had authorized Olsen to let Otter pass on what he knew in case Otter didn't get to wherever he was being taken, and as a further precaution Olsen had included Marie. It wasn't as if the information was something that Sovereignty would want kept secret.

Otter lay sprawled along a couch in the living area watching a movie. Bert was in a room at the back, sorting and checking through various items of equipment. Vera had kept night watch and was sleeping. The number of beds and amount of kit scattered through the rooms and closets suggested that more people used the place, but at present were elsewhere on undisclosed errands. Marie paced restlessly behind Olsen, who was seated at the table in the room that served as his quarters and office, talking to the taxi driver who had been sent to make the collection in Atlanta. He held the phone away suddenly, and cursed beneath his breath. "What is it?" Marie asked, going over.

"A woman showed, but it could be a setup. He thinks she's being watched."

"*What?*" Marie stared at the phone in his hand, as if it could tell her something. Roland wouldn't be involved in something like that. Not knowingly, anyway. She felt embarrassed and guilty, as if she had led them into this. "I can't believe it," was all she could say.

"Let's see what Len thinks." Olsen used a mouse to click the "Call" box of a communications dialer already displayed on one of the screens in front of him. Moments later, Len's voice answered from a connected speaker.

"Watcher here."

Len was at the Metro in Atlanta, observing from back inside the motor lobby entrance. The situation had demanded that somebody else be on hand in case of problems developing, not just the cabbie. The phone that Len was carrying had a video pickup.

"Collector thinks the subject may have a tail," Olsen said at the mike. "How do you read it?"

"Yes, I've got him too. The subject's a woman. It looks like they know each other. Collector came by and then took off. Subject is making like 'What do I do?' The tail is shaking his head." As Len spoke, the screen in front of Olsen switched to show a crazily angled shot of a woman in a light blue coat, wearing a yellow hat, standing beside two bags. Her face was indistinct in the light under the roof outside the lobby doors. She was looking to her right, then turned away in the other direction. The scene cavorted as the camera swung, then settled on a tall man in a light-colored jacket, keeping farther back in the shadows. The figure became clearer as Len moved out toward the doors, then jumped into closeup. It was a man his midthirties, angular cheeked with narrow eyes, and brown wavy hair combed back at both temples.

"Oh my God!" Marie whispered weakly. "What's he doing *there*?"

Olsen turned his head. "You know him? Who is he?"

"It's him . . . the person it came from. My ex-husband. That's Roland. . . . He must have come with her, to make sure things went okay."

Olsen studied the image thoughtfully. "That means

we don't have to listen only to this woman we don't know. We can get his input too. You're sure he's likely to be straight?"

Marie nodded affirmatively. "Oh, yes."

"Then let's bring him along." Olsen leaned forward and touched a key. "Watcher?"

"Here."

"The tail is friendly. In fact, we're glad he's here. So include him in the party too."

Rebecca was getting agitated, looking back at Cade and making empty-hands motions. Cade didn't know what was going on. It had seemed that the cab driver had spotted her and pulled over; then he seemed to change his mind at the last moment. Cade signaled back tersely for Rebecca to stop making it so obvious that they were together. She seemed to get the message, calmed down, and directed her attention back toward the motor lobby entrance. An airport shuttle that had been filling with departing hotel guests started up and departed.

Perhaps the business with the cabbie had been genuinely a case of mistaken identity. Cade checked his watch. Seven minutes past the hour. Was it reasonable to expect people in this kind of line to be punctual—especially with all the trouble that was going on? He opened the newspaper that he'd been carrying under his arm and stared at it. He felt like a ham in a spy movie. Well, hell, what was he supposed to know about this kind of business? He found he was looking at the sports section. He didn't even understand the rules of baseball. A white limo appeared and disgorged a couple both with long hair and in blue jeans. While the driver came around to begin unloading luggage from the trunk, a bellman appeared from inside the hotel, pulling a cart.

And then a cab appeared in the entrance and slowed. Cade wasn't certain, but it seemed like the same one that had passed through before. This time it drew up directly in front of Rebecca. She stooped to peer inside uncertainly. The nearside window lowered, and the driver leaned across to say something. Rebecca nodded. The cab's trunk lid popped open, and the cabbie got out to take care of the two bags. Finally, everything seemed to be going well. Rebecca opened the rear door, and climbed in, glancing out from the window to nod quickly. Cade watched the cabbie slam the trunk lid shut, then go forward and get back in. Just a few more seconds now, and the whole business would be out of Cade's hands. He exhaled a long sigh of relief.

"Take it easy. Don't turn around. Just get in the cab too." The voice spoke close to his ear. It was low, little more than a murmur, but had a distinct no-nonsense quality.

Cade tensed reflexively, then forced himself to relax again, realizing that anything else was futile. "What is this?" he breathed.

"I don't know either. It seems that the people meeting your friend want to talk to you."

"I'm just a delivery man. I don't know anything about what goes on."

"That's not for me to decide. I've just got orders." There was a pause. Cade hesitated. "Come on," the voice said. "You don't want to mess with us. Let's move."

Cade sighed and walked over to the cab, the stranger following. Somehow, the cabbie seemed to know they would be coming and was waiting. Cade opened the door, shrugged in response to Rebecca's bemused look, and got in next to her. The stranger squeezed in beside Cade and closed the door. He was maybe sixtyish, Cade saw as he sat back. Tanned, wrinkled features; hair going white; dark, indecipherable eyes—the kind that never gave away exactly where they were focused. He was wearing a hiplength coat of brown suede over a tan, crew-neck sweater. The cab pulled back out onto Peachtree, negotiated several blocks, and descended an on ramp to a highway that signs said were Interstates 75 and 85 South, which led back toward the airport. But after a few intersections it exited again onto a road leading among industrial premises, where it entered a parking area and stopped beside a black, windowless van. "Here, we change," the stranger informed them. "Not much of a view from here on, I'm afraid. But I'm sure you understand that these things are necessary."

The three got out. A driver was waiting in the van, wearing a hat over a full head of hair, who could equally well have been male or female from the brief glimpse they were able to get. Before they had even walked around to the rear doors, the cabbie had deposited Rebecca's bags and was on his way. Interestingly, the stranger hadn't paid him anything, Cade noted. The stranger opened one of the van's rear doors, picked up the suitcase, and ushered the other two in. Cade took the travel bag. The interior had seats on both sides and across the front, and was lit by lights in the corners. Cade and Rebecca settled down facing each other across the rear end. The stranger moved past them to sit looking back. He banged his hand a couple of times on the wall behind him, and the van moved off.

Cade quickly lost track of the turns, so that by the time he felt the van accelerating back onto what felt like the Interstate again, he was unable to tell whether they were still going south or had about-turned. As

time wore on he made sporadic attempts to start some
kind of conversation with the stranger, but the
responses were brief and noncommittal, except to say
that they could call him "Len" and it was okay for
Cade to call Lou Zinner's pilot and say he had been
delayed. Cade was mildly surprised that he had been
allowed to keep his phone, and concluded that he
wasn't some kind of prisoner. Hence, if this dragged
on past the pilot's deadline for returning, he didn't
think he would have much difficulty getting a regular flight back. Maybe on principle he should ask
CounterAction to cover the fare.

A little under two hours passed. Since the people
they were going to meet hadn't known how they
would be traveling, it made sense that the initial
rendezvous should have been set in a regional center like Atlanta. There was no reason why the ultimate destination should be conveniently close, of
course. But it puzzled Cade that Len, and presumably those he represented, seemed unconcerned about
the possibility of police checks on a journey of this
length. The most likely explanation he could think of
was that in their own territory they had the highways
staked out and were able to pass warnings of roadblocks in time for them to be avoided.

Eventually, the van's motions signaled that they
were leaving a highway. A few minutes of intermittent turns and stops followed before it halted, and
the engine died. Len got out, turning to retrieve the
bags. Cade and Rebecca followed, stretching cramped
legs and flexing arms, to find themselves outside the
rear of a typical midrange motel.

Len led them to room 127 and rapped on the door.
It was opened by a petite woman in a thin, knitted
pattern sweater, loose slacks, and lightweight hiking
boots. She had wiry hair that wavered between dark

blond and burnt auburn, styled short and easy to manage, sharply defined features that couldn't be called "cute," yet were attractive in their own in-depth kind of way, and dark, almost black eyes that in moments gave the impression of never being still, darting over the arrivals and already seeming to have gleaned all the information there was to see. The eyes came to rest on Cade and softened into mischievous liquid pools at the astonishment on his face.

"So hi," she greeted. "I guess, for once, I get a turn with the surprises. It's been a long time."

It was Marie.

CHAPTER SEVENTEEN

It was so sudden and unexpected that Cade found himself at a loss for anything to say that wouldn't have seemed inane. For several seconds, all he could do was stare. While he was still getting over his surprise, Marie brought them all inside. She had doubtless come from a hideout or safe house somewhere in the area to make the initial contact. Cade and Rebecca wouldn't expect to have been taken straight there.

It was a standard motel room with a pair of double beds. A woman's topcoat was thrown on one of them; a couple of magazines lay on the other, which was rumpled, as if Marie had been reading while she waited. Coffee was brewed in the pot provided, and some deli sandwiches, chips, and soft drinks laid out alongside it. Len threw his coat on top of Marie's and handed her a phone that he had been carrying, which Cade saw was a video type. *Now* he realized why

Marie hadn't been surprised on seeing him. Len had sent back an image, even before he accosted Cade in Atlanta.

Marie positioned the phone on a corner table to take the room in its viewing angle and attached a speaker extension. Evidently, the proceedings were to be monitored remotely. Cade wondered how normal it was for any face-to-face contact to be permitted at all in a first meeting. It seemed dangerous. Had they relaxed their usual precautions, perhaps because Marie had vouched for him?

"We need you sitting here, Rebecca," Marie said, waving to indicate the nearest of the two beds. "You can munch while we talk." Rebecca moved the coats aside and sat down. "Roland, I'm going to have to ask you to take a walk outside with Len," Marie said. "You'll get to talk later. I'm sure I don't have to explain." Cade nodded, shrugged in a way that said it was okay, selected a sandwich to take with the coffee cup he was holding, and moved to the door. Just before Len opened it, Rebecca got up again, went into the bathroom, and came back out with a towel, which she spread by her on the bed to put her sandwich plate on. "Okay? Let's get started," Cade heard Marie say as Len closed the door behind them, hanging the "Do Not Disturb" sign outside.

He sipped his coffee and stood, looking around. The van was gone—or at least, moved from the slot it had been in. Extending away beyond the fence were the trappings of what could have been the outskirts of virtually any city. In the distance, however, in a direction that Cade judged to be the west or south from the position of the sun, stood a high, flat-topped mountain, forming one side of a valley. He had noticed that the room's call terminal carried the area code 423. Offhand, he didn't know where that was.

Two hours driving from Atlanta? . . . But then, he didn't know if all of that had been in the same direction.

"Kestrel suggested we take a walk," Len said. "Let's walk."

"Kestrel?" Cade grinned. "Is that what you call her these days?" Len grunted, seemingly irked at having given away more than necessary. They moved to the end of the block and stood chewing sandwiches and finishing their coffees. Then they crossed to a dumpster standing on a corner of the parking lot to dispose of the cups. Vehicles were parked here and there. It was early yet for the evening arrivals to begin showing up. Cade saw license plates from Georgia, Alabama, Tennessee, one from Florida, another, Indiana. It didn't really tell him much. They strolled back to the room. The sign was still hanging outside the door. They made another circuit of the block. When they came back, the sign had gone. Len knocked, and Marie let them back in.

Now it was Cade's turn to talk to the camera and answer questions. Len stayed, while Rebecca left with Marie. There were no surprises. Cade told his story as it had happened, omitting details of precisely who had initiated the contact into CounterAction for him, because he wasn't asked. The question that caused him the most difficulty was regarding his motivation: Why had he done it? Why had he gotten involved? He couldn't say it was to help with their cause—truth was, he had never given much thought to it. His own life was pretty comfortable, thanks to no one else, because *he* had made it that way. It was up to others to worry about what he considered to be their problems. He didn't feel that whoever he was talking to would appreciate a discourse on personal philosophies of that nature, however.

"Julia—the person I'm with now. It seemed important to her," he said. "Apparently, they were close friends back in college. . . . I guess I just wanted to do what I could. I didn't have any thought then of getting involved." He gestured to indicate the room he was in. "Not like this." Which was true; but somehow not enough. Cade didn't find it satisfying.

"There was nothing of a more . . . 'personal' nature, maybe?" the voice from the phone speaker queried.

Cade sat back, jolted by the question. "No. . . ." But he wasn't sure. He realized how impossible this would have been had Marie remained present.

There was a pause. Then the voice on the phone said, "Very well." Evidently, Cade had passed muster; the subject was closed. So was that what he had been brought all this way for? It needled him.

"Well, I'm glad that you're satisfied," he said. It was one of those rare times when he was unable to keep an edge of sarcasm out of his voice. "My plane back to LA will have left already. I'm going to have to get some kind of a regular connection instead from here, wherever this is—unless you've got rules that say we have to go on another mystery tour first. You realize that you've cost me my whole evening."

The person who the voice belonged to seemed unimpressed. "There are people out there right now for whom it's costing their homes, their families, their lives," he replied coolly.

The remark hit Cade as disconcertingly as it came unexpectedly. He sat back on the bed, finding himself too troubled and confused to respond. He had never thought of it that way. Somehow, the thought of putting in an expense claim didn't feel like such a good idea.

Marie and Rebecca came back. Len held a muted conversation over the phone. It seemed that business was concluded for the moment. He would need to go back to confer, he announced. Rebecca would probably be moved to another location later that night and arrangements made to send Cade home. In the meantime they were to remain here. Marie would keep them company. Len collected his coat off the bed. When he opened the door, the van had magically reappeared. As he was leaving, Marie caught Cade's sleeve, and drew close to keep her words private. "We have to take care of business first," she murmured. "Maybe we'll be able to talk a little later. There must be lots. It's been a long time." Cade nodded.

While Marie rinsed out the coffee pot and prepared another brew, Rebecca lay back along the bed they had been using and stared at the ceiling. Cade paced disconsolately to the door and back several times, then settled down on the other and picked up one of the magazines still lying there. An ad at the bottom of the page it was opened at was for a restaurant called the Chattanooga Chew Chew. Its phone number had the area code 423. Well, that answered one question, anyway, he told himself.

The miniature locator that ISS operative "Ruby," currently operating under the field name Rebecca, had attached beneath the collar of Len's jacket while it lay on the bed updated its position from satellite fixes every five seconds and had connected with the national security network via booster relays covering the area. The computers at ISS Regional Command in Atlanta had found voiceprint matches with two samples from previously tapped recordings, both established from interrogation leads as belonging to members of the Scorpion cell. The male was the operative known as "Len"; the female went as "Kestrel."

For ten minutes, the plot from the locator traced a route northwest of Chattanooga to coordinates shown on a large-scale map as pinpointing one of a number of mobile homes situated in a wooded area just over the Tennessee River. Conversation picked up later inside the house identified the Scorpion member, believed to be cell leader, known as "Olsen," and a female voice not on file. Then, after a further fifteen minutes, another male voice was detected. Within seconds, the analyzer monitor in Atlanta started beeping and flashing a box with the caption PRIORITY. An operator transferred spectra samples to an auxiliary screen and ran a full Fourier and time series comparison. He picked up a red phone that connected directly to the section supervisor.

"Bingo!" he reported. "It's him, Reyvek. We've found the defector."

A Status Report, Operations Plan, and Request for Action Approval were flashed to Washington within eighteen minutes. Before a half-hour was up, the response came back: GO.

Choppers from a base in the mountains between Chattanooga and Nashville, experimentally fitted with quiet-running Hyadean ducted fans in place of conventional rotors, landed strike teams a mile from the target in opposite directions along the north bank of the river. Their orders were to identify and take out the designated Subject, along with all other opposition on sight. When that objective was confirmed, a second unit would go in to relieve operative Ruby in the motel on the south side of the city, and eliminate the two remaining hostiles there.

CHAPTER EIGHTEEN

Cade lay propped against the headboard and watched as Marie poured two coffees. She added some creamer and a sachet of sugar to his, left hers black, and brought them over. Rebecca was in the bathroom, and from the time that had passed, could conceivably have fallen asleep there. Cade took the cup that Marie offered. She sat down with her own at the foot of the bed and regarded him over the rim as she took a sip. He returned the look evenly for a moment, saw that she was simply being open, inviting things to take any turn from here, and let his face soften.

" 'Mole Woman'! What ever made you remember that? I thought you'd be a million years past any sentimental stuff by now—whatever used to be there, anyway."

"They wanted something personal. You see, you never could get it into your head that I had a side like that. You only saw this cold intellectual . . . and you invented most of that yourself."

"Oh, come on."

"You still can't see it?"

Cade gestured at her. "Look at you, for Christ's sake."

"So there's a side that wants to do something about things I take seriously, too. The two aren't mutually exclusive. It's just as well some people do. . . . Besides, why just talk about me. What's this 'red coal' thing I'm hearing about all of a sudden?" Her eyes flickered over him. "Trying to tell me something, Roland?"

Cade made an exaggerated show of sighing at the ceiling, missing the impish twist of her mouth. "Oh, we're not about to go off into some Freudian excursion are we? The guy I was talking to threw the question across a table, and that was what I came up with. It's not as if there's a huge list of alternatives."

"Oh, I don't know. You could have picked . . ." Marie thought for a few seconds. "Let's see, there's 'red cola,' 'real cod.' Then you've got 'old acre' or 'old care.' Does 'earl doc' work?" She frowned. "Yes, it does, doesn't it?"

"Okay, okay." Cade cocked a complimentary eyebrow. "You're still as quick, I see." Marie showed an empty palm and made a face that said "if you say so." But she wasn't about to drop it. "So why did you come here?" she said.

Cade let his head fall back against the headboard. "Why is everyone around here trying to psychoanalyze me? Look, it wasn't *me* that wanted to come here. I just planned on coming as far as Atlanta to make sure she was collected okay. The rest was your people's idea. I didn't get a lot of say in it. They went through all this while you were out of the room. Why not ask them when you get back, eh?"

Marie stared at him for a moment or two longer, then nodded. She took another sip from her cup. "So is life still being kind to you?" she asked.

Now Cade felt on familiar ground. He answered automatically. "It is, because I let it." Despite the qualms that had assailed him earlier, he couldn't resist being provocative. "You know how I am. I mind my own business. If other people want to make problems for themselves, that's their right, I guess."

"Oh, how can you blame people for what's happening to them? Ordinary, decent people, I mean. They work hard, believe what they're told. They're being sold out."

Cade raised his chin. They were at it again, already. It seemed that the amnesty had been short-lived. "So who are you blaming, the Hyadeans? Well, some of them happen to be friends of mine, and they can be pretty ordinary and decent, too, believe it or not."

"But that's the whole *point*! It's not a simplistic 'them' or 'us' situation. The power on both sides is in collusion. It's like, oh . . . when the Romans used to provide palaces and protection to the local chiefs for keeping the natives in line and the taxes coming in. This whole regime that they've set up in Washington is getting to be just like one of those puppet—" The room's phone units sounded an incoming call. Cade picked up the handset from the bedside stand, pressed the "2" button to select audio only, and offered the phone to Marie. "Dictatorships you used to hear about," she completed as she took it. The latch of the bathroom door clicked barely audibly.

A look of alarm seized Marie's face suddenly. As Cade started to mouth a question, she touched "3" to activate the screen and speaker phone. Sounds poured forth of voices shouting indistinctly, some seeming to be barking commands, others yelling warnings; confused scuffling and banging; then a torrent of what could only be gunfire.

"*What in hell*—" Cade began, swinging his legs down off the bed.

Len's face filled the screen, twisted by fear and desperation. "*Kes, get out! It's a bust! They're already coming in here! We've got*—" Half his head erupted in an explosion of flesh and gore. He vanished to be replaced by a brief image of a black-hooded figure holding a gun in one hand and gesturing to somebody with the other, then disappearing off-screen.

"*Jesus Christ!*" Cade cried.

"*State Security. Freeze right there!*" Cade looked around at where the voice had come from. Rebecca had come out of the bathroom, clasping an automatic in a two-handed grip. He gaped, paralyzed. But she made the mistake of swinging the weapon from him to Marie and back again to cover both of them. As the muzzle moved away, Marie swept her arm up, throwing the contents of her coffee cup into Rebecca's face, then almost in the same movement bunched herself to go in low under it, crashing her shoulder into Rebecca's midriff with her full weight and momentum behind it. The action was instant, reflexive—before Cade had even tuned in to what was happening. The sound of an explosion followed by more shooting came from the phone's speaker.

The bullet went into the wall a foot away from Cade. Rebecca was hurled backward, going down and cracking her head on the drawer unit by the wall, which had the snack leftovers on top. Marie pulled Rebecca's head up by the hair, thudded it back against the floor, then used her knee to pin the arm holding the gun and twisted it from Rebecca's grasp. Rebecca made a V with the fingers of one hand and jabbed upward viciously, aiming at Marie's eyes, but

Marie deflected it, then struck sideways at Rebecca's head with the gun, left then right, and then again—pure survival instinct reacting to lethal danger. Cade looked on, horrified, as blood welled from a gash on Rebecca's temple and ran down her face, mingling with the coffee that Marie had thrown. Marie stood up, breathing shakily. But Rebecca was still not out, nor was she finished. She sat up and lunged for the gun, but was too groggy to judge the distance. Marie shot her twice in the center of the forehead.

Cade was still too shocked to have moved. Marie killed the phone and stood looking uncertainly around the room, thinking to herself furiously. "Len must have carried something back. . . ." She went around to the other bed and picked up her coat, still lying where Len's had been, and began searching rapidly through the folds and pockets. Cade rose in a daze, looked disbelievingly at the body crumpled on the floor while he picked his way past it, and moved over to see what Marie was doing. She turned back the collar and held the coat up to reveal a black, rectangular object, about the size of a printed-circuit chip, attached underneath. She pulled it off, and making a sign for Cade not to say anything, went over to the closet beside the bathroom, where Cade had hung his jacket. A quick check found an identical device under one of the lapels. How or when Rebecca had put it there, he had no idea. Marie thrust the jacket at him to put on, handed him the automatic, and then as an afterthought went into the bathroom and added several extra ammunition clips that she found in Rebecca's toilet bag. As Cade pocketed them, Marie put her hand to her ear and made the motions of using a phone. Cade took his unit out and showed it to her questioningly. She shook her head and pointed at the bed. He tossed the phone down, and then after taking a last look back at the body, turned to follow Marie out the door.

Marie had keys to a spare car that had been left around the back of the block—a white Toyota. They got in, Marie driving, and left as quickly as was practical without drawing attention. As they turned at a traffic light to enter a ramp signed as leading to I-75 North, three military trucks painted in dark camouflage shades and moving fast passed them, heading the other way. Still numbed, Cade felt the unfamiliar bulge in his jacket pocket. Why had Marie given the gun to him? Obviously, because she was already carrying one, was the only answer to suggest itself.

CHAPTER NINETEEN

Marie drove tensely, moving the wheel in quick, jerky motions to weave through the evening traffic, constantly watching the mirror. She had switched on the radio and tuned it to a local country-music channel where a deejay was playing phone-in requests. It seemed odd to Cade. Maybe it calmed her nerves. A helicopter appeared from the west and went into a wide circle above the highway. Marie slowed down and eased into the traffic stream to be less conspicuous.

"Was it really such a good idea to leave that phone there?" Cade asked. "I mean, it's traceable to me. They'll know I was there."

Marie smiled humorlessly. "You think they didn't know anyway? Rebecca was ISS, or whatever."

Cade shook his head as if clearing it. Of course. His mind still wasn't functioning. "So what do we do?"

"We'll need to get off the Interstate," Marie

answered. "They might seal off this whole area, which means everything on the exit routes will get stopped. They'll have voiceprints on both of us—maybe visuals as well. They'll already have yours in any case."

"Great. . . . So where are we heading, right now?"

"Just covering as much distance as we can, while we can. I don't really know this area. I only just arrived here. . . . We have to make contact with local people who are sympathetic."

"How do you propose doing that if you only just arrived in the area?" Cade asked. It didn't exactly sound like the kind of thing someone would advertise.

Marie seemed to be of two minds as to how to answer. "There are ways," was all she said, finally.

The radio deejay prattled on amiably. "Well, that was a good one from way back. And now we have another caller on the line. Hello there? Who are we talking to?"

A man's raspy voice answered. "Hi, Mike. Name's Al. Folks call me Big Al. Been listenin' to that show o' yours for aw . . . must be close to five months now. Moved out here to Cleveland, a little under twenty miles north o' the Big Nooga. Wouldn't go any farther'n that mind you, 'cause I'm kind of a city boy originally. I've always thought that somebody oughta—"

"Well, it's real nice to hear from you, Al. So what kind of a song can we play for you today?"

"Oh yeah, right. Well, what I'd like to hear is one that I used to—"

Marie switched the radio off. Cade glanced at her questioningly, but she kept her eyes ahead. She passed the next exit, and then left the Interstate at the one after that. Cade noticed that it was signposted Cleveland.

They came to a small town center and crossed to

the far side, away from the highway. Marie left the main street and found a minimall with a convenience store, several smaller shops, and a Burger King, and pulled in. Outside the convenience store were a couple of public net-access booths. "Stay here," was all Marie said as she got out of the car. Cade watched her go into one of the booths, sit down, feed a bill into the machine, and peer expectantly at the screen. Police sirens were sounding in the direction of the town center, where they had just passed through. Cade eased back in the seat, stretched his head upward, and exhaled shakily. Only now was his mental machinery beginning to operate anywhere near normally again.

Rebecca had been a plant, sent to infiltrate CounterAction. Very probably, an inflammatory piece denouncing President Ellis and the Washington administration had appeared from opposition sources, but she hadn't authored it. That had been part of a cover story exploiting the opportunity. Presumably, the aim had been to uncover a part of CounterAction's routes and methods for moving people out of the country. Cade could think of nothing further. That was all he had asked Udovich to convey in the message—along with the information that would identify Cade as the sender, to Marie.

He looked back at the booth and saw her speaking into the phone handset, at the same time writing hurriedly on a scrap of paper. Whom could she be talking to if she had only recently arrived in the area herself? Maybe they had a way of inserting coded information in local ads and announcements that would give a number to call if you knew what to look for. His mind drifted back to where it had been previously.

Information to identify Cade *to Marie*!

Could finding CounterAction's conduits have been just another part of the cover story too? Had the real objective all along been to track down Marie? Anything was possible for all he knew. How was Cade supposed to have known what she might have been involved in?

And then a more uncomfortable thought hit him. If Rebecca hadn't been what she said, then what kind of a coincidence would just happen to make her an old college friend of somebody living with a man on the ISS watch list whose former wife was a suspected CounterAction operative? A pretty unlikely one, to put it mildly. In fact, the more he thought about it, the more he was forced to conclude that it couldn't happen. So she hadn't been an old college friend of Julia's at all. But if that were true, then Julia had to have been part of the setup as well.

Surely not. After all that time? . . . It had to be impossible.

Then he remembered the strange way in which Julia had suddenly started asking questions about Marie, whom she had never expressed curiosity over before, and insisting that surely there was some way of contacting her again. . . .

He was still grappling with the implications when Marie came back. She got in and sat looking for a minute at the paper she had written on, as if memorizing it, then folded it and slipped it into a side pocket of her coat. "There's a coffee shop we need to find and wait in for a while," she said. "Someone will get back to us there." Cade merely nodded. If she had wanted him to know more, she would have said. He was completely out of his depth by now.

They drove out of the mall parking area and took a backstreet route, slowing occasionally for Marie to check street names and landmarks until they were on a road leading out of town. They followed for about twenty minutes to another township, smaller this time, standing below tree-covered hills looming into the dusk, which was closing in by now. Marie stopped under an intersection lamp to check her directions again, and then stayed on the main street to a traffic light, where she turned right and stopped two blocks farther on outside a diner billed as "Dean's." It was workaday and nondescript, with a few old cars and pickup trucks drawn up facing the building.

Cade had been thinking over events yet again. He looked at Marie as they were about to get out. "That guy who called in on the radio earlier. Was that some kind of code that the station broadcasts? The exit we turned off at was the name of the town that he said. He made it sound like some old fool just chatting, but he said something about not going any farther than that. Were they stopping the traffic farther on up? Was it something like that?"

Marie gave him a look that said he ought to know better than to ask; but there was a hint of a compliment there too. "A lot of people are getting really tired of what's going on," was the most she would admit before opening her door. On the way in, she stopped and took out a lighter to burn the piece of paper she had written on, stirring the ash into a cigarette sand-tray standing outside the door.

Inside was a counter with stools, a row of booths by the window, and tables and a few more booths at the back. The place was moderately busy with people who looked like local farmers and tradesmen, a group of teenagers, and several casual customers, none of whom gave Marie and Cade more than a glance as they entered. Cade found he had no appetite and ordered just a coffee at the counter. Marie took a sweet cold tea. Cade carried them to an empty corner booth, with nobody in immediate proximity.

They sat for a while toying with their mugs and stirring the contents needlessly, looking around with intermittent glances at each other, each adjusting to the situation in their own way. Despite whatever impressions he might have had earlier, Cade got the feeling that this wasn't exactly what Marie did every day. He wanted to talk, but it seemed pointless to start asking about what was supposed to happen next, which would reveal itself in due course.

Taped music was playing from speakers overhead, which would mask conversation. Finally, he brought up the subject of Julia, which was still nagging at him. He summarized the conversations that had led him to attempt contacting Marie, and his sudden suspicion just now, while Marie was making her call, that Julia must have been part of it. "But how could she have been?" he concluded, turning up his palms. "It's been over a year. . . . Yet why else would she pretend to have known Rebecca?"

Marie didn't seem to find it so surprising. "Tell me more about her," she invited. "How did you meet?"

Cade did his best to describe Julia and their relationship in a way that was sensitive to Marie's situation, mentioning her former husband who ran night clubs and how her social life as a consequence had clicked with Cade's own agenda. "I met her at a dinner party somewhere. She had a spare ticket to a show that someone had canceled out of and asked me if I wanted to fill in. It developed from there."

"It sounds ideal." Marie regarded him dubiously, as if not quite sure that what he'd said was adequate grounds for what she was thinking. She ran a fingertip around the rim of her mug, then said, finally, "Doesn't it strike you that it could have been just a little *too* ideal?. . . I mean, a bit over year ago, right? That is, by the time I'd have been marked as a CounterAction active."

Cade shook his head, at the same time smiling as if this had to be some kind of joke. "Surely not. I mean, would they really go so far as to set me up with my own permanent live-in agent?"

This time Marie nodded without hesitation. "Oh sure. It would be routine to put a watch on anyone connected with a marked name like mine. With a person in your position, constantly in touch with influential Hyadeans, they'd want to know everything about your deals and interactions. What better way to do it than that?" Cade could only stare at her aghast. Marie seemed amused. "Are you only starting to notice for the first time, Roland? We're being turned into a Hyadean colony. There might be some friendly ones that you can meet and party with, but the system they work for is ruthless about imposing its own ideas. Their style of security is being introduced into the U.S., and *our own people*—the ones who run the machinery that serves the interests that stand to make big—are collaborating." Cade felt a twinge of discomfort, wondering where that put him. But Marie's phone beeped before he could say anything. She took it out and answered, then produced a pen and another piece of paper and proceeded to jot down more instructions, answering in monosyllables. "Right. . . . Yes. . . . No, I've got it. That'll be okay." She closed the phone and put it away. "Time to go," she said to Cade, rising.

They followed a different road a few miles to a disused gas station, which Marie entered, parking on one side of the forecourt. They waited in the darkness for a little under twenty minutes. Then a car drew up on the roadway outside and flashed its lights once. Marie started the engine, turned on the lights, and exited to pull behind it. The car led them about a mile and then pulled off onto an expanse of open ground that seemed, in the moonless night, to be bordered by trees. Marie's phone beeped again. She answered it, listened for several seconds, and announced that she was to leave Cade here for a while. Meanwhile, the car ahead had moved on a distance and doused its lights. Marie got out, closed the door, and disappeared on foot in the same direction. Cade waited for about another fifteen minutes, feeling as if he had been pitched into the middle of one of those movies that he'd never really managed to connect in his mind with reality; or maybe a country that you read about but never thought about long enough to realize might actually exist. If he got out of this in one piece, that was it, he told himself. No more heroics or dabbling with intrigue and subversives. From now on he would . . . But even as the thought formed, he realized he was no longer so sure. The voice on the phone in the hotel room came back to him. *There are people out there right now for whom it's costing their homes, their families, their lives.* The picture of himself running back to his world of comfort and security didn't sit very well with him either.

Figures materialized from the shadows outside. A flashlight played on him through the glass. Another light showed papers with a picture in somebody's hand, being scrutinized. Finally, the door was opened, and a voice directed, "Come with us, please." Cade got out and found himself between two muffled figures wearing hats. Another was visible on the far side of the car. Cade and the two with him began walking the way Marie had gone, over uneven gravelly ground. When they had covered twenty yards or so, the car started behind them, and its headlights came on. Cade looked back to see it begin moving, turning back toward the roadway. "It's okay. You won't be needing it again," the same voice told him. For a chilling moment Cade wondered how he was supposed to take that. Getting too imaginative, he told himself.

A pickup was waiting along with the car that they had followed, he saw as they got closer. Marie was standing with two more figures. "Okay, it looks as if there's a place where we can stay for a few days at least," she told him. "This isn't the best time to hold a conference. It's been a rough day. We can talk more about options in the morning."

A big man with a bearded face and pulled-down baseball cap ushered them into the pickup and then got in on the other side. As he started up, the car with the three others departed back in the direction of town. They pulled back onto the road, continuing in silence in the same direction as before for a couple of miles, and then turned off onto a dirt track climbing uphill through trees. It led to a camper trailer standing in the corner of a field behind what looked like a farmstead outlined dimly in the darkness. "There's linen inside and some grub. Just help yourselves," the big man said as he dropped them off. "You've got a phone that connects to the house. It would be best if you didn't show yourselves there, at least for a while. . . . Oh, and you can call me John."

The camper had seen better days, but the power and the plumbing worked. From the clothes in the closets and other signs of occupation, it seemed the place had been vacated for Cade and Marie's benefit. They made themselves a salad and cooked a couple of pork chops. Were it not for the day's events, this might have been a little like old times. The news on TV described a "terrorist hideout" in Chattanooga, which security forces had surrounded following a tipoff; they'd been met by gunfire. Five terrorists had been killed in the ensuing assault, and two had escaped. There was no mention of any incident at a motel. Cade's and Marie's pictures were shown as the two escapees, described as armed and dangerous.

By that time they were both too exhausted to talk more. Cade took a fold-down bunk in the camper's living and dining area. Marie used the bedroom, farther back. As Cade lay thinking back over the day, it occurred to Cade that the photograph of him that they had shown on the TV was one that had been taken around six months previously. How had the authorities gotten it? The only thing he could think of was that it must have come from Julia.

CHAPTER TWENTY

By daylight, the farm revealed itself to be in a dilapidated condition, with little to mark it as a going concern. The fields, for the most part, had been left fallow, and rusting machinery stood among the outbuildings. A few scrawny looking cattle were penned in a muddy patch on the far side of the house.

John called on the phone to ask how things were. Marie took the call, said they were comfortable, and thanked him again for helping out. Right now, they needed a little time to make plans. She listened for a short while longer and then hung up.

"The police are all over the area and still stopping traffic," she told Cade. "They're showing our pictures everywhere." She shook her head. "It was stupid for both of us to have gone into the coffee shop like that. We shouldn't have been seen together. Let's hope there weren't any wrong people there with sharp eyes and good memories." It wasn't something that could be changed now. Cade put on the coffeepot, popped a couple of slices of bread into the toaster, and turned back to the eggs he was about to scramble. Marie set dishes and cutlery on the table, poured two glasses of orange juice, and slid into the narrow bench seat behind.

"Roland. . . . In case we end up going separate ways in all this, or maybe if we both don't come through . . . there's some information that I need to give you. It's important that it doesn't get lost." Cade got the feeling she had been thinking hard about this. He looked over his shoulder to indicate that he was listening. Marie paused, as if searching for the right place to begin.

"Rebecca wasn't infiltrated so much to find me. It was the particular group I was associated with. It's the group that was blamed for that assassination in Washington a couple of weeks back—when the Hyadean flyer was shot down. What the media are saying is all a lie. We had nothing to do with it. No part of CounterAction did. You have to believe that."

Cade slowed his stirring, and then resumed again just in time to avoid burning the contents of the pan. That was right. . . . The ISS people who came to the house two days after it happened had told him Marie was suspected of being with the cell the Hyadean plasma weapon supposedly found its way to. With all that had been going on, he had forgotten about that connection. "A senator, wasn't it?" he said. "Farden. . . . And some general . . . ?"

"Right. Meakes."

"A couple of Hyadeans too."

"They shouldn't have been there. The targets were Farden and Meakes. The reason the cell I was with got picked was that it had been compromised somehow.

Therefore, it could be targeted to be taken out. Get the idea? Nobody who had been implicated would be around to deny it. That was the intention, anyway. But we were warned ahead of time, and disbanded."

Cade turned, frowning, as he scooped the eggs out onto the plates. "So that wasn't what happened yesterday at wherever that call came from—where Len went?"

Marie shook her head. "That was a place in Chattanooga that we were using in transit to wherever next. But there was another man there, who went by the name Otter. He had the information on how those assassinations were really carried out. That's the information I'm going to give you now. The more chance it has to get around, the better. His real name was Captain Wayne Reyvek of the ISS. He'd had enough of what he'd seen and decided to switch sides. They couldn't afford to let somebody like him talk. *That's* who I think Rebecca was sent to track down."

Cade added bacon strips from a plate he had set aside earlier and sat down to pour the coffees while Marie buttered the toast. "But they set me up to lead Rebecca to *you*," he pointed out. "What reason would they have to think that you and Reyvek . . . I guess he's history now?"

"Seems like it."

"What reason would they have to think you and he would be together?"

"I've been wondering that too," Marie said. "All I can think of is that they guessed he'd be asked to compare notes with the people who were being blamed." She shrugged. "The controllers monitoring a trace that Len took back found they had hit lucky, sent in a hit team—and you saw the cavalry heading the other way when we were leaving the motel. Guess who'd have been next."

Cade had already figured that much out. He went over what had been said so far while he began eating his breakfast. It still didn't make sense. "Why go to all that trouble?" he said finally. "If Reyvek knew who really did it, then presumably the ISS knew too. So why not simply go for them in the first place? Why go out of your way to lie about some other group, and then have to take them out in case they get a chance to disprove you?"

Marie sat back and smiled, as if something about the way he still couldn't see it delighted her. "*Because they did it themselves!* It was engineered within the ISS! Reyvek was involved in obtaining the Hyadean plasma cannon. It came from some that disappeared in South America, were recovered but not acknowledged, and found their way into an unofficial stockpile at Fort Benning in Georgia. It was fired by a colonel called Kurt Drisson, who specializes in deniable dirty work for friends in high places. Reyvek wasn't sure, but he believed that a financier called Casper Toddrel was behind it. Toddrel is mixed up in big land deals that are going on in Brazil and Peru. Reyvek had evidence to substantiate his story, which he mailed to a private box in Baltimore. I guess the key's lost, but there are ways around things like that."

Cade was listening, but he couldn't relate any motive to what he was hearing. The story the two ISS agents had given when they came to the house seemed straightforward enough. He shook his head uncomprehendingly. "But why? Farden was pushing bills that would open up big markets for cheap minerals that the Hyadeans are pulling out of Bolivia, right? Now, okay, sure, I can see how that might drop the bottom out of a lot of industries here that have seen their day, and make him unpopular with a lot of people. That would make him a natural target for an outfit like CounterAction, that looks for popular support. But why should somebody like Toddrel care? He's not a titanium miner who got let go last year with no place to go."

"You're buying the standard line that they put out," Marie told him. "Simple. Easy logic. Gives us an instant Enemy of the People to hate."

"Well . . . what other line is there?" Cade invited.

"Farden had enemies within the Terran Globalist elite. He was working with other interests—I suspect British, but I'm not sure—who were being paid by South American land agencies and development investors to expand the Bolivian extraction operations. That earns the Hyadeans the foreign currency they need for their land deals, and in recycling it everyone in the loop gets rich."

Cade still couldn't quite buy it. "But that still doesn't explain why Toddrel should want to get rid of Farden. I mean, isn't he in the loop too?"

"It's a different loop," Marie answered. "Farden's scheme is undercutting a lot of U.S.-capitalized mining, which makes it too radical for some people. Toddrel is part of a more cautious approach to cashing in on the Hyadean economic system by marketing Terran creative skills, which sell at a huge margin on the alien worlds. That means selling out middle-class professionals instead, which doesn't create powerful enemies. Also, you're not giving foreign governments a green light to rush into handing over big chunks of this planet, which not everyone is happy about." She waved her fork by way of conclusion. "Hence, eliminating Farden was convenient for a lot of people you don't find at Washington protest rallies. If you can do it and discredit the opposition at the same time, then so much the better."

Cade nodded reluctantly. It was starting to make

sense now. "How come you know so much about all this?" he asked curiously.

"Oh, come on Roland. You know that reading between lines and finding sources that I believe has always been my thing."

"Yes, right. Let's not get into that. . . ." Cade picked up his glass and drank. "So what about General Meakes? The version I heard was that he wanted to beef up our defense capability by introducing more Hyadean weapons and methods, which countries like the AANS didn't want to see happen. So they spread the story that he was going to put our military under alien control, and that made him unpopular enough for CounterAction to target. What's your take on that?"

"From what I've heard, Meakes was sincere," Marie replied. "He genuinely wanted a stronger capability. But that was so the U.S. could run its own security operations independently. But the same people who didn't want Farden bankrupting Western industrial interests *want* an expanded Hyadean military presence here to protect their investments, with our own forces maybe eventually under their command."

Cade was astounded. "You're kidding!"

"I wish I was. The joke is that what they're pushing for is exactly what Meakes was accused of, but which in reality he was obstructing. So they had reason to want to get rid of him too." Marie looked across. Cade had no more questions for the moment, but sat absorbing what he had heard.

"So that's what you need to know," Marie told him. "If I don't come out of this for some reason, get it to the right people in the organization." She finished her toast, thought for a moment longer, and then added, almost as an afterthought, "Unless you still don't want any part of it, of course."

After half an hour of brooding, shuffling restlessly around in the cramped confines of the camper, and saying little, Cade sat down opposite Marie as she sat staring through a window at the tree-covered slopes rising beyond the end of the field. "It's not enough," he declared. "Yes, we need to get this information to the right people in your organization. But it has to go further than that. It has to get to the Hyadeans too—the *right* ones. They need to know what kind of people their government is collaborating with. Because they don't question things, they'd be easy to take advantage of. But that would make them all the more appalled if they knew the truth. Maybe I have spent a lot of the last few years staying out of things that matter, but one thing it's done is put me on more than just speaking terms with a few who would be ideal to start with. One in particular that I'm thinking of is very close to Dee. Do you remember her?"

For a moment, Marie registered too much surprise to be capable of saying anything. She collected her wits quickly and nodded. "Dee? Yes. She's okay."

"We need to use her."

"How? What are you talking about?"

"Well, obviously we can't risk alerting Julia," Cade said. "What are the chances of getting a message to Dee somehow, through this network of yours?

"They could do it, sure," Marie agreed. "But in a situation like this, it's best to assume that anyone who comes to mind as a natural contact will have been marked by the other side too. That means they're likely to be watched and their lines tapped. It could take some time."

"Then the sooner we make a start, the better," Cade said.

CHAPTER TWENTY-ONE

They gave John details of how Dee could be contacted, along with an instruction that she was to mention it to *nobody*. After that, there was little else to do but wait. There was no way Cade could use a credit card, write a check, or present ID without being picked up. The confidence of the people sheltering them evidently grew over the next two days, or maybe their story was authenticated somewhere. More of John's friends began showing up at the house, many of them at night. John himself stopped by from time to time to check up on things and drink a coffee or beer with Cade and Marie. Times had grown bad since the coming of the aliens, he told them, and that seemed all that was needed to establish cause and effect. Cade wasn't aware of any activities on the Hyadeans' part that would depress U.S. agriculture, and from what he had heard attributed it more to rising Third World productivity and changes in East-West relations, but there was no arguing with the local wisdom. Cade wondered how typical this might be of thinking across the country. Maybe he had been getting more out of touch than he had realized. Marie borrowed a laptop and encrypted as much as she knew of Reyvek's story in a file that she entrusted to John for consignment to Sovereignty. So at least there was some safeguard now in that respect.

Meanwhile, the news brought reports of more operations by security forces, and an apparent act of retaliation in Minnesota, where a stretch of roadway was blown up while a military convoy was passing over, causing over sixty fatalities. Globalist Coalition fighter-bombers were shown in action against "bandit" forces in South America, long portrayed as organized by drug and other criminal elements to disrupt lawful land transfers and development programs that threatened their business. Cade didn't believe it anymore. Another clip showed Hyadean military advisors training Brazilian counterinsurgency troops in the use of prom guns, which were apparently being introduced into the bush fighting with devastating results, along with other Hyadean innovations and methods. Cade recalled what Marie had said about the real motives behind the assassination of Lieutenant General Meakes. He wondered how long it would take for similar provisions to be introduced in the U.S.

He found he was beginning to see things in a new light. In one of their conversations he asked Marie what was going on behind it all, the big picture. What was it all intended to bring about? She told him he had already half figured it out. It was to serve the elite who controlled the Hyadean power structure. Did she mean by profiting from dumped products that had no value back among the Hyadean worlds, and the resale there of cheap Terran labor? Yes, he could see all that. Hadn't he been involved on the fringes of it himself?

But it went further than that, Marie told him. They were moving in to take over choice parts of Earth as their own private preserves. Huge tracts of places like western Brazil, eastern Peru—and now they were talking about South Africa—were being transformed into estates and palaces for the Hyadean ruling clique to escape to from the drabness and overdevelopment of their own worlds. And the properties came with willing managers and domestics that outperformed Hyadean AIs, and none of the political difficulties associated with hiring subservient labor back home.

A freshly sculpted planet, Cade recalled. Unique in its biological vigor and stunning geology among the planets the Hyadeans had spread to. So finally, he had gotten to the bottom of it. *That* was what was really going on.

"So what happens to the people who live there?" he asked Marie in one of their ongoing debates between games of bézique, rummy, napoleon, and taking in the news and a few movies.

"The old story," she replied. "Obviously, if you want to take over their land, they have to go. So you call them bandits and send in the gunships."

"I never realized."

"Most people don't. It's been a long time since there was any genuinely free reporting."

Cade thought about his conversation with Vrel and Krossig when they were out on the yacht. "I'm not sure it's all that different for the average Hyadean," he said. "They think they're here to protect Earth from itself and introduce it to the benefits of a superior system. This is supposed to be an outpost to protect us from the Querl. It's kind of crazy, isn't it?"

Marie snorted. "I don't recall hearing anything about us ever asking for protection. From what? We don't even know who the Querl are. What have you been able to make of them?"

"Supposedly, they're too unruly and ideologically misguided to make the Hyadean system work," Cade replied. "So one day they'll try and take what they need." He showed his hands and shrugged. "But I've even heard Hyadeans questioning that line."

"You amaze me. I didn't think they were capable of questioning anything."

"I'm beginning to think the Querl are something like their version of our bandits. They want to get away from the glorious Hyadean system."

"Which means they can't really be the big threat that we're told, can they?" Marie said. "So why do the Hyadeans need a military capability?"

Cade could see only one answer. "To keep their system together. They talk about orderliness, but the truth is it has to be held in place by force too. Just the same as ours have always had to be."

"My, you really have been doing some thinking. Is this really the same Roland?"

"Don't be patronizing. Or is it matronizing?"

"But seriously, the aim is to gain control of the U.S. as the focal point of global affairs. That's what the AANS nations are resisting, and why we support them."

"You think that terrorizing people over here is the right way?"

For the first time, Marie's manner became short. "That's pure propaganda. The people's own government has become the terrorists. We're trying to wake the people up!"

"But you'd take it to an open struggle, maybe eventually involving Terrans and Hyadeans directly."

Marie spread her hands. "Look at what's happening. You've got us on the verge of a civil war here, right now."

Cade looked hard at her, as if trying to gauge how serious she really was. "Training programs in the mountains and rhetoric are one thing," he said. "But can you really condone it: firing on American defense forces?"

"Hell, Roland. What kind of defense? They're mounting military assaults on American citizens already!"

The next day, John delivered a reply from Dee. Vrel was anxious to learn whatever it was that Cade wanted to convey. Not knowing where Cade was or his situation, he had arranged in his official capacity as observer to visit a U.S. military base near St. Louis and report on the activities of a Hyadean contingent sent there as technical advisers. That, of course, left the question of how Cade and Marie were to get to St. Louis, since with violent incidents escalating nationwide, all modes of travel were subject to routine checks and searches.

The answer came in the form of two nameless people who arrived the same evening to dye and restyle Cade's hair, stain a distinctive birthmark onto his forehead, and then photograph, fingerprint, and voiceprint him for a false set of ID documents, according to which he was now "Professor Wintner," described as a political scientist. Marie was similarly transformed into a social psychologist called "Dr. Armley." Cade doubted if it was mere coincidence that the professions fitted so well with Vrel's official work. The document forgers obviously knew their business, and came across as being intimately familiar with the official records systems. But those systems were interconnected, which meant that for the false IDs to work, appropriate data profiling the personas would need to be in there. Could it really be that thorough? Cade was intrigued.

"I said you'd be surprised how much support there is out there," Marie told him when he asked. "Sometimes the ones who work for government in the day are secretly our biggest allies. They *know* what goes on."

And they did work. Notification came via John that accommodation had been reserved for Professor Wintner and Dr. Armley at the St. Louis Hilton as guests of the Hyadean Office of Terran Cross-Cultural Exchange, which was the department that employed Vrel. They could book themselves a flight first-class, charged to a Hyadean account. It made a crazy kind of sense, Cade had to admit on reflection—the last place that Terran security would be looking for fugitives. Sometimes Hyadean logic managed to surprise him still. Being Hyadean, Vrel wouldn't be subject to the same scrutiny and restrictions as a Terran trying to make comparable arrangements.

They disposed of the guns and other possibly incriminating articles, and Cade handed over his own ID papers and personal effects for mailing to a collection address where he could pick them up later. A woman from the local network drove him and Marie to downtown Chattanooga, where they got a taxi to the airport. Although, as far as Cade knew, no civilian flights had been affected, much was being made of the dangers of terrorist missile attacks, with signs in the airport warning that passengers flew at their own risk. Cade read it as part of a campaign to promote fear.

With their official credentials and new identity documents, Cade and Marie cleared the airport check-in routine without incident. They departed an hour and fifteen minutes later on an early afternoon flight to St. Louis, changing at Atlanta.

CHAPTER TWENTY-TWO

On arrival at the St. Louis Hilton, Cade and Marie found themselves booked into a twentieth-floor suite consisting of a comfortably furnished and stocked lounge area in addition to two bedrooms—a typically prim Hyadean consideration, although it suited the circumstances. The desk clerk produced a package for collection by Professor Wintner that contained a phone—presumably with "clean" programmed-in identification and serial numbers—a number at which Vrel could be reached, and two thousand dollars in cash. Cade called Vrel as soon as they got to the suite. Vrel was relieved that they had made it, but was tied up in the city on business right now. He would join them at the hotel later.

"I see your lifestyle hasn't changed much, Roland," Marie commented. She had been wandering around, inspecting the contents of the mini-bar and refrigerator while he talked to Vrel. "Always the man with

151

the right friends. It's a change from that camper on the farm." She didn't sound entirely approving.

"Well, suit yourself if you want to stake out a claim on the moral high ground," Cade replied. He picked up the wads of hundreds and fifties and ruffled it at her. "Wearing the same clothes for three days makes me feel kind of grubby. I don't know about you, but I'm going out to do a little shopping, and then freshen up for dinner. Are you coming along, or going to start preaching?" Marie thought about it, sighed, and decided preaching was out for the rest of the day. "So now you're sullying your image by dipping a finger in Hyadean wealth too," Cade said. "What's happening? Are you converting me, or am I corrupting you?"

"I don't know. But you're right. I just want to feel clean clothes again," she said.

By the time they sat down in the hotel restaurant, they were chattering and swapping banalities almost like old times. Despite the public exposure—or maybe as a consequence of surviving it without incident— Cade felt more secure than he had for days. Inwardly, a part of him was waiting for Marie to get around to politics or principles, because she always had—it was usual. Less usual was his realization that the anticipation wasn't bothering him. In fact, he found he wanted to talk more about such things. The irony was that Marie, for her part, seemed to be heeding his preferences for once by avoiding them. It was Cade, finally, who brought the subject up.

"What's happened to the fanatic I remember of old? If this goes on, you'll have me thinking we might actually get through dinner without stepping into quicksands."

"This has been such a change. I didn't want to spoil

it." Marie pushed some salad into a wad with her fork and looked up. "Was I always a fanatic?"

"I used to think so," Cade affirmed candidly. "Now, I don't know. Julia asked about it a lot lately—but I guess we know why now." He chewed thoughtfully for a while. "What makes people do a job like that? . . . Live a life of deception. Could you?"

"Some people would say our whole lives are nothing else," Marie said, seemingly not to make any particular point.

"Greed, hatred, and deception," Cade intoned. "What about them?"

"Those are what the Buddhists say are the root of all of life's evils."

"What's this, a new Roland? How long have you been into stuff like that?"

"I'm not, really."

"Yes, I *had* noticed."

"It was something that Mike Blair was on about once. Do you remember him—Mike Blair, the scientist?"

"I only met him a couple of times, I think. Hair with bits of gray in? Wears glasses?"

Cade nodded. "That's him—except the hair's probably a bit grayer now. He's been getting into Eastern philosophy as well as science. It seems our religions are making a big impression with some of the Hyadeans. They don't have deep philosophical views about things. They just look at what the basic facts are saying and leave it right there. Mike says it has something to do with why they're flying starships and we're not. I didn't really follow it."

Marie stopped eating for a moment to frown dubiously. "In that case, why should they care about deeper philosophies? What do they need one for?"

"Because they live their lives stressed out on

treadmills tied to getting better ratings on this 'entitlement' system of theirs, which I don't understand either."

"Right. Like taking a day out fishing in a boat off California."

"I told you, a few like Vrel are different. . . . Well, they're changing. To them, a view of life that values other things beyond just status and material success is a revelation—literally. They've never heard of anything like it. Krossig—he's another Hyadean, who works with Vrel in LA, being moved to Australia— says it's catching on among the kids back home. They talk about Earth as the home of a deeper spirituality: ways of getting in touch with reality that the Hyadeans had once, but lost."

Marie pulled a face. "I guess I'm a little more cynical with regard to human spirituality. I've been too much in touch with conventional reality these last few years." She eyed him for a moment before spearing more of her salad. "Isn't this a bit out of your line, Roland? Are you changing or something, or did I just never see it?"

Cade shrugged in a way that said surprises happen all the time. "I see a lot of aliens."

Marie studied him curiously. "I don't think you realize what an unusual insight it's giving you into alien psychology," she said. "I'll admit, I've tended to see them as all alike—and not all that nice."

"I do an unusual job," Cade replied.

Vrel arrived later in the evening and joined Cade and Marie in their suite. To show off his expanding repertoire of acquired Terran tastes, he started off by refreshing himself after the day with a cool beer, and then settled down to follow it with black, unsweetened coffee. Marie's manner was guarded to begin with, in the presence of possibly the first alien she had spent any time with at close quarters, but she loosened up as time went on.

Vrel was anxious to make it clear that Dee hadn't known Rebecca was a setup. Even with his exposure to Terrans, he didn't seem to grasp that the possibility that she might have had never crossed Cade's mind. His concern seemed to imply that a Hyadean in Dee's position might have sold Cade out knowingly if it gained points somehow in the game-plan calculus that they lived by, and hence by their norms some defense of Dee should be necessary. Cade didn't really follow but accepted it as well meant. It was beyond Marie's experience or comprehension.

Then they got down to the reason why Cade had needed to contact Vrel so urgently. They related the true story of the assassinations of Senator Farden, Lieutenant General Meakes, and the two Hyadeans who had died with them. Vrel listened with growing incredulity, then outrage as Marie explained how the U.S. security services themselves had been responsible, with the implication of possible high-level Hyadean knowledge and collusion. The Hyadeans' nature was not to question what they were told, Cade concluded. It seemed that an unprincipled faction among them were taking advantage of the fact to enrich and empower themselves. Vrel knew the Hyadean system better than they did. There had to be ways of making the truth known in the right places for things to change.

"And you can substantiate it all with evidence?" Vrel said when they were done.

"Not by producing Reyvek anymore," Marie replied. "Although the way he was taken out should be evidence enough. But we have the names and the details, and we know where the documents in Baltimore are."

"Sovereignty will put the story out here," Cade said. "But how much will find its way back to Chryse? That's where any change in policy will have to come from. How can we get a channel back to there?"

Vrel left, promising to contact other Hyadeans that he knew. In the meantime, Cade and Marie could remain in the Hilton at Chryse's expense. Vrel even gave special instructions to the on-site Hyadean security personnel who watched over their official guests to make a particular effort to keep "Professor Wintner" and "Dr. Armley" out of sight and incommunicado. He explained that CounterAction had them listed as Hyadean collaborators, and they were possible targets for retaliation. The hotel's regular security staff were notified and agreed to keep the presence of the two academics highly confidential.

CHAPTER TWENTY-THREE

Casper Toddrel had once fired an assistant who referred to Laura as his "hooker." She could discuss Dostoevsky or Freud, Hegel or Brahms, Dow Jones or the Bolshoi Ballet in four languages, knew how to get a floorside table or instant theater ticket anywhere in New York, and had preferred accounts at Tiffany's, Bendel's, and Saks. The Upper East Side apartment suite that he provided for her had come in at half a million and cost two thousand a month to maintain. He didn't object to how she used it when he wasn't in town, so long as she was discreet. The place had more than paid for itself in the information it yielded from loose-tongued business rivals, whom Laura was an expert at playing. She seemed to get a kick out of it—as if it put her in a role of intimate collusion with Toddrel. Since he never detected any similar ploy being made toward himself, he felt reasonably safe in concluding that she wasn't overextending by trying any double-agent games.

A coalition of churches had staged a demonstration in Dallas to protest the passing of new laws aimed at curbing the dissemination of politically subversive material from pulpits and in parish magazines, and the local police had responded too zealously for prudence. Toddrel sat at the desk in the suite's den, brooding at a picture that had come in over the net, showing a priest holding his arms up protectively against a riot trooper brandishing a baton. This couldn't be allowed to get out. He finished composing a message putting a hold on media release and ordering the removal of the official responsible for security arrangements in Dallas. As he sent it off, Laura's hands began massaging his shoulders through the robe that he was wearing.

"Hey, Big Guy, haven't you had enough of that for one day?" her voice murmured. The scent of perfume touched his nostrils. A lace-covered breast rubbed the side of his head. "Tammy's in the Jacuzzi already. We've got a surprise."

Toddrel slid his hand up to find hers and smiled distantly. "This was urgent. But you're right. . . . There are times when enough is enough." He returned fully to the present and rose from the chair, his manner lightening. "Have you really? This sounds interesting. . . ." And then his phone emitted the tone for his priority-secure channel. "I have to take this."

"Oh, Casper. . . ."

"It probably won't take a minute. Run along and wash Tammy's back." Laura knew better than to argue further and disappeared. Toddrel patched the call through to the desk unit. The screen showed the face of Francis Denham, a British investment banker whom Toddrel had talked to during a recent European visit. The effect on world prices gave Denham his own reasons for wanting to curb the Hyadean mining operations in Bolivia. Before Toddrel departed, they had agreed on the need for a face-to-face meeting with representatives of like-minded Hyadeans. With Senator Farden out of the way, the time was ripe for coordinating further action.

"Good day, Casper—or whatever time it is wherever you are," Denham began. "I trust you had a pleasant trip back?"

"Good enough. What's the news?"

"I've heard back from our friends." He meant Hyadeans who were raising Terran currency by marketing Terran skills back home rather than undercutting Terran industry. "We seem agreed in principle. The official agenda will be on armaments movements." Toddrel had suggested that as the ostensible reason for getting together. Preventing Hyadean and foreign-manufactured Terran weapons from reaching subversive groups was a concern both in the U.S. and Europe. In the latter case, overland movement from Asia was becoming a major problem, and closing of the Canadian and Mexican borders was being considered on the other side of the Atlantic. Another potentially controversial measure that had been proposed was the stopping and searching of ships bound for U.S. or European waters.

But that would be a smokescreen. Denham went on, "One thing that we have to give due consideration to beforehand, I think, would be the question of, how would we say? . . . extending the principle exemplified by Echelon to more general operations."

Toddrel smiled. Even over a secure line, the Englishman couldn't bring himself to state a delicate matter directly. Echelon was code for the action taken to eliminate Farden and Meakes. What Denham meant was engineering ways of not only concealing but publicly blaming the other side for actions that could not be admitted to. "We'd both like to see the scale of activity in Bolivia cut back," Toddrel supplied. "And there's a guerrilla war going on down there. What I'm hearing is that some destabilization in that part of the world would work to our advantage."

"Er, yes. . . . I think we are on the same wavelength," Denham agreed.

"I'll get proposals from our experts in that department," Toddrel said. "I assume that's what this meeting is for." He bit his lip as he spoke. He still wasn't happy about the security situation concerning Echelon. The ISS's confirmation that Reyvek had been among those killed in the Chattanooga raid had come as some relief; on the other hand, the loss of their undercover operative in the motel meant that nobody knew how much information the two who had escaped might have taken with them. He didn't want to divulge any of that now.

"Yes. . . . Exactly," Denham said.

"Where will this meeting be? Do we know yet?" Toddrel inquired.

"Not for sure. I thought we might go to them this time, and make it somewhere in South America. That sounds like an interesting trip, and to be honest I've never been there. What would you say?"

Peals of laughter accompanied by splashing noises came from along the passageway beyond the door. "Well, New York does have its attractions, but there are times when I could use a change too," Toddrel said. "Sure. Put me down as seconding it."

Vrel reappeared intermittently for two days, during which Cade and Marie remained out of sight in the hotel. Gradually, they opened up, talking more about their lives in the years since they had gone separate ways—he having nothing to conceal; she, more circumspect for obvious reasons. They had drifted apart into different worlds. Now, suddenly and unexpectedly, they were thrown together in the same world. Cade began to remember Marie again as he had known her—living life with an intensity that made each day a unique experience. The difference now was that he was sharing it in a way that he would never have thought possible. Marie, for her part, had to accept that her world hadn't protected them, and their security now stemmed from Cade's world which she had once contemned.

Cade couldn't decide if the erosion of barriers between them was simply a pragmatic reaction to the situation or signified something deeper and more personal. Even in his own case, he wasn't sure. One night, after they had sat up late in the suite talking over a bottle of Grand Marnier and then gone separate ways, he returned and stood outside Marie's door undecidedly. The drink and the closeness had left him mellow, and he found it easy to create scenarios in his mind of reliving lost intimacies. But in the end he turned away and went back to the other room. Something didn't feel right. He marveled at this apparently newfound sensitivity that he was able to muster. Udovich would surely have approved.

The next morning, Vrel appeared and announced that they were going to Bolivia. Marie wasn't used to the Hyadeans' blunt, unceremonious way of going about things once they had set their mind.

"Just like that. Out of the blue. We're going to Bolivia," she repeated lamely.

"Roland, do you remember Corto Tevlak? Wyvex talked about him at that last party of yours," Vrel said.

"The art promoter who was developing Chrysean outlets, right?"

"Yes. He's been worried for some time about the way things are going here in the U.S. and on Earth generally, too. Erya talked to him on her way back. He knows others down there who feel the same way, including some Chrysean media people. The public back on Chryse is being misinformed, but questions are starting to be asked. Earth and its cultures are big news right now. This could be a good moment for getting attention in the right places." Vrel paused to let them absorb that much, then shrugged. "You're not safe here in the U.S. in any case. I'm told that from South America it would be easier to get you somewhere where you can stay out of the way for a while."

Just like that.

"Well, it's a nice thought, Vrel," Cade agreed. "But just how do you imagine you'll get us to Bolivia—when every security agent and surveillance computer in the country will be looking for us?"

"In the same way that we're hosting you now," Vrel replied. "As guests of the Hyadean government. We fly you there ourselves, VIP class." He shook his head. "Sometimes I think that Terrans just look for problems, not solutions."

Cade stared at him strangely. "You do realize what you're doing, Vrel?" he said. "A pure favor, probably at considerable risk, with no immediate payoff. Doesn't it feel just a little bit odd?"

"The idea of being motivated by helping others. Yes, I agree—it's very odd." Vrel paused to consider the question fully. "My honest answer is that I find it . . . strangely uplifting." He grinned apologetically. "I can't explain it either."

The following day, accompanied by two other Hyadeans whom Vrel introduced as Ni Forgar and

Barto Thryase, they drove out from the city and were admitted to the fenced compound that the Hyadeans maintained inside the military facility that Vrel had been visiting. A flyer carried them to a Hyadean air base in Maryland, where regular alien traffic connected to other points in the U.S., the Hyadean South American enclave, places in Europe, and elsewhere. They departed several hours later in a suborbital supersonic transport bound for the Hyadean mining center at Uyali, in the southern Altiplano region of Bolivia.

CHAPTER TWENTY-FOUR

Bolivia is a land of color, contrast, and change, which has been nicknamed "the rooftop of the world." The western third of the country is covered by the Andes, extending southward from Peru in two roughly parallel chains a couple of hundred miles apart. The western chain, known as the Cordillera Occidental, marks Bolivia's border with Chile and is the continuation of a high mountain range that begins in northern Peru. Few passes open westward, the lowest being at thirteen thousand feet, and the stretches between are studded with volcanoes, many of them active, with peaks rising above nineteen thousand feet. The eastern chain, or Cordillera Real, consists of a series of great crustal blocks tilted eastward, rising sharply on the western side and descending through a region of rugged, densely forested terrain and mile-deep canyons to the eastern lowlands that make up the remaining two-thirds of Bolivia.

Between the two mountain chains lies a basin of plateau and highlands known as the Altiplano, or high tableland, extending over five hundred miles north-to-south and varying in elevation from twelve to fourteen thousand feet. The northern part of the Altiplano, bordering Lake Titicaca and containing the seat of government, La Paz, is the industrial hub and home to the bulk of the population. Nowhere else does such an industrial area, with cities, railroads, and highways, exist at such an altitude. The southern Altiplano is more arid and barren, consisting of vast salt wastes and rolling plains of steppe vegetation broken by fingerlike remnants of eroded escarpments standing between deep river valleys and basins.

The Spaniards began mining in the sixteenth century, finding large deposits of silver that made Potosí the largest and richest city in the New World at the time. Although later centuries saw developments in the extraction of tin, bismuth, tungsten, antimony, lead, zinc, iron, and copper from accumulations of volcanic ash and ancient sediments, much of the region's mineral potential remained untapped because of political instability and want of capital investment. Then the Hyadeans moved in, and applying such techniques as nuclear-driven particle beam mining, and plasma ionization with magnetic separation, which no Terran operation could rival, began exploiting on a massive scale fabulous deposits along the inner slopes of the Cordillera Occidental in the southern-most reaches of the country. They sold the processed minerals to Terran manufacturing industries in exchange for land-purchase currency on terms highly profitable for the Terran enterprises concerned and also for the national land-management agencies. Development of transportation northward opened up the Amazon route for exporting processed minerals, especially to Europe, and a newer, current project involved blasting a tunnel through the Cordillera Occidental to a new shipping and handling facility being constructed at Iquique in Chile.

The Hyadean residential settlements were farther north in the more picturesque parts of eastern Peru and the highlands in the tip of Brazil, west of the Amazon basin. Their main spaceport for connection to the interstellar ships parked in orbit was at Xuchimbo, in western Brazil, near the point where the borders of the three countries meet. The Hyadean presence had brought a prosperity boom to local businesses, and workers and unions were more than happy with the wages. This provided a broad popular base of political support for the Hyadean-backed government operations being conducted against the insurgency forces active throughout the area.

Cade's reality—the accumulation of perceptions and experiences that he lived in—had always reflected the world of the affluent and the comfortable. Having taken twenty-first-century global communications for granted as part of growing up, he had paid a token concession at the intellectual level to the existence of other places ruled by other conditions; but despite the background detail woven into movie presentations and the vividness of travel documentaries, the places he acknowledged at that detached level of awareness had never before, somehow, taken on the deeper, emotional quality that brings on a sense of being *real*.

"Vast," "rugged," "empty" were the words that formed in his mind as he took in the cabin displays while the SST slowed for its vertical descent into the landing zone. It was now late in the day. To the west, broken ramparts of reds, browns, yellows and grays, rising in ranks of fading ridges to a line of snowy peaks barely visible in the distance, were darkening against the background sun. Arid hills and rocky basins extended away north and south, opening out and leveling eastward into barren salt flats. Amid it all stood the installations at Uyali.

Uyali was Hyadean-built to serve as the center of their extraction operations, sprung out of the Altiplano desert south of previously worked Terran mining areas. On the western side was what Ni Forgar, who seemed to be some kind of engineer returning to base, said was the reduction and processing complex. With its metal domes, cylinders, and spherical constructions standing among large, white boxlike structures, it looked more like a refinery than what Cade would have expected, though with less clutter and piping. It seemed ugly and sprawling, but visiting Terran engineers had apparently been amazed at its compactness for the volume of material that it handled. This arrived by way of two gigantic moving-belt conveyors converging in a V across the landscape, carved through hills and spanning canyons until they were lost from sight; farther on, Forgar told them, the root conveyors divided repeatedly to form a branching tree probing its way through to extraction points scattered among the mountains. He described the processing complex with typical Hyadean bluntness, never slow to make a point of what he thought they did better.

"That's where the rock is crushed, vaporized, and separated into its various elements," he told them. "It doesn't have to be high-grade ore. Any shovelful of desert contains traces of just about everything you can name. But low grades aren't economic with your methods. You know how to produce nuclear heat but you don't use it. It reduces all materials to a plasma state of charged particles which can be separated magnetically. All clean and efficient. Tuned radiation fields direct the recombination to whatever compounds, alloys, and other forms you want. Surplus energy is tapped for generating electricity and process heat as byproducts. The refined output is sent up to the rail links and Amazon system." Forgar indicated a wide roadway disappearing to the north, on which processions of robot trucks could be seen moving both ways. "The Pacific coast will become the most important outlet when the tunnel is completed." Forgar looked at Cade and Marie as if expecting questions, but neither of them had any for the moment. He turned toward Vrel.

"Terrans stumbled upon the beginnings of low-energy transmutation years ago, but they didn't read it right. We run reactions at levels far below anything their scientists believed were possible."

"Was that what they called cold fusion?" Vrel queried. This really wasn't his field.

"Bad name. 'Nuclear catalysis' would have been better. They misinterpreted what was going on, then abandoned it because they couldn't explain it."

Vrel looked at Cade. "Is that beginning to sound like someone we know?" he invited.

"Mike Blair?" Cade guessed.

"Because it didn't fit with the theory," they both quoted together.

Forgar looked mystified. "Theories! They'd rather stay with products of their imagination? I don't think I'll ever understand it."

A couple of miles east from the reduction complex was the "town" of Uyali itself—more the advanced-alien equivalent of a mining camp. Stark and utilitarian even for something conceived by Hyadeans, conceding nothing to adornment or elegance, it provided living space, services, and administration for the area. From above it resembled an irregular, colored-tile mosaic. As the SST descended, the tiles took on the form of rectangular boxes and cubes aligned and stacked like creations of children's blocks, making bridges here, adding a level there, the whole giving the impression of being added in haphazard leaps according to need rather than resulting from any unifying design. Beyond, separated by an expanse of fenced open ground, was a sprawl of familiarly styled Terran office units and prefabricated buildings thrown together into streets, blending on the far side into a shantytown of cabins and trailers.

The SST landed and taxied from the touchdown point to a handling area where a mix of Hyadean aircraft stood amid service buildings, maintenance gantries, and cargo conveyors. A driverless bus took the passengers to a jumble of more Hyadean domino and shoebox constructions that Cade took to be the terminal facility. Along the far side of the landing area were huge, hangarlike enclosures giving glimpses of sleek shapes surrounded by service platforms and access stairways within, standing in front of clusters of storage tanks, various unidentifiable structures, and tall towers bristling with antenna arrays. To one side, away from the main scene of activity, stood a line of what were unmistakably Terran-built military jets. Armored cars and other camouflage-painted vehicles were parked in a fenced compound nearby. Cade could only speculate as to what they were doing here. They passed a construction area where Terran work crews, some in shirts and jeans, others wearing orange coveralls, using unfamiliar machines, were excavating a new site for something. Evidently, local labor was being employed even inside the air base.

From closer range, the terminal revealed itself as a composition of what appeared to be prefabricated modules and tubelike connecting units stacked and combined in various ways to form office units, living quarters, or work space as desired. The resulting outlandish creations had ends of boxes projecting out into space; blocks straddling gaps and leaving holes through to daylight on the other side; connecting tubes emerging from walls to make right-angled turns in midair, as if changing their minds as to where they wanted to go. It seemed odd that with their obsession for efficiency, Hyadeans should be so incapable of realizing anything that on Earth would be regarded as "pleasing."

The interior was predictably functional. The mission in Lakewood had used a regular building adapted to Hyadean use. This was the first time Cade had been in an environment that was Hyadean in origin. The part of the building they had entered consisted of several large and irregular interconnecting spaces rather than the linear arrangements of rooms and corridors that typified Terran buildings. The predominant color was unfinished metallic gray, with a rigid white mesh in most places serving as ceilings below tangles of cables, pipes, and ducting that were plainly visible. Dividing up the area was an assortment of structures functioning as partitioning, shelving and storage, seating, control consoles aligned and combined in various ways, making it difficult to distinguish furnishings from parts of the architecture. They seemed to be both. One of the Hyadeans working nearby said something to the unit near him and got up to move to another station. The unit reconfigured itself to present a counter and convenience shelf that hadn't been there before, lost a corner, and moved after him to attach itself to a different part of the surroundings. A voice spoke from somewhere in the wall; the Hyadean grunted a reply and carried on. Cade noticed that Marie was staring in surprise. Not being familiar with the ubiquitous Hyadean low-level AIs, she had thought for a moment that the Hyadeans were talking to themselves.

A Bolivian immigration agent processed their papers as well as those of Vrel and his companions. Once again there were no hitches with the system, and Professor Wintner and Dr. Armley were officially admitted to the country. The party came through into what appeared to be the central concourse, where a number of armed Hyadean military were on duty. It was the first time that Cade had seen Hyadean combat troops close-up. They wore dark brown uniforms and black helmets, with lots of gadgets and pouches, and carried short weapons suggestive of assault rifles but stubbier, wider at the muzzle, and studded with controls. They had superb physiques and looked tough, a suggestion enhanced by the blockish, square-faced Hyadean build. Cade decided he could get by without tangling with them.

Forgar left them there to go his own way, along with most of the other passengers from the SST. Several, however, rode with Cade and Marie, Vrel and Thryase, in a transparent-topped car running on a monorail into another modular hodgepodge, only on a larger scale. They learned that this was the Hyadean residential part of Uyali. The area beyond, looking more like a familiar if somewhat ramshackle town, which they had seen during the descent, was the Terran sector. The two areas were segregated because of an ongoing problem of insurgents from the north infiltrating into the work force to spread discontent and conduct sabotage.

The two Hyadeans checked with some kind of office and then conducted Cade and Marie to separate quarters in a hive of cells sprouting off in different directions. They turned out to be quite comfortable accommodation units, plain but serviceable, yet surprisingly spacious. Cade's first problem was with the unfamiliar wall units and gadgets intended for Hyadean voice-direction, which were supposed to have been adapted for English but in reality rapidly became confused. In the end, he settled for the prospect of making do with minimal luxuries and conveniences. He got the shower to work, and in the course of a learning experience that involved a few minor scaldings, freezings, and flow surges, succeeded in taming it. Afterward, he laid out the collection of casual slacks, plaid, check, and plain shirts, lightweight tan jacket, straw hat, reserved sweaters, zippered topcoat, and other items that had seemed an appropriate wardrobe for a visiting academic—all very conservative compared to his customary choices—and considered what might be appropriate for the evening. He really had no way of telling, since he didn't know what the plans were. But before he could give the matter much thought, he felt himself being overcome by a shortness of breath and acute muzzy-headedness. Minutes later, Marie tapped on the door, and when Cade found the right word to open it, tottered in saying that she felt the same way. Then Vrel called to say that he had talked to Corto Tevlak, who was anxious to meet them. Cade groaned that right now neither of them wanted to meet anybody. They'd picked up some kind of South American bug or something already, he was sure.

"Bugs don't work that quickly," Vrel assured him. "It's altitude sickness. Terrans seem to be more affected by it than us. Get some rest. Most people adapt after an initial lousy night. I haven't arranged anything for tonight. We'll be going to see Corto first thing tomorrow."

CHAPTER TWENTY-FIVE

Cade felt better on awakening, able to take on the world again. After showering and shaving, he selected olive pants, the lightweight jacket, and a narrow-check shirt with knitted tie as his attire for the day. When he stopped by Marie's room, it turned out that she had recovered too. Vrel and Thryase arrived soon afterward to collect them. Although there was a communal canteen on the ground floor of the accommodation complex, they ate in a private room nearby to avoid needless questions as to who the Terrans were. It was gray with metal furnishings and exposed pipes, reminding Cade of the wardroom in a Navy ship that he had visited once. Breakfast was an insipid Hyadean vegetable-based pseudo-sausage covered in a kind of synthetic liquid cheese, accompanied by yellow bread and a warm, fruity drink. Only then, through talking to Thryase, did Cade appreciate fully the audacity that Vrel had displayed in spiriting him and

Marie out of the U.S. The normal Hyadean, inured to authority and needing orders from above before acting, would have been incapable of conceiving such a scheme, which was probably why nothing Vrel did had been questioned. Thryase wondered if Vrel's stay on Earth was turning him into a Terran—a remark that Vrel seemed to find pleasing. They departed for Tevlak's in a Hyadean flyer shortly afterward, heading northeast across the southern extremity of the Altiplano.

From the conversation during the flight, it seemed that Thryase was visiting Earth on behalf of a dissident movement of political "doves" who questioned the militant Hyadean policy toward the Querl. The Querl had not been expelled because of their inability to merge into the Hyadean system, Thryase maintained, but had separated because of their refusal to submit to it. He had entertained doubts about the official line for some time, but surrounded on all sides by a majority steeped in the conventional mindset, like many others he had hung back from speaking out strongly. Coming to Earth had opened his eyes to a lot of things and given him more confidence. What the Hyadeans were told represented lawlessness was nothing more than the expression of independent people free to live as they chose. He saw the variety and richness of Earth's cultures as a consequence of the same thing. Marie didn't quite share Thryase's idealistic view of universal freedom on Earth, but she seemed encouraged. It was the first time she had heard the official Hyadean line being questioned by a Hyadean.

They flew low over white salt wastes and reedy marshes where flamingos rose in sunlit flurries of orange and magenta reflecting from the pools like fireworks displays. Ahead, the land became more hilly, rising toward mountains with the snow line of the

Cordillera Real visible distantly behind. A valley opened out to reveal a huddled township set astride a meandering creek and giving way at the outskirts to patches of green cultivation crisscrossed by trails. The flyer dipped to pass over red-roofed, Spanish-style houses looking aged and dusty, and singled out one of several residences standing apart among clumps of yucca bush and a scattering of trees along the creek bank on the far side. It was built of adobe with a tile roof, and enclosed by a slatted fence running down to the creek on two sides. Outside the fence, a ramshackle assortment of maybe a dozen cars, trucks, and other vehicles was drawn up haphazardly along the roadside among the boulders and trees. Brown-skinned figures sitting in the open doors or under leanto shelters of blankets or plastic sheeting poles looked up curiously as the flyer descended. It landed inside the enclosure, alongside several auto-mobiles, a newish-looking pickup truck, and a couple of Hyadean personal-model flyers. There was also a larger, more impressive model of flyer, sleek and businesslike, consisting of a dark blue body riding on two yellow nacelles. The Hyadean equivalent of a Learjet, Cade decided. Two men with the high-cheeked, long-nosed features of Andean Indians, neatly groomed and wearing loose white shirts with black pants, but tough-looking nevertheless and car-rying sidearms, had already appeared from the house and were standing in front of the door when the arrivals got out.

Before anyone had moved a pace, a rotund figure, chunky-looking even for a Hyadean, swept out of the doorway, arms extended as if greeting long-lost friends. In all Cade's time of dealing with them, this was the most incongruous Cade had seen. His skin hue was dark, varying from blue to purple at the nose and cheeks, and what could be seen of his hair was crimson, protruding at the sides below a native-style, wide-brimmed derby. Along with the hat he wore a poncho embroidered with brightly colored designs, and voluminous trousers tucked into calf-length boots. He recognized Vrel and Thryase, doubtless from video exchanges, and greeted them exuberantly in Hyadean, gripping each in turn in the customary Hyadean fashion, Roman style, hands gripping the other's wrist. Then he switched to Terran handshakes. "You must be Dr. Armley, whom we've heard about. . . . And you are Professor Wintner. . . ."

"This is Corto Tevlak," Vrel managed to squeeze in.

Tevlak waved at the surroundings. "We don't have much in the way of campus life here. But welcome anyway. There are three more waiting inside to meet you." He turned to usher the party back toward the doorway, at the same time speaking in short, simple, but well-formed sentences. "And how are you shaping up this morning? Flew in last night. The altitude sometimes affects Terrans. We don't seem so bothered by it."

"Last night was a bit rough," Cade said. "We're okay now."

"Splendid."

They passed on into the house. In the hallway, Tevlak took off his derby and jammed it on top of one of several gaudily painted Indian devil masks glaring down from the wall above a carved rack bearing coats and cloaks. The interior admitted little sun but was well lit artificially. It was virtually a gallery of art, dress, ornaments, and furnishings, not just local forms but mixing styles from everywhere. Besides Indian blankets and tapestries adorning the walls and covering chair backs, and pottery pieces emblazoned with Inca or in some cases possibly Central American designs, Cade picked out a couple of Benin bronzes, ebony carvings and figurines that looked African, an Arab burnous, and a Cossack astrakhan hat. Crossed Maori throwing spears commanded the rear of an alcove between an arrangement of Navajo sand paintings. The bureau at the rear of the large room that Tevlak led them to was Victorian European or North American; a hand-cut glass decanter atop an ivory lacework corner table that could have been Turkish held a decorative wax candle (ugh); the Easter Island head set on the sill of the high window was wearing a French kepi. Marie caught Cade's eye and gave a short, bemused shake of her head.

Two of the Hyadeans that Tevlak had mentioned— a youngish-looking man and an older female—were seated together at one end of a large central table, which from the litter of bric-a-brac on the surrounding shelves and side cabinet had been cleared to make room. A shiny cylindrical object with what looked like a lens was set up on a stand at the other end, and a couple of similar devices were to the sides of the room. They looked like cameras. A flat box with a screen lay near the one on the table. There was another box with a screen and controls, along with an opened case of papers, pieces of auxiliary equipment, and other oddments in front of the younger Hyadean. He looked at Cade expectantly and seemed tempted to grin, though uncertain if he should. He had dark green hair blending into black in parts, and had acquired a T-shirt with an animal design and inscription in Spanish, though still worn beneath a regular Hyadean tunic jacket. His features were familiar.

"I know you, don't I?" Cade began. "Where was it . . . ?"

"Veyan Nyarl," the Hyadean supplied. "We met at

the mission in Los Angeles a few months ago. I was passing through the West Coast."

"Yes, right! You were the . . . 'investigator'—from some Hyadean reporting outfit that worked with the news media."

"I still am." Nyarl indicated the female with him. "And this is the person in charge of my . . . I suppose you'd say something like 'section': Hetch Luodine."

"Hello, Mr. Cade." Luodine extended a hand. "Hetch," Cade knew, was a Hyadean form of female address, something like "Ms."—not part of the name. It was appropriate for Nyarl to use it when referring to his boss. She had traveled to most parts of Earth, putting together what she described as stories about "more interesting and unusual" sides of Terran life for Hyadean consumption. The blue-and-yellow flyer outside was hers and Nyarl's.

Cade indicated Marie. "This is Marie . . ." He looked at her uncertainly, realizing he didn't know. "Cade?" She nodded. "My, er . . . a very good friend." Marie and they exchanged greetings.

The remaining Hyadean had meanwhile stood up from an armchair—embroidered Queen Anne, fitted with tasseled silk cushions that looked Chinese—where he had been sitting when they entered. He was broad, with curly brown hair, which was unusual, and an exceptionally Hyadean face composed of solid horizontal lines, looking as if it had come out of a press. He wore a loose, dark shirtlike garment tucked into baggy black trousers secured by a belt, which carried a hand-weapon in a gray, holsterlike pouch.

"This is Brezc Hudro," Tevlak informed them. "He is with the—"

"Military," Marie supplied.

Tevlak looked surprised. "How did you know? He is out of uniform."

"I can tell," Marie said.

Cade looked the Hyadean up and down again. He could picture him as one of the Hyadeans they had seen on duty at the air terminal the day before.

"You are from CounterAction," Luodine said to Marie. "Are soldiers so much alike everywhere?"

"Something like that. You develop a radar."

Hudro seemed unperturbed, simply spreading his hands in a gesture that asked what he could add to that.

Tevlak fussed around, finding seats and clearing chairs of trinket boxes and framed prints. An Indian housekeeper appeared, and went away again with orders from Tevlak for refreshments and drinks. Vrel opened the warm-up talk. "You have a genuine native dwelling," he remarked to Tevlak. "Most Hyadeans that I know prefer our own prefabs, even away from the bases. Does it go with the Terran art, somehow?"

"We were just asking the same thing when you arrived," Luodine said.

Tevlak, who hadn't sat down himself but continued moving around the room, made an expansive gesture that could have meant anything. "I like native Terran surroundings. They create a stratosphere that helps me think."

"*Atmosphere*," his veebee corrected from somewhere beneath the poncho, which Tevlak had left on.

"Whatever. You don't have to talk and be prattled back at all the time. We back home have forgotten it."

"Do you feel safe out here, away from the bases?" Thryase asked. "With the trouble that's going on among the Terrans? A lot of them don't like us. I've seen it myself in the U.S. Did you know that we're training their police and military?"

Tevlak guffawed loudly. Cade suspected it was an

acquired mannerism. Hyadeans didn't laugh much, tending more just to smile when amused. When they did, it usually signified embarrassment. "It's different here. I am a threat to nobody. Everyone here is aware of it. Do you know what the prices I can get mean to them?" He gestured in the direction of the window. "Did you see those people outside? They travel miles to bring me their work. I am the big father-number."

"*Figure.*"

"Figure." Tevlak laughed again. This time it seemed Hyadean. Hudro seemed to have reservations but chose not to press them at this point.

Vrel, who Cade gathered was the organizer of the meeting, looked at Luodine. "Let's get started. It's your show now. How do you want to do it?"

"I've got a list of things to cover. We go through a dummy run first." Luodine nodded at Roland and Marie. "That'll give you a chance to familiarize and get your lines together. Then we do it again live, a bit more formally. Don't worry about getting it perfect. We do a lot of editing."

"Wait a minute," Cade said. "What are we talking about here, 'live'?" He remembered the direct communications to Chryse that he had seen in the Hyadean offices in LA. "Is this going out over your network back home?"

"Well . . . of course." Luodine looked surprised. "Isn't that why we are here? It's not just to drink coffee."

"You mean it'll be going out right now, as we speak?" Marie queried. She glanced at Cade uneasily.

"Not that directly," Luodine replied. "I said we do preliminary editing here. Then it would be reviewed and cleaned up by the directors back home. But within a few days or so, sure. I'd hope you're going to be big news—the other side to what the people there have been told. Hyadeans involved with Terran leaders who plot assassinations and lie about it. What an exposure! We got the idea from watching how the media works here. Didn't you know? Vrel, didn't you tell them? "

"I was more concerned with getting them out of the country," Vrel said.

Cade shook his head, bewildered. Yes, it was the kind of thing he'd wanted; but it was happening so soon. The thought of talking to aliens at distant stars rendered him momentarily speechless. A week ago he had been just a guy in California making a living and minding his own business. Now he was hours away from possibly becoming an interstellar celebrity.

"What's the problem?" Luodine asked. "I thought you'd be in favor."

Marie began, "It's just that . . ." She faltered, looking to Cade for a moment. "Well, it isn't as if they're not in communication with Earth. In two days the powers back here will have the story, know our faces. Then where do we go?"

"But that's no different from the position you're in anyway," Vrel pointed out. Which of course was true. Cade looked blankly back at Marie. Her expression said she couldn't argue with it either. "You're already wanted by the ISS," Vrel went on. "So I assumed you'd want us to make a version of the take for the U.S. network as well. That's what I told Luodine."

"We're set up to do it," Luodine confirmed.

Cade had a glimpse of how Terrans must look through Hyadean eyes—forever finding reasons why not to. He decided to try being a Hyadean instead. "Okay," he heard himself say. "So let's do it."

Luodine lapsed into Hyadean exchanges with

Nyarl, who carried out what sounded like some kind of programming dialogue with the equipment, checking responses on one of the screens. Then they were ready to go. Thryase opened by answering some questions from Luodine, then going off into longer monologues. Since this version was for a Hyadean audience, the language was Hyadean. For Cade and Marie's benefit, Vrel summarized in murmured asides. Essentially, Thryase was repeating the skepticism he had expressed on the way from Uyali regarding the Hyadean depictions of the Querl. He offered the conclusion that the hostility with the Querl was an outcome of the same kind of policy that he saw being enacted on Earth now. What kind of policy was that? Luodine asked. Exploitation, Thryase answered. The Hyadean power elite sought to subdue the Querl in order to establish overlordships for themselves, away from the drabness of their own tired, worn-down planets. But the splendors of Earth went far beyond anything ever seen on the Querl worlds. Now Earth represented the premium pickings for luxury resorts and estates, to be made a quasi-feudal reserve where the privileged could get rich from Terran labor and resources. Financial control was being effected with the collusion of Terran leaders in return for the Hyadeans conferring wealth, power, and protection.

"That's exactly what the AANS is fighting," Marie whispered to Cade. "The West is told it's about Asia wanting to hang on to its economic advantages."

"Now, you will be shown back on Chryse, right?" Cade checked with Thryase when he had finished. "So what kind of risks will that mean? I thought that independent coverage outside the official guidelines was unheard of." He felt strange as the Hyadean cameras, which had been tracking the speakers automatically from different angles in the room, caught his voice and turned toward him.

"I came here as an observer. I described what I observed." Thryase shrugged. "You see, I've been learning a lot since I came to Earth."

That set the background. Next it was Cade and Marie's turn. Luodine briefed them that the object was to get their version of the Farden-Meakes affair, the cover-up and attempt to lay the blame elsewhere, and the bid to silence the witnesses. Luodine had obviously been well versed by Vrel. She put Cade and Marie on-screen together, beginning by asking them questions and then leading them into elaborating in their own words. They spoke in English, naturally, which they were told would be dubbed by a translation for the final version. Vrel explained that the voiceover would describe them as being interviewed after escaping pursuit in the U.S. Exactly where they were and how they had gotten there would, understandably, be left vague. After a few repeats and reruns, Luodine declared that she was satisfied.

Cade still wasn't sure what Hudro's role here was. The "Brezc" turned out to be a designation of military rank, which from his description Marie guessed came closest to "colonel." He had been following the proceedings with a deep, brooding expression. While Nyarl was tidying up notes and details with the equipment, Luodine gave Hudro a questioning look. "So what do you think now?" she asked him.

Hudro took a second to respond. "Even worse than I realize," he said.

"Does that mean you're with us?" Luodine asked. "You'll help?"

Hudro hesitated again, then nodded. "Yes." Cade and Marie were watching, not really comprehending. Hudro turned and explained, "I am like the defector

that you talk about. I have been in operations farther north. I see things there that our publics are not
told that disturb me." It seemed Hudro was making do without veebee prompting. "For a long time
I am not sure if all is bad. Now I hear it is so. I
decide that Hyadean way is wrong. Our training
deadens minds. Terrans who know love and carings
and make fine things are killed, and their beautiful
world is taken. I cannot agree with such things. So,
as Hetch Luodine tells, I will help."

"What kinds of things are you talking about—that
you say you've seen, Brezc?" Vrel asked curiously.

Hudro gestured toward Thryase. "Is as he says.
We train and equip Terran government soldiers that
news tells are protecting peoples from bandit terrorists who make own laws. Is not that way. They
are moved out of lands. Make space for big-money
Hyadeans. Clear forest. Make gardens, big palace
houses. Is bandits who try to protect them. We send
missiles and terrorize. The Asians—they know."
Hudro produced a square, flat container, about the
size of a box for a finger ring, from a pocket, opened
it on the table, and pushed it toward Luodine. It
contained what looked like shiny black pellets, held
in restraining slots. "Here you have proof. I show
you air strikes, and what it looks like from the
ground. Did you ever see children burning or shredded by cluster bombs? Or whole village exploded
under fuel-air vapors? All this I have. You show it
with what Thryase and Mr. Roland and Ms. Marie
all tell. Show all is so."

Luodine took the box, handling it almost reverently.
"Can we see some of this?" she asked Nyarl. He
nodded. Luodine passed it to him but continued
looking at Hudro. "This sounds like . . ." She looked
uncertain, then asked her veebee. "Dinosaur?"

"*Depends what you mean. What context?*"

"Something stunning. Sensational."

"*Dynamite.*"

Luodine didn't bother repeating it. "We need more than just pictures," she told Hudro. "We need an explanation—by someone who was there, who can interpret them. Will you go on-camera too?"

Hudro shook his head. "I can't be identified. You know that." Luodine seemed unwilling to let it go at that, but finally nodded reluctantly. There was a drawn-out silence.

Then Thryase said, "It doesn't have to be Hudro. Why can't the Terrans do it? Let them go on-screen and say it's as told to them by a senior Hyadean officer. That wouldn't even be lying."

Everyone looked at everyone else, waiting for another to come up with a reason why not. Nobody did.

"It's a thought," Vrel agreed finally.

"It's *brilliant*!" Luodine whispered. "The impact on Chryscans would be even greater. The Terrans could present it as what's happening to *their* people." She shifted her gaze back to Cade and Marie. "Will you do it?"

By this time there was nothing to ponder. They were already far enough in that it made no difference. Marie nodded. "In any case, I want to see those clips," she told them.

"Tell us what you want us to do," Cade said.

"First, let's take a break," Luodine suggested. "After that we'll play the videos and hear Hudro's story. Then I'll transpose it into interview format and we'll take you through the same routine as we did before."

"You also wanted some native stories from me," Tevlak reminded her, anxious in case he might be left out. "Don't forget that."

"I know, and we will. In the meantime, I'm getting hungry. How about a snack or something?"

"I'll see what we can do." Tevlak drew in his poncho and bustled out of the room.

Marie picked up a coffee that she still hadn't finished and sat staring distantly at the wall as she sipped. Nyarl rose, stretched, and moved over to do something to one of the cameras. Thryase began dictating in Hyadean to his veebee, which also functioned as portable secretary. Cade went over to join Hudro, who was still in the armchair.

"I'm curious, Colonel," he said. "What turned you around?"

"I haven't moved."

"What changed your mind? Most Hyadeans don't seem to question. And as you said, military training doesn't help. Why were you different?"

Hudro stared at him. He had troubled, introspective eyes, the kind that were never at rest. "Here I discover your Terran teachings of the spirit. Hyadeans know power and violence, but not your God who saves people who cannot help Him. In our way, you kick when the other is down. The ideas of Earth feed the mind. So I question what I do. One day I will save lives too."

Cade looked around the room. Here, in one house, they had Vrel, who was risking all because he had discovered ethical values previously unknown to him; Thryase had found a new politics of individualism and freedom; Tevlak had forsaken security to immerse himself in a culture; and now here was a military officer finding religion. Bombs and guns—the way that Marie had committed herself to—would never break the Hyadean stranglehold taking hold of Earth. But somewhere, Cade sensed, in these things that he was seeing here, was the way to prevail against them. Not to defeat them, for in a straight contest of strength they couldn't be defeated. But where was the need to defeat anyone, when Hyadeans could become even more Terran than Terrans themselves? Somehow, that was the key. It was all just a question of finding the direction of the flow, and then going with it.

Tevlak's name had been on the list that Julia had forwarded to her ISS controller as a matter of routine after its mention at Cade's party. One of the items that subsequently found its way into his house was a slightly damaged—hence unsalable—set of nested Russian dolls now standing in a niche in the hallway, next to a Norwegian carved-horn mermaid. The location was not ideal, but even so the chip concealed in the base of the outermost doll had collected a smattering of conversation from all of the occupants of the house, if not a comprehensive account of what was going on there. The chip responded to its periodic interrogation code sent from a Hyadean satellite as it passed overhead, and uploaded the file of what information it had managed to accumulate.

CHAPTER TWENTY-SIX

The U.S. was in uproar. Sovereignty had made public an account that it claimed was by an ISS defector they named as Reyvek of how the ISS had engineered the Farden-Meakes assassinations, along with documentary evidence. Officials denied it, of course. Nobody of that name had ever been employed by the ISS, they said. The documents were forgeries. Sovereignty retorted that Reyvek was killed in an assault that the security forces had admitted in Tennessee, the expunging of the record was standard cover-up, and they would soon produce proof of that too. Coming on top of the continuing challenges being voiced to the administration's legality, the story was causing a furore. There was open talk about a secession of western states. National Guard units in California, acting on orders from the state governor, had intervened to obstruct ISS operations.

Besides being concerned at the possible effects on

his own personal future, Casper Toddrel was also disgruntled. The news detracted from what would otherwise have been a timely escape to an idyllic setting that he had been looking forward to. The Hyadean estate known as Derrar Dorvan had been built in the Andean foothills of southeast Peru for a leading government figure who had come to Earth on his retirement, accompanied by a retinue of family and special friends. It consisted of a thirty-room principal villa constructed Roman-style around a central court, designed by a specially commissioned Terran architect, situated on a clifftop facing a spectacle of foaming waterfalls plunging between forested mountainsides and rocky towers. A hundred acres of landscaped parkland, pools, and gardens on the reverse slope contained domiciles for lesser members of the tribe. With fast, convenient transportation always at hand, they enjoyed a rich and varied social life with other Hyadean immigrant groups scattered around the region's maze of uplands and canyons, revolving to a large degree around parties and sports, sightseeing trips, and elaborate social games played for recognition, prestige, and romantic intrigue.

Toddrel had arrived the day before with several others also attending the unofficial conference that Denham had arranged. The guest accommodation rivaled the best European hotels. After a champagne breakfast on a glazed veranda looking down over cataracts and greenery, he walked with the Englishman and the ISS colonel Kurt Drisson to the Hyadean hoverbus that would take them to the part of the estate where the talks would be held. With them was General Insing, who was Meakes's replacement—hand-picked by Toddrel and his associates, far more cooperative and understanding than Meakes had been. A significant improvement in relationships with the military was expected from now on. Thoughts for the immediate moment, however, were on damage containment following the story that was breaking in the U.S. The biggest threats right now were the Californian influence peddler Cade and the CounterAction woman known as Kestrel, who had gotten away from the motel in Chattanooga minutes ahead of the security forces after killing the ISS undercover agent Ruby. It was virtually certain that Kestrel was the only surviving witness to have heard Reyvek's story firsthand; Cade would be able to testify for her, and had possibly talked to Reyvek also, if only by phone. Producing them when the moment was right had to be what Sovereignty meant when it promised that proof of the Reyvek cover-up would be forthcoming. Hence, finding and getting to them first was imperative. Combing the Chattanooga area and putting a watch on communications and on Cade's listed contacts in California had turned up nothing. Some of the intelligence people working on the case wondered if the pair were still in the country.

"Cade was friends with a Hyadean political observer called Vrel at their place in Los Angeles," Drisson told the other two. "Three days after the Chattanooga bust, Vrel took a trip to a military base near St. Louis, organized at short notice. Then, yesterday, the Hyadean records show him escorting a couple of academics, who happen to be a man and a woman, to the Hyadean mining center at Uyali in Bolivia."

"You think it's them?" Denham ased.

"I'd bet my next promotion on it. The names are in the system, but so far there's been no independent corroboration that they're real. They were accompanied on the flight by another Hyadean called Thryase, who's a critic of their policy toward Querl and is now questioning what's happening here. It smells from end to end."

"Why Uyali?" Denham asked.

"Who knows? Maybe it seemed out of the way and different—the kind of place nobody would guess. And who would?"

"And she's his ex-wife," Toddrel grumbled. "Does that mean he's been a source for Sovereignty all along? Didn't it occur to anyone?"

"That's exactly the reason Arcadia was put in there more than a year ago," Drisson said defensively. Arcadia was the ISS's live-in agent planted with Cade. "She never found any indication of communication between them."

"A strange way to rekindle an old romance, then," Toddrel commented. "So where are Vrel, this other Hyadean, and the academics now?"

"If they've left Uyali, the vehicle they used isn't registering," Drisson said. "We're giving it maximum effort. The minute anything comes up, I'll be informed."

"So is Arcadia still there—at the house in Los Angeles?" Insing asked.

"For the present, yes."

"Isn't that risky? They must know now about Ruby. If she was supposed to have been an old friend of Arcadia, that implicates Arcadia too."

"Right now, the group in Uyali are the only ones who know," Drisson said.

"All they have to do is get a message back to LA."

"And what would the people there do? Cade's friends are just good at making money. And Hyadean clerks?" Drisson shook his head. "This isn't their line of business. If they're onto her, Arcadia will know in time to get out. In the meantime, with all the uncertainty out there, she's still a valuable resource. She's also the bait if we're wrong about Cade and Kestrel, and they show up there again suddenly."

"It still sounds like a hell of a risk," Insing said heavily. "I read Kestrel's profile. She's good. And she has a big score to settle here."

"Arcadia's a professional. She can take care of herself."

"So was Ruby."

They arrived at the bus and waited while several others ahead of them boarded. Chen, a youthful Hyadean member of the household, was waiting, smiling, to usher them inside. Two of the native house stewards were standing with him. An additional attraction for wealthy Hyadeans acquiring estates on Earth was the availability and willingness of domestic help, which they regarded as a big status symbol. Employing menial labor on Chryse entailed political problems and was generally a privilege enjoyed by only the most prestigious or influential. Screening the flood of native applicants was a full-time job for specialized Hyadean security experts aided by Terran psychologists. Armed native guards supervised by a Hyadean officer watched from a discreet distance in the background.

The interior of the bus was like a luxurious but uninspired waiting room, with Hyadean-size seating and a front-end display screen, at present blank. The doors closed. The bus rose on an invisible cushion and moved away smoothly and silently. The sight of rolling lawns, lakeside walks among trees alive with birds and crossing ornamented bridges, knots of llamas and alpacas staring curiously from grassy glades and rocky stream banks dispelled further thoughts of assassinations and political coverups for the moment. Toddrel lounged back and looked enviously out over the scene and at the mountains beyond. What, he wondered, would be the prospects for somebody who cooperated sufficiently with the Hyadeans one day finding a niche in a place like this too? What a change it would make from the familiar environments he had come to detest, of stultifying boardrooms and choking, congested cities.

Denham's voice brought him back. "One item that the Hyadeans are going to bring up is a proposal to supply remote-detonatable munitions to Earth from now on, and retrofit existing stocks. It's the ideal answer to matériel disappearing. Wherever it's gone to, you can press a button and explode it. How's that for a deterrent?"

Toddrel frowned. "Hmm. . . . It's inviting high collateral. There'd be a lot of outcry, bad press. Do we need more right now?"

"That could actually help us," Denham pointed out. "The scarier the publicity, the better. Nobody would dare touch any of the stuff. Just what we want."

"Let's see what the general reaction at the meeting is when it's proposed," Toddrel suggested.

They came to one of the outlying residences, which had been made ready with conference facilities, a catering and domestic staff, and additional guards. They got out, and Denham and Insing moved ahead as they approached the building. Just as they entered, a high-pitched tone came from the compad in Drisson's jacket. He drew it out and looked at Toddrel meaningfully. "Emergency band. This could be something new." Denham and Insing stopped to look back. Toddrel motioned for them to go on, and that he and Drisson would catch up. They looked around and moved into a more secluded space off the entrance hallway. Toddrel watched the screen as Drisson activated it. The face and shoulders of a Hyadean appeared, in a tunic carrying military insignia. "Borfetz—Hyadean security," Drisson muttered.

The Hyadean peered out at them guardedly. "You are not alone. I need to speak urgently."

"It's okay," Drisson said. "This is Toddrel. He's with us."

Borfetz nodded but didn't look happy about it. "We have located them, both—the man and the woman," he reported. "They are at a house that belongs to an eccentric Hyadean, two hundred miles from Uyali. They don't seem to be planning to depart anytime soon. We can be there within an hour."

"Not another cowboy circus this time," Toddrel murmured in Drisson's ear. "We need them to talk. I have to find out how much they know and who else they've passed it on to. Everything could depend on this."

"Minimum force, no lethality," Drisson relayed. "They're wanted alive."

"I understand," the Hyadean acknowledged.

CHAPTER TWENTY-SEVEN

The midday news brought reports that two of the freighters used to transport Hyadean-processed minerals out via the Amazon had been sunk by planted bombs. The Brazilian Air Force was conducting retaliatory strikes against suspected guerrilla bases and support centers in the area. In Bolivia, a section of one of the conveyor lines in the extraction region west of Uyali had been blown up. The newscaster expressed fears that this might be the beginnings of a major sabotage campaign against the Hyadean operations. A government commentator attributed it to a sudden increase in external aid to MOPAN—Movimento por la Autonomía Nacional was the name of the general resistance movement formed out of various opposition groups that had grown throughout the region. Asian sources were suspected. Weapons of Asian manufacture in captured guerrilla supplies were presented as evidence, and there was some insinuation of Chinese companies acting as fronts. The commentator feared that more potent Hyadean weapons might find their way through via the same route. He cited the recent assassinations carried out in the U.S. with a Hyadean plasma cannon as a precedent.

Hudro was stationed in Brazil and had taken a few days leave to come down to Bolivia. After hearing the news, he announced that he had to return to his unit immediately. Vrel decided to go with him as far as Uyali. Security would be tightening up everywhere, and he wanted to make discreet inquiries on his own regarding the options for moving Cade and Marie onward. In the meantime it would be better for them to remain where they were. He would return or send the flyer back for them when he had a firm plan. Vrel and Hudro departed shortly afterward.

The others got back to rehearsing and then recording Cade and Marie's narration of the material they had gone through with Hudro. Luodine then moved on to the take that she had promised for Tevlak. Finally, she settled down with Nyarl to editing the preliminary version for transmission to her organization on Chryse. "This might start another sensation," she said as Nyarl worked with the equipment. "Direct news from the front, bypassing the official system. I don't know if it's ever been done before."

"So why are you doing it?" Cade asked her. "Why are you risking your . . . What do you call it. Career? Entitlement."

Luodine looked at him oddly for several seconds. "Because that's all we've ever lived for. It's the way we were conditioned. But Terrans find meaning in life beyond whatever it is that our entitlements measure. I want to find it too. So I suppose I'm experimenting."

"We all are," Thryase said.

Cade found his curiosity over this strange effect that Earth seemed to have on Hyadeans who spent any time there increasing more and more.

Marie had gone outside. Cade followed and found her standing by the door, taking in the scene of the mountains on one side, the creek running down toward the town on the other. Tevlak was outside the fence with the people who had been waiting there and were now talking excitedly, seemingly all at once, showing him various wares. One of the house guards was standing a few paces behind him.

Marie heard Cade come out and spoke without turning her head. "Why can't the whole world be more like this? People just living their lives, leaving each other alone. Why does anyone have to care what others believe or think?"

"You tell me. Aren't you the one who understands causes?"

"I hate it. But what are you supposed to do about the ones who take everything that other people produce, and give nothing back? They couldn't build a house or make a shoe or even feed themselves without ordinary people like these. . . . Yet because they can steal from them, they call them inferior. I don't like them getting away with it. It doesn't matter if they're ours or Hyadeans."

The sun was picking out the almost blond parts in Marie's hair, the sharp angles of her jaw and cheek. She still looked slim and lithe, even in the loose sweater and shapeless dun-colored pants. "Anyway, it may not stay so peaceful for long, by the sound of things," Cade said. "I guess that'll slow down all that production we saw yesterday."

"I wonder who benefits," Marie said distantly.

Cade moved closer behind her. He could tell that

she sensed his nearness, but she didn't move. "Did you really go to China?"

"Sure. I did the full training routine there: guns and explosives; computers and codes; murder and mayhem. The works. Skiing at Aspen was getting to be so ordinary. You know I have uncommon tastes."

"I thought they were all totalitarians there. Turn you into marching zombies. Doesn't it work like that?"

"Oh, that's all over. They're discovering individualism now, and hurling themselves into it with the same fanaticism they've always shown for everything. They're like the Arabs—with a tradition of resisting outside influence and interference. That's why Asia has become the natural center of opposition to what's going on."

Cade was about to reply, then snorted. "You see: it isn't me. You turn everything into politics."

Marie turned to face him. "But you *asked* me!"

"About China. You could have talked about the Great Wall, or real wonton soup."

"But China *is* politics right now. All of Asia is. Resistance isn't going to come from anywhere else. Not on any organized scale."

"Okay, so I don't care about China. Right now, I—"

At that moment, a commotion broke out among the people outside the fence, where Tevlak was. Marie and Cade turned to see what was going on. Some were gesturing toward the sky. Aircraft of some kind had appeared to the north and were approaching low and fast. They resolved themselves rapidly into three flattened oval shapes, black in color, flared at the tail, spreading out to make a circuit of the town. As Cade wheeled to follow them, a second flight of three came into sight, following the first.

Nyarl appeared from inside the house. "What's happening?" he asked, then followed their gaze.

"Hyadean troop carriers," Marie said tightly. "Their security forces use them. I can only think of one reason that would bring them here."

"There's some kind of problem inside too. Luodine is trying to send the file out to Chryse. The system won't accept. It's been blocked."

"Bad news," Marie muttered.

The first three carriers came out of their turn on a direct course for the house. Two descended toward points a short distance upstream and downstream along the creek bank, while the third passed overhead to the opposite side, presumably to cut off escape in that direction. The second three carriers were heading directly in for the house to complete its encirclement.

"The phone!" Marie said suddenly. "Hyadean communications might be blocked, but ours could still work. We've got to get that file out!"

Nyarl turned and stumbled back into the house, Marie following. Cade stopped to look back the other way. Figures in combat gear were leaping from the carriers that had landed, spreading out and advancing. It looked like a mixed force of Hyadeans and Terrans. The people around Tevlak were drawing back, alarmed, some already running instinctively toward the gate as if the house offered protection. Tevlak was standing, bewildered. The house guard drew his gun and ran forward to stop them. Tevlak waved him aside to let them through. As the second wave of carriers touched down, an amplified voice boomed, "YOU ARE SURROUNDED. DO NOT ATTEMPT TO RESIST, AND NO ONE WILL BE HARMED." Cade turned away and hastened inside after Marie and Nyarl. Marie was handing a phone to Nyarl, who plugged in a data lead, then frantically connected that to an adaptor hooked to a piece of the Hyadean equipment. Luodine was watching one of the screens with an agonized expression. "I have to reformat," she told Cade. "Our codes won't work with the Terran system."

"Where do we send it?" Nyarl asked. Marie seemed at a loss.

Cade thought furiously. "Vrel's got a clean phone. Send it to him. He'll figure out a way to forward it."

"You know the number?" Nyarl asked. Cade nodded. Nyarl passed him the phone. The housekeeper came in, jabbering in Spanish; at the same moment, the other house guard appeared at the opposite end of the room. The guard yelled something. They disappeared toward the rear. Screams punctuated by shouted commands were coming from outside, getting nearer.

"*Done!*" Luodine exclaimed. Cade hammered in the number.

A musical tone sounded. "Acceso inválido. Servicio negado," an impartial voice enunciated.

"*Shit!*" Tevlak's phone was being blocked too.

"What is it?" Marie asked tensely. Cade didn't answer. For several seconds he stood glaring from side to side like a trapped animal. Then he threw the phone down and rushed back out of the house. The yard was filled with milling figures. Tevlak was inside the gate, uniformed Terrans restraining him on both sides, a Hyadean calling orders to others moving forward. More Hyadeans had taken up positions around the perimeter. Some genius ordered a burst of warning shots to be fired. The milling and shouting turned into panic. Cade grabbed a fleeing Indian, wide-eyed with fear, by the shirt front.

"*Do you have a phone?*"

"Eh? No comprendo."

"Jesus. . . . Teléfono. ¿Tiene un teléfono?"

"No."

Cade pushed him aside. A woman in a straw hat and red wrap was screaming and waving her arms aimlessly. Cade saw a phone attached by a loop to her shoulder purse. He pointed at it. *"I need that phone!"* The woman wasn't listening. He tore the phone from the purse and rushed back inside. Nyarl ripped the data lead out of the useless phone and jammed it into the one Cade thrust in front of him. Cade tried the number again.

Ri-ing. Ri-ing.

The front door banged open, and a voice shouted, sounding like the guard who had been outside. The second guard reappeared from the back of the house and ran out toward the front.

"Christ! Christ! Christ! Come on. . . ."

Ri— The tone cut, and a voice answered in Hyadean.

"Vrel?"

"Yes."

"It's Roland. No time to talk. I'm downloading the file. You have to get it to Chryse somehow."

"What—"

"Just do it!"

An endless pause. Then, "Ready." Cade nodded at Nyarl. Nyarl barked something at the Hyadean electronics. A crash followed by splintering noises came from the rear of the house, and then the terrified yelling of the housekeeper. More thuds from the front door. Indignant shouts, a couple of shots, then more screaming, getting louder as the door was battered in.

"It's going through," Luodine murmured.

Boots hitting the floor at a run; shouts; other doors in the house being thrown open.

An officer in peaked cap and army uniform,

brandishing a pistol, appeared from the rear rooms, followed by troopers in helmets and flak jackets. *"Everyone stay where you are! Hands high! Stop that!"* Seconds later, armed Hyadean figures came through from the front, thrusting aside Thryase, who was trying to block the doorway. The leader barked something at Luodine, while another hauled Nyarl away from the table.

"Sent and deleted!" Luodine whispered to Cade. He released a sigh of relief. They straightened up to face the intruders.

The Terran officer came forward. "Ms. Marie Cade, otherwise known as Kestrel, I believe. And Mr. Roland Cade. You are under arrest as terrorists wanted for extradition to the United States." More soldiers appeared from the rest of the house, making negative signs. One of the Hyadeans began checking the recording equipment. Luodine and Thryase were protesting in response to questions from another Hyadean, answering in English for Cade and Marie's benefit.

"We're simply doing our jobs. . . . I'm a political observer. She is a media investigator."

"Tevlak doesn't know anything about them. They were introduced as visiting professors."

"No, I don't know anything about a Teera Vrel. . . . Hyadean officer? What Hyadean officer?"

In the end, it was announced that the four Hyadeans would be detained pending a ruling from a higher authority somewhere. Cade and Marie were taken out to one of the craft that had landed, and boarded with a mixed Terran and Hyadean guard detail. The carrier took off immediately, accompanied by a second flying as escort.

CHAPTER TWENTY-EIGHT

Toddrel learned just after the evening banquet at Derrar Dorvan that the two fugitives had been captured. They were being held in a detention facility at a base used jointly by Hyadean and Peruvian military forces near Cuzco, pending further instructions. Hyadeans had been at the house too, but there seemed to be some confusion over their motives and circumstances. In any case, Hyadean security was dealing with it. Toddrel's concern at this stage was purely in establishing how much the two Americans had found out, and whom they might have divulged it to before leaving the country. And then silencing them. He skipped the next morning's session of the meeting and left for Cuzco with Drisson, curious to meet face-to-face this couple who had been the cause of so much trouble. They flew south, with the wall of the Andes standing clear in the early sun, far off to the right.

"I've been thinking about those remote-detonatable munitions that Denham was talking about," Drisson said. "If the Hyadeans are moving troops into the south Altiplano region to protect their action, it means they'll be stashing a lot more hardware around there. If some of the munitions they bring in are of the new type, and someone could get the remote-access codes . . ." He looked at Toddrel meaningfully.

A lot of damage and confusion could be caused, slowing down if not halting operations completely, which Toddrel and associated interests would appreciate. It didn't need spelling out. "And the media have already set up MOPAN with Chinese backing as the obvious culprits," Toddrel completed.

"My thinking, exactly."

"Hm." Toddrel decided that it had possibilities. "It could be tough on a few of our Hyadean . . . allies." He looked at Drisson questioningly.

"Hell, if it's the way to win the war . . ." Drisson left it unfinished.

"Something to bring up with Denham when we convene again tomorrow," Toddrel pronounced.

Cade sat hunched on a coarse mattress covering the single cot, his legs drawn up, arms resting on his knees. The cell was part of a detention facility in the place they had been brought to. It seemed some kind of military base from the glimpses that he'd managed to get. He hadn't seen anything of Marie since they were taken separate ways on their arrival the previous day. Sounds from outside came intermittently through the barred, glass-slatted window, of vehicles, tramping feet, voices calling orders, and aircraft taking off and landing. Besides the cot, he had a chair, a table, a wooden shelf, a washbasin with a faucet that dribbled brown water, and a toilet. Light was from a bulb, hanging by its cord. It all felt very far from Newport Beach.

They had fastened a metal collar around his neck. When he started protesting and demanded legal representation, a jolt that felt as if it were tearing his head apart knocked him off his feet, impressing the message that he wasn't in a position to demand anything. It had been a sobering and effective lesson. In movies, people always breezed through such experiences to perform acrobatic escapes or deliver comeuppances with interest on their aggressors. The reality turned out to be very different. His head still throbbed, and his nerves felt shredded. His body seemed to have gone into a protective shock. Worse was the feeling of humiliation and outrage, the disorientation that came with the realization of his utter helplessness. And he'd had plenty of time to reflect that this could be just the mild beginning. Perhaps that was an intended part of the process. He tried not to think about Marie.

Footsteps approached outside. Keys jangled in the door. It opened to reveal two of the guards— dark-skinned and hefty, with mean, indifferent faces. One of them said something in Spanish and motioned for Cade to get up. The other was holding a unit resembling a TV remote, which controlled the collar. Cade's body had chilled and stiffened, but he wasn't arguing.

They took him past a row of doors with shuttered grilles, down a flight of metal stairs, and along a corridor of walls painted green up to a brown dividing line and yellow above. Steel lockers stood at intervals along one side, and red fire extinguishers hung on the wall at the end. A soldier in fatigues came out of one of the doors and passed them going the other way. They stopped at a door farther along. The guard who was leading knocked. A voice from inside called, "*Sí.*" The guard opened the door. The other jabbed Cade in the back to propel him through.

It was a bare room of painted brick walls and a concrete floor. A man in a tan jacket and white, open-neck shirt was sitting at a metal desk, empty except for a file folder, some scattered papers, a lamp, and an open laptop. He had a balding head fringed by dark, oily-looking curls, and a rounded face with brooding eyes that followed Cade curiously as he came in. Another man, leaner, with fair, cropped hair and a mustache, wearing ISS uniform with rank designation that Cade wasn't sure of—colonel, maybe—was standing, arms folded, with his back to the corner on one side. An upright wooden chair faced the desk. The guard prodded Cade toward it while the other closed the door. He sat down, and they stationed themselves behind.

The interrogator let his eyes flicker over Cade for a few seconds, as if looking for a visual cue as to how to open. "So, the other half of the duo," he said finally. He was American. "You two have caused a lot of problems." He didn't seem to expect any response at that point. "Okay, let's save us all a lot of time. We know you were at the motel in Chattanooga, how you got there, and that you were brought out through St. Louis by this Hyadean from California, Teera Vrel." He went on to supply some of the salient details. Maybe the idea was to sound as if he knew more than he did, with the implication that telling untruths could be risky. Cade figured that Rebecca and Julia between them would have supplied everything up to the incident in the motel. With surveillance everywhere and taps into all the computers, who knew how they had traced them to St. Louis? Anything relating to the three days between his and Marie's fleeing from

Chattanooga and their arrival at the St. Louis Hilton was notably absent from the interrogator's account.

"Did you at any time meet the person who was referred to as Otter? His real name was Reyvek, formerly with the security forces." Cade didn't answer. The man nodded to one of the guards behind. A pain like a three-second migraine headache seared through Cade's skull, then stopped. Just a warning. He realized that the rush of fear had almost caused him to loose bowel control. A sour taste welled in his mouth. His chest was pounding, palms slippery.

"I'm not here to do all the talking," the interrogator told him. "You *will* tell us, so you might as well make it easy on yourself. Again, did you at any time meet Otter?"

Cade licked his lips. Conflicting impulses tore at him. He had never known that the urge of self-preservation could be so strong. In his confusion he couldn't form a coherent answer. The pain began again, rising slowly this time, like a dental drill probing a nerve, only in his head. "*No!*"

"No, what?"

"No, I never met him."

"Did you talk to him at all—by phone, maybe?"

"No."

"You *will* tell us," the interrogator reminded him again.

Cade felt sweat running down his back inside his shirt. "I didn't talk to him! What else can I say?"

"CounterAction arranged his defection. Weren't you involved with that?"

"I don't know anything about CounterAction."

"Don't give us that," the colonel said from the corner. His voice was clipped. "You've been an under-cover informer of theirs for years. That's what that whole setup of yours is in California. Isn't it?"

"No. That's not true."

"Isn't it?" the interrogator at the desk echoed. The drill started probing again.

"It's not true, I told you!" The drill stopped. Cade gasped for breath. "You've had your spy there for a year. What did she see?"

"Why did you go to Chattanooga?" the interrogator asked.

"You just told me a few minutes ago. I didn't intend going to Chattanooga. Only Atlanta."

"That was the story," the colonel said. "We want the real reason."

"That's all there is."

"Wasn't it to rendezvous with Kestrel, your former wife, whom you'd been in communication with all the time?"

"No. I didn't even know she was there."

"You expect us to believe that?" the interrogator asked.

"Probably not, if you've already made your minds up. . . . But it's true."

The interrogator glanced at the colonel, apparently deciding not to pursue the point for the time being. He jotted something on the papers in front of him and looked back up. "Where were you in the three days after Chattanooga—before you showed up in St. Louis?"

"I don't know." Cade felt a tingle building up. He gulped. "It was dark. We followed a car somewhere."

"So you were still in the general area," the colonel said.

There couldn't be any denying it. "Yes."

"How many hours did you drive from Chattanooga? Which direction?"

"One, maybe two. North . . . I think."

The interrogator made more notes, then consulted

something on the laptop. "Vagueness won't get you anywhere in the long run," he murmured, still looking at the screen.

The colonel moved across the room to stand looking down at Cade, giving him no respite. "Where did Vrel go?" he demanded.

"When?"

"Quit stalling, Cade. Vrel wasn't at Corto Tevlak's house. Where is he?"

"He went to check up on some things."

"Back to Uyali?"

"He didn't say exactly where, and I've already been mixed up in this long enough not to ask." Cade looked up. The colonel was watching him distastefully. "Look, whatever you think, I haven't been working with CounterAction. I just make trading deals and mind my own business. If Julia's been any good to you, you know that."

"Who was the other Hyadean who disappeared with him?"

"I'd never met him before."

"I didn't ask that. What was his name?"

Cade couldn't bring himself to answer. He gripped the edges of the chair and stared at the front of the metal desk, feeling himself perspiring in rivers. "It doesn't matter for now," the interrogator's voice said tiredly from above. Cade raised his eyes, half expecting a trick. "We don't want any undue unpleasantness here. This is only a transit facility, you understand. Shortly, you'll be taken to a more permanent location, where they have experts who are more skilled at this kind of thing than I. I'm sure you'll be more cooperative by the time we next meet." He eyed Cade dourly for a moment. "Even if you do discover a reserve of unsuspected heroics, there are usually other avenues of weakness that can be explored. The other person that we're holding, for example, seems to be becoming an object of restored affections, even assuming that your alleged estrangement was genuine. I trust you take the point?"

"Bastards!" Cade started to rise and was checked by a jarring sensation in his neck. A hand from behind seized him by the hair, yanking his head back, forced him back down, while another cuffed the side of his face painfully. He glowered across the desk, panting shakily.

The interrogator studied Cade's face pensively. It must have registered abhorrence that a Terran could be capable of selling out his own kind to such a degree. His expression changed to one of amused contempt. "Don't tell me you've fallen for some campus ideology. Our files describe you as a realist. There's only one kind of realism in the universe, and its proponents all understand each other. There aren't any rules to the game. Its sole object is to take care of oneself. You make trading deals, you said? Very well. We can make you an offer to come over to the winning side in return for being sensible. Isn't that what any realist wants?"

Cade didn't hold much stock in any offers. Whichever way things went, he had the distinct feeling that knowing what they knew now, the chances of he and Marie ever getting back to the States were pretty slim. Losing them somewhere would hardly present a problem. After all, they had never officially left.

CHAPTER TWENTY-NINE

The Hyadean transport hummed through the air. Cade had no idea in what direction. The view panels were set to opaque, leaving just the stark, metal-ribbed interior and its austere fittings. Marie was next to him, with two Peruvian guards in the row in front, three behind, and their Hyadean officer facing from a bulkhead seat in front. The captives had been issued with baggy gray prison garb, and each wore one of the diabolical Hyadean collars. They had both spent a second uncomfortable night. But at least they were together again—for the time being. Perhaps a chance to renew concern between them was part of the intention—to make things that much tougher later. There had been little opportunity to discuss their experiences. Cade didn't know if she had been exposed to threat along the lines the interrogator had implied. He wouldn't have mentioned it in any case.

"Look. . . ." He kept his voice low, glancing

sideways to be sure she was listening. "It's been a long time. A lot's happened. In case we don't get out of this, I just want you to know that a lot of things that seemed smart once don't seem so smart anymore. What I mean is . . . Hell, you know what I'm trying to say."

"Roland groping for words?" she murmured. "I don't believe it."

"Asshole, then. How's that for a choice of word? I was an asshole."

"No talking between the prisoners," the Hyadean officer said.

Cade sensed Marie smiling. Her hand found its way around the metal tubing holding the armrest, to where his was resting. Their little fingers touched and entwined surreptitiously. If only just a little, he felt more at peace.

About fifteen minutes later, the transport dipped suddenly without warning and went into a steep descent. The officer grabbed a handrail on the wall to steady himself and asked something in Spanish to the guard who seemed to be second in command. The second answered negatively. The officer called out in Hyadean to the vessel's control system. There was no response. He called something else, then broke out a manual control panel that hinged down from the bulkhead. The guards began jabbering in alarm as they clung for balance. "¡Silencio!" the officer shouted, tapping frantically at the panel. "¡Espera para órdenes!"

Cade and Marie exchanged ominous looks. "You might just have made that last-words speech in time," Marie whispered. They clutched hands tensely.

The transport leveled out suddenly, causing more disorder; then there was a bump and a swish that sounded as if they had brushed a treetop, followed by sudden deceleration, throwing everyone forward onto the floor and flattening the officer against the forward wall. Cade was pitched fully between the two seats in front and went down in a heap with the guards. Before anyone could begin untangling themselves, there was the *bang* of a hole being blown in the side of the cabin, and then something exploded in a blaze of light that left Cade blinded and helpless except for a bizarre reverse-colored image etched into his retina. He was vaguely aware of shouts, scrambling noises, bodies colliding around him. Fragments of vision began coming together again to reveal the door partly burned away and hanging open, two large, helmeted figures silhouetted against the daylight, coming through, and then others, smaller. A guard tried to rise and was clubbed down. Two of the assailants seized Marie. One threw something like a blanket over her head and held her, while one of the larger figures leveled a device at her throat. "*No!*" Cade screamed. He tried to hurl himself at them, but strong arms gripped him from behind. Then a metallic mesh came down over him, and he felt his head being pushed back.

"Don't resist!" a Hyadean voice shouted near his ear. "It scrambles signals to the collar! They can still blow your head off!" Cade forced himself to relax and felt some kind of shield being forced up between his neck and the band of metal. Moments later there was a *clunk*, and the collar came free. The mesh was removed. He looked over, his eyes still dim with aftershock from the light, and saw that Marie was rid of hers too. He turned back to the Hyadean, who was regarding him in what looked like a jaunty stance, hands on hips, while armed Terrans shepherded the dazed guards and their officer out through the ruin of the door. The details cleared slowly to show him in Hyadean combat garb, belt and shoulder harness loaded with pouches and accoutrements, grinning and waiting while Cade's vision cleared sufficiently to recognize him.

It was Hudro.

"You were going the wrong way," Hudro said. "We figured you needed help." There had to be a response that would go down in history. Cade couldn't think what it was.

Meanwhile, the second Hyadean, who was female, had been locating and smashing key parts of the transport's communications equipment. "That's it," she announced. "Let's go."

"We need to move fast," Hudro told Cade. "The traffic-control system will be flashing alarms already."

The vessel was tilted among a tangle of vines and trees. They climbed out carefully and crossed an open area, where Terrans in forage caps and jungle gear had the officer and two of the five guards sitting on the ground, disarmed, hands on heads, while two others assisted one who seemed to have hurt a leg. There didn't seem to be any more Hyadeans. The female who was with Hudro frisked the captives for personal communicators and took those too.

In a clearing a short distance away was an olive-painted military helicopter, rotor running. The two Hyadeans guided Cade and Marie over to it, where a Terran waiting in the doorway helped them aboard. He shouted to the others, who began backing away from the guards, keeping their weapons trained on them. The guards were looking scared. For a sickening moment Cade thought they were about to be gunned down in cold blood. But the rescuers turned to run the last few yards to the waiting helicopter and threw themselves aboard. Hudro shouted something to the pilot, and it began rising. A couple of weapons were thrown back to the guards as the helicopter cleared the treetops. Minutes later, it was skimming over a green ocean of forest.

"I said that one day I save people," Hudro shouted above the engine noise. "Is good feeling."

"I'm glad you don't waste time once you make your mind up," Cade yelled back.

Hudro gestured to introduce the other Hyadean, crouching next to him on the floor, gripping the side netting—the helicopter's cramped side seats didn't admit to Hyadean proportions. She had taken off her helmet to reveal orange-yellow hair and smooth features for a Hyadean. Cade had the feeling that by their standards she would be young and pretty. "This is Yassem. A long time we know each other. It is she who shows me the Terran God. We decide that Hyadeans who bomb Terrans from homes here are criminals. Terran powers that they act with are criminals. We want no more part." He hesitated, then said something to Yassem in Hyadean. She laughed, which Cade remembered meant embarrassment. "I guess is okay to tell you now," Hudro said to Cade. He gripped Yassem's hand. "Until yesterday, Yassem works with Hyadean intelligence service. Communications technical specialist. Is how we meet. We fall over love. Go away, live together as Terrans now. Who knows where? Away. Maybe Asia someplace."

Marie laid a hand on Yassem's shoulder and smiled. "Good luck," she said.

"Thank you."

The rest of the company in the helicopter comprised a mix of tough-looking characters in parkas, sweaters, flak jackets, combat smocks, decked with equipment belts and bandoliers, nursing an assortment of weapons. One who appeared to be the leader—with a black beret worn forward, sunglasses, and a black mustache—was eyeing Cade and Marie curiously from a jump seat on Hudro's other side.

"Here is Rocco," Hudro supplied, following Cade's gaze. "I know too for long time now. My work with Hyadeans makes me live close with MOPAN bandits, try to spy. But it works backward. I get to know them. Yassem tells me about God, and I learn bandit peoples know God too. So I am on wrong side. Maybe live with bandits for time before go to Asia. Teach defense to Hyadean devil weapons. Many tricks. Makes me the big prize, eh?"

Rocco acknowledged Cade and Marie with a nod. Cade returned it. "We owe you a big thanks. I never realized we were so well known here already."

"If Hudro says you're two important people who could make some difference to this war, that's good enough for me," Rocco said.

"So how did you pull it off?"

Rocco indicated Hudro and Yassem. "You have to ask them. They got into the system that controls the Hyadean robot flyers. Brought it down where it wasn't supposed to go. We were waiting."

"Where are you from, Rocco?" Marie asked.

"It doesn't matter anymore. No family left anywhere. All wiped out in the fighting. Now I just live to fight Globs."

"Globs?" Cade's brow creased.

"Globalists," Marie supplied.

"Forces of governments that work for the criminals," Hudro said. "Is more complicated here than Earth is told."

"And every day getting more complicated," Rocco said. "What do you think is going to happen in the north?" he asked Cade and Marie. "Places in the western states ordering federal troops out. Air bases being taken over."

"We hadn't heard about it," Cade said.

"A lot of people say they're gonna split."

Cade turned his head to Hudro. "After you left Tevlak's, we tried to send a file to Vrel via his phone. Did it come through?"

Hudro nodded. "It comes through. But we cannot send to Chryse. Vrel think he knows somebody in California instead. If they ever get it, I don't know."

"Where's Vrel now?" Cade asked.

"Waiting for us. Is with Luodine and Nyarl. When—" Hudro looked away as a call from the pilot up front interrupted. Rocco got up, ducking his head, and shouldered his way forward between the rows of figures hunched over guns and packs. Hudro straightened up on the floor in readiness to rise. Next to Cade, Marie pulled herself closer.

Rocco came back and shouted down to Hudro. "Segora is under attack. We are being warned off. The pilot wants you up front. We've got incoming radar from somewhere."

"What's Segora?" Cade asked Hudro as he unfolded up from the floor.

"Is where we were supposed to land. Maybe have to change plans now." Hudro followed Rocco forward. The guerrillas had become alert, straightening up in their seats to watch something outside. Cade turned to look out of the open hatch, past the machine gun. Several miles away, perhaps, an aircraft shaped like a black arrowhead was climbing away from the ground, followed by a second a short distance behind and to one side. A boiling cloud of black smoke mixed with flame rose behind them. More planes were visible as dots higher up.

"Air strike," Yassem commented needlessly. Smoke was also coming up from other places among the trees. Whether it was due to air attack, artillery, or conflagrations on the ground was impossible to say. A brilliant pink light flashed past the open gun-hatch; then came the jolting of objects hitting the helicopter's structure. The cold realization came over Cade that they were being shot at. Yassem put her helmet back on and secured it.

At the front, Rocco turned and shouted back instructions. One of those behind clambered up to man the machine gun, while another hooked up the ammunition belt from the feeder box. Everyone else clung tight as the pilot went into a violent evasive maneuver. Cade was thrown outward from his seat, then hard back on the wall. He and Marie braced their arms on the sides and tried to steady themselves against each other. . . .

And then nothing.

Fragments of awareness. Blurred smears of sensations coalescing from a vacuum.

Spinning patches of light. . . . Churning noise. . . . Lurching motion.

Thirsty. Sweating. Touch of damp fabric.

Cade was lying down. Every lurch tossed him to the side and back again, causing pain to shoot through his head. His head didn't feel good at all. It felt bloated on one side and numb at the back. The thought came and went hazily. His head was wrapped in something. Stiff. Aching everywhere. . . . None of him felt good at all.

He heard the whirr of an engine revving, then gears being shifted. The lurching resolved itself into the jolting of a truck on a rough road. He tried to open his eyes but they seemed to be stuck. Even the effort made the shooting pains in his head worse. The thirst was unbearable, as if his throat were filled with dry furnace ash. He groaned.

Voices somewhere floated incomprehensibly. A hand lifted his head. He winced, feeling as if his neck would break. Something touched his mouth. *Water!* Not cool, but priceless. He tried to gulp greedily but the hand restrained him, allowing him only to sip. A wet cloth was swabbed over his face and eyes. He tried opening them again and succeeded with an effort. A face was looking down at him. His faculties still hadn't returned sufficiently for him to recognize anything. He sipped more from the water bottle and registered slowly that he was in a truck. Only then did he begin to remember that he had been in a helicopter.

Another face, blue-gray in hue, materialized behind the first. He flexed his lips. "Vrel?" he managed.

"No." The face looked concerned. "This is Hudro."

Oh, right. Vrel hadn't been there. So how come a truck now? "What . . . ? Did we crash?"

"Was more than a day ago now," Hudro said. "Was fighting at Segora. We were hit."

Cade contemplated the statement in a detached kind of way. It didn't take on any immediate great significance. His head had been injured, and it hurt. Pink lights. He remembered the gunfire. Then it all started coming back.

"Marie!" He focused and looked up. "How is Marie?" The Hyadean face stared down at him in what seemed a long silence. "Where is she? What's up?

"I'm sorry, Mr. Cade," Hudro said. "She didn't make it."

CHAPTER THIRTY

The flyer sped low on a southwestward course, a few thousand feet above the barren salt wastes of the southern Altiplano. Ahead and to the right, the line was coming into view of the new roadway with its procession of robot trucks carrying produce from the extraction operations north to the Amazon outlet, and a return flow of vehicles either empty or bringing construction materials and supplies. Vrel and Hudro were over an hour out from leaving Tevlak's house and getting close to Uyali.

"What do you make of it?" Vrel asked Hudro. He meant the news they had heard at Tevlak's that morning of the escalation of sabotage and guerrilla attacks in the Amazon region, and the retaliatory actions by government forces. They were speaking, naturally, in Hyadean.

"Somebody, somewhere gave them a signal. Someone who has been building up backing and support."

"The Asians?"

"They get a lot of the blame publicly, but I'm pretty sure there's more to it. The Asian economy isn't affected that much. A lot of Western finance would like to see a slowdown in the operations here."

"I thought they were supposed to be with us," Vrel said.

"It's all complicated . . . trying to understand what goes on. I don't really understand it."

Vrel watched Hudro staring out through the view panels. His face was troubled. "So what are you going to do?" Vrel asked. There was a pause.

"There is a girl that I know up in Brazil—it's best if you don't know her name . . ." Hudro seemed to think better of whatever he had been about to say. "We have plans," he ended simply.

"A Terran girl?"

"No. She is Hyadean."

"I know a Terran girl in Los Angeles," Vrel said. "Very pretty. Blond hair, cut like this at the front." He made a line with his hand to indicate a fringe. "Sometimes I think of going off to live a Terran life— like Tevlak."

"You do?" Hudro seemed more than just casually interested. He was about to say more, when a tone interrupted from the Terran phone that Vrel was carrying. Vrel frowned, took it out, and answered guardedly, "Who is this?"

"Vrel?" A Terran voice.

Vrel switched to English. "Yes."

"It's Roland. No time to talk. I'm downloading the file. You have to get it to Chryse somehow."

File? It could only mean the file they had recorded with Luodine. Vrel was confused. "What—" he began.

"Just do it!"

Hudro was looking at him questioningly. Vrel waved

a hand to indicate that he couldn't explain. "Some
kind of trouble," he muttered, at the same time keying
in the code to direct input to the phone's integral storage. "Ready," he said into it. He could make out noise
at the other end: voices shouting; distant bangs and
crashes. An indicator showed that the file was coming through. In a few seconds, it was done.
"Hello? . . . Hello, Roland?" Vrel tried. But the connection was already gone.

"Roland? You mean it was Cade? What did he
want?" Hudro demanded. "What kind of trouble?"

"I'm not sure. It sounded as if there was fighting
going on there. Roland sent the file. It's here, in the
phone. He wants me to get it to Chryse."

Hudro thought for a few seconds. "Security must
have traced them there."

"How?"

"I don't know. There are all kinds of ways."

Vrel tried to think what it meant. If they had been
traced to Tevlak's, Cade's and Marie's aliases were
already blown. Vrel's association with them would be
revealed by the Hyadean flight records from St. Louis
to the base in Maryland and from there to Uyali.
Thryase had used his diplomatic pull to keep the
flyer's movements out of the system, but it was a safe
bet that a reception party would be waiting at Vrel's
room in the Hyadean sector of Uyali. "I can't go
back," he told Hudro. "They'll be onto me as well."

"How can you be sure?"

"I came in with the two Americans yesterday. It
will be in the flight log." Vrel looked at Hudro dubiously. "How sure can you be about you?"

"Impossible to say."

"You can't just report to the military desk at Uyali,"
Vrel said. Hudro's intention had been to find transportation back to his unit in Brazil. "They could be

just waiting for you to show up. Maybe that's why you haven't had a recall. Why alert you that something's up? We don't want to land back there at all—not until we've found some way of checking the situation."

Hudro frowned, obviously not liking Vrel doing his thinking for him. But he couldn't argue. He interrogated the on-board system about other options and directed it to reroute the flyer to a construction area thirty miles north, where a power generating installation was being built. There, they could try to find some kind of ground transportation, which would be less conspicuous.

Since anything could happen after they landed, the file from Cade needed to be forwarded now. Vrel couldn't use the flyer's system to access the direct net link to Chryse, however. The message protocols would involve his personal ID codes, which were bound to have been watch-listed, and reveal his whereabouts. The only alternative was to use his Terran phone and hope that it was clean. That, of course, couldn't get the file to Chryse. The only way he could think of to do that would be to send it via the mission in Los Angeles. But communications into there were still likely to be subject to surveillance, as would any to his known contacts if he was being sought—which ruled out using Dee or anyone at Cade's house.

"You'd better come up with something soon. We've got less than five minutes," Hudro said.

There was a dealer that Dee used for work on her car. Vrel recalled that he was called Vince something. Something to do with ducks. . . . The service manager's name was Stan. He had wanted to introduce Vrel to golf. Vrel thought, tried to remember. . . . Beak? Drake? Bird? No . . . Walk, waddle? *Web!* That was what they called their funny feet. Vince Web! Vrel called information but didn't know enough Spanish to make himself understood. "Can you connect me to an English-speaking operator?" he pleaded. "Er . . . *Operador. Habla inglés.*"

"Give it to me." Hudro took the phone. "What do you want?"

"United States directory information. California, Los Angeles area. An automobile dealer called Vince Web—somewhere around Venice."

While Hudro was waiting for the information, Vrel copied the file into the flyer's system and encrypted it into Hyadean Code along with a message to Wyvex for it to be forwarded to Chryse. He attached a plaintext note to "Stan, Service Department," asking him to pass it on urgently to "Wyvex, care of Dee Rainier, who drives the white Pontiac." Meanwhile, Hudro had obtained the number. Vrel loaded the package back into the phone and sent it off just as the flyer was touching down.

The first thing Hudro did after they landed was get rid of his military-issue Hyadean communicator, which was traceable. Until he knew whether he was compromised or not, he didn't dare use it. If his name was hot, any message sent from it could trigger a surveillance computer.

They arrived at Uyali late in the afternoon in a Terran truck making a run from the construction area to pick up a piece of equipment that had been ferried from the spaceport at Xuchimbo. Hudro had found a friendly plant engineer, showed his military pass, and explained with a wink that he and his friend needed a ride back to town after a hot double date in one of the villages farther north. The flyer was "borrowed" and would make its own way back. In recognition, Hudro promised to send back a bottle of Terran "risky"—a Hyadean pun based on the

English rhyme with "whisky"—with the truck driver from Uyali. "I'll take two," the engineer had said, which was the Hyadean way of asking who you think you're kidding. Hyadeans saw no point in fulfilling one-time obligations. But he had found them a place in the truck anyway.

Hudro had told Vrel that he had a friend he trusted in Hyadean Military Intelligence back in Brazil, who might be able to find out if Hudro was being watched for and what else was going on. Vrel wondered if it was Hudro's girlfriend, but Hudro didn't say. Whoever it was, Hudro would only be able to talk about such things over a secure link, which would mean going into the sprawling Hyadean military base at Uyali and getting access to the communications there. He was willing to gamble that even if Hyadean military police were checking the air terminal, the alert would not involve every guard and gate sentry in the area, and that his papers would get him in. Vrel couldn't offer any better idea. The only thing for Vrel to do in the meantime would be to lose himself, away from prying Hyadean eyes. The best place to do that promised to be the Terran sector. Accordingly, the truck dropped them off outside a store on the part of the road that ran nearest, and Hudro dutifully purchased a half bottle of pisco brandy for the Hyadean driver to take back for the engineer. The driver accepted it appreciatively and seemed amused. Whether or not it would get where it was supposed to go was beyond Hudro's control.

They had a meal of spicy meat and vegetables on rice in a café on the outskirts and then strolled around to familiarize themselves with the area. It seemed to have grown around three main streets, one crossing the other two like the lines of a Terran English *H*. The Terrans were happy to see Hyadeans in their sector because Hyadeans drew large paychecks. After further thought, Hudro bought a man's leather wallet—hand-sewn and richly decorated—some pieces of jewelry, and a mechanical, spring-powered Terran watch that had to be wound by hand every day, which Hyadeans found intriguing and prized even on Chryse, where the twelve-hour cycle meant nothing. "You never know. I might need to bribe somebody in there," he explained to Vrel as they came out of the store. "It never hurts to be prepared."

"I'm impressed," Vrel complimented. Coming from a Hyadean, it meant just that.

"Military training," Hudro said.

"Out of curiosity, just what *do* you do in the military?" Vrel asked.

"Counterinsurgency intelligence. Infiltration. The guys you don't hear about, who live on the other side of the lines."

The final item that Hudro bought was a regular Terran pocket phone with clean codes and a prepaid call quota that he could use without opening an account. So at least, he would be able to make calls over the Terran system that wouldn't attract attention. He left after arranging to meet up with Vrel again later. If there were an emergency, now they could call each other.

One thing about being on an alien planet was the guarantee of always getting a lift from one's own kind. Hudro waited no more than a few minutes on one of the approach roads to the base before a Hyadean military vehicle carrying both uniformed figures and others in regular dress pulled up in response to his wave. He would arouse less curiosity that way than if he arrived on foot, he had decided. The crew turned out to be surveyors and construction supervisors who had been out planning a water pipe-line, and a detail of Army guards. There were no Terrans, and at the gate they were waved straight through, although the occupants of a bus taking Terran workers inside were being rigorously checked and searched. So obstacle number one was out of the way as easily as that.

Hudro was back in the Hyadean world now. Already, it felt different. The surroundings were functional, businesslike, designed for getting things done. Time seemed to snap along at a Hyadean pace. People moved briskly, with purpose. They wore uniforms and working clothes that he recognized, giving them roles that were familiar—like a picture that had suddenly come into focus. There were weapons emplacements inside the perimeter fence, a transportation depot with a landing area inside the gate, where an officer was supervising a fatigue detail unloading an air-truck, and other figures crossed to and fro on various errands. A Military Police post stood on the other side, with signs indicating directions to such locations as 12TH CLOSE SUPPORT BATTALION; 76TH AIR ASSAULT HQ; TAC COM CMD OPS; QMSUP OFF. 19TH INFTRY REC GRP. Hudro followed a path of fused rock chippings painted white to a multistory configuration of office and service modules designated the Administration Center, which was where Headquarters Command was indicated to be situated. He found it after checking with the desk sergeant inside the door, taking an elevator up two levels from the lobby, and following a corridor into the next riser. Inside the door was a waiting area consisting of seats set around three sides of a low table, with the fourth open to a desk-counter at which sat a female Officer of the Day—a captain. Hudro took a seat, picked up one of the reformattable, universal-book folios from the table, loaded a journal at random, and for maybe fifteen minutes scanned it idly while getting a feel for the place and watching the routine. Then he went back down to the entrance. Just as he was about to leave the building, he turned back as if struck by an afterthought, and went over to desk.

"Excuse me, Sergeant." Although not wearing a uniform, he had presented his pass showing his rank when he entered earlier.

"Sir?"

"Can you bring up the Forces Directory for me there?" He indicated the desk terminal. "I need this base's address for somebody to send something to me here."

The sergeant called up the file giving publicly posted information on Hyadean military installations and units, on Earth, Chryse, other worlds, orbiting stations, and elsewhere. He located the entry for Uyali, giving permanent offices, units currently stationed there with addresses, mail codes, commanding officers, and other details. "There. That's us here."

Hudro studied the screen. "So for the HQ Command office upstairs I'd use . . . that one?" He pointed.

"You've got it."

Hudro asked for something to write the details on. The sergeant raised his eyebrows as he passed across a slip of paper. The normal thing would have been to copy it into one's personal communicator. Hudro had thrown his away after landing at the construction site. "In my jacket," Hudro said. The sergeant frowned. Hudro sighed. "I know, I know." He cited the regulation: " '. . . to be kept on the person at all times.' If it were you I could give you a citation." He noticed that the sergeant was wearing a Terran windup watch. "Nice piece of work," he said.

"You like it? It's got elegance, hasn't it?" The sergeant turned his wrist to show the band.

"It's amazing what these people can do." Hudro produced the watch he had just bought in the Terran sector. "What do you think of that?"

"Wow! Pretty nice."

"I just got it—for someone when I get back home."

The sergeant held it admiringly alongside his own. "Do you know something?" he confessed. "I don't even know how to read what they say."

"Me neither," Hudro whispered as he took it back. There was a rapport. So at least he had a friend here already if the need arose. Infiltration training. Think and prepare.

Outside the building, he found a quiet spot and used his phone to call the Terran number of the Hyadean intelligence unit at the Brazilian police facility in Acre province that Yassem worked with. A clerk located her and transferred the call.

"Who is this?" her voice asked.

"The guy who questions."

"Yes?" Since he hadn't used his name, she knew the subject was sensitive.

"We need to talk privately. Here's where I'll be to take it." He read out the code he had copied for Uyali Headquarters Command. "Make it thirty minutes. There's something slightly wrong that'll need straightening out. That's important. Okay?"

"Okay. . . ." There was anxiety in her tone. "Is there—"

"Later."

Yassem would know what to do. The remark about something being slightly wrong was a code they had agreed previously for emergencies.

Hudro went back into the Administration Center, sent a cheerful nod to the desk sergeant, and made his way up to the Headquarters Command office. The female captain was still at the desk. Hudro approached her.

"Yes?" she inquired.

"My name is Hudro." He showed his identification.

"Sir!"

"I was here earlier. I'm expecting a call on a secure channel. Did it come through yet?"

"I haven't heard anything." The captain called a log onto a screen and consulted it. "I'm sorry, there's no sign yet."

"Thanks."

Hudro took a seat, browsed through some journals again, and made a show of looking irritable and restless. "Are you sure there isn't anything through for a Colonel Hudro?" he called over to her ten minutes later.

She checked again. "I'm sorry, sir."

Two soldiers appeared, conducted a brief conversation, and were taken by a clerk to one of the rooms. "Who's your commanding officer?" Hudro demanded after another ten minutes or so.

"That would be Major Sloorn, sir." She was getting rattled. Just what he wanted. He sat glaring at the folio, flipping the pages and moving his head in short, jerky movements. Finally, her voice almost cracking with relief, the captain called, "Colonel Hudro, sir!"

"Yes!" He got up and strode over.

But already she was looking uncertain. "A secure-channel call just came in. . . . But it's specifying a Colonel Mudro. I don't know if . . ."

"*Well, of course it's the one!*" Hudro snapped. "Some native clerk somewhere."

"Well, I really should call them back and . . ."

"Look, this is an important matter, and I need

privacy. I've waited long enough. Where can I take it? Just connect it through, please."

"Room 1304. It's just along the corridor."

"Thank you." Hudro strode away in the direction she indicated. Being a communications specialist with an intelligence unit, Yassem would be able to make the call without its being logged as official procedure required. In the past, some of the things she had managed to extract from official files had been astounding. Misspelling his name by one letter—the "something slightly wrong"—would be a fairly elementary error—to any *person*. But it meant that the surveillance computers wouldn't have found a match.

A minute later, he was looking at the features of Yassem. "Are you all right?" she asked. "Where are you? Still in Bolivia? That was the longest half hour I've ever spent. I've been so worried!"

"I'm not hurt or anything. But I might have been compromised. If so, then we might have to move our plans forward and get out right away. Is that still what you want to do?"

Yassem swallowed and nodded her head. "If we must."

God, how he loved this girl, Hudro thought. Had he just appealed in his mind to the Terran deity? Yes, he had. "Look, this is what I want you to do," he said. First, he needed to know if his name was on any surveillance lists. That would be fairly straightforward. The next thing was trickier. He summarized what had happened at Tevlak's and named the persons, Hyadean and Terran, who had been there when he and Vrel left. Could Yassem find out if the house had been raided by security forces— maybe from operations lists? If so, what had happened to those who were there? Yassem promised to see what she could do. Some of the things she had extracted from official files in the past had amazed him. Hopefully, she could turn up something within three or four hours, she said. Hudro thought he could lose himself in the officers' club or somewhere during that time.

CHAPTER THIRTY-ONE

Luodine had engineered her posting to Earth to escape from the banality of life among the professional and social elite on Chryse that her work immersed her in. She had to find something different, far away, she had decided—before she either destroyed her career by reporting what she really thought, or became one of them. As an executive investigator with one of the major media organizations, she had specialized in exploring success stories, which was an approved and well rewarded choice because it put her among the molders of the role images that it was felt healthy for average Chryseans to emulate. It kept them busy, distracted them from thinking too much about what it all meant, and the economy as a whole remained prosperous.

The only problem was, just about everything she saw brought out the side of her that was decidedly not average for a Chrysean. She met officials in charge of government bureaucracies that dreamed up forests of regulations and employed thousands who buzzed around importantly day after day, intent on their mission, no end result of which, as far as Luodine could see, added up to anything of actual *use* to anybody. All that the elaborate machinery did was get in the way of the few left who *were* trying to do something useful. A long, red curvy fruit called an *iliacen* grew on parts of Chryse, not unlike a Terran banana, but larger. There were specifications giving the limits of size, weight, color, water content—even curviness as determined by a procedure spelled out in detail—that defined what was a permissible *iliacen*. Any commercial transaction involving one that didn't conform was illegal. They couldn't even be given away by producers. Huge numbers of perfectly good, edible fruits had to be thrown away because they were a little bit too straight or a little bit too curvy. This was considered "efficient." Efficiency, Luodine discovered, had little to do with what was obtained for the cost. It had to do with the extent and effectiveness of *control*. When she pressed for an explanation of why it mattered, and how the enormous effort expended on preventing people deciding for themselves what kind of *iliacen* they liked could be justified, nobody could give her one. It seemed that the regulators were simply unable to function without books of rules and numbers telling them what to do. They had become extensions of their own machines.

She had once talked with the head of a large contractor involved in developing and supplying advanced space weaponry deemed essential for meeting the threat posed by the Querl. Said to be among the richest thousand on Chryse, he worked in his office from early morning until after the staff had left, and hadn't taken private time off for two years. When

Luodine asked why he didn't do something else now, he had looked at her blankly and asked in seriousness what else there was. "Build a house with your own hands. Learn to sail a boat," Luodine had said. "When you were a young man, weren't there things you dreamed of? Things you told yourself you wanted to do some day, when you had the time, and circumstances permitted?" The executive had become angry and terminated the interview.

She had listened, smiling, to wives whose lives revolved around hosting ever-more bizarre parties, the principal aim of which was to achieve prominent mention in the socialite gossip columns—one had been set on an island park stocked with over two thousand animals from one of the Querl worlds; another was held orbiting in freefall. She dutifully recorded the wisdoms of generals who measured the cost-effectiveness of a battle with a formula that mixed money, fatalities, and five categories of casualty; of media chiefs who sold rights to dictate what slant should be put on news stories; and of "image consultants" who had built a respectable profession out of presenting things to the world as other than they were, and coaching influential people in the art of lying convincingly from a screen.

Somewhere, she had told herself, there had to be a place where words meant what they said and not the opposite, and reality was what it seemed. And then she heard of the amazing planet that had been discovered in the course of exploring more distant star systems following development of a new, long-range drive—a planet whose inhabitants wove dreams into worlds of thought, created forms for no other purpose than to delight the senses, and described realms of vision and being that confounded all of the professors and scientists. Fads and fashions extolling

Terran art and creativity appeared all over the Chrysean worlds. The ingenuity and imaginativeness of Terran minds stimulated great demand among Chrysean industries. And Luodine talked her way into an assignment there.

At first she had found herself bewildered by this world of chaotic, colorful craziness. But then, as she traveled and learned to reorient her thinking, she began to discover ways of looking at life, its values, that Hyadeans could never have conceived—unless, as some maintained, they had once known such things in a distant past age and forgotten them. There was the advertising executive in Sweden who gave up a secure, lucrative career and mortgaged his house to raise capital because he had always wanted to make a movie. She met a couple in Iran who for two years had been bicycling around the world—utterly pointless to the average Hyadean; captivating to Luodine. There were the religious missionaries in Africa who taught and treated the children of strangers with no prospect of gain other than the following of their convictions. There were dozens of stories from every continent.

And then Luodine found that the real policy being enacted was to turn them all into Hyadeans. Not only that; they were expected to be grateful. Sometimes, apparently, a little help was needed to make them see the benefits.

"Look, I've already told you, one of them had come from the United States; I don't know who the other one was." Luodine turned in front of the table in the room at Tevlak's house and regarded the officer in charge of the Hyadean security unit, who was dictating notes to a communicator pad. Cade and Marie had already been taken away in two of the six personnel carriers that had arrived. Since the officer had disclosed that Vrel had been identified, she wasn't giving anything away by repeating it. "We refused even to consider recording the kind of story they wanted. They realized they were wasting their time, and they left."

"Heading where?" the officer asked.

"I don't know. It's not the kind of thing people in their situation would shout to everyone."

The officer looked at her uncertainly. He was young and seemed not very experienced. Luodine was taking the only line that held any promise of getting her and Nyarl out. "You're saying that none of this was actually used?" He gestured at the equipment set up in the room, which the technicians had examined and pronounced clean of any recent recordings.

"They were talking about *subversive* material!" Luodine looked and sounded shocked. "Claims directed at undermining our Terran policy! Would you believe that?" She shook her head. "We'd simply been told there would be an interview involving some important, undisclosed people. After all, that's our job. That's what we're here for. We didn't know anything about fugitives from the U.S. We set up and prepared, sure. When they arrived, and we found out what it was all about, we said no." Luodine shrugged, turned away, and then back again. "And the rest I've already told you."

The officer seemed perplexed. He went outside the door to consult with a colleague for several minutes, and then retired to another room for privacy while he sought instructions from a remote higher authority.

The remaining Terran security soldiers—those who had not gone with Cade and Marie—had dispersed to other parts of the house or were carrying out routine searches of the people and vehicles outside while the Hyadeans settled their own affairs. Thryase was in the next room, where he could be heard protesting vehemently to officials at the Hyadean General Embassy at Xuchimbo, the principal diplomatic presence on Earth. He was here as a political observer, he insisted. When he was approached in St. Louis to accompany two Terrans introduced to him as social-science academics to South America for what he was told would be a major political news event, of *course* he had accepted. What did they think he was—some kind of parasite who came to Earth to enjoy the scenery and avoid the work he was paid to do?

Tevlak had taken the line of simply knowing nothing. Sure, he had agreed when somebody from the U.S. contacted him to ask if they could use his house—he was Terran in his ways now: hospitable to everybody. Had he known who they were? No, he didn't care. How had they known of him? As far as he could make out, Tevlak said, his name had been mentioned at a party in California.

The officer came back in. Luodine confronted him, hands on hips. "Well? Are we supposed to have committed some kind of offense?"

"Ah, no. It appears not. . . ."

"Then I take it we are free to go." Without waiting for confirmation, Luodine began disconnecting pieces of equipment and motioned at Nyarl to start packing up.

"It would be considered cooperative if you remained while the rest of our business is being concluded," the officer said.

"Are you making some specific charge or charges?" Luodine asked him.

"No. All the same—"

"Well, we have our business to think of too, and we've lost too much time already. If your people in the U.S. had been doing their job, we wouldn't have their renegades coming down here in the first place. Now, I suggest you follow after them, wherever they've been taken, and make sure they don't get away again, instead of wasting more of everyone's time here."

The officer capitulated. Luodine and Nyarl stopped to say a brief farewell to Tevlak and Thryase on the way out to their blue-and-yellow flyer. "We'll come back when the atmosphere and the company are more conducive to something constructive," she told Tevlak. "I *must* do a piece on these art collections of yours! Absolutely fascinating! The viewers back home will love it." She left, giving them a brief glance that conveyed there had been nothing else she could do. Their looks in turn said that they understood.

Ten minutes later, Luodine and Nyarl were airborne, heading north along the eastern edge of the Altiplano. Evening was approaching. The first thing they needed to do was warn Vrol and Hudro against going back to Tevlak's.

Luodine still had the phone that Cade had used to send the file. Vrol's number would still be in its log. After the way Vrel and the others had been traced to Tevlak's, however, Nyarl was leery about using it. "I wouldn't risk calling direct," he said. "It would be safer to go through an intermediary."

Luodine thought for a moment. "You're right," she agreed. "But who? We don't even know where they are."

"Hudro was going back to his unit in Brazil, which means they were heading for Uyali. Who have we talked to there, that we know can be trusted?"

Luodine thought back to a documentary they had made about Hyadeans who worked at Uyali and the lives they lived there, and slowly, a smile came into her face. "I think I know just the person," she said.

CHAPTER THIRTY-TWO

It was getting dark in the Terran sector of Uyali. The streets of the shanty city that had grown in months from a jumble of prefabs and mobile units were filling as workers back from the mining operations and construction projects headed for the restaurants, the bars, and the clubs. Vrel still hadn't heard anything from Hudro. A few other Hyadeans out shopping or curious just to visit the Terran sector had stopped to talk and in a couple of cases invited him to join them, but it had seemed prudent to keep his own company. He sat nursing a fruit juice and nibbling on a roll of flat, crispy bread filled with some kind of cooked vegetable paste in a dingy coffee shop that he had found near one of the three main thoroughfares. It was quiet but not empty, out of the way but not isolated in a way that would make him conspicuous—good for losing himself in for another half hour, say, before moving on to somewhere else.

The more respectable Hyadeans were drifting back to their own sector, which was fenced, orderly, and felt safer after sunset. Those who remained prowled around in ones and twos or groups, acting too self-assuredly: off-duty troops; engineers with billfolds full of Terran money; lonely clerks light-years from home—all curious to sample the forbidden fruits they'd heard about. Mind-altering drinks that it was illegal to possess on Chryse; the atmosphere of a place where Terrans sang, danced, and for a while let their feelings take over—some Hyadean doctors said it could be beneficial; an experience with a Terran woman, perhaps? Hyadean and Terran military police patrolled the district in pairs of either one race or the other. Vrel felt himself tensing when any of them came too close or treated him to anything more than a cursory glance. But so far he hadn't been troubled. If anyone was looking for him, he could only presume they were concentrating on the air terminal, where he would be expected to appear.

Six years ago, Vrel would have looked at a scene like that around him now with a sense of incomprehension at the purposelessness of the ways Terrans chose to spend so much of their lives, and contempt for their inability or refusal to do anything to improve themselves—especially with the Hyadean example before them. So much time and energy wasted on things that weren't needed. No plan. Contrived evasion of what should have been duty. The incredible *inefficiency* of it all. And underneath, there would have been a feeling that didn't need to be expressed, since the facts were so obvious, of the innate superiority of the Hyadean—the kind of smugness that he had detected in so many Hyadeans since, and now found mildly sickening. It was only in the latter part of his time here that he had finally come to grasp one of the most profound insights that the whole Terran worldview and way of life expressed, which most Hyadeans weren't within a lifetime of understanding: The purpose of existing, what mattered, was simply to *experience* it. Just that. Nothing more. If one chose to seek additional satisfaction from achieving or striving, then that was fine too. But it didn't *matter*. Dee had told him once that she thought they put statues up to the wrong people: usually those who had lasted the longest in contests of wiping each other out, or invented the most ingenious ways for legalizing thievery.

"Who should they put them up to, then?" Vrel had asked her.

"The people who do the important things. Except, there wouldn't be enough room."

"Why? What are the important things?"

Dee had shrugged. "Raising kids. Fixing roofs. Clearing drains. I think the others are really Hyadeans with unblue skin. Why don't you take them back?"

A musical tone sounded from the phone in Vrel's pocket. He snatched it out and said "Yes?" in Hyadean, just checking himself from blurting Hudro's name. But the voice that answered was that of a Terran female.

"Is this Mr. V.?"

"Er . . . yes." Instant befuddlement.

"I am Ramona. I get a message from Luodine asking me to call you."

Vrel faltered, then managed finally, "Where is she?"—probably irrelevant, but nothing else suggested itself.

"The person who called me didn't say. But it's important that you don't go back to the house. I guess you know what that means, eh?"

"Yes. . . . I had already figured it out."

"And there is more. Luodine needs . . ." Ramona's voice trailed off, as if something had just occurred to her. "She said you would most likely be in Uyali. Is that right?" Her English was simple—not her natural language, Vrel guessed. Probably, she had been told he was not a Spanish speaker.

"Yes," he replied.

"I am here too. Maybe it is easier if we meet somewhere. Do you know the Terran sector?"

"Yes."

"How long it would take you to get there?"

"That's where I am now," Vrel said.

"No kidding?! Where in the Terran sector?"

"I'm not sure."

"Okay, then I tell you where I will be. There is a bar called the Gold City. You find Central, which is the street in the center—it makes sense, eh?—and the bar is halfway along. Or ask anyone."

"I think I know where that is," Vrel said. "It'll just take a few minutes. How will I know you?"

Ramona laughed. "I think is better if I look for you, no?"

Vrel found the Gold City without difficulty. It had a window with orange lights inside looking out over the street, a flashing neon sign overhead, and a bright red door. It was only when Vrel was halfway through the door that it occurred to him that he might just have walked into the most elementary trap imaginable. But if so, the place would be staked and he was already spotted. Hudro would never have done this. He swore inwardly at his own naïveté, braced himself, and went in.

Inside was a long bar with mirrors behind running the length of one wall, a dance floor taking up one corner of the room, the rest being filled with tables and chairs. The place was busy and crowded. The throng included several Hyadeans, all male, in a knot clustered at one end of the bar, clearly military although out of uniform. A few others were scattered around at the tables, and two somewhat clumsily and self-consciously working hard at mastering the mystique of dancing. While Vrel was still looking around, a petite dark-skinned girl with wavy, shoulder-length hair and wearing a bright red, tight-fitting dress materialized in front of him. "You are Mr. V.?" she said.

"Yes. How did you know?"

"I learn to tell these things." Without further preliminaries, Ramona took Vrel's elbow and steered him toward some tables by a wall forming the side of some stairs going up. None of the tables was empty, but Ramona said something in Spanish to two girls seated at one of them, and they got up and left after a brief exchange. Ramona sat down and waved for Vrel to take the other chair. She had a lot of the artificial coloring that many Terran women wore around the mouth and eyes, he saw. Makeup was unknown among Hyadeans—although he had heard recently that some youngsters were causing all kinds of reactions by introducing the practice back home. A waiter came to take their order. Ramona asked for simply "a beer." Vrel decided he had better stick with fruit juice.

"So Luodine didn't talk to you directly," Vrel said.

"No. A friend that she has called me. I guess maybe she thinks someone might be checking her calls, eh? Sounds like some kind of trouble." Ramona shrugged in a way that said whatever it was, it didn't worry her. "Luodine has many friends everywhere. She travels around, makes movies of people. People like her. She listens to what they say. Too many of the aliens, they don't listen." She gave Vrel an approving nod. "See, you are listening. You're okay too."

"Have you met Luodine yourself?" Vrel asked.

"Oh sure. A couple of months ago, when everything here is like a camp. She is making a movie about the Terrans that Hyadeans meet when they come here to work—and then when they are not at work. She is very interested in the working girls who come to the mining town. It sounds like a lot of people where you come from are not too happy about it, eh?" Ramona eyed Vrel saucily and smiled. Vrel realized with a start that she was one of the Terran women who hired themselves out for sexual pleasure. Such a thing was highly illegal on Chryse, even its depiction in fictional settings being banned. There had been calls from home to have the Terran authorities close such practices down on parts of Earth where young Hyadean soldiers were posted. The Americans that Vrel had met in California called them "fishers" . . . or something like that. His first impulse was to express some kind of disapproval. But he controlled it and forced himself to see things the way he had learned to since coming to Earth.

"The girls, they all like her too, when they get to know her better," Ramona completed.

Vrel pulled himself back to matters of the moment. "On the phone, you started to talk about Luodine needing something," he said.

"Yes. The person who talks to me for her says that she thinks her . . . what do you call those things like little airplanes without wings?"

"Flyer?" That was what most Terrans seemed to call them.

"Right. Luodine thinks hers is being tracked somehow. Anywhere she goes, the computers will know. Maybe is normal for you guys, I don't know. But it sounds like she doesn't want this."

The drinks arrived. Vrel paid. "Okay," he said slowly

after the waiter left. It meant that Luodine was mobile. So, assuming that Tevlak's house had been raided after his and Hudro's departure, it sounded as if she—and probably Nyarl too—had been released. But she thought it likely their blue-and-yellow flyer was being monitored, which was probably true. That all made sense.

"She says you have a 'clean' flyer," Ramona said. "I guess that means one they're not watching, eh?" That could only mean the flyer that had brought Vrel, Thryase, Cade, and Marie to Tevlak's from Uyali, and which was now at the construction site thirty miles away where Hudro and Vrel had left it. Thryase had somehow arranged for its movements not to be recorded by the traffic system (which eliminated that as an explanation of how they had been traced to Tevlak's).

"Go on," Vrel said.

"Well, it sounds to me like she wants to go someplace without them knowing all the time. She needs to use yours."

Vrel leaned back on the chair, sipped from his glass, and thought about what he should do. In the end, he decided it would probably be best not to do anything until he heard from Hudro. He glanced at his wrist unit unconsciously. Still nothing. Where *was* Hudro? They had agreed to call only in an emergency. Vrel wondered much longer he ought to give it before deciding that this was becoming one.

Ramona had shifted her attention to another presence that had appeared by the table. Vrel looked up to find a Terran glowering at him. He was tall and lean bodied, with a short beard and hair tied by a band at the back, wearing a black shirt under a leather vest, and pants held up by a wide, ornate-buckled belt. Two more were behind him, looking equally mean and ugly. He shot something in Spanish at Ramona, causing an abrupt change in her manner. She gripped her glass tightly, as if to throw it; her eyes flashed. She retorted just as sharply, and an angry exchange in rapidly rising voices followed, accompanied by gestures and challenging looks from the man, at Vrel. Conversation around them died. The Hyadean military by the bar looked questioningly at each other and started to move closer. Somebody ran out the door, and his voice could be heard calling along the street. A man across the room called out in English, "Leave them be. You are assholes. Why don't you mind your own business?"

"When they come here taking our women, it *is* our business," the leader of the three shouted back. "Who the hell are you, pig shit? *You* mind your—"

"I am not anybody's woman!" Ramona spat.

Two Terran military police appeared in the doorway—peaked caps with red bands, white gaiters, drawn batons. Fingers pointed across to the table. They came over. One of them asked what was going on. Several onlookers began telling the story all at once. The Hyadeans by the bar drew back but remained alert. Ramona dropped her aggressiveness, shrugged and shook her head, and answered the MPs' questions meekly. Their attention turned to the three men, still standing their ground, and an argument broke out between onlookers supportive of both sides. The MPs began shouting and waving their batons to try and calm things down.

Ramona looked at Vrel resignedly. "Should I call this friend of Luodine's and give some answer?" she asked him.

"No. There is a colleague of mine here somewhere that I need to hear from first."

"What you want to do now?"

Vrel shook his head. "I don't know. Just wait."

"You don't need this trouble. My place is near here. We can go there and wait to hear from your friend. Will be easier, no?" Ramona looked at him as if there was nothing more to say. Vrel hesitated. She laughed. "If you worry about I might be losing business, you don't need to. Is good for everyone to have a break sometimes. Besides, if it helps get Luodine out of some kind of trouble, then there is nothing to think about. Okay? So, we go." It seemed a good idea. All Vrel needed was for this to turn into an incident that would result in his being identified. They left unnoticed while the argument was still proceeding furiously.

They walked along Central to one of the two major intersections and crossed it to enter a maze of narrower dirt streets and alleys twisting among trailers and instant buildings, dark except for isolated lights outside doors or occasional glows from some of the interiors. Ramona led the way to a small, flat-roofed cabin set on blocks. It had a split-height door behind a screen, and an outside lamp showing a green cross on an orange background. Vrel waited while she went ahead up several wooden steps to unlock the door, and then followed.

The interior, when she turned on the light, was what he supposed a Terran would describe as feminine and homey—but to Hyadean eyes a riot of decorative ingenuity. "You drink coffee?" Ramona asked.

"After a day like today? Sure, why not?"

Colorful woven tapestries and prints of animal and plant themes filled the walls; a carpet of rich designs covered the floor. All the pictures and curios that Vrel had come to expect of a Terran dwelling were there, with the added touch that females seemed to show for softening the effect with cushions and flowers, and frilly edgings to covers and drapes. It brought to mind Dee's apartment in Los Angeles, though with a distinctly different "style."

"You like it?" Ramona said, seeing him looking around while she filled a pot and took cans and mugs from a closet. "Is not like your Hyadean places, eh? Like army barracks or factories. How can anyone live in those? I buy it from a Chilean girl who is singer with a band, but has big gambling problems. Owes maybe ten thousand dollars to the clubs. You don't mess those guys around. So she comes here to work in Uyali temporarily. Tells husband the band is on foreign tour. Is funny, eh?" Vrel wasn't sure why, but grinned obligingly. "Do Hyadeans gamble?" Ramona asked him.

"No. The statistical demotivations are too obvious."

"Oh? I guess I'm not too smart. What does that mean?"

"I'm beginning to doubt that. It means that nothing is more mathematically certain than that the class of gamblers as a whole loses. So why would anyone pay to belong to that class?"

Ramona put the coffeepot on and stared at it as if for advice. "Really so, eh? But what if you win?"

"It's possible, of course," Vrel agreed. "But the chance you buy isn't worth what you pay for it."

"Okay. . . . If you say so." She didn't seem convinced but wasn't about to make an issue of it. They tossed the matter back and forth while the coffee was making, then sat down with their drinks in a couple of easy chairs in the living area adjoining the kitchenette.

"So what's your story?" Vrel asked her curiously. "How did you come here? Any plans for the future?"

Ramona leaned back and sighed. "I am from Rio

a long time ago, you know—over on east?" Vrel nodded. "Is big difference, who is rich and who is poor. I come from wrong part." She laughed suddenly. "Maybe you are right after all: Luck doesn't pay off, eh? The only way you're gonna get rich is maybe be big soccer star if you're a boy, or a girl, do this. Or maybe else you can sell drugs, either one. But is not for me. Too much nasty people—all the time killing, violence. And after? . . . I don't know." She winked. "Big savings already. Maybe buy my own bar someday. Lots of music, dance. I like to see people having fun. Maybe a Hyadean bar. They need teaching how to have fun, no?"

Vrel grinned tiredly. "Maybe." He looked at his wrist unit again.

"Where you go tonight if your friend don't show up?" Ramona asked him.

"I hadn't thought about it. I didn't think it would get this late."

"You think he is okay?"

Vrel shrugged. "I don't know."

Ramona looked him up and down over the rim of her mug. "You can stay here if you want." The color-enhanced eyes widened suggestively. "Maybe relax and make the best of it a little if you stuck anyway. Is okay, on me. I'm not working tonight."

Vrel found himself flummoxed, even after years on Earth. "Really, no. . . . It's a nice thought, but I'm okay. Aren't there any hotels, places that'll do a bed for the night?"

"I thought you say they look for you. Maybe is not so good idea out there. Better off here." Ramona emitted a sigh that said she really didn't understand but if he insisted, and waved a hand to indicate the part of the cabin beyond the living area. "Is okay, anyway. I have two bedrooms. One is for work, the other where I sleep. Just one would be like living in the office, eh? You take one of them. Either is okay."

At that moment, a call came in on Vrel's phone. He pulled it from his pocket. It was Hudro. "Can you talk?" Hudro asked.

"Sure."

"Okay, we have news. Where can I find you?"

Vrel paused, momentarily perplexed. "You're not going to believe it," he answered.

"Why? What's happened?"

Vrel couldn't think how to begin. "Look, I'll pass you over to someone else. She'll give you directions," he said finally.

Hudro recovered quickly from his astonishment. It seemed he had found more tolerant grounds for his religious convictions than some that Vrel had encountered on occasions. Vrel updated him on the message he had received from Luodine via Ramona, and offered his conclusion that Tevlak's had been raided as they had suspected, and that Luodine was now free but her movements were being tracked.

Hudro was able to confirm it. Since his business in the military base was not Ramona's affair, he spoke in Hyadean. Tevlak's house had been visited by a combined force of Terran and Hyadean security following a surveillance alert that Cade and Marie had been identified there despite their aliases. How surveillance had found them, Hudro's contact didn't know. Proof of criminal activity sufficient to justify detaining the Hyadeans who had been there—Tevlak, Thryase, Luodine, and Nyarl—had not been established, and they had been released but would no doubt be subject to continued surveillance—as Vrel had surmised. Cade and Marie, however, who were wanted by U.S. federal authorities, had been arrested. Finding out what happened to them had taken the contact a lot longer. The essence was that they were at a detention facility in Peru, awaiting some VIP with an interest in their case who wanted to conduct a preliminary interrogation personally. After that, they would probably be moved to a military prison farther east, in Brazil.

Hudro continued: "If that happens, it won't be good news, Vrel. What they know could be too damaging to some powerful Individuals, both Terran and Hyadean. They'd never get out alive. If we're to do anything at all to help them, it will have to be before they get there. That may not give us very long. So this is the plan.

"Do you remember when we were on our way here, I told you about a girl that I have here? I said that one day we intended disappearing to Asia or somewhere and living as Terrans? Well, she is the contact I've been talking to today. We have decided that the time must be now. My work here has brought me into contact with some of the Terran so-called terrorists that we are sent to fight, and I have found that more often than not they uphold Terran ideals more faithfully than the governments do. So I can no longer fight on the side of Terran governments—you heard me say all this at Tevlak's. I know some resistance fighters up in Brazil who I think can be persuaded to help."

"To rescue them?" Vrel checked. "Roland and Marie. You can get Terrans to work with you?"

Hudro smiled faintly. "I said I wanted to save somebody one day, didn't I? My name is clean so far—not on any watch lists. Tonight I will get regular transportation back north to Brazil as I originally intended. My partner and I will make our arrangements to meet a Terran guerrilla leader there whom I have known for some time—we have both helped each other in the past. We can only hope there will be enough time to come up with something. It would have to be while Roland and Marie are being moved."

Vrel was couldn't help feeling apprehensive. "You really think you can rely on Terrans that you're supposed to be fighting?" he said. "Is it wise to trust in them that much?"

"What other choice do we have?" Hudro answered. After a second or two more he added, "Anyway, I trust in their god."

Having established that much, they got Ramona to call Luodine's intermediary and pass on instructions for her and Nyarl to fly to Uyali the next morning, setting the regular air terminal as their destination. When they were on final approach but not before, they were to change the landing point to a pad area in the Terran sector, which Ramona said would be busy and crowded all day. Vrel would meet them and take care of things from there. With that, Hudro left for the terminal to find a ride back to Brazil. Vrel stayed the night in Ramona's "office."

The next morning, after preparing them a breakfast, Ramona took Vrel to the part of the Terran sector that she had told them about, which turned out to be a nonstop commotion of people, activity, and vehicles coming and going as she'd promised. Vrel used his phone to summon the flyer that he and Hudro had left at the construction site to the north. It arrived ten minutes later. A little under an hour after that, Luodine and Nyarl's blue-and-yellow craft appeared overhead, descending steeply. Vrel greeted them as they emerged and indicated his own waiting flyer. While Ramona and Luodine embraced and laughed like long-lost sisters, Vrel helped Nyarl transfer recording and other equipment across. In order not to be lose touch with other events that might develop, Nyarl set a link in the blue-and-yellow flyer's communications system to forward any incoming messages to a code that he set up in Vrel's flyer. Even if it were seized and the link code found, it wouldn't mean anything to anyone else. Finally, Vrel thanked Ramona and conceded a hug.

And then they were airborne, heading north to get clear of the area before anyone following the movements of Luodine and Nyarl's flyer would have time to react to what had happened. To add further confusion, Nyarl had set it instructions to take off again, empty, and head away in a different direction as a decoy. After a hundred miles or so it would land near a village picked at random off the map, and anyone monitoring it could make of it what they would.

They continued northward to be nearer to where anything involving Cade and Marie was expected to happen, and put down around midday in a remote spot past Lake Titicaca. They waited there through the middle part of the day, eking out the fruit juices and snacks that were all the flyer had to offer, talking over the events of the past days, trying to guess possible outcomes, and speculating about future plans. Vrel talked vaguely about making for Asia or Australia, maybe trying to join Krossig. Luodine wasn't sure she wanted to leave just yet. She was an investigative journalist, after all, and the things that seemed to matter were happening here.

Hudro called around the middle of the afternoon and informed them that the operation would take place tomorrow. He gave no details apart from the map reference of the place where he and the Terran guerrillas would meet them afterward, which was farther north, inside Brazil. Vrel and the others were to head there tonight and were expected. The name of the place was Segora.

CHAPTER THIRTY-THREE

At last, Luodine could breathe easily again, not feeling that their every movement was probably being tracked by surveillance computers.

From maps retrieved via the flyer's communications system, Nyarl had determined that Segora was in a low-lying forested and swampy area around one of the southern headwater tributaries of the Amazon. Luodine had expected it to be something like a village, in the sense of dwellings clustered in some kind of clearing, but it turned out to be more a general name for an extended area of huts, houses, and other constructions loosely strung together beneath the forest canopy with little attempt at forming any identifiable center. It could be an unconventional type of living arrangement that put seclusion before neighborliness, she supposed as the flyer descended out of gray overcast; equally well, it could have been contrived for harboring an illicit militia in a way that afforded anonymity, concealment, and dispersal.

The flyer landed in a slot cut between high trees, at the bottom of which nothing more could be seen than a strip of bare earth and a couple of tin-roofed shacks. On touching down, they found that the strip was just the edge of a larger, undercut space concealing an assortment of trucks, cars, and other vehicles that had been invisible from above. A group of figures in shirts and jungle smocks, some with weapons slung on their shoulders, watched the flyer roll in. Two of them directed it to park by several helicopters standing to one side. A reception committee came forward as the occupants emerged. Vrel was not conversant with the local languages and left the talking to Luodine. Her experience was more with Spanish whereas the prevalent speech here was Portuguese, but with help from her veebee and a smattering that Nyarl had picked up, they were able to manage.

The spokesman was small and wiry with a beard, wore a soft-peaked forage cap, flak jacket, and string vest, and carried a basic Terran automatic firearm. He didn't give a name but described the three Hyadean arrivals to the others as "the alien news team who are here to tell our story"—which, discounting Vrel, was close enough. The others seemed suspicious all the same, and regarded the Hyadeans warily.

They boarded an open-topped Terran military truck, along with the guide in the peaked cap, another, and the driver, while the rest of the party piled into a second vehicle behind. Whether they were guards or an escort, Luodine wasn't sure. As the vehicles moved away, she saw sandbagged positions under the trees commanding the landing strip and its approaches, with bunkers and entrenchments concealed among the vegetation behind. Farther on, they passed cabins and houses, what looked like a storage dump, some kind of a water landing, and a workshop for vehicles. The road became a leafy tunnel, in places crossing stretches of swamp on wooden causeways. There were tent cities mingled with the undergrowth; squads training with weapons; at one point, a pit with earth protecting walls under camouflage nets, that looked like a missile emplacement.

"This might go on for miles," Luodine said to Nyarl. "They could have the equivalent of a whole town hidden down here."

"Or an army," he replied.

Luodine became more certain in her own mind, and more excited. "*This* is the story we should be working on, Nyarl!" she told him. "Right here, not in Asia. I want to see for myself those things that Hudro showed us. What do you think? Would you stay if we could?"

"Yes, I'd stay," Nyarl said.

A spur off the roadway brought them to several low wooden buildings standing together beneath the trees. The vehicles pulled up in front of one, and everyone dismounted. While the guards or escorts—whichever—dispersed themselves around the outside, the leader in the forage cap and his second conducted the three Hyadeans in and through to a large room, bare except for several closets, a central table with chairs, and kitchen facilities at one end. An adjoining room contained six double-tier bunks arranged around the walls, and there were several more rooms with stacks of boxes, items of kit, and further oddments of furniture. Evidently these were to be their quarters for the night. In the meantime, apparently, they were to wait.

A window looked out toward the way they had come in off the road. As dusk was closing in, two trucks appeared, embarked armed figures from one of the other nearby buildings, and drove away again. The roadway itself seemed to be busy with an irregular but continuing flow of vehicles and porters on foot carrying loads. "Something's going on. There's a buzz in the air. Don't you feel it?" Luodine said to the other two. She asked the squad leader in the forage cap. He seemed uneasy but would divulge nothing.

After about half an hour, headlights appeared, and a Terran open-topped military car sped up and screeched to a stop outside. Two figures jumped out and marched up to the door, while two more began lifting out cartons and boxes, helped by a couple of the guards who had been posted outside. The man in the forage cap went out, and there was an exchange in lowered voices outside the door. Then two of the arrivals came in. The first was tall, swarthy skinned with a thick mustache, and wore a belt with sidearm over a bush jacket, jungle camouflage pants, canvas boots, and a black beret. He identified Luodine as the spokesperson and introduced himself as Rocco. The man with him, black, shorter, stockily built, wearing an olive shirt and bandolier of cartridges slung across his body from one shoulder, was called Dan.

As the Hyadeans had already inferred, they would be staying here until tomorrow. In the morning, Rocco would leave with a guerrilla force to meet up with Hudro and Hudro's unnamed companion, and attempt to rescue Cade and Marie. Where and how this was to happen Rocco didn't disclose, but from the things that had been said before, Luodine presumed it would be while the two captives were in transit somewhere. Afterward, assuming the operation was successful, they would all return to Segora. What the plan was after that, Rocco didn't say. Dan would remain to take care of the Hyadeans and deal with any needs or problems if he could.

The other two who had arrived with Rocco and Dan were women. While Rocco was talking, they brought in the cartons that had been unloaded, put them on the counter at the kitchen end of the room, and began taking out bread, vegetables, cans, and other provisions. Rocco left shortly afterward, explaining that he had preparations to attend to. If all went well, he would see them again tomorrow.

When the meal was ready, the two cooks took portions out for the guard detail around the building. Dan and the man in the forage cap, now revealed to be "Zak," joined the Hyadeans at the table in the large room. Dan told them they were the first Hyadeans he had seen brought here as guests, although it appeared he had met Hudro previously somewhere. The rest of the men had seen the aliens only from a distance, and then on the other side. They were not clear what was going on, which made them understandably wary.

"Could they learn to accept us, do you think?" Luodine asked him.

Dan seemed puzzled. "Why should they have to? What do you mean?"

She indicated herself and Nyarl. "We are journalists from Chryse who are a little different. We've been reporting what *is*, not what's supposed to be—even if it has been causing us problems. We think our work is here. Suppose we wanted to stay. Could something like that be arranged, do you think?"

"I don't know. Maybe. . . . You'd need to talk to Rocco and Hudro tomorrow, when they get back."

Luodine noted the same edginess in Dan's manner

that she had detected in Zak earlier. "Something is making everyone nervous tonight, isn't it?" she said. "I saw it in Rocco too. What's happening?"

Dan glanced uneasily at Zak, as if acknowledging that he wasn't sure this was the right way to be talking. "There's a lot of Glob activity everywhere. Air strikes, troop drops. This area has to be targeted. Rocco's got bad feelings about staging this mission tomorrow, but it seems like it can't be any other time. I'm not sure why."

"I think we already know," Luodine said.

Dan shrugged in a way that said he didn't need to hear. "My job is just to make sure you're all here, ready and waiting, when they get back."

It had been an eventful and arduous day, and the three Hyadeans turned in early. Just as she was drifting off into sleep that promised to engulf her in seconds, Luodine was brought back to reality by the sound of what could have been distant thunder coming in through the screen of the open widow, but with a sharper, more percussive bark. "What was that?" she asked into the darkness.

"It could be artillery fire. Or maybe an air attack somewhere," Vrel's voice replied.

The sound continued for maybe fifteen minutes, sometimes seemingly a little closer, then farther away. In the next room, Dan and Zak were engaged on a radiotelephone with others elsewhere. They sounded tense and agitated. Dan poked his head in around the door a few minutes later. "Sleep in your clothes and keep your boots near at hand," he told the Hyadeans. "We may have to move out in a hurry."

It was daylight when sounds of loud explosions accompanied by a shrieking roar tore Luodine out of a deep sleep. She sat up, struggling to integrate the impressions into some kind of coherence. Aircraft, passing low overhead. Bombs! Vrel and Nyarl were already tumbling out of nearby bunks, finding shoes and grabbing coats. The door was thrown open, and Dan entered. "We're under attack!" he shouted. "Glob forces moving in on the area. We're taking you back to the strip now."

They stumbled through into the large room where the table was. One of the two women was waving her hands at Zak and wailing something. The other was nowhere in sight. A guard stuck his head in from outside. "The truck's coming now," he called. Dan ushered the Hyadeans across to the door and outside. Smoke clouds were billowing skywards from somewhere not far away, where flames could be seen among the trees. A truck was turning off the approach lane from the road. As several of the guards moved out from the building to meet it, the sounds of approaching aircraft came again, followed by staccato chattering of gunfire. The guards threw themselves down into the undergrowth or beside the wall of the building, a couple under the truck.

"*Down!*" Dan yelled. Luodine stood outside the doorway, confused. "*Get down!*" She came to her senses, ran a few paces, and hunched herself awkwardly by Nyarl against the base of a tree. The roars grew to a screaming din overhead. Luodine covered her head with her arms. A series of jarring concussions came, numbing the ears, and then a sharper *crack,* followed by what sounded like a tremendous blast of hail slicing through the trees, shredding leaves and cutting branches. Fragments of metal *pinged* off the truck and embedded themselves in the wall of the building. Somebody screamed.

"Come! Now! We have to go!" Dan's voice shouted. Luodine straightened up, dazed, her ears still ringing. Somebody grabbed her elbow and steered her toward the truck. Figures were already clambering aboard. Vrel was there. Nyarl appeared from behind her. Someone was reeling drunkenly, gushing blood from a partly severed shoulder. It was the second cook. Hands pulled Luodine up over the tailboard. The truck began moving.

The attack had hit on the far side of the roadway. Smoke was pouring from the remains of several demolished buildings among the trees, which nearer the center of the blast area had been stripped practically bare. A vehicle was hanging upended in the branches; another lay on its side, surrounded by bodies, some moving. As the truck turned right onto the road and headed back in the direction of the landing strip, Luodine made out more figures crawling and staggering amid the smoke. The sound of the attacking planes faded, and the steadier, deeper drone of higher-flying aircraft became noticeable behind the engine noise and rattles of the truck, and the voice of Dan shouting into a hand radio. A series of muffled crumps sounded somewhere off to the left. "ATG," Zak said tightly. Luodine looked questioningly at Nyarl as they clutched the sides of the wildly bouncing vehicle.

"Air-to-ground," he supplied. "Missiles. Incoming."

"Troops are landing to the south and east," Dan announced. "They've already taken the main river crossing. Gonna sweep the whole area."

"Will Rocco's group have to call off the mission?" Vrel called from the other side of the truck.

"Too late for that. They left hours ago."

They drove past armed guerrillas hastily forming up, squads with packs running at the double along the roadside; vehicles being loaded, others racing in both directions. The background of explosions and gunfire was now continuous. At one point they had to drive off the road on a bypass flattened through the undergrowth around a truck and a car that had collided. Just past them was a blackened area, still smoking, everything flattened, where Luodine was sure she had seen a mobile missile launcher the day before. Exactly as she had wanted, she was right there in the middle of everything, and far sooner then she had ever expected. Yet she and Nyarl could capture none of it. They had left all their equipment in the flyer.

They arrived back to find the landing area in pandemonium. One entire side—fortunately, not where Vrel's flyer was parked—was a mass of blazing vehicles and storage sheds, while across the remainder of the area figures ran frantically to load what could be salvaged onto departing trucks and carry over the wounded. Two helicopters were wrecked, but another out on the open strip took off as the truck bringing the Hyadeans pulled up. Dan waved toward the flyer and shouted at Vrel, "Make it ready, whatever you have to do."

Vrel spread his hands. "What about Cade and the others? We were supposed to wait for them."

"I'm going to try and find out what I can now," Dan threw back, already running toward a frond-covered bunker protected by sandbags and logs, partly dug into the ground nearby. Vrel turned toward the flyer. Luodine followed after Dan, Nyarl close behind her. Inside the bunker was a map table and cabinets of electronics, weapons and kit slung along one wall, and a half dozen or so people, two talking into phones, two more following something on screens, one marking a map, a girl in a camouflage smock watching the scene outside through a firing embrasure in the bunker wall. Dan was talking tensely with a man in a peaked cap who seemed to be in charge. He waved for Luodine and Nyarl to wait a moment as they entered. One of the operators was calling into a microphone. "Emergency! Repeat, emergency! Divert! Do you read me, Yellow Fish? You must divert. The LZ is under attack."

"It's them," Dan told Luodine and Nyarl. "They're on their way here now. They've got Cade and the woman. But they can't land in this."

"Where will they go?" Luodine asked, daze at trying to take it all in.

"I don't know. They'll . . ." Dan's voice trailed off as the operator became alarmed.

"Hello? . . . Hello, Yellow Fish. . . . Yellow Fish, come in. . . ." He waited, looked across, and shook his head. "We have lost contact. They were taking fire."

"Jesus! What's this?" Eyes turned to the girl watching the outside. A peculiar violet light was coming in through the embrasure. Dan and the officer in the peaked cap stared uncomprehendingly for a moment, then moved toward the entrance, practically pushing the two Hyadeans out ahead of them. They emerged to find the surroundings bathed in a strange radiance of an eerie, electrical quality.

"What is it?" the officer asked, bewildered.

Dan shook his head. "I don't know. I've never seen anything likes it."

Then, abruptly, it was gone. Their eyes took several seconds to readjust to normal illumination. Then Dan touched the officer's arm and pointed across the open stretch of landing strip. The violet had shifted to an area beyond the far tree line and was now revealed as a pencil of light coming down from the sky. Even as they watched it shifted again, as if probing. Then the column flickered briefly in several pulses that turned it brilliant orange, and the entire area surrounding the base of the beam erupted into a fireball expanding above the trees. Moments later, a concussion wave swept across the landing area, followed by a blast of wind that bent the treetops, sent a storm of leaves, sand, and pieces of wreckage swishing across the open ground, and toppled Luodine over a wall of logs fronting the entrance to the bunker. A rain of torn branches and debris began falling over the entire area.

The flyer, already moving from its parking spot, lurched visibly and then steadied. Dan pulled Luodine to her feet. Nyarl was holding onto the top of the log wall. "What about the others?" Vrel called from the doorway of the flyer as it neared, at the same time turning.

"They're down somewhere!" Nyarl yelled. "We have to go! Now!"

"Go where? We have no plans."

"*It doesn't matter! Just GO!*" Dan shouted, pushing Luodine toward the flyer. Vrel heaved her in, Nyarl followed with the door closing, and the flyer began accelerating toward the open ground. Then it was under the strip of sky, airborne, climbing. It rose to skim the treetops. Smoke and fires were everywhere, with aircraft dotting the sky in all directions.

"That light. What was it?" Luodine gasped as she buckled into one of the seats.

"Orbital bombardment maser," Nyarl said. His voice sounded strained. "Ours. Area obliteration weapon. I didn't know we were using anything like that here."

For a while they flew north toward the main basin of the Amazon, away from the combat zone, debating what to do. Returning to Tevlak's seemed risky, with no idea of the situation there. Vrel had lost his

Terran phone somewhere in the confusion. Nyarl was reluctant to use the flyer's system, since incoming calls to Tevlak's would probably be monitored and could be traced back. In the end, Luodine remembered an Indian tribe that she had spent some time with as part of putting together a program on Terran cultural diversity. They lived in a remote area north of the main river and had no interest in worldly affairs. And they were friendly—not to each other, especially, but they were to the blue-giant aliens, to whom they apparently attached a religious and mystical significance. Nyarl found the location in his records, and in less than two hours the craft was descending toward a forest clearing showing leaf-thatched huts scattered around a stream, watched by an awed crowd of brown-skinned figures and children, most of them barely clothed. They remembered Luodine well, and greeted her and her companions with laughter, much excited chatter. A spicy meal was arranged for the evening, attended by the whole village and accompanied by dancing apparently put on for the aliens' benefit, despite their exhaustion, and the presentation of gifts ranging from a sweet fruit preparation to a necklace made from flowers, beads, and the dyed shells of nuts. The arrivals fell asleep in the hut provided for them, still too numbed by events of the day to be capable of discussing any further options objectively.

When morning came, the whole situation had changed. News via the flyer's system brought the staggering announcement that the Western part of the U.S. had seceded and declared itself a sovereign federation governed from Sacramento. As fugitives on an alien planet, by no means sure where they stood with their own authorities, none of the Hyadeans was sure of the implications or what they should do. The easiest and perhaps safest choice seemed to be simply to stay on in the village, making the best of the peace and seclusion it offered, get the rest that they all needed, and give things a couple of days to see what happened. The villagers and their headman had no objections, and the children found the blue aliens fascinating, following them everywhere.

But before they had finalized any plans, an even stranger thing happened. A call came in over the flyer's system, forwarded by Luodine's blue-and-yellow flyer, still landed far to the south in Bolivia. It was routed via Chryse, but had been sent by the Hyadean girl that Hudro had returned to Brazil to collect before joining Rocco's force for the attempt to free Cade and Marie. Her name was Yassem. The operation had succeeded, but the helicopter bringing them all back to Segora had been shot down. As far as Yassem knew, she and Marie were the only survivors. She was relieved to learn that all three Hyadeans had got away safely from Segora. Right now, Yassem and Marie were at a Brazilian military base on the southern side of the Amazon basin. For the moment, they were managing to pass themselves off as affiliated with the security forces under a story that Yassem had dreamed up, but that cover could only last so long. Using codes obtained from registration records on Chryse, Yassem had located the blue-and-yellow flyer down in Bolivia. She wanted to use it to get them away. Now that they knew where Luodine and the others were, she and Marie could fly there and join them. Nyarl was worried about surveillance risks. That was okay, Yassem assured him. Military communications was her job. She would take care of that.

CHAPTER THIRTY-FOUR

Pink lights flashed past the open gun-hatch; then came the jolting of objects hitting the helicopter's structure. Yassem, crouched on the floor in front of where Marie was sitting, put her helmet on and secured it. Rocco shouted back instructions from the front, and one of the men clambered up to man the machine gun, while another hooked up the ammunition belt. Marie and Cade braced their arms on the sides and tried to steady themselves against each other as the pilot went into evasive maneuvers. And then a giant fist seemed to slam the helicopter, bursting the wall behind them inward and tearing Cade away from her grasp.

Impressions kaleidoscoped together of bodies tumbling and hurtling about the interior, cries of pain and fear, a blast of wind. The figure that had been at the hatch was gone. Everything was turning. A force pinned Marie with her face and chest to the wall, unable to move. Yassem rose from somewhere and then fell against her, entangling them. Past Yassem's shoulder, Marie saw Cade caught in the side webbing, blood pouring from his head and down the back of his jacket, and Rocco nearby, clinging to the edge of the hatch. The helicopter hit the ground to a cacophony of screams, objects crashing against the sides, and the shriek of metal rending and buckling. Marie heard herself cry out as Cade and Rocco collided and disappeared. The helicopter carried on sliding downhill, slewing, and coming apart, spilling bodies, equipment, and debris. A limb of a tree reared up through pieces of disintegrating cabin and floor, and Marie was pitched forward onto a headless body that gushed blood over her face and chest. There was a wrench that felt as if she were being pulled apart; sudden light; leaves and branches rushing and tearing at her. . . .

She was underneath a section of what had been the fuselage, ensnared in foliage among pieces of wreckage. Her face felt on fire. Her whole body ached. She became aware of guns firing, sounds of aircraft, explosions. They had come down in the middle of a battle. She tried to move, and winced as every muscle and joint protested. But there was no other way out of this. Testing herself warily, she concluded nothing was broken. Then, gathering her breath, she bit her lip against the pain and forced herself to move, first freeing the thorns and vines from her clothing. The activity seemed to help. She extricated herself gradually, straightened up, and took stock. The headless corpse was doubled grotesquely over a seat attached to part of the cabin wall. The only other figure in sight was in Hyadean military garb, lying facedown and motionless on a section of buckled flooring. Marie hauled herself across and turned the helmet to reveal a flash of yellow-orange hair against the blue skin. It was Yassem. She was breathing. There was no sign of Hudro. Marie could smell smoke and burning. Forcing herself onto her feet, she turned the Hyadean's body over and secured a grip under the arms. Yassem was spattered with blood too, but there was no way of telling if it was hers. There were no obvious gashes in her clothing. Gritting her teeth and straining, Marie dragged her inch by inch clear from the wreckage.

They were on one side of a sloping, rocky-sided ravine filled with dead trees. The rest of the helicopter was in parts farther down, with seats, pieces of rotor, parts of the tail assembly, and more bodies strewn in between. Flames were licking around the largest section. Somehow, Marie pulled Yassem's inert form through the thickets of dead branches and thorn bush to the rocks higher up the ravine side, where she collapsed with her burden into a hollow. A dull *whoosh* sounded as the wreckage ignited, and black smoke curled upward from below. The crackle of small-arms fire was coming from very close, interspersed with bursts from a heavy machine gun. At one point, Marie heard voices shouting. She lay still, too numbed with delayed shock to know what she should do. Time passed. She nudged and tried to shake Yassem. The Hyadean groaned but wouldn't stir. Marie located the water bottle on Yassem's belt, unscrewed the cap, and pressed it to her lips. "Yassem, can you hear me . . . ?" This time Yassem reacted, feeling for the water bottle and holding it to her mouth. "How bad does it feel?" Marie asked. "Does it hurt anywhere?"

Yassem gulped and took in a series of long breaths. "Hudro?" she whispered. "We were hit. Is he here?"

"Don't worry about that now. We have to move."

Like Marie, Yassem was torn and bruised but

seemed otherwise uninjured. After waiting perhaps
a half hour for her to orient herself and collect her
strength, they began moving, stopping frequently for
rests. Marie had no clear plan. Her vague thought
was to find a river or creek and follow it downstream.
Water led to habitation. Yassem seemed too dazed or
perhaps overcome by grief to object or offer anything
more constructive. The sounds of fighting drew farther away. They carried on, movement still painful,
making slow progress over the rough, forested, hilly
terrain.

Nightfall brought them to a deserted collection of
huts and trailer cabins by a dirt road, several demolished, and the rest riddled with bullets—clearly the
scene of recent fighting. A number of bodies lay scattered around, including some charred black in a
burned-out gun pit. Despite the macabre surroundings, Marie and Yassem could go no further. Finding some packs and cases with unused rations, they
scraped together a meal of sorts—even a dash of
brandy—and lay down with makeshift blankets in the
corner of a relatively unscathed house, away from
what appeared to have been the center of the action,
to spend the night.

They were found and awakened next morning by
Brazilian soldiers sent to clear up the scene and bury
the corpses. Seeing Yassem and her military garb, they
fetched the Hyadean officers accompanying their unit.
The Hyadeans were tough-looking, confident, reminding Marie of the ones she had seen in the air terminal at Uyali. Yassem had regained much of her
strength by now, and answered their questions in
Hyadean. From their general manner, Marie got the
impression that she and Yassem were considered to
be on the same side—certainly not prisoners.

A medic was summoned to check both of them. He pronounced no major injuries but used up a lot of adhesive dressings and gauze on minor things, including a lot of superficial lacerations to Marie's face, which he said would heal. Shortly afterward, a Hyadean military flyer landed, and they were put aboard. One of the Hyadeans and two Terrans would be apparently coming too. Just before entering, they turned to exchange a few final words with others outside. It was Marie and Yassem's first moment of privacy since their awakening that morning.

"What's happening?" Marie asked in a whisper as they sat down.

"I told them I'm one of our communications liaison officers, and you're a Terran aide who works with me," Yassem replied. "We were attached to a Terran unit mixed up in the fighting here, and we were separated. They're taking us back to their base."

Marie couldn't feel totally happy about it. "Won't they check?" she queried.

"Eventually. But it will give us some time."

Marie looked down at the drab gray tunic that she was still wearing, which she had been given at Cuzco. "I'm surprised nobody noticed this prison garb."

Yassem looked Marie up and down. "With all that blood, I'm not sure anyone could tell what it is," she said.

They arrived at a camp of wooden and corrugated steel huts, depot facilities, an airstrip, and defensive positions, set inside a perimeter of double wire fences. Beyond were grassy hills cloaked by scatterings of trees. The camp was bustling with Terran and Hyadean aircraft arriving and departing, presumably in support of the operations still in progress elsewhere. Yassem declined a suggestion of the base medical officer to put her and Marie in the sick bay for a couple of days, which would straightaway have required information on who they were and from what unit. Staying on their feet would leave them more in control of their own affairs. So instead, they were shown to quarters where they were given clean clothes and left to freshen up.

Later, when they came out, and tottered over to the officers' mess for breakfast with more effort than they let show, it turned out that their story was not anyone's special concern just for the moment, anyway. The big news was that in the north, the governor of California, William Jeye, had declared the secession of the Federation of Western America. The talk among the Brazilian officers was about whether an all-out North American war was imminent, and if so, where they would stand in it. But the most astounding thing was when the newscaster replayed notable incidents from the days leading up to the declaration. One event cited as having had a profound effect on the American people was a documentary released from unofficial Ilyadean sources to the Western news media. It was none other than the one featuring Cade and Marie that Luodine had made. *It had gotten through!* At least, it had as far as California. Marie stared disbelievingly. Yassem watched her in puzzlement before making a connection between the face on the screen and the swollen, discolored one next to her swathed in dressings—and even then, probably only because Hudro had told her about it. Marie excused herself to go back to their quarters. It wasn't only to recover from the shock and absorb the implications. Even with the dressings, she couldn't rid herself of the conviction that it would only have taken minutes for somebody in the room to recognize her. Some time passed by before Yassem joined her.

"I've been getting a picture of the situation," she told Marie. "It doesn't sound good. Segora was heavily attacked yesterday. It's in government hands now. Vrel and the others would have been right in the middle of it all if they got there the night before. We have to try to contact them. Obviously we're on borrowed time here. Do you know the number of Vrel's phone—the one Roland sent the file to?"

Marie shook her head. "There was never any reason to think I'd need it."

Yassem looked vexed. "Communications is my specialty. We talk routinely to people on Chryse. There *must* be some way. . . ."

It took Yassem ten minutes of pacing about the room and frowning out the window to realize what she had said. "Chryse!" she exclaimed suddenly. "Luodine and Nyarl's flyer—the one that's still in Bolivia, somewhere. It carries Hyadean communications that can be reached from there. The registration record to Luodine's agency on Chryse will have its call code, and it's accessible via the Hyadean equipment here at the base. We can get through to them that way!"

"You're going to connect via some other star system, to talk to somebody maybe a couple of hundred miles from here?" Marie was incredulous.

"Probably safest," Yassem said, smiling. "With the situation, all the local systems are likely to be watched. But Hyadeans make calls home all the time. Let me go see if I can find a friendly operator."

For once, things went as straightforwardly as hoped. Yassem got through, and it turned out that Vrel, Luodine, and Nyarl, after narrowly escaping the day before, were still shaken but all right. Currently, they were at a remote Indian village to the north that Luodine had known, and hadn't formulated any plans yet. Of course they would wait there if there were some way Yassem and Marie could join them. Once again Yassem was determined that it had to be possible. Marie could only marvel at Hyadean tenacity, once they had set their minds to something.

And again, there was a solution. The flyer sitting in southern Bolivia, where Nyarl had sent it as a decoy, was no doubt being kept under observation and its log monitored. Using access codes to its control system that she retrieved from the vehicle registry on Chryse, Yassem was able to delete its connections to the Hyadean South American traffic control network, thereby rendering it invisible to the tracking computers. Then she obtained the coordinates of its present location from the on-board local control and fed it instructions to fly to the base in Brazil where she and Marie had been brought. Thus, when the Hyadean adjutant asked about scheduling their return, Yassem could tell him that it was okay, they had made their own arrangements. Transportation was arranged for them. So, little curiosity was aroused two hours later, when the blue-and-yellow flyer landed itself on the airstrip. Yassem and Marie bade thanks and farewell to the two Hyadeans who walked out with them to see them aboard. Minutes later, they were climbing and turning north on a course that would cross the Amazon basin. Yassem made sure that the flyer would return a "friendly" identification code if interrogated by a Hyadean or Brazilian antiaircraft fire-control system.

Marie gazed out at mile after mile of rain-forest canopy sliding by below like a sea of frozen green waves. Finally, she could feel some respite from the chaos assailing her life for the last . . . was it nine days? Ever since Roland walked back into it. She laid her head back into the roomy, Hyadean-size seat and put a hand to her brow wearily. It met bandages. Roland. . . . Years ago she had tried, despaired, and given up. Then he had come back, starting to become what she had always known he could be. . . . And now this. She replayed scenes of the crash in her mind, trying to tell herself there might be a way he could have survived. It had been only a moment before impact when he and Rocco disappeared. They couldn't have been more than a few feet from the ground by then. But there had been blood pouring from Roland's head. It was no good. She was trying to create wishful fantasies. Eventually, whatever the reality was would have to be faced. She looked across at Yassem and found the Hyadean watching her with an expression that seemed to read her thoughts. But then, Yassem was having the same problem.

"Hudro's pretty tough," Yassem said. "Sometimes I think he is, what did you say once, 'charmed'? Like Roland."

Marie took in the crisp, clean Hyadean military fatigue garb that Yassem had been issued. Everything was so mixed up. Marie was used to thinking in terms close to black and white. There were "us" and "them," good guys and bad; you knew who was on which side. Hyadeans had always been "them." In the last week she had found herself trusting them as much as she had ever trusted anyone—which was ironic, for it seemed that the concept of "trust" itself was something that they themselves were learning from Terrans. Now one of them might have died helping to save her and Roland. And the person to whom that one had meant the most was now Marie's confidante and companion, whose life Marie had recently saved, yet wore the uniform of those who were hunting them. Marie could no longer make any sense of the world.

"How does this happen?" she said. Yassem raised her eyebrows but said nothing. "Hudro was with your counterinsurgency forces. You were with communications, attached to Terran intelligence." Marie shook her head uncomprehendingly. "I *know* how people are selected for jobs like that. They look for a particular kind of personality, the kind that identifies with the system it serves and takes pride in loyalty. People like that don't change their minds and go over to the other side. The one from the federal ISS, Reyvek, that you saw Roland and me talking about on that recording this morning, was an exception. He was very disturbed in some ways that went deep, and the system must have missed it. But normally that doesn't happen."

Yassem had to think for a while, as if the subject were something new. "On Earth, you mean," she said finally. "That's the way it is here."

"Well, yes. . . ," Marie was surprised. "Wouldn't it be the same anywhere?"

Yassem paused again, searching for words. "Here you have these 'religions' and ideologies—big schemes that try to explain everything."

"Are you saying they're bad? I thought you and Hudro wanted to understand religion. That was why you left."

"No, they're not especially bad. They can be wonderfully inventive. But sometimes they program your thinking. Who is right and who is wrong becomes accepted as part of the indoctrination. Then life is simple, and killing who you're told to becomes easy."

"So how is it different with Hyadeans?" Marie asked.

"We just accept what we see. We don't try to make it something else because of ideas of what it should be. So who is right and who is wrong depends not on who people are, but on what they *do*."

Marie still didn't follow. "So why is your planet supporting a government that's working with the powers here who are exploiting Earth's peoples? Isn't that supposed to be wrong? Why won't they accept that when they see it?"

"*Because they never have seen it!*" Yassem replied. "Don't you understand? It works both ways. Because Hyadeans don't question, they accept what they're told. And what has happened on Chryse is that for longer than I know, a powerful ruling caste has controlled what Chryseans are given to believe. But when they come here and see for themselves that what they have been told is not true, it's easier for them to decide that what they are doing is wrong and change sides. It happened to Vrel, to Hudro and me, and to others I have known. And it sounds as if it happened to some of the ones you know. *That* was why Luodine was so anxious to make the recording and get it to Chryse. She knew the effect it would have there. Terrans assume they will be lied to and regard it as normal. But to Hyadean minds that have never questioned, the realization would be devastating. You should have seen the effects in the Hyadean officers' mess this morning after you left. For the first time, some of them are questioning what they are doing. You see—until now they have been told they were helping the people defend themselves against terrorists. It never occurred to them that there might be another story. That was just from watching a news item here, put out by the new Western federation. Can you imagine the effect if it were broadcast all over Chryse?"

Marie stared at Yassem fixedly. Finally, she could see what Roland had glimpsed but not had time to understand. The scientist in Los Angeles that he'd talked about had credited the Hyadeans' ability to see things as they were as the reason why they had built ships that could bring them to Earth, while Earth's scientists were still trying to divine from abstruse mathematics whether or not it was possible, and arguing over whether they had evolved from molecules or been created by a god—neither of which the Hyadeans saw any point in caring about. That same faculty could determine whether or not they would tolerate what was happening on Earth. The Hyadean ruling element and the force they controlled could never be defeated in a straight, stand-up firefight—despite her commitment to CounterAction, deep down Marie knew that. But they would topple if the people back home ever learned the truth. And they knew it too. No wonder they fought with all the fear and repression that came from insecurity. Marie snorted to herself at the offbeat humor: "Security" forces described them pretty well.

They arrived to a warm but sad welcome from the others, and expressions of added delight from the villagers. Vrel in particular was devastated by the news that both Cade and Hudro were lost. There was concern at Marie's appearance, but she assured them the damage was not as bad as all the bandages and tape suggested. The villagers provided a meal, but even before she was halfway though it, Marie, her body stiff and protesting everywhere by now, felt her eyes closing and exhaustion sweeping over her. Yassem seemed to be in about the same condition. The Indian medicine man, assisted by two of the women, applied medications and poultices of pastes and leaves that worked wonders, and the two new arrivals were asleep before there was a chance to discuss anything further.

❖   ❖   ❖

It was late in the morning when Marie awoke. Yassem was already up, but as yet nobody had agreed on any firm plans. Luodine had wanted to stay to cover the South American situation, and Vrel's thought had been to head across the Pacific, but now they were wondering about trying for the newly formed Federation territory in what had been the U.S.A. Both the flyers were personal short-haul vehicles and didn't have the range for such a journey. However, Nyarl ascertained from the web that commercial flights into western North America were still operating from Quito in Ecuador, which was reachable. To check on the American situation, Vrel tried calling his colleagues at the Hyadean mission in Los Angeles, which he seemed surprised to find was still functioning. He asked to speak to a Hyadean called Wyvex.

CHAPTER THIRTY-FIVE

The physical similarities between Terrans and Hyadeans, not just in general appearance but in terms of chemistry and genetic codes as well, had been devastating to Earth's prevalent theory of life and its origins, but had come as no particular surprise to the aliens. They had listened skeptically but with interest to the idea of how ooze could turn itself into a jellyfish and a jellyfish into a horse by selectively accumulating random mutations, and when the evidence claimed to support it proved not to, they dismissed it as another of Earth's secular religions, invented to displace an earlier one.

In a way that fitted well with the Hyadeans' cata-strophic account of the origins and development of planetary systems, Darwin's original notebooks were filled with observations of evidence written worldwide of epochs of sudden, cataclysmic change. But twenty years later when he published, he had come around to adapting to biology Lyell's principle of gradualism, by then established as the guiding paradigm of geology. Under the new scheme of things, no catastrophic upheavals needed to be invoked to explain the past. Everything could be accounted for by the processes seen to be taking place in the present, provided they were allowed operate for a sufficiently long time. Hence, from an ideology were constructed the immense spans of time that the Hyadeans found it astonishing anyone from Earth could look at the surface of their own planet and believe in.

Earth's history fascinated the Hyadeans. Revolution in the American colonies and then France had terrified the ruling houses of Europe. Napoleon's armies had carried notions of rising up against traditional authority from Catholic Spain to Tsarist Russia, and by the middle of the nineteenth century the continent was seething with militant political movements advocating socialism. All it needed now was for science to declare that violent upheaval was the natural way of change. The new scheme, however, depicted change as a slow, gradual accumulation of tiny advantages—so slow that little significant difference should be evident even in the course of a lifetime. And on the other hand, an explanation for life that did away with the supernatural served the new, technocratic wealth, based on commerce and industry, by completing the undermining of the authority on which the old power structure rested. Expedient and intellectually satisfying, it was embraced from all sides and rapidly enthroned as science. When the evidence that had been predicted failed to materialize, and contradictions continued to accumulate, ingenious and imaginative possibilities were devised to explain the facts away. No serious consideration was given to the possibility that the reason so little proof *could be found of life's having evolved from simple molecules on Earth might be simply that it hadn't; it had arrived there.*

Yet it had long been known that bacteria and other microorganisms exhibited an extraordinary tolerance to extremes of such quantities as radiation, temperature, and pressure, that was difficult to account for by any selection process on the surface of the Earth, where such conditions had never existed. But it made them ideally preadapted for space. Carbonized structures uncannily suggestive of familiar forms of microbe had been discovered inside meteorites—and yes, with the possibility of contamination excluded beyond reasonable doubt. Refractive indexes in part of the interstellar clouds matched those of biological objects more closely than any of the alternatives put forward to explain them. Some scientists over the years had pointed to these findings as a case for supposing that the genes that directed life had originated from somewhere else. The mainstream scientific community saw warnings of the theological can of worms opening up again, and their general reaction was to ridicule the suggestion or leave it alone.

The Hyadeans had made the same observations. Having neither supernatural nor secular fundamentalism to defend, they accepted the evidence as meaning what it said and concluded that living organisms were constructed on planetary surfaces from local materials under the direction of genetic information with which space was seeded. These incoming code units were combined into complex genetic programs that built organisms suited to local conditions. Infection was the principal mechanism for spreading new genetic combinations around and establishing initially compatible breeding populations—much faster and more efficient than sexual transmission, the slowness of which was another problem with Terran theory—especially given that the enormous time spans contrived to make it seem plausible were wrong anyway. The programs were ruggedly constructed in possessing a degree of adaptability to cope with environmental fluctuations, and this had been extrapolated into an explanation of everything.

The upshot was that similar kinds of places would originate similar kinds of life. Life did indeed evolve on planets, but not in the way Terran scientists had thought. Chryse was roughly like Earth, even if worn down and not reworked as recently, and that was why Hyadeans were roughly like humans.

Since they had never observed genetic information originating either through a mechanistic or an intelligently guided process, the Hyadeans hadn't asked how it came together in the first place. About the only possibility they seemed to have considered was that it could be an advanced culture's way of propagating itself through the galaxy using a radically different form of starship. Where that culture might have come from wasn't the kind of thing that Hyadeans were going to spend a lifetime worrying about.

Hence, the Hyadeans rejected Terran evolutionary theory as a construct having more to do with Earth's political religions than scientific reality. What captivated them, however, and came as a totally new revelation to their thinking, even if the Terrans who had first dreamed it up were now rejecting it, was the concept that life itself might have a purpose. So while Terrans were contriving mechanisms to deny all the meaning in, and reasons for, existence that they had once believed, the Hyadeans were discovering questions that it had never occurred to them to ask.

CHAPTER THIRTY-SIX

In the room that he had just about taken over as his permanent office in the Hyadean West Coast Trade and Cultural Mission in Los Angeles, Michael Blair hung up after taking a call from Krossig, now established in Australia, and pushed his chair back from the desk to stretch. The Hyadean scientific station was on the outskirts of Cairns, in the northeastern coastal highlands of Queensland, which over the last twenty years had grown into a sprawling, medium-size township of cosmopolitan flavor following "discovery" of the region by wealthy escapees from Asia, the U.S., and elsewhere, attracted by the region's combination of independence, rugged informality, and the chance of a quiet life. His previous experiences having been limited to the U.S., Krossig was rapturing about the racial variety and contrasts of lifestyle that he was finding here. Blair had assured him there was a lot more of Earth to be sampled yet.

285

The latest home news was that Texas had declared for the Federation. The Eastern part of the country was staking claim to legitimacy by resurrecting the Civil War term "Union" and threatening the use of armed force to suppress what it insisted was rebellion. Federation spokespersons, by contrast, referred to it as the "Globalist puppet regime" to emphasize its non-American underpinnings and backing. Already, the Union was challenging the Federation's hegemony by sending armored units forward between the Mississippi and Dallas, and flying provocative military demonstrations over the seceded territory. There were rumors that Mexico was already under Globalist diplomatic pressure to allow supporting operations from the south. To the north, Federation forces, for their part, were advancing eastward to secure a flank along Lake Superior. What Canada would do, nobody knew.

Although it had been threatened for some time, the secession when it finally happened had come with a suddenness that took everyone by surprise. And the Hyadean mission in Los Angeles, due to its being in unusual circumstances at the time, had played a big part in bringing it about.

Following disagreements with the Hyadean Office in Washington that Blair neither understood nor wanted to, the Hyadean head of the legation had been recalled east along with key members of his staff for "policy discussions." Orzin, the political official who was still visiting, had taken it upon himself to manage the day-to-day operation of things in Los Angeles until whatever was going on got sorted out. And while this was the state of things at the mission, an event occurred which some said was a key factor in bringing about the secession. The story was so bizarre that Blair hadn't, even yet, been able to construct in his mind the beginnings of an explanation.

Dee had appeared at the mission, asking to see Wyvex, and handed him a storage cartridge containing a file encrypted in Hyadean code. The file was from Vrel, who had last been heard of five days previously, when he left saying something vague about visiting a place near St. Louis. Somehow, he had ended up in South America. Dee had known no more than that. The cartridge had been given to her by the service manager of the dealership that took care of her car, who said the contents had come in over the phone. He'd suggested that next time she wanted her car checked, she should take it to the phone company. Why Vrel couldn't have used the regular communications to contact Wyvex was a good question. Presumably, he was in some kind of trouble and his access was blocked; or he didn't want to broadcast his whereabouts by using a system that would need his ID codes; or he was worried about general surveillance on mission traffic.

The reason became clear when Wyvex decoded the file and ran it. To his astonishment, it featured none other than Roland Cade and his former wife, Marie, giving an account of the truth behind the Farden-Meakes affair and the measures taken to suppress it. Along with their allegations was a portrayal by other Hyadeans that nobody at the mission knew of what was happening in South America, including harrowing clips of the aftermath of air strikes, Hyadean-equipped ground units in action, with Cade and Marie again, relaying the narrative of a disillusioned Hyadean officer. Coming at a time when emotions were high everywhere following Sovereignty's release of the Reyvek documents, it was enough to finally demolish official denials and the entire government position. Vrel, in his message to Wyvex, asked for the recording to be sent to Chryse.

Blair didn't know what Wyvex would have done if the mission's official head were still in charge there. He doubted if Wyvex would have had the nerve to forward the recording on his own initiative as Vrel had requested, and had he sought higher approval, the legation head would surely have quashed it. Orzin, however, standing in temporarily, was more flexible. He had become a familiar face in Cade's social circle and mellowed to Terran ways, learning to enjoy the entertainments, turning a blind eye to staff dealings in illicit exotics, and some said not being beyond having a hand in a few himself. The important thing was that he had developed an affection for Earth that many Hyadeans seemed eventually to come to share. When Wyvex showed him the documentary, Orzin had been very disturbed. After much talk and deliberation that Blair had not been a party to, he had decided it *should* be forwarded to Chryse—which meant straight from the mission, since it would never get through Washington. Not only that: Orzin had authorized a version in Terran format to be released to the Western news media. Whether it had constituted a prime cause or not, the Federation had declared its secession within forty-eight hours of the broadcast's going out.

What Cade, who hadn't been heard of for days either, was doing in South America was anyone's guess. Nobody that Blair had talked to at the house had a clue. Even Julia had professed being at a loss, saying he'd gone to Atlanta on personal business and that was all she knew. Equally mystifying was what Marie was doing with him, since as far as they were all aware she had long been history in Cade's personal life. But it would all presumably be revealed in time, and until then there was nothing they could do, since Vrel had given no means of contacting him.

They were in no position to devote a lot of thought to such matters, in any case. Right now, there was an impending war situation to contend with.

Blair propped his heels on the desk and clasped his hands behind his neck. He hoped that all this was not about to disrupt the progress he was making toward a better understanding of the way Hyadeans thought, and how those who spent any period of time on Earth began to be affected by it.

Earth had been dogmatizing itself into a virtual Dark Age for the best part of a century, discovering little that was fundamentally new, concentrating on technological improvements that it persuaded itself constituted science. The cause was a system of social dynamics that encouraged the pursuit of rewards in the form of accolades and funding, and then conferred them in recognition of what was "right" rather than what was true. The result was an Establishment that repeated the history of the medieval European Church by selling out to the political system as purveyors of the approved Truth in return for patronage, prestige, and protection. The irony, Blair was beginning to suspect, was that the solution might well lie in what all the great religions of the world, in essence, had been teaching all along: controlling passions and cultivating the ability honestly not to care what the answers to supposedly objective questions turn out to be. An even greater irony was that the Hyadeans, who seemed to possess this quality innately, seemed bent on imparting to their discoveries the significance and deeper meaning that generations of Terran scientists had been working diligently to expunge from theirs.

The Hyadean account of subatomic phenomena was close to what had become known on Earth as the Many Worlds Interpretation of Quantum Mechanics, and described a vast, fantastic, virtually infinite super-position of everything that had happened, would happen, or could happen. In making the decisions to follow one path rather than another through this ever-branching labyrinth of possibilities, the individual assembled together the sequence of perceptions and experiences that were interpreted as the universe and its flow of time. In fact, there were uncountably many universes, but isolated in such a way that at their normal, day-to-day level the inhabitants of any one had no knowledge of the others, or awareness that they even existed. Other "nearby" realities did, however, interfere at the quantum level, which was another way of saying that information could travel between them.

People had been insisting for centuries on the reality of things that science was unable to explain. Now, instead of dismissing such possibilities out of hand, it had become fashionable for scientists to grant that there might be something to some of the claims and to cite quantum "leakage" as the answer. Hence, there was still no case for invoking any "supernatural" phenomena beyond what science could account for. It was just that "science" covered more now, the world was a bigger place, and "natural" meant more than it used to.

The Hyadeans saw things the other way around. Whereas the Terran physicists found an ultimate mechanistic explanation that removed the illusion of purpose from all equations, the Hyadeans were beginning to see the whole, immense totality as a framework ideally suited to making morally meaningful choices possible. From there, having no preconceived notions to get in the way, they had followed their propensity to simply accept what the facts said and seemed to be arriving at the—to them, utterly new and revelational—conclusion that it had been designed that way, by an intelligence, for a reason.

At first, Blair had been taken aback. Since graduating, he had generally accepted uncritically the materialist doctrines that underlay his training, and their assumptions had become habit. But now, since meeting the Hyadeans—and particularly after having to forget so much of what he had believed before—he wasn't so sure. Even before the Hyadeans came, increasing numbers of Terran biologists had been astounded by the complexity that they were finding even in allegedly primitive organisms, and saying that such organization couldn't have come together of itself. Blair tried to fit this in with the Hyadean picture of the cosmos as initially hot, high-density entities spinning off progressively lower-energy objects from quasars down to stars and eventually planets. What else were planets but assembly stations for constructing living organisms and providing an environment for them to develop in? If it was purposeful, then the purpose of life was to evolve consciousness; and what other purpose could consciousness serve than to provide the means of undergoing experience? It was all so uncannily close to what Krossig was getting so excited about. What did Blair make of it? He really didn't know. Maybe he was becoming a lapsed atheist.

All the same, even if the Age of Materialism should turn out to have been overhasty and based on misplaced confidence, it would be wrong to conclude that no good had come of it. Blair had never understood what the horrors of the Inquisition, wars of extermination, and witch burnings had to do with a creed supposedly based on tolerance, kindness, and compassion. Perhaps a pause in social evolution to forget the old vengeful, spiteful god hadn't been such a bad idea.

Earth had invented religion, even to the extent of turning its science into one. The Hyadeans had produced a science free of unsupported beliefs and irrational convictions, and now they wanted to project religion into it. Maybe the future would see a merging of the two: the Hyadean form of science, restrained by the notions of modesty and humility that stemmed from an awareness of powers greater than oneself—what earlier ages had idealized but never been able to make a reality. There was so much that they could be working toward together, instead of the conflict that seemed to be relentlessly approaching.

An incoming call sounded. Blair swung his feet down and sat forward to take it. It was Wyvex, in the communications room on the floor above. "We've just heard from Vrel again," he announced. "A direct call this time."

"Okay! Are they still in South America?"

"Yes, but he wasn't specific about where. He said something about being in a village and trying to get a flight from Ecuador."

"You mean they're on their way back?"

"It sounds like it—soon, anyway. They've added more to the party. The journalist who made that documentary is there. Her name is Luodine. Her associate, Nyarl, was here a while ago."

"I remember him. Striking hair—kind of green and black."

"Yes. And there's another Hyadean woman, called Yassem. None of us knows her. Some kind of communications specialist."

"So when should they be here? Any idea?"

"As soon as they're sure there's no problem entering Federation territory. We can't think of any reason why there should be, but we don't really know. Orzin is checking with Sacramento now."

"Of course there won't be a problem. They're heroes. Roland and his ex are celebrities."

There was an unnaturally long pause. Then Wyvex said heavily, "She's there, but Roland isn't. Apparently, he was in a helicopter that got shot down over a combat zone. Yassem and Marie were there too. As far as they know, they were the only survivors."

Blair exhaled shakily, and then nodded. "I see." He had to swallow a lump in his throat

"I'm not sure how Terran social conventions work with regard to Julia," Wyvex said. "What's the way to handle her situation?"

"I'll take care of it," Blair told him.

CHAPTER THIRTY-SEVEN

Cade's gray prison garb was gone, and in its place he had acquired a pair of baggy white peasant-style trousers, a colorfully embroidered shirt something like a vest with sleeves, and a coarse woolen cloak that also doubled as a blanket at night. He even had a floppy, flat-topped hat with a brim. As his faculties slowly returned sufficiently for him to be able to follow, Hudro told him the story.

The helicopter had been downed by a proximity burst and crashed in a rocky ravine full of fallen trees, spilling bodies as it tumbled down the side. Rocco had found himself thrown out near Cade and dragged him clear. Hudro joined them, hauling another of the occupants, also unconscious. They found another stumbling around, dazed, and another impaled on a shattered tree limb—he died later that day. And that was it. There had not been time to search for any more. They had come down under fire in an area where MOPAN guerrillas were retreating before part of the government force that was endeavoring to encircle Segora, where the helicopter had been heading. A group of MOPAN had gotten to them before the regular soldiers and rushed them away.

Faced by regular troops deploying Hyadean weapons that they had not encountered before, and for the first time in some places by Hyadean ground troops who turned out to be not especially adept at using the terrain but commanded fearsomely effective firepower, the guerrillas had been routed. What remained of them were straggling southward, still hunted and harassed, to regroup. Besides Hudro, Rocco, and the two other survivors from the crash, one of whom was immobilized with leg injuries, a local MOPAN leader called Miguel was riding in the same truck, along with five of his troops—three youths and two girls. The truck was also laden with a miscellany of weapons, equipment, and supplies lashed to the sides and the cab roof, or piled in the rear with the passengers underneath netting woven with leaves that were changed twice a day. The local population had long been in the habit of aiding in concealment by lighting plenty of fires to clear undergrowth and burn trash, and scattering incendiary devices about to confuse infrared imagers. The high-resolution satellites had to be told where to look, so that with experience it was possible to remain invisible to a surprising degree. Even so, Miguel was wary of moving when the skies were clear of cloud cover.

What of the others? Cade wanted to know. Had Hudro or anyone heard from Vrel, Luodine, and Nyarl since the attack at Segora? No. It had all been too sudden and confusing. Cade borrowed a phone and tried calling Vrel's Terran number. It rang somewhere, but nobody answered. Was there any news of Tevlak? No, nothing.

Cade listened dully to a summary of events elsewhere. The sensation was that in what had been the U.S., the mountain states—Montana, Wyoming, Colorado, New Mexico—along with Texas and those toward the Pacific, had formally denounced the Washington regime as illegal and seceded as the Federation of Western America, its capital Sacramento, with the former governor of California, William Jeye, as president. Already there were reports of clashes with federal and security forces in the region who refused to come over or be disarmed, and military overflights being shot down after ignoring warnings to turn back. The South, essentially, had declared neutrality and been occupied at key strategic points within hours by Hyadean-assisted Eastern forces.

Hounded in the jungle, wary of using communications, the guerrillas hadn't pieced together the full story. Hudro thought the recording they had made at Tevlak's house could have been a factor. He confirmed that Vrel had received it and sent it on. But Cade no longer cared; or maybe a defense mechanism in his mind was protecting it from something that it wasn't yet ready to deal with. He had already been coming to terms with the realization that his life was going to change in some fundamental ways from what it had been. Now, the alternative that he had glimpsed had been snatched away before he'd even begun to understand fully what it meant.

"You're sure nobody else could have made it out of the crash?" he asked Rocco.

"What was left of the helicopter went up in flames while we were dragging you away. If anybody did, the Globs have them now. So we'll never know."

Cade had gashes in the side and back of his head,

and a mild depressed fracture that had been treated during the two days he was unconscious, and which with luck would now heal; also, a strained neck and a collection of body cuts and bruises. Events passed for him as a series of incoherent impressions, like disconnected fragments of a movie that was no longer of interest. Whether this was due to his condition or the drugs that the medic who checked him periodically and changed the bandages on his head gave him to dull the pain, Cade didn't know. . . .

The truck was bumping past people who look strained and exhausted, trudging along the roadside leading pack animals, pushing loaded carts and bicycles, or carrying bundles on their backs. A woman sat looking blankly, her belongings strewn around her, heedless of her crying child. The man propped against the tree beside her didn't move. . . .

It was night. Houses were in flames, with explosions sounding distantly. There were cries and wailing all around. People crowded around the truck, pleading to ride. The truck had already picked up as many as it could. There was no more room. . . .

The noise came of aircraft flying low overhead. The figures under the netting strung between the parked truck and the trees fingered their weapons nervously. An Indian woman tried to quiet her restless baby, as if the pilots might hear. . . .

They had pulled off the trail. Gunfire was sounding somewhere ahead. Two men came back from another truck to report that the Globs were holding the bridge over a river. They had to go back and try another way. . . .

Never had Cade seen such human misery and suffering. What was it all for? Who benefited?

CHAPTER THIRTY-EIGHT

The commander-in-chief of the Hyadean military forces on Earth was called Gazaghin. Normally, he was based in his headquarters near the General Embassy in Xuchimbo. When he stopped by Casper Toddrel's Washington club to meet for lunch the day after Toddrel's return from Brazil, however, it was from the liaison office that the Hyadeans had established in the Pentagon just across the river. He had flown up on an emergency visit to discuss strategy and coordination with the Eastern regime's forces following the secession of the FWA two days previously.

Toddrel didn't like him and never had. Besides having an extreme case of innate Hyadean bluntness and an inability to grasp even the rudiments of finesse or subtlety, he held a disdain for anyone outside the military caste, which he made no attempt to conceal. His basic attitude seemed to be that the task of the military was essentially to clean up the messes that others—and in particular, financiers and politicians—had created yet again and learned nothing from, and it was just as well the soldiers had a better grasp of reality.

"I want to talk because I want to warn you," Gazaghin said, tearing into a quiche salad, to which he had allowed some grilled salmon to be added. His hair varied from black to dark blue; his features were purple-gray, compressed and fleshy. He wore a dark green tunic with designations of rank on the shoulders, breast pockets, and cuffs, and a cap which he continued wearing at the table. "We have ships sunk in the Amazon areas. Now, I hear sabotage begins in our operations at Uyali. Four Hyadeans killed in explosions there this morning." He pointed menacingly with his fork. "I hear sayings that all is not straight with you, Toddrel. Too much Hyadean production from Uyali means your friends lose big money. So maybe your left hand is holding up what your right hand plays at knocking down. You see what I say? These terrorist rebels get money from somewhere."

"That's the most outrageous suggestion I've ever heard," Toddrel said tightly, his color rising. "We know their backing comes from Asia."

"North America has more interest for Asia, now maybe even more after the secession." Gazaghin waved a hand. "They don't care about Uyali. You care about Uyali."

Toddrel felt himself gripped by a mix of guilt and fury. He couldn't afford to be put on the defensive. "I'd have imagined you'd have business enough looking into the ineptness of your own people than questioning my motives," he retorted curtly.

"What you mean by this?"

"How were the Hyadeans who were with Cade and his woman at that art dealer's house permitted to leave? How was it possible for them to be snatched out of one of your transports and vanish without trace? Today I've just learned that the Hyadean journalist's aircar that's been sitting in Bolivia, which you've been waiting for to lead you somewhere, has vanished from the surveillance log. When an observation team went to check, the vehicle had vanished too. So it's obviously gone to pick them up somewhere, and not one of your experts with all their satellites and gadgetry can tell us where. And *you* are the ones who will instruct *our* military services?" The strata of Gazaghin's features seemed to puff up, like a saggy beach ball being inflated. Toddrel saw that his words had hit home and pressed on with a quiet inner satisfaction. "These two people have become a personal issue with me now. I *want* them found. It may be just a job to you, General, but because of the inability of the security forces to stop them in time, what they've done has cost me an immense personal fortune. How much has it cost you?"

Gazaghin waved it aside impatiently. "Pah! Still all you can think of is your money and fortune. You don't understand what this secession by west states means. If new Federation and Asia unite with Querl powers, it would make big troubles on home world. Could be end of everythings for you and for me. This Federation must be crushed quickly. But who is there that will do it? Too many U.S. weapons in California, Nevada. Your forces not reliable. So it must be with Hyadean forces. Little get-rich power games don't matter now." Gazaghin's face darkened, even from its normal hue. He wagged a threatening finger. "I know story about assassinations in Washington is true. Now I don't have time to worry if you are behind sabotage of Amazon ships and Uyali also. From here on we have serious war business. If we find you interfering to make different plans, is all finish for you, Toddrel. You go back tell your friends too. If Hyadeans direct this war, we do it Hyadean way." Gazaghin flipped an olive off his plate and ground it into the tablecloth with his thumb. "That means anyone who gets in path is crushed. Like little vegetable. You understand what I tell you, Toddrel, yes?"

Toddrel seethed but had to contain it. Every adversity that had befallen him, including his humiliation at the hands of this barbarian now, were due to that infernal couple. Whatever other priorities might intrude, he would have them hounded down. That much he vowed.

The caller who appeared on the screen in Laura's apartment suite on New York's Upper East Side had lean, firm features with dark hair cropped short, and a cleanly trimmed mustache. Although she was unable to register a detailed impression because of the dark glasses he was wearing and the low level of lighting— no doubt deliberate—at wherever he was speaking from, her instincts and experience at once tagged him tentatively as "military."

"Hello, Laura," he opened. "Who I am doesn't matter for now. Let's just say that we're both acquaintances of Casper. I know quite a lot about you— knowing things about people is my business. In particular, I know you're an astute and discreet business lady. We have certain interests in common that we should discuss."

Laura smiled in a way that was part professional but at the same time genuinely curious. She assumed already that the end-objective would be for her to take on another client. Some men thought the mystery image added appeal. Others overaffected assertiveness as a cover for awkwardness. She had seen all the lines: candid, humorous, businesslike, nice-guy. . . . Or this could be someone Casper needed to know more about, being set up. "Do I take it you just happen to be in town at the moment?" Laura asked, treating him to a knowing look. "People should get to know each other a little before they commit to things. Suppose we meet up for cocktails someplace?"

"No, I think you misunderstand. Recent political events could have bearing on the personal safety of both of us. I'm talking about mutual protection."

Laura's expression at once became serious. "I don't understand," she said guardedly.

"Of course not. That's why we should talk. I expect to be in New York within the next week or so. I'd like to meet sometime then. Unobtrusively would be best. Is that agreeable?"

"Well . . . of course." If this was just another line, Laura told herself, it was the weirdest one yet.

"I'll contact you again before then."

"Do I get a name to recognize you by?"

"For now, call me . . . Timothy."

In a public net-access booth a few blocks from Internal Security Services headquarters in Washington, D.C., Colonel Kurt Drisson cut off the screen and turned up the interior lighting. Blonde, tanned, shapely, and sophisticated. Toddrel knew how to pick them, he was forced to compliment inwardly. There was no reason why adding a more personal dimension when the time was right should interfere with business.

Toddrel's position was shaky. And when people like

Toddrel felt insecure, those closest and with the most inside information had cause to worry. Not that Drisson feared any imminent danger for as long as he continued to be useful. But he believed in taking out early insurance.

CHAPTER THIRTY-NINE

They were back in Bolivia, at the north end of the country, east of the frontier with Peru. The truck, accompanied by an escort riding in a captured military Hummer, had continued south and crossed the border at night. Hudro showed how to put patterns of absorptive paint on the vehicles that would minimize the profile on image enhancers. Also, it turned out that playing static out of the speakers at full volume to disrupt acoustic patterns transmitted by sensors scattered from the air was more effective than coasting silently on the downhill stretches. The computers looked for engine frequencies and harmonics, and didn't know what to make of white noise.

Cade was slowly becoming himself again. "Are you getting over Yassem yet?" he asked Hudro as they stared back at the dusty trail winding away behind. They were out of the denser forest now, entering more open, hilly country.

"No. Maybe never. Why you think it?"

"You get on with your job. You don't seem to let it bother you."

"Inside it bothers. Must get on with job and get done. Is Hyadean way."

Cade decided there was something to be learned, and tried to find useful things to do. It seemed to help his head.

The altitude became higher, the surroundings more rugged. They came to a settlement of adobe houses, farm buildings, and sheds, tucked in a fold of the hills. Miguel had sent word ahead of their coming. Food and accommodation would be provided for the night. Also, a white-haired leader of the local arm of MOPAN, called Inguinca, was waiting to meet them with some of his followers. Ahead lay the most populous region, around Lake Titicaca and La Paz. From here on, Rocco and his escorts would merely attract attention. Their job was done, and they would turn back. Miguel volunteered to continue with Cade and Hudro to act as interpreter and general lookout.

A special evening meal was prepared for the occasion, consisting of a bean soup followed by meat, sweet potatoes, and a vegetable dish, with a plentiful supply of dryish red wine. It was held in a large, smoky room spanned by wooden beams and lit by oil lamps in one of the larger houses. There was nothing secretive or furtive. Just about the whole settlement, it seemed, from wide-eyed children and dark-braided women—several of them puffing pipes—to old men, squeezed themselves in around the walls and by the stove to take part, or at least be an audience. Maybe this was one of the things that passed for entertainment in these parts. It was clear that most if not all of them had never seen a Hyadean in the flesh before. Apart from curiosity that none tried to

conceal, reactions were varied. Some, encouraged and
not a little surprised by the alien's familiarity with
Spanish, did their best to be polite to the guest in
the ways they had been taught. Others seemed hostile, showing their feelings by glowering or staring
sullenly from far parts of the room. Cade was unsure
of the risk they might represent, but nobody else
seemed unduly bothered. Maybe the closeness of
these communities was such that betrayal was unthinkable. Hudro seemed to accept such variations without surprise.

Inguinca told of the intensive search going on
everywhere for the two Americans who had been
snatched from a military transport intercepted
between Peru and Brazil. All the Andes passes were
under close surveillance; air connections out of the
region were being watched. Although it might have
seemed at first glance that the Amazon system would
offer a choice of routes impossible to police effectively, they all converged in a gigantic funnel through
a few checkpoints that it would be risky to try passing
through, especially with all the military activity in the
region following the outbreak of sabotage attacks.
Inguinca denied that MOPAN guerrillas were responsible for these. Their fight, he said, was against the
operations to clear populations farther west. Other
groups were being funded from somewhere, and
MOPAN being made the scapegoat.

Inguinca's recommendation, therefore, was that
Cade and Hudro should press on southward, even
though their ultimate aim had not yet been agreed.
Clearly, they had to get out of the South American
continent. Poring over a map that Inguinca produced,
Cade thought of getting past the Andes into Chile,
somehow, and then south to Santiago. The Hyadeans
were boring an outlet from the Uyali region through

the Andes to the Pacific. If it was too risky to go over the mountains, with the kinds of friends he was collecting there might be a way to get himself and Hudro smuggled under them, through the tunnel workings. The idea became less crazy as he recalled the highway with its procession of robot trucks as a possible way of getting there. From Santiago it might be easier to get a commercial flight over the Pacific, perhaps to New Zealand, where Neville Baxter was, and then return on a regular flight into the Western Federation, avoiding the politically doubtful areas on the direct line between. Hudro could perhaps go on from New Zealand to join the Hyadeans with Krossig in Australia, and work out a new life from there.

That still left the question of how to get them through the populous area around Lake Titicaca and La Paz. Someone made a suggestion that brought laughter from some quarters and ridicule from others. Cade couldn't follow, although Hudro seemed to be able to. As the noise fell, an old man near the stove began speaking. Miguel moved closer and translated in a low voice for Cade's benefit. "He says the two of you can't travel together. The American is no problem. It's easy to make you invisible among the people, even if we have to darken your skin a little. But how do you hide a blue giant with a face like a rock statue?"

At that point, a man in a dark shirt, with straight hair combed forward and a thick mustache, rose and began talking loudly, pointing a denouncing finger at Hudro and making appealing gestures to the room. He was angry and had maybe taken a bit too much wine. The gist was that he wanted to know why they were talking about helping an alien at all. The aliens were behind the people who sent planes to destroy their villages, and soldiers who took their land. He had lost his farm and his son. Why was this alien here, eating their food and expecting them to save him? Heated words and admonishments followed, with Miguel getting involved and hence failing to keep Cade informed. It ended with the man in the dark shirt stalking from the room.

A clear-skinned boy with deep, dark eyes, probably around fifteen, brought them back to the subject by reminding everyone that next week would be a time of festivals and parades, with devil dancers in costumes designed to exaggerate their height, and masks that covered their heads completely. What better way could there be to disguise the blue giant?

Hudro said something that brought laughs from all around. "What was that?" Cade asked Miguel.

"He says does that mean he has to learn to dance too?"

A woman pointed out that seeing devil dancers in a parade was one thing, but how would you explain one out on the highway or halfway across the Altiplano? Eventually it was conceded that ingenious though the idea was, it had too many difficulties.

As Cade watched and listened, he contrasted the company to the kind he was used to at his own parties. These were just simple, self-sufficient people, asking no more than to live as they chose and be left alone. Nobody was coerced or robbed to provide their needs. Dee had said something to him once about the people who did the really important things, but he hadn't understood what she'd meant. Now, he did. The people he had known were as incapable of turning wilderness into food, rocks into a home, plants into a coat, or a dead tree into a table as they were of levitating. They depended for their very survival on the knowledge and skills of others. Told that their comfort and affluence arose from their innate excellence and the free interplay of market forces, they were happy to accept it. But Cade had seen what really went on.

As the debate continued, Cade remembered how Vrel had concealed him and Marie in St. Louis. Seizing a moment, and using Miguel again as translator, he told everybody, "If somebody is that conspicuous, then instead of trying to hide him, the thing to do might be to put him out in the open as something everyone would be expecting to see."

"Such as what?" Miguel asked.

"Would it be possible to get hold of a Hyadean military uniform somehow? Miguel and I dress as Bolivian army. We ride through openly in a jeep or something—a Hyadean officer and two Terran troopers." Cade looked around. The idea seemed to have merit.

"The uniforms might take some time. . . ." Inguinca said finally. He sounded dubious. "And then a suitable vehicle? . . . I don't know. That might be more difficult still. You would need papers to get gas. . . ."

More debate followed. Then a girl that Inguinca had introduced earlier as Evita, wearing jeans and a red shirt, her hair woven in braids, said, "Let me be the guide who will take them through. There is no problem with the vehicle. I drive a van for the telephone company, which passes everywhere. Hyadeans work with the telephone people sometimes when they put in special equipment. So he can wear his own clothes." Evita nodded toward Cade. "The American's idea is good. Let the Hyadean ride up front with me where everyone can see him. Hiding him in the back would look suspicious if there was a check. Miguel and the American come as workmen. When a pretty girl drives, the soldiers want to be nice guys. It is the best plan."

Nobody came up with any objection.

"Is this van of yours here?" Cade asked Evita.

She hesitated for a moment. "Yes. . . ."

"And I assume it would have a phone in it too?"

"Sure. All the regular phone company equipment."

It was the first prospect of being able to use trustworthy communications since Cade and Hudro were shot down. "Maybe we could call Baxter ahead and see how it looks," Cade suggested. "Get him started on making arrangements at his end."

"I guess. . . ."

At that point Rocco raised his hands. "This, I will leave to you. It is no longer our concern. It is time for us to be leaving now. So, we will say farewell and good luck, my friends."

A gaggle from inside came out to get some of the night air and watch as Cade and Hudro walked with Rocco to where the truck was waiting behind the Hummer, which was already filled with figures, engine running, ready to go.

"Remember to piss on body-scent detectors that they drop from the air when you find them," Hudro said. "And wear fresh flowers in hat. Works pretty good too."

Rocco's smile showed against the black of his mustache in the feeble light. "I'll remember. And the other thing I'll remember is that who are the good guys and who are the bad guys is more complicated than people think. But they have to learn it if this kind of thing is ever going to stop. That's the most important thing to learn."

He shook hands with Cade, then Hudro, and turned to heave himself up onto the tailboard. Somebody banged on the roof of the cab, and the truck started up. It flashed its lights for the Hummer ahead to move, and then followed twenty yards behind. Cade and Hudro stood watching, their arms raised, until the tail lamps disappeared, and then turned to go back to the houses.

Afterward, Evita took Cade to the van, where he used its phone to call Neville Baxter in New Zealand. Baxter was surprised and delighted. "What the hell gives?" he demanded, ever indomitably jovial.

"A long story that I'm not even going to try to get into, Neville. Look, I need help. I might be taking you up on that offer to visit you there sooner than you thought."

"You sound like you're in some kind of trouble."

"You could say that."

"Something to do with that documentary you did with your ex? We saw it here. It was dynamite." There was a pause, as if Baxter were putting the pieces together. "You were in South America when you made that. Is that where you still are now?"

"Right. And we need to get out."

"Who's we? You mean the ex? What was her name . . . ?"

"No, I told you it's a long story. I'm with a Hyadean—not one that you know. Heading directly north might have problems. The easiest way might be to come out your way. We're trying to get to Chile, and then down to Santiago."

"Where are you now, exactly?" Baxter asked. "We've got associates in a number of places down there. Maybe they can help."

For a second, Cade was unsure whether to answer. But then it was he, a moment ago, who had said he needed help. "Bolivia," he said. "Should be arriving in La Paz sometime tomorrow."

"Leave it to me. We might be able to come up with something."

Next, Cade called Luke at the house in California.

To his surprise he learned that Julia was still there—
acting about as normally as could be expected after
a secession, and with war breaking out. Cade cau-
tioned Luke to be careful of her. There was reason
to believe she wasn't what she said. Until he got back,
Luke shouldn't trust Julia with anything confidential.
That, of course, included any mention of the fact that
Cade had been in touch.

CHAPTER FORTY

The city of Nuestra Señora de la Paz, Our Lady of Peace, had seldom lived up to its name since its founding in 1548 by the envoy to whom the King of Spain had entrusted the rule of the empire seized from the Incas. It was supposed to mark the peace after the original Conquistadors, their companions at arms, sons, brothers, and heirs finally wiped themselves out after sixteen years of senseless civil war. Then, revolts plagued the nearly three centuries of Spanish rule. Aymará Indians besieged La Paz for six months in 1781, when latter-day Inca uprisings extended from Peru to Argentina. In 1825, Simón Bolívar, the liberator after whom the country was named, became the first national leader, only to resign the next year and be succeeded by six presidents in the next three years. Over the following two hundred years, sixty-odd men held the top spot, many lasting only days or weeks, tumbled by one another in more than 150 uprisings during the period. Twelve were assassinated.

Cade's first view of the world's highest capital city came as he, Hudro, Evita, and Miguel drove down off the Altiplano along a concrete boulevard of wide, sweeping curves overlooking an immense, tightly packed labyrinth of streets and terraces sprawling across the slopes of a river-gouged canyon cutting into the edge of the tableland. In front of them as they descended, dwellings, business premises, and office buildings clung to the steep, red, slide-prone slopes, while beyond the plateau line above, the snow-capped triple peaks of Illimani rose to 21,000 feet. Cade was taking a stint up front in the cab with Evita and Hudro. Miguel was in the rear. The drive southward had passed without incident, although news of sabotage attacks in the Uyali area and consequent tightening of security made the prospect of journeying farther in that direction worrisome.

The chief inspector in the city's police headquarters had received instructions to contact military security immediately if anything was heard concerning the American man and woman who were being hunted, and the two missing Hyadeans, again a male and a female, believed to have been involved. Hence, the oaf responsible for sifting intelligence reports had been looking for *couples*, and a whole day had slipped by before it occurred to someone else that the tipoff from a disaffected rebel in a remote village to the north might refer to the two males in question. If so, then what had happened to the females was anyone's guess. But it appeared that half their quarry might be on its way to the city right now.

"My information is that they are traveling in one of your vans," the chief inspector said over the phone to the general manager of the telephone company. "The driver is known as Evita. I don't know if that is her correct name, but I have a description. . . ."

"You can never get lost in La Paz," Evita said as she swung the wheel first one way, then the other to negotiate the series of downward bends. "Just keep going downhill. The whole city is a funnel that comes together onto one big main street that runs out the bottom." She lifted a hand momentarily to indicate two boys doing something to the wheels of an upturned coaster wagon. "They can go twelve miles without a break in that. Twenty-three hundred feet drop vertically. Good sport for boys, yes?"

Inguinca had given them instructions for contacting a highway construction foreman who could make arrangements to hide them in one of the robot trucks returning southward. However, as they came onto the main thoroughfare that Evita had mentioned—a tree-lined mall of shops, offices, and restaurants, called El Prado—the phone in a receptacle on the dash panel rang. Evita took it as she drove, listened for a moment, then passed the handset to Cade. "It's for you," she told him. "Neville Baxter again, from New Zealand."

"Hi, Neville."

"Roland. Is it all right to talk?"

"Sure. What's up?"

"Are you anywhere near the city yet?"

"Just coming into it now."

"Good. Look, this might be short notice, but I think we can do better than that schedule you talked about. I'm going to give you a number for somebody there—a business associate of my company. His name's Don. Call him right away. He'll tell you what it's all about. If you move fast, we might be able to swing something your time tonight."

They pulled off and stopped in a side street. Cade called the number. Don was with a shipping office at El Alto Airport, a few miles from the city, that handled local dealings for Baxter's business. He arranged to meet Cade and Hudro in town within the hour.

The general manager of the telephone company called the chief inspector back. "Okay, I have it. Her name is Carla Mayangua. She is one of our area service technicians." He gave a description of the van and its license number.

The chief inspector wrote down the details and passed the slip to his assistant. "Get a call put out to all units to look out for this vehicle. It is believed to be in the possession of a woman and man who go as Evita and Miguel, harboring two fugitives who are wanted for questioning: Roland Cade, alias Professor Arthur Wintner, an American, and Gessar Hudro, a Hyadean military officer who has gone missing. The occupants are to be apprehended immediately. Have any units sighting them call for full backup."

Evita and Miguel dropped the two off at a sidewalk cafe along El Prado, where Don had arranged to meet them—he said that Hyadeans were becoming a familiar enough sight in the capital. Don was already waiting at a corner table inside, sipping a Cinzano. He was small and dapper in a dark business suit, with a white handkerchief folded in the breast pocket, and a pencil-line mustache. Cade ordered coffee; Hudro, a Coke. Don's manner was nervous and fastidious. After preliminaries, he began, "Baxter's company imports agricultural machinery."

"I know," Cade said. "We met at a party I held about a month ago—"

Don held up a hand. "Please, it is best if I don't know your backgrounds." Cade nodded for him to continue. "Currently, he is experimenting with fitting his machines with Hyadean low-level Artificial Intelligence control units so they will be able to operate semiautonomously. The units come in at Xuchimbo, and we ship them out from here. Briefly, we have a consignment going out tonight to Auckland via Papeete, in Tahiti. I can get you listed as a Hyadean technical adviser traveling out there to instruct on the equipment, and Mr. Cade as a member of the flight crew. The controls are not strict for people leaving Bolivia. It's the contents of the shipments that they check. They're worried about Hyadean weapons and munitions getting out of the country."

"What about entry to New Zealand?" Cade queried.

"Neville knows people at the Immigration Department. You'll be brought in as political refugees. Low-key, no questions."

Cade recalled what Marie had said about AANS support being widespread, and how they had obtained false papers before traveling to St. Louis. He turned his head toward Hudro in an unspoken question, but there was really nothing to deliberate. At that moment, the wail came of approaching sirens. Traffic on El Prado pulled sluggishly aside as two police cars sped past with lights flashing and turned the block. More sounded distantly, coming from the other direction. Evidently, whatever was going on was quite close.

Don turned his head back and licked his lips. "Something's happening. Maybe it would be better if you lie low in the city for the afternoon. I know somebody who has an apartment you can use. When it gets dark, we'll send a car to bring you to the airport."

Cade looked at Hudro again. This wasn't something for them to judge. "How do we get there?" Cade asked Don.

"I'll take you now. It's not very far, but uphill. Everywhere from here in La Paz is uphill."

"Yes, we heard." Cade looked around. "First, we need to say goodbye to the people who brought us. Can we call them?" Don signaled a waiter and asked for a table phone.

"Maybe see Australia after all very soon now," Hudro said.

"One day at a time," Cade told him. Just one agonizing afternoon to get through. Then they might be finally out of it.

The phone arrived. Cade called the van, while Don sat back to sip his drink. The phone seemed to ring for an unnaturally long time. Then Evita's voice said, "Hello?"

"It's us," Cade said. "Okay, we're done. I guess we can—"

"Hello?" Evita said again.

"Can you hear me?"

"Yes, I hear."

Only then did Cade register the fear in her voice. "Is everything okay? You—"

"*No! Not okay. You must—*" There was what sounded like a slap, followed by a cry of pain. Cade stared at the phone in his hand, for an instant mystified, and then horrified.

"What's up?" Don demanded.

Cade turned the phone off and stood up suddenly. "Move!" he snapped. "We have to get out of here!"

Don fished a key from a niche above the door, let them in and then left, saying he would be back later. The apartment was small, plain, modestly furnished, but clean. A man's coats hung on hooks inside the front door, and a couple of soccer posters brightened the kitchen, along with a corkboard showing postcards, local business cards, and family snaps. A corner of the bedroom had been made into a religious shrine with a Sacred Heart statue, flowers, and a candle in a red glass. Cade and Hudro ate a lunch of tortillas and rice that they had picked up on the way, and settled down to wait.

"So how might it affect things for tonight?" Cade asked. They had agreed that what he heard over the phone could only mean that Evita and Miguel had been picked up. Cade still hadn't recovered from the shock of realizing that they themselves must have escaped by mere minutes.

"Is likely they are watching everything at airport," Hudro replied.

"How would they know anything about the airport?"

"Don't have to. They suspect everywhere. Is way police mind works. We just have to wait if plans changed now. Is not our thing to control anymore."

They turned on the news. In the former U.S., the provocations and responses by both sides had escalated to open belligerency. Twenty years ago it wouldn't have been possible. Incredulous, Cade watched Union fighter-bombers attacking bases, rail centers, and highway interchanges in Texas, Colorado, and Utah, apparently to slow communications to what looked like becoming a war front. The situation was confused, and the commentator couldn't make much sense of it. No city areas had been targeted as yet, but tensions and frustrations that had built up over years were suddenly being released, and things could heat up rapidly. Hudro was apprehensive of the effects if Hyadean weaponry were introduced on any significant scale. "So far we only use people-control tactics here," he told Cade. "Police action. You haven't seen what Hyadean war weapons do."

"What if Asia comes in and backs the Federation?" Cade asked.

"Then Asia is finished too."

"That would be practically an all-out planetary war."

"Is not first time. Hyadeans call it imposing the peace. Their way of peace. So you learn order and civilization, and everyone is happy and grateful."

"Unless Earth turns into another Querl," Cade mused. He found he didn't particularly like the image of passive submission.

"Not happen, Mr. Cade. Earth doesn't have Querl army and weapons."

They watched the lights going on across the canyon slopes as day darkened into evening. The phone rang, persisted for a while, but they left it alone. Don returned about thirty minutes later.

"We have to change the plan," he said. "Every Hyadean inside the airport is being checked. But we're going to try something that maybe nobody expects." That was all he would tell them.

He led them back downstairs, where they found a small Fiat waiting with a figure in the driver's seat. Cade and Don got in the back, and Hudro squeezed his bulk into the passenger side in front. The driver had a floppy hat, hooded zipper jacket over a sweater, and features impossible to make out in the darkness. He pulled away in silence and drove up from the city. When they came out onto the plateau he doused the headlights, and for the next half hour they picked their way carefully along roads and tracks, sometimes at little more than walking pace, with Don getting out twice to guide them through a difficult spot with a flashlamp. This brought them onto a dirt track following a chain-link fence with orange and blue runway lights beyond on one side, and knee-high grass on the other. The airport terminal facilities, outlined dimly in a halo of glows, were visible maybe a mile away to the right. After a few hundred yards, they came to a tube-frame gate. Don got out and stood scanning the area for several seconds. Then he walked up to the gate, tried it, then turned and waved his arm. Hudro and Cade got out with muttered thanks to the driver and hurried forward, while the car backed away among some rocks and scrub. The gate had been left unlocked. Don ushered them through, closed the gate carefully behind, and motioned them forward through the grass, checking from side to side at intervals to keep track of their bearings. Finally, he whispered, "Here," and motioned them down. They settled into the grass to wait.

Lights appeared in the distance above, grew brighter with the sound of approaching engines, and a plane landed. Several minutes later, another moved out from the terminal, taxied up along the perimeter-way, turned onto the main runway, and took off. Soon after, another followed. Both of them halted within fifty yards of where the three figures were crouching before making their turn prior to the takeoff run. Don checked his watch in the light from his flashlamp, shielding it with a flap of his jacket. "Should be the next one now," he whispered.

The night air was clear and getting cold. There seemed to be activity at the far end of the airfield, where vehicles were moving and searchlights probing, but nothing came closer. Then the sound carried across of another jet starting up, and a low, sleek shape moved out from the terminal area. It rolled toward the perimeter about a mile away and swung around, causing its landing lights to brighten suddenly.

Cade tensed as the plane moved toward them. It had four engines slung beneath the wings, he saw as it enlarged, and the tailplane carried atop the fin. Several hundred yards away, it slowed. Cade thought he saw what looked like a light flash several times from a window of the flight deck. Don stood up, raised his flashlamp, and pressed the switch several times. The aircraft moved in front of them—a windowless cargo transport with low-slung body and tail loading doors. As it came to a halt in the gloom, Cade made out the side door already opening and its internal stairs hinging down. Cade and Hudro rose from the grass.

"Now, go!" Don brushed aside their attempts to shake hands and waved them on. At the top of the steps Cade turned to send back a salutation from the doorway, but he had already disappeared.

The convulsions had caused Miguel to bite through his tongue. Congealing blood covered the front of his bruised, naked body. Evita, her own faced swollen, lips split from the softening-up process, watched with dull horror creeping over her as he was dragged unconscious from the room.

The interrogator turned toward her. "Now, I ask you. Where did you leave the American and the Hyadean?" Evita felt dryness in her mouth. She was unable to swallow. She had heard that the best thing was to say nothing. Once you began to give a little away, there was no stopping it. The voice barked. "Where were they heading for? What was the plan to get them out of the country?" She felt herself shaking, tears running uncontrollably down her face. The interrogator's hand moved toward the box connected to the electrodes. Evita closed her eyes and began to pray.

✧   ✧   ✧

The jet lifted into a clear sky filled with stars. Minutes later, the ghostly shapes of Andes peaks were drifting by in the night below. Then they were high over Chile. The Moon appeared slowly over the horizon, and in its cold, expanding light, the dark mass of the Pacific opened out before them, extending endlessly toward the west.

CHAPTER FORTY-ONE

Dee had always been of that independent turn of mind that led her to be her own person. She didn't like others trying to program her thinking, and when it suited her, took an inner delight in shocking them by daring to be different. That was probably why, when Vrel had contacted the office not really knowing what a travel agent was but needing a guide to show some Hyadeans from the mission around the area, she had elected to take charge of the party personally; and then, when Vrel turned out to be an intriguingly different alien also in his own kind of way, probably been a little forward in propelling things toward a more personal relationship. The simple Hyadean readiness to accept words for what they meant and people for what they said had come as a welcome relief after the minefield of California dating politics that she was accustomed to, and from then on whatever friends and neighbors thought hadn't figured into it. Vrel had introduced her to Cade and his seemingly limitless list of friends who supplied, arranged, or were looking for just about anything one could name. And life had taken on a progressively more interesting slant ever since.

Then Rebecca had appeared, trying to trace Julia after being referred by a friend of Julia's former husband, and disappeared with Cade about two weeks later. Three days after that, Vrel left for St. Louis suddenly and hadn't been heard of since. There had to be some connection, but without Cade around there were few leads she could follow. Julia had professed to know nothing—and seemed curiously impersonal about it for someone in her situation, for what Dee's opinion was worth. Then, less than a week after Vrel's departure, when the whole country was in uproar over allegations of political assassination by the government, Cade and his former wife, long supposed to have become part of the past, appeared in a Hyadean news documentary, filmed in South America of all places, that exploded the official denials. In something approaching a dream state, Dee had listened to the announcement two days later that she was living in a new country. . . .

And now this.

The Residents' Committee of the condominiums where she lived on the edge of Marina Del Rey had sent maintenance staff around to tape all the windows in case of air attack, and check fire extinguishers. Other measures were spelled out in an instruction sheet that Dee had just retrieved from her mailbox: a list of first-aid and emergency supplies that everyone should acquire; the ground floor of the community block would be made into a casualty clearing station and bomb shelter; part of the parking lot was to be kept clear for emergency vehicles. Gasoline restrictions were already in effect, and coupon books were being printed to ration essential foods. A Labor Directorate had been established in Sacramento, empowered to shut down nonessential businesses and transfer labor to war-related work. She didn't know yet how her own job at the travel agent's would be affected. Guesses yesterday had been that a percentage of those in the business could expect to be assigned to other work. Vehicles and weapons assembly and munitions production were being expanded with emergency priority and already taking in drafted trainee labor. Males over eighteen were registering for the draft. There had been missile attacks on West Coast military bases and two aircraft assembly plants near Los Angeles.

Dee sat in her kitchen area drinking a coffee and blinked disbelievingly as she checked through the rest of the mail after skimming the morning's paper. These things didn't happen in the U.S.A. They happened to other people in other places that had never been quite real anyway. . . . Then she remembered that there no longer was a U.S.A. No, even though she had heard the air-raid warning sirens tested yesterday and seen the damage on last night's news, she couldn't believe it. Older folk talked about the erosion of freedoms her generation had never known, such as being able to drive coast-to-coast without having to give a reason, or not being profiled in the federal records system, and said that things had been heading this way for a long time. But all the same, Dee had grown up feeling a fond familiarity for the country she'd learned about at school with its flag and list of presidents, Fourth of July tradition, and national institutions that ranged from the Football League to the Postal Service. It *couldn't* be over. When her father died, she had taken weeks to accept it and continued seeing figures on the street that for a moment she would believe were him, telling herself there had been some huge mistake. She felt something similar now, as if suddenly she would wake up and everything would be back again the way it was supposed to be.

The door chime sounded from the hall. Dee got up, went out, and peered through the spy hole in the door. It was Mike Blair from the Hyadean mission.

"Hi," he greeted as she let him in and led the way back to the kitchen. "I probably should have called first. Have you got a minute?"

"Sure." Dee gestured toward the newspaper and mail scattered over the table. "I can't believe all this, Mike. Tell me it isn't real."

"I know. I've got the same problem. We don't do this to each other because someone tells us to. That's what people in other countries do." He spread his hands. "But what else do you do when the other guys are coming over here with bombs? And the crazy part about it all is that they probably think exactly the same about us."

"Can I fix you a coffee or something?"

"Thanks, no. I'm in a rush."

"So what gives?"

"I talked to Wyvex earlier today. And guess what. He got a call from Vrel. Vrel's okay!"

"*What?!*" Dee stared disbelievingly. "*Really?!*"

Blair grinned and nodded. "I just told you—really."

Dee threw her arms around Blair's neck, and kissed him on the side of his face. "So what happened? Where is he? What's going on? Did Wyvex say when he's coming back?"

"South America someplace. It sounds as if he's with some kind of Hyadean news outfit. They're making sure they've got clearance into the Federation. It could be in the next day or two."

"Terrific!" Dee sat down and looked around ecstatically. She was still having trouble absorbing it. "News team? You mean the ones who made that documentary? So are Roland and his ex coming too?" Blair became solemn and shook his head. "What's up?" Dee asked.

"Marie's there, but Roland isn't. It seems they were in a chopper that got shot down. It's . . . bad news, I'm afraid."

"Oh." Dee's jubilation died abruptly.

"Someone needs to break it to Julia before they get here. I told Wyvex I'd take care of it. I'm on my way over to the house now."

"I'll come with you," Dee said.

Blair arrived with Dee at Newport Beach a little under an hour later. En route he had received a further call from Wyvex, saying that Vrel and the others hoped to arrive the following day. Julia and Luke were both at home, and Blair broke the news to both of them together. Julia received it stoically. "I see," was her rejoinder. "How certain are they of this?"

Blair could only shake his head. "I don't know if Wyvex knew any more than he said. I didn't press him for details. As far as he knew, Marie and the Hyadean girl were the only two survivors."

"So there weren't any actual witnesses."

"Not as far as I could gather, no."

"I'm so sorry," was all Dee could say, again.

Luke had been watching Julia's face long and thoughtfully throughout. He said nothing.

A half hour after Blair and Dee left, Julia told Luke that she had some errands to run and left in her cream-colored Cadillac. Two miles from the house, she pulled into a parking area and used the phone that she carried in her purse to call the ISS unit that she reported to under the field name Arcadia. The phone was a special-issue model and connected directly on an encrypted channel. The duty controller took down the details and advised Arcadia to expect further instructions later. He then relayed the information immediately to Kurt Drisson, as per standing orders. Within minutes, Drisson was through to Casper Toddrel, still in Washington, at that moment in an office of the Senate Building, sorting through notes he had made during meetings that morning. Toddrel found a more private room, and Drisson related what he had just learned. For once, it seemed that the intelligence services had better information than Cade's friends did.

"Obviously, these people in Los Angeles don't know about Cade and the Hyadean defector," Toddrel said.

"Check."

They had been tracked to La Paz following a lead from an informer, and then missed by a matter of minutes. An agent at El Alto Airport had picked up something about two illegals being smuggled out somewhere but hadn't been able to fix the destination. Now it seemed clear.

"What's your assessment?" Toddrel asked.

"If the bunch who skipped in Brazil are heading for Quito, that's where Cade and the Hyadean were heading," Drisson replied. "They're all going to meet up there, then fly up to LA together."

"That's the way I'd be inclined to see it too," Toddrel agreed. "But why wouldn't they mention Cade and the Hyadean to the people in Los Angeles?"

"If they're not all in Quito yet, it would be premature to presume it. . . . Or maybe they just didn't want to talk too much about their movements."

It sounded probable. "And then we'll have all our

problems together—in one place," Toddrel said. The implication was clear.

"Mmm . . . It would be difficult to arrange an incident there, in Quito, with the time scale we've got," Drisson said. "We don't have readily available operatives there."

"I'm not sure I'd want that in any case," Toddrel told him. "Ecuador is trying to stay out of things politically. We don't want to risk any embarrassments there. Wait until they get to California. With the current situation, anyone could be suspected. You could use Arcadia. She's right there, on the spot. Then pull her out immediately afterward." Toddrel quite liked that idea. It seemed poetic. Keeping her there had been a risky decision. Maybe it could pay a dividend now.

"I'll get on it right away," Drisson promised.

Late that night, a message appeared in Julia's phone via its special channel, giving a number and instructions to ask for "Laredo." She called the number, and shortly afterward drove out through roads busy with military traffic to a rendezvous not far from LAX, Los Angeles International Airport. Laredo gave her a heavy black suitcase, which she stowed in the trunk of the Cadillac.

Next morning, in the residential quarters of the Hyadean mission in Lakewood, Wyvex took a call from Julia on his personal number. "Mike Blair and Dee gave me the news," she told him.

"I'm sorry it couldn't have been better about Roland," Wyvex replied.

"It's one of these things we have to learn to live with. They're due in today, right?"

"Yes. At five this afternoon."

"What's the plan? Were you planning on collecting them?"

"Yes." Wyvex hesitated, unsure of the correct Terran etiquette in view of Marie's presence. "Why? Did you want to be there?"

"I'd rather see them later. But look, I know that with the way things are, Hyadeans are trying to keep a low profile and stay out of sight. I could arrange for Luke to pick them up instead."

"Well . . . that would probably be a good idea. You're sure it's no trouble?" Wyvex said.

"Of course not," Julia told him. "No trouble at all."

CHAPTER FORTY-TWO

Between quitting the Navy and running into Cade, Luke had been a professional bodyguard and security consultant. That meant he was suspicious of anything that didn't quite feel right. The seeming matter-of-factness with which Julia had accepted Cade's disappearance, and the little inclination she had shown to try locating or contacting him since had seemed unusual even before Cade's call warning that Julia might not be what she appeared to be.

What did it mean?

Because she'd been installed into Cade's life around a year ago after a romance that had bloomed too smoothly and easily, a clear possibility was that she had been planted. With Cade commanding a growing social circle of influential Hyadeans and Terrans who did business with them, and then having a former wife connected with CounterAction, it was the kind of thing they should have expected. And then the broadcast had told of his almost being killed after going off with Rebecca, who had been introduced by Julia. It reeked of "setup."

Midway through the day that the flight bringing Vrel and the others from Quito was due to arrive, Julia asked Luke to have the limo ready to collect Wyvex and Dee from the mission and then go on to LAX to meet them. She explained that it would avoid the Hyadeans having to venture out in public at a time when hostility was being shown from some quarters.

Luke would normally not have thought twice about it, but the present circumstances caused him to question everything. Why was Julia showing such concern, when nobody from the household would be among the expected arrivals? It felt odd. Had the Hyadeans asked her to arrange for the party to be collected? Luke called Wyvex to check. No, Wyvex said. Julia had called him to suggest it. Even odder. If it were merely to keep the Hyadeans out of the way, why not use any of the commercial limo or shuttle companies at the airport? Why did it have to be *this* limo? His suspicions fully aroused, Luke went out to the garage and checked over it from end to end. And concealed in a cardboard carton in the trunk, he found a heavy black suitcase that shouldn't have been there. He took it out and stood it out of view between the wall and the rear of Julia's Cadillac. By now it was almost three in the afternoon. Luke went out the back of the garage, across the rear yard to the dock, and boarded the yacht. Warren Edmonds, the *Sassy Lady's* skipper, was in the main cabin, taking in a movie with Charles, the boat's cook. "Warren, I need to talk to you," Luke said. They went out onto the foredeck, Luke closing the door behind them.

"What's up?" Warren asked.

"I'll explain it all later—I have to leave for the airport in a few minutes. But there's a black suitcase by the wall in the garage. I think it might be a bomb."

"*Jesus*, you're joking! Where—"

"I said, later. What I want you to do is pick it up after I'm gone, take it out over the water in one of the dinghies, and drop it down on the end of a line. It's just a precaution." Luke looked around and lowered his voice. "Look, I haven't told anyone this, but Roland is okay."

"*What?!*"

"He called me a couple of days ago. I'm not sure, but I think he might be arriving this afternoon with the others. If so, then we'll be able to straighten everything out after he gets here. You mustn't mention anything to Julia about this. But in the meantime, just to be safe, I want that thing out of the way."

Warren nodded. "Okay, Luke. If you say so."

Julia finished packing the black leather pilot bag and set it alongside the garment bag, red suitcase, cosmetic bag, and shoulder purse on the bed. She made a final check through the drawers of the vanity and added a few final items to the blue carryall containing her jewelry boxes, personal papers, and some casual clothes and shoes. Then she moved to the window, which overlooked the rear of the house, and peered past the drapes. Luke was just coming down the steps from the yacht. He crossed the rear yard and disappeared from sight into the door at the back of the garage. Julia went from the bedroom to the far side of the suite, where the window commanded a view of the front. A minute or two later, the limo backed out of the garage, turned in the circle at the top of the driveway, and left. Julia went back to the bedroom, picked up two of the bags, and carried them down through the house. "Henry," she called out as she approached the door into the garage. "Are you anywhere around, Henry?" He appeared as Julia put the bags down behind the Cadillac.

"Yes, ma'am?" His face registered surprise.

"Something has come up suddenly. I have to make a trip. There are some more bags on the bed upstairs. Fetch them for me and load them, would you, while I collect some other things?"

"Er . . ." Henry waved a hand undecidedly and looked perplexed. He seemed far from happy, as if some explanation were called for, yet at the same time conscious of his station.

"It doesn't *matter* why, Henry," Julia said sharply. "I do not have to justify myself to you. Just kindly do as I ask, please."

"Yes. . . . Yes, of course." Henry turned and went back into the house.

Julia followed, going to the den, where she retrieved the briefcase and book bag that she had previously filled with documents and files from her own drawers. She took them through to the garage along with her laptop, placing them by the bags that she had left previously just as Henry came back with three from upstairs. He was agitated and unsure, depositing the bags with the others and departing, as if to spend as little time around her as possible. As Henry was about to leave, Warren Edmonds came in through the door from the rear yard. He stopped, seemingly confused.

"Ah . . . has anyone seen Luke?" he asked. It sounded like an excuse. Evidently, he hadn't expected to find Julia and Henry here.

"He's just gone," Henry said from the doorway. "Picking up Vrel and the rest at the airport, remember?"

"Oh . . . right." Warren gazed around the garage as if reluctant to leave.

"He'll be back in a few hours. Was there something else?" Julia said impatiently.

"Er, no. . . . No, I guess not. Okay." Warren turned and went back the way he had come. Henry exited into the house. Julia went through to the front hall to sort coats and jackets from the closet. By the time she returned to the garage, Henry was back and had just lifted the last of the bags into the trunk. Julia opened the driver's door, threw the coats onto the back seat, prepared to get in, then saw that Henry was watching her strangely. Something needed to be said. It didn't matter what. Five minutes more and she would be out of this place permanently. "I told you, something unexpected has come up," Julia told him. "I'll be back in a day or two." Henry nodded but didn't look as if he believed her. She climbed in, started the motor, and backed the car out.

As she came onto the freeway, Julia called her ISS control unit and left a message that said, "Arcadia checking in. Rooster is on schedule. Gamecock. Surfing." The code words meant that Luke had left on time, the device was planted, and she was on her way out.

A couple of miles farther south, she pulled into a service area to fill up with gas. She decided it would be a good time to eat too, rather than stop again later. On her way into the coffee shop by the gas station, she threw her regular domestic phone into the trash bin by the door. That part of her life was over now.

Warren found Henry in the kitchen, doing something with the program of the autochef. Henry was looking worried, but Warren was too flustered to notice. "Henry, drop that and come this way. I've got a problem." Warren led the way back through to the garage, then waved a hand around. "There's supposed to be a black suitcase here somewhere. I've looked all over. You were in here a few minutes ago. Have you seen it?"

"I loaded all the bags into the Cadillac," Henry said. "Julia's orders."

Warren looked around, as if noticing for the first time that it was gone. "Where'd she go?"

"I don't know. She didn't say. But she was acting strange. Packed. Gone. I don't know what it's all about."

Impossible thoughts raced through Warren's mind. "*All* the bags?" he repeated.

"That's what she said. The mood she was in, I wasn't asking questions. Why? Is something wrong?"

Warren thought frantically, then went out into the yard and called Luke's number from his pocket phone. "Hello?" Luke's voice answered.

"Luke, it's Warren. We may have trouble. There isn't any black suitcase in the garage. Henry says he put it in the Cadillac with a bunch of other stuff of Julia's that he just loaded. She's gone."

"Gone? Where to?"

"We don't know. She's blown. Taken off. She was set to go right after you left. Henry says she was acting strange." Warren paused, but there was no immediate response. "What does it mean?" he asked finally. The silence persisted for a long time, as if Luke were wrestling with all manner of imponderables. "Luke?" Warren prompted.

"Don't worry about it," Luke's voice said at last. "Just leave everything to me."

CHAPTER FORTY-THREE

It was different from the last time he had looked down over Los Angeles from an incoming flight, Vrel reflected. Then, he had been traveling on official business for the Hyadean authorities, returning to their West Coast office of the United States. This time he was a renegade seeking asylum at an unofficial enterprise in a new, rebellious Federation gearing up for war. He really had no comprehension of the political and economic tangles that had led up to it, he realized. Perhaps he was still only at the beginnings of understanding anything about Earth and its squabbling, disorganized, variously colored natives.

In the window seat next to Vrel in the First Class section, Luodine stared out, looking for signs of the war. After her experiences in Brazil, she hadn't been sure what to expect, but Los Angeles still looked very much the way it had when she last visited. They had been fortunate in getting a flight into the Federation at all. Many airlines had suspended operations because of the military risks. The morning had seen a major attack by air-launched missiles on the naval installations in San Diego, farther south, which the Federation had taken over. Also, Union aircraft had been allowed across Mexican air space to lay mines and other underwater devices at points along the West Coast. The Federation was reinforcing its southern border. Luodine looked to the future with a mixture of excitement that the big story she had been working toward was about to break here, and trepidation as to what it might entail.

In the row in front, Nyarl was despondent that at the end of it all, nothing they did would have any measurable impact on Chryse. The control over what Hyadeans were told was too effective. What had Luodine and he been thinking to imagine they could change it? They had become too distracted by what they had seen on Earth, and then in their minds projected it into Chryse. But Chryse was not Earth. The flyer had given them a direct connection to Chryse before they had to leave it at Quito. The documentary that they made at Tevlak's had not been aired there. The director of the agency that Luodine and Nyarl represented had balked when he saw it and requested guidance from the authorities. That meant it never would get aired. Oh yes, Luodine would get her story here. And nobody would ever get to see it.

Across the aisle, Yassem and Marie sat together, saying little. Each, in her own way and for her own reasons, had imagined that if this journey ever took place it would mark the beginnings of a new life. Hopes for that were now gone, and both of them faced a life that opened up to a long prospect of uncertainty leading nowhere.

The plane landed and taxied to the terminal.

Military vehicles and personnel were scattered along
the airport perimeter, where work crews were constructing antiaircraft defenses and dispersal bays, and
digging slit trenches. There were fewer civil aircraft
than had been normal for LAX, although many
painted olive drab or camouflage. An official from the
newly inaugurated Federation immigration office met
them as they deplaned and took them through arrival
formalities in a secluded area, away from the public
facilities. Wyvex and Dee were already waiting beyond.
Police escorted the group out through one end of the
regular Baggage Claim level to the pickup zone, where
Luke was waiting with Cade's maroon limo. They
climbed aboard amid an arriving military unit jostling
to sort out packs and kit bags on the sidewalk.

Inside, Vrel and Dee hugged warmly, but then Dee
put a restraining hand on his arm and eased him away.
Vrel frowned at her, puzzled. She moved her eyes in
Marie and Yassem's direction. Vrel returned a faint
nod that he understood, at the same time reproaching himself for needing reminding.

Introductions were completed as the limo pulled
out into the traffic. Wyvex and Dee already knew
Marie's face from the documentary she had made with
Cade. Vrel indicated the front, where Luke had left
the limo's privacy screen down. "And that's Luke, who
was Roland's right-hand man, I think you say." Luke's
eyes left the road for a moment to glance into the
mirror showing the rear compartment.

"Luke, hello," Yassem said. The eyes found the
mirror again, and Luke nodded in acknowledgment.

"Hi, Luke," Marie said. "It's been a long time."

"You're right about that. So how was China?"

"Oh, I didn't know you already knew each other,"
Vrel said.

"Maybe we never really did," Marie told him. She

looked toward the back of Luke's head again. "It feels as if it's all my fault, Luke. I'm sorry I didn't bring him back. . . . Things could have been so different. One day I'll tell you the whole story."

Luke didn't reply. Marie was hoping to begin building a bridge between them to close a gap that had existed in the past. His failure to respond struck her as strangely insensitive, even for Luke.

The gray Dodge following several cars behind had pulled out from the sidewalk parking strip opposite as the limo left the baggage claim pickup area. With the intervening traffic and melee of soldiers, Laredo hadn't been able to positively identify all of the expected arrivals. But the importance of carrying through the mission there—before any of them had an opportunity to meet people from the media or Federation government—had been stressed, and in his judgment that didn't constitute sufficient grounds to reconsider. He slid the detonator control out from the map receptacle under the armrest and flipped the primer switch to the ARMED position. An amber light came on to confirm.

Luke put the phone back in the holder on the limo's dash panel. Still no answer. He wasn't sure why, since there was hardly any reason to feel sentimental, but he had been trying to raise Julia ever since Warren's call. It hadn't required an effort of genius to fit the pieces together. If Julia had played her hand and gone, then nothing Luke said could make any difference now. He chewed on his lip as he drove, trying to decide if he should tell them.

" . . . the Midwest states might be about to come over," Wyvex was saying behind. "But the East is pushing solidly into Texas. Everything's confused."

"Might Hyadeans be getting ready to play a bigger part?" Luodine asked in a worried voice.

"Nobody knows."

"We heard there's been a lot of air fighting," Nyarl said.

"Especially in the center, yes," Wyvex confirmed. "We've had raids here too. NATO is mobilizing in Europe."

Marie was being very quiet. Luke glanced in the mirror again. She was still watching him, her face showing hurt and confusion, on the verge of fighting back tears. Drawing a long breath, he turned his head to call over his shoulder. "Hey, everyone back there . . ." His tone brought immediate quiet. "There's something you all ought to know." They waited. "Roland and Hudro are both okay. They made it through the crash. The MOPAN got them to Bolivia. Roland called me from there a couple of days ago. There were reasons to keep it quiet. He was talking about trying to get back via New Zealand. I thought he might have changed his plans and met up with you people somehow."

The traffic on I-405 south was noticeably thinner due to the gasoline restrictions. Laredo moved out a lane and accelerated gently past the limo. He watched in his mirror as it fell back a comfortable distance behind, then released the safety latch over the FIRE button. A red warning light confirmed that the circuit was active. He kept the Dodge well ahead and waited for a clear stretch in the traffic pattern.

Marie and Yassem were hugging each other in delight, Yassem smiling and trying to suppress a compulsion to laugh at the same time, Marie openly weeping. Vrel was speechless; Dee flung her arms around his neck. Luodine and Nyarl were grinning and smacking palms together in the way they had picked up from Terrans.

"You mean we can call them?" Marie said, finally managing to speak coherently.

"I don't have the number here," Luke answered from the front. "But sure, as soon as we get back to the house."

"But . . . why couldn't you have told us?" Wyvex stammered.

"I said, there were reasons," Luke replied. "But they don't matter anymore."

Laredo pressed the FIRE button. A green light indicated positive function. Yet nothing had happened. The limo was still there in his mirror, a couple of hundred yards back in a gap behind a truck and a Chevrolet sitting close together. He shook his head bemusedly and pressed the button again.

Nothing happened.

Thirty miles farther south, traffic braked and swerved wildly to avoid the remains and falling debris of what, a few seconds before, had been a cream Cadillac moving fast in the direction of San Diego and the border.

In the trash bin outside the coffee shop by the gas station, the phone rang again for a while, then fell silent.

Back in the limo, Luke replaced the phone for what he decided was the last time. He had done all anybody could do, he told himself.

CHAPTER FORTY-FOUR

After a scheduled stop in Tahiti, Cade and Hudro arrived in Auckland without further incident. Neville Baxter, jovial as ever, met them personally with several other people from his company to make sure there was no hitch with the arrangement for them to enter the country as political refugees. They were granted temporary visas, and then Baxter took them to an apartment in Auckland that he had procured and placed at their disposal, recommending that they rest, relax for a few days, and adjust to the world as seen from the other side. After that, they could consider their options.

The first thing Cade did was call Luke in California to let him know that he and Hudro were safe. It turned out that Luke had some news for him too. "Vrel and those two Hyadeans that made the movie, they're here. They arrived yesterday on a regular flight from Ecuador."

"Hey, that's great!" Cade exclaimed. He looked up. Hudro was staring at him from the far side of the room. "Vrel and Luodine and Nyarl are okay. They're in California."

"Yes, I heard." Hudro got up and came across.

"That's not all," Luke said from the screen. "Are you ready for this? You guys weren't the only ones to make it out of that chopper crash. Marie's here too—a bit thinner than when I last knew her, but looking pretty good." Hudro gripped Cade's shoulder as he looked past him, squeezing hard enough to make him wince.

"I'm happy for you, Roland," he murmured.

Luke went on, "And the Hyadean girl is with her, Yassem. She's the one who got out with that other guy there, yes?"

"*Yeaaah!*" Cade exulted. He held out a palm. Hudro gripped it. They squeezed and shook deliriously, both unable to find words. Eventually, Cade looked back at the phone and managed, "But they don't know about us yet, right? You're still having to clam up because of Julia."

"Oh, they know," Luke replied. "The Julia problem kind of solved itself. It's complicated. She's history. Mind if I wait on that till you get back?"

Cade had suddenly decided that Julia's story could wait anyway. "They know?" he repeated. "So is Marie there at the house? Can I talk to her?"

"Sure." Luke's head turned away as he called offscreen. "Hey, Henry. You wanna go tell Marie she won't believe who's on the line here? And you'd better check around and see if you can find Yassem while you're at it."

The next day, Cade contacted Krossig at the Hyadean scientific center for fieldwork that he had gone to in northeast Australia. Naturally, Krossig had also seen the documentary that Cade, Marie, and the others had made in South America. "So where are you calling from now?" he asked.

"You won't believe it."

"Mr. Cade, if you told me it was from the far side of the Moon, I would believe it."

"I'm a lot closer to you now, as a matter of fact— in New Zealand."

"Ah, that means you must be with that man, what was his name . . . ?" Krossig probably asked his veebee, "Neville Baxter."

"Fast, Krossig," Cade complimented. "But there's more. Look, I have another Hyadean with me. You probably won't know him. His name's Hudro. To cut a long story short, he needs a new start in another part of the planet. I thought that Hyadean group that you're with there might be able to take him in—at least for a while."

They talked for a little longer, Cade giving the gist of how they had ended up in New Zealand.

"I'll make inquiries," Krossig promised.

Two days went by, during which the news brought reports of growing turmoil in America. Hyadean ground forces, apparently from several ships of reinforcements that had recently arrived in orbit, were occupying the Panama Canal Zone, which was generally interpreted as presaging operations in the Pacific. Already, there was talk of Asians "defending" Hawaii, which everyone understood meant securing trans-Pacific supply routes. The Hyadean move also prepared for the possible arrival of Globalist forces from South America in Mexico. The Mexican response was an outbreak of insurrection by a movement that had obviously been organizing for some time, no doubt linked to MOPAN, opposing the government's Globalist supportive policy.

The Dakotas, Minnesota, and Wisconsin joined the Federation, anchoring its northern frontier solidly along the Great Lakes. Washington was making accusations of Canadian railroads moving Federation supplies inland from Vancouver and through the Rockies. Significantly, perhaps, Canada had refused overflight permission to the Union. In the southern sector, the Unionist drive into Texas was continuing, with ground forces now coming into contact, maneuvering for positions, and with actual outbreaks of skirmishing in places. Cade watched shots of tanks with familiar white star markings firing on positions a few miles west of Fort Worth. If he hadn't seen it with his own eyes, he would have said it was impossible.

Then Krossig called back. Yes, indeed, his superiors at the Hyadean field center would be extremely interested in meeting Cade and Hudro. Arrangements would be made to receive them as soon as they wished.

And so, just five days after their arrival in New Zealand, Cade and Hudro bade Neville Baxter farewell before boarding a New Zealand Air Force jet transport bound directly for Cairns, on the Queensland coast.

While Cade and Hudro were looking out over the sunlit blue of the Tasman Sea, it was a close, muggy evening in New York. There had been air-raid alerts, fire drills in offices and schools, and a lot of merchandise moved to safes and basements, but nothing had come of it.

Drisson met Laura for dinner in an out-of-the way but highly rated Greek restaurant frequented by gourmet aficionados on the East Side above 70th Street between Second Avenue and the river. He had decided that some investment in up-market taste could be justified in this instance. They got around to business after the appetizers and salad, and a second choice of wines to suit the entrées.

"People in my line of work don't trade social niceties," he said. "That way, we save time and avoid misunderstandings. You and I are both in situations where we know things about Toddrel that he wouldn't have wanted his mother to know. You keep him happy at playtime and know how he really does business. I know what happens to people who get in his way. It isn't pretty." He paused for a reaction. Laura continued watching him silently over her glass as she sipped. Drisson went on, "His South American operation has backfired, which put him right next to the big fan when the secession hit. When people like Casper are in trouble, life for everyone around them tends to get insecure."

Laura looked mildly reproaching. "You're not trying to tell me I could be in some kind of danger, surely?"

"I think you should be certain you know the person you're dealing with." Drisson studied her for a second or two, as if weighing whether to elaborate. "He had a wife once. I assume you know that."

"She drowned in a boating accident seven years ago."

"Right. They were heading for a divorce that was going to be bloody. She knew a lot about him that he wouldn't have wanted to see in the papers, and she meant to use all of it." Drisson shook his head. "It wasn't an accident."

"How do you know this?"

"I told you, my job is to know things."

Laura's expression registered the more serious dimension that this was taking on. "What are you asking me to do?" she asked warily.

"I'm suggesting that you change your insurance. Or at least, take out extra cover."

"Which your company, of course, happens to deal in."

"Very professional and experienced. Long established in the business."

"Why? What's in it for you? It sounds as if you can take care of yourself."

"Information. Access. If it ever comes time to claim on the policy, it can work a lot smoother with help on the inside." Drisson indicated her with an extended hand. "Like I said before, separate, we're both vulnerable. Working together, we could look out for each other pretty good."

Laura's gaze flickered over him, reading the face and the eyes, comparing their message with that of the words. If things really could get that ugly, it was beginning to sound as if she might need this person around. But then she would end up in an even stronger position of knowing enough to compromise him if events took such a direction, and she felt so inclined. And he had already shown how much he believed in taking precautions. She was going to have to play this carefully, she decided. Very carefully.

CHAPTER FORTY-FIVE

The group waiting to greet Cade and Hudro at Cairns, which boasted a modestly sized airport in spite of its billing as "international," consisted of Krossig; his Hyadean boss, Freem; and an Australian biologist by the name of Susan Gray, who worked with them. With them, local officialdom was represented in the form of a grinning Aborigine in the full regalia of khaki shorts and a white shirt worn shirttails out, and an equally affable Asian in a casual jacket and slacks. They were called Tolly and Hueng. Both were nominally based at the local authority's offices in Townsville, two hundred miles south, which served as an outpost of the state government in Brisbane. They maintained a loose contact with the Hyadean presence in Cairns and had flown up to "coordinate" with Cade and Hudro, and make their stay comfortable.

Accommodation had been arranged in a hotel called the Babinda farther in toward the city—

although Susan was from Melbourne originally, and said that nobody in Queensland knew what a real city was. They drove there in a bright orange minibus through grassy, hilly farmland and spread-out suburbs of broad streets and modern frame buildings tucked among palm trees and stands of tropical greenery. On the way, Freem talked among other things about the inefficiency of internal combustion engines. The hydrogen atom, he explained, could be catalytically induced to assume lower energy states than the "ground" state held by Terran science to be the lowermost possible, and in the process released energies hundreds of times greater than conventional combustion. It was inherently clean, using water as a fuel and producing degenerate hydrogen as exhaust, which was totally inert and diffused up out of the atmosphere. Cade had heard this from Vrel, but he didn't want to spoil Freem's line by saying so.

"But here's an angle that these guys never thought of," Tolly said.

"I suspect we did, but it got suppressed," Krossig interjected.

Tolly continued, "Cars powered that way could run all the time without choking up the planet. So how about this: Instead of owning a big chunk of capital investment that spends most of its time depreciating in driveways and parking lots, you use a turbine driving an electric generator-motor system to make it a mobile power plant as well as a vehicle. When it isn't going anywhere, you plug it into the grid and get credited for what you deliver. Millions of people take care of their own power requirements. We reckon an average car could net the owner around ten thousand dollars per year."

Cade was intrigued. "You think something like that could happen?"

"We're working on it."

"So who would own it?"

"I don't know. Scientists from all over are working here with Hyadeans."

"Mike Blair's due to be joining us anytime," Krossig said.

Hueng, who it turned out was on some kind of loan from the Chinese government, chimed in. "The Western Federation has the right idea. This side of the world is the way of the future. The interests that the Globalists are trying to hang on to are finished. When a system has to resort to force and deception to preserve itself, you know it's only a matter of time before it collapses. I am Chinese, Mr. Cade. I know. The military empires of earlier times have passed away. The fascist and socialist political empires of the last century are gone. Now we're seeing the end of the Western- and Hyadean-style financial empires. Everybody will manage their own affairs." He grinned broadly. "So we still call it the People's Republic. It fits the reality rather well."

"Maybe Hyadeans are discovering their own version too," Krossig said. "Away from the restrictions of the system we've known."

"The same kinds of restrictions that Americans and Europeans have come to regard as normal," Susan Gray put in. She was in her thirties, Cade guessed, with neck-length blond hair, sun-bronzed and frighteningly fit looking, dressed in a tan shirt and light green jeans. "We do things kind of casually and informally around here. The region has a strong independent tradition of minding its own business and not trusting the central government. Somehow it seems to provide the right atmosphere for everyone to get along. That was a big reason why the Hyadeans stayed."

"I feel I have begun to awaken," Krossig said. "Many Hyadeans that I've met here say the same thing."

Cade stared out as they drove into the outskirts of the city. All it took was to experience what free thinking could be like. Then there was no going back. If this was what the Hyadeans who came here were finding, could exposure to Earth eventually cause their whole population to wake up?

The hotel was in the tradition of the architectural cloning which for decades had been creating airport environs and urban peripheries that were in danger of becoming indistinguishable the world over. But it was cool, clean, and comfortable. Cade and Hudro were given separate suites and then left to freshen up, change, and spend the remainder of the afternoon relaxing with beers by the pool among palm-tree-enclosed gardens at the rear.

That evening, there was a dinner in town for the occasion, hosted by Tolly and Hueng on behalf of the state and attended by Krossig, Freem, Susan, and others from the scientific center, several more Hyadeans connected with other enterprises, and a mix of a few business figures and other local notables that it seemed fitting to invite or who had otherwise wangled their way in. It was all very colorful and cheerful, especially as the drink continued to flow generously, and at midnight they called Cade's house in California, got Marie and Yassem, and toasted them over the phone. Cade promised he would be back before much longer. Hudro hadn't decided yet what his intentions were.

The late stayers then retired to a private bar. Krossig, by then well stimulated and loquacious, told Cade, Hudro, and Susan about his discovery of Asian philosophies from his dealings among some of the area's varied populace. He was particularly enthralled by the notion of reincarnation, according to which individual personalities were created for the purpose of assisting a soul on its path of development. The circumstances of each incarnation were chosen to provide the experiences and lessons that the soul needed in order to heal itself and grow. This seemed to follow so naturally from the many-worlds view of quantum reality that Krossig and Mike Blair back in California saw as a purposefully contrived learning environment in which the choices that a consciousness made created its path of experiences. Their latest thought was that despite all the things that were heard about Eastern mysticism and Western science converging toward saying the same thing, perhaps both were missing the whole point of it all equally. Krossig explained:

"Physics exposes the backstage machinery. Eastern insight says that what the machinery supports is illusion. But surely the whole purpose of it is to *experience* the illusion." The company was listening intently. "It's a bit like a physicist finally figuring out that the movie is a product of electrical patterns and photons, and the mystic observing that what they depict isn't real. But all the time, neither of them sees that the purpose of the movie was to . . ." He waved a hand about. "Whatever the movie is made for."

"Tell a story. Teach a lesson," Susan supplied. She was now transformed in a close-fitting black cocktail dress and looking devastating.

"Exactly."

Susan looked at the others. "Interesting. I've always thought of myself as a hard-boiled science type too. But you know, fellas, I like it."

"You see, it needs Hyadean and Terran brains combined," Freem said.

Hudro was enraptured. "So, is all designed for consciousnesses to make choices and learn," he said to Krossig. "What is it does the designing?"

Krossig spread his hands. "I don't know. Not my department."

Hudro turned to Cade. "Here is what I seek. Is as you say, like fresh air. We bring Yassem here. Already I think we stay in this country."

Cade looked inquiringly at Susan and Freem.

"I don't think that would be too much of a problem," Susan said. "There's a good community of Hyadeans here—all learning to be individuals. Sounds like they'd fit right in."

For the next couple of days, Cade and Hudro were given a tour of the area, particularly to see some of the ways in which Hyadeans and Terrans were working together without organizing directives from above or centralized policies favoring corporate economics. The scientific station was larger and more diverse in its activities than Cade had imagined. He toured the labs and workshops, saw prototype rigs of the catalyzed hydrogen turboelectric system that Tolly had talked about in the bus on the way from the airport, and didn't really understand a lot else. Like the mission in Los Angeles, the station had gravitic communications equipment in touch with Chryse via the orbiting Hyadean relay system, and Cade watched Terran scientists still spellbound at the thought of interacting with counterparts light-years away.

"This makes the web look like Pony Express," one of them told him.

They were from a surprisingly wide range of places and backgrounds, brought in one way or another through influences of the cosmopolitan influx of the individualist-minded from Asia, Europe, and the Americas to what had already been a mixed region. There were also a lot more Hyadeans than Cade would have expected. Freem said that most had paid their own way privately to come to Earth in search of the independent way of living they had heard of that was new to them. Krossig felt there was more going on here than just a collaborative scientific center. It could be a microcosm of how an alternative might evolve to the imposed, top-down form of organized dealings between the two races that had taken root in the West.

But there was another side that was disconcerting. "China's policy," Susan said when she and Cade were with Freem in Freem's office, next to the gravcom room. "What we think is their real aim in leading the AANS—and we've talked to Hueng about it, and he agrees. They see the lineup of Hyadean and America-Europe as an attempt to preserve a Western-dominated economic order that should have died after the twentieth century and two world wars. They made the Hyadeans a symbol for the rest of the world to rally against. Beijing seems to think that now the U.S. has broken up, it's as good as over. All it has to do is deliver a knockout blow. They're underestimating what they could be up against. We could never beat Hyadeans by taking them on in a straight fight—if it ever came to that. Hudro understands that. But there's no need to. From the things we're hearing here, they're ripe for their own form of revolution. Why confront when you can undermine? With the right strategy, we can win enough of them over that their system caves in."

Cade was both intrigued and gratified. In effect,

this was stating in other words what he himself, Vrel, Luodine, and others had also concluded. At the same time, he was mildly perplexed. "I agree with what you're saying," he told them. "But why are we going through all this? You sound as if you expect me to do something about it."

"I talked to Hueng," Freem replied. "His connections in Beijing go higher than you perhaps imagine. I'm sure he provides an efficient direct conduit back of anything of interest that goes on here." Freem held up a hand before Cade could respond, as if to say that was of no consequence. "But he also shares our concern. Naturally, he has made his superiors fully aware of the presence here of the American featured in the South American documentary, and the Hyadean officer whose story he helped narrate. Hueng put out some feelers, and it seems they would be interested in inviting you there. You have a chance to present our case maybe where it stands the most chance of having some effect."

Cade blinked. "You mean go to Beijing? Me?"

"While there's still a chance," Susan said. "You understand Hyadeans as well as anyone."

Cade didn't have to think too much about it. He was prepared for just about anything by now. "It would need Hudro there too," he told them. "The documentary wasn't only me. He'd carry a lot of weight there too."

"Then let's talk to Hudro," Freem suggested.

Hudro returned that evening from visiting an experimental school the Hyadeans had set up for teaching their way of science, which was proving to be a big hit with the local children. Cade and the other two put Hueng's proposition to him over beer and burgers in the station's canteen. "There are people in Beijing who have the power to make decisions that will affect many people, but I'm not sure they understand what a full-scale conflict might bring," Freem told him. "You are a former Hyadean military officer. Also, your experiences in South America give you insights that they do not share. If you really want to prevent what could happen, there would be your place to try."

Cade and Susan stared at each other somberly. Hudro gave Freem a long, searching look. Finally, he nodded. "Very well. I will go to Beijing with Roland and say what I know and what I think. Then I come back to you here. Yassem comes across from over ocean. Then we live here in Australia as Terrans. Is what we dream."

"That would be understood," Freem said.

CHAPTER FORTY-SIX

They stayed in Cairns a little over a week. Everything Cade saw reinforced his impression that it modeled on a small scale the way things could have been: Australian whites and blacks, Europeans, Asians, Americans, Hyadeans, working out their own ways of getting along.

Meanwhile, three Eastern Union nuclear supercarrier groups had put to sea in the Atlantic and were heading south, presumably to enter the Pacific via Cape Horn. The confrontation in Texas was heating up, with both sides using air support. Oil installations along the banks of the Houston ship canal were ablaze under artillery fire. A suburb of St. Louis had been hard hit by overshoots from an attack on an air base.

Then the formal invitation that Hueng had set up came through from Beijing. A farewell party that included Krossig, Freem, Susan, Hueng, and Tolly but

which had grown significantly from the one that had
greeted them accompanied Cade and Hudro to the
airport, where they boarded a Chinese government
executive jet sent with two officials from the Department of Foreign Affairs to collect them. The flight
north lasted six hours and brought them to Beijing's
International Airport, ten miles south of the city
center. A white limousine flying the new pennant of
the Democratic Republic of China from its hood,
preceded by a police escort that seemed to delight
in using its siren and lights to clear regular traffic
grudgingly out of the way, conveyed them to the
seventeen-story Beijing Hotel on Wangfujing Avenue,
the busiest of Beijing's shopping streets, marking the
eastern edge of the old Imperial City.

The atmosphere was very different from the colorful, provincial informality of Cairns. Even with the
time together through the plane trip, the two officials who accompanied them seemed stiff and formal
after the easygoing smiles of Tolly and Hueng. The
talk was of things hypothetical and impersonal, gran-
diose schemes for the future, and how people would
need to adapt and be educated to play their part—
not of people simply allowing life itself to determine
whatever kind of scheme took shape.

The same mood set the tone of the obligatory
dinner that was given later in one of the hotel's private
rooms. Cade had the feeling that in addition to paying
the requisite courtesies, it was designed to send a
political message. The ranks and numbers of the
guests seemed calculated to convey that Cade and
Hudro's presence, while acknowledged to be of interest, shouldn't be seen as carrying cosmic significance.

The speeches dwelt on political theory and abstract
ideals. China might have made heroic efforts to
change the form, but the old habits of thinking were

still there, Cade thought as he nodded, smiled, and applauded. It was still the thinking of Earth, which created vast, imaginative symphonies of fantasy setting out what ought to be, and then tried forcing reality to fit. The community that had grown at Cairns embodied, even if it probably didn't understand, what Hyadean thinking had been before opportunism took advantage of it, and conformity stifled it—the thinking that had accepted reality as it is, and pointed the way to building starships; understood it the only way it could be understood: spontaneously, by living and expressing it.

It would have been an oversimplification to say even that Asia stood for one side or the other of the tussle that was dividing Earth. Should that be resolved, then Asia itself would break up into factions, as would other alignments that seemed stable for as long as the greater common threat persisted. Cade was beginning to see Terrans from something like the perspective that he imagined Hyadeans saw them. Whether one agreed with and liked what one saw depended on where in the Hyadean social order the viewing was from. The true dividing lines were complex. There were bulky, blue-to-gray "Terrans," and there were slender pink-to-black "Hyadeans." What better words might have more accurately described which of both groups stood for what was far from obvious.

The next day, they were taken on a tour of the city by four intense young people, two men and two women, polite, impeccably groomed, dressed, and mannered, all speaking English, and two, to Hudro's surprise and commendation, ably versed in Hyadean. One couple was from the public relations office of the Department of Foreign Affairs, the other from the Central Military Directorate. Beijing had been China's capital city since its founding in the Yuan Dynasty during the thirteenth century, and the layout was still dominated by its imperial past. The city proper, as opposed to the greater metropolitan area of modern times, consisted of two distinct sections: the square Inner, or Tartar City to the north, and adjoining it to the south, the more cosmopolitan and commercial, oblong Outer, or Chinese City. The Tartar City, dating from the earliest period, had originally been enclosed by walls forty feet high, removed only during the 1950s, in the Communist period. Within its fifteen-mile perimeter, it enclosed two other nested walled cities erected during the fifteenth-century Ming Dynasty: the Imperial City, with parks, temples, secondary palaces, and residences and offices of the nation's leaders; and within that the moated Forbidden City, containing the Imperial Palace with its 9,000 chambers, as well as audience halls and terraced courtyards extending over 250 acres, now maintained as a museum. Cade and Hudro stood in reverence at the shrines and temples of wooden beams, red clay walls, and massive, yellow tiled roofs with upturned eaves; admired the broad marble steps, carved stone lions, and ceremonial gates; and walked among the gardens with their ornamental lakes. But it was all an enclosed wonderland, a preserved relic of a past that had gone. When they came back outside, the humorless office blocks of glass and concrete, and imposing government buildings with brooding stone frontages pushing their way in and joining up like a rising tide around the shrinking islands of times gone by, reminded them that the serious business of the world at large and its future set the tone and the rhythm now.

The four young guides talked eagerly about plans

for the future and a new society to be built. Yes, mistakes had been made in the past, but they had brought their lessons. In essence, the global conformity that the Hyadeans would impose on Earth if they were allowed threatened the same kind of exploitation that the West's imperialism had the century before. Eastern Asia had resisted successfully then, and it was natural and inevitable that it should form the nucleus of the resistance growing across the world today. Cade heard the total self-assurance that can come only from minds incapable of conceiving the possibility that they could be wrong. The belief that the future could be molded as desired, given determined planning, and guidance remained unquestioned. Only the plan had changed.

"You're still inventing the perfect society in your minds, then trying to figure out how to shape people to fit in with it," Cade commented to one of the young women.

"Yes. It gives purpose and requires dedication." She looked at him bright-eyed, as if waiting for a revelation. "Is there a better way?"

"Leave people the way they are, and accept whatever society comes out of it," Cade said. "Like the Hyadeans do with facts. You're making your society a theory. Just let facts and people be what they are, and lead to whatever becomes. That's the way to build starships."

But she couldn't make the connection. Her programming didn't include such a concept.

Cade and Hudro were subdued by the time they returned to the hotel. This was going to be tougher than they had thought. That evening, they dined less ostentatiously with a half dozen people from foreign affairs and military departments. Conversation focused on plying Cade and Hudro with questions about

Hyadean-Terran relations in the former U.S.A., their impressions of the guerrillas in South America, and Hudro's experiences in counterinsurgency operations. The undisguised object was to gather advance material for the more senior representatives whom they would be meeting in the morning.

The meeting was held in a large, somber room of paneled walls with portraits of mostly forgotten military and political leaders in one of the government buildings off Tiananmen Square, a couple of blocks from the hotel. There were shelves of ornately bound books that Cade could never imagine anyone opening, brown leather armchairs arranged with side tables along the sides and in the corners, and a bench seat below the end window. Cade and Hudro sat at one end of a polished table forming the centerpiece. The chairman, who had been introduced as Brigadier General Zhao Yaotung of the Army, faced them from the far end. Arranged along the two longer sides were five other principal participants and their several secretaries and translators. Two microphones on the table and a video camera commanding the table from a corner indicated that the proceedings would be recorded.

The other five were: Madame Deng Qing, an undersecretary of the Directorate; Liu Enulai, military scientific adviser; Colonel Huia Xianem, of the Air Force; Abel Imarak, an Iranian liaison officer from the Muslim side of the AANS; and Major Charles Clewes, from a Canadian military mission that was apparently visiting. The Muslim and Canadian presence was revealing. It seemed that coordination within the AANS was farther advanced than Cade had realized.

Zhao began by working through a list of questions

compiled from the things the deputies had raised the previous evening. He was heavily built with a saggy face, and spoke with a tired detachment, as if used to commanding an authority that was never questioned. His points covered tactics and logistics of the ground operations in South America, the morale of the guerrilla fighters there, their training, equipment, and attitudes toward receiving support from Asia. When the questions zeroed in on specifics of Hyadean weaponry and ways of countering it, Hudro reiterated what he had already told Cade: Although he had come to the conclusion that the Hyadean military intervention on behalf of the Globalist Coalition was wrong, he could not justify saying anything that might contribute to causing casualties or deaths among his own kind. He had left all that now, to begin a new life. Mme. Deng, sharp of face and manner, her hair tied in a bun, wearing a black skirt and jacket over a high-necked, lilac floral-pattern blouse, wanted to know, with a hint of disapproval, if that was the case, why had he come to Beijing? Because he had been asked to, Hudro said. He had accepted in the hope of finding some way to avoid escalation, not to promote it.

That seemed to open up the latent course that the meeting had been predisposed to follow. Zhao launched into a recitation that flowed smoothly and monotonously as if he had been through it many times, of why the time to strike hard and fast was precisely now. In North America, the Washington regime was still taken by surprise, its forces divided among themselves and disorganized, with reports of defections. The day before, at Amarillo, an entire Union armored brigade had come over to the Western Federation. Their drive into Texas was running down. Mexico was heading toward open civil war against cooperating, which blocked the threat of a Globalist outflanking move from the south for the time being.

Meanwhile, the Federation was solidly established across the north all the way to Lake Michigan. The underground front and irregulars that the AANS had been cultivating for years were emerging as an effective auxiliary arm of the regular forces. Alaska was pro-Federation, although formally maintaining a neutral stance, and Canada, for a long time seeking ways of easing itself from domination by Washington, was supportive. Zhao gestured across the table toward Clewes, as if by way of vindication. And on the European front, Russia had declined to follow the NATO Globalist alignment, securing Asia's position from the west. It was a time for decisiveness and vigorous action. Nothing worthwhile in history had ever been attained by half measures.

Imarak, the Iranian, took up the torch. "At this moment, China and the other Asian AANS nations have over five million men under arms. Our air forces started equipping for something like this a long time ago. Hawaii has agreed to cooperate in staging operations and is being reinforced." He looked at Zhao for a moment as if for approval to divulge further detail. The general returned a curt nod. Imarak continued, "With the transportation at our disposal right now, we can airlift five divisions with supporting armor and artillery into Mexico in ten days, followed within a month by landings to intercede in South America. With such a demonstration of support, the South American states will arise." Imarak waved a hand. "From the things you have said yourselves, the *people* are with us already! What's left? A few tottering governments that are rotten on the inside anyway. With the South gone, Canada denied, and the western two-thirds of the U.S.A. effectively part of the AANS already, the Washington-based Union reduces to an extension of the decaying remains of Europe. We can swing practically the rest of Earth behind us now. How could a few nonrepresentative states—states that do not have the support of their people—backing an alien power stand against that?"

Cade had a foreboding that they were not going to penetrate this kind of euphoria and overconfidence. "You're not allowing for the aliens," he said, nevertheless.

Liu Enulai, the scientific adviser chimed in, taking up the party line. "That is the reason why it is so important to move fast," He was lean and hollow cheeked, with close-cropped white hair and skin stretched tight over his skull, looking as if it were about to crack. "We are here *now*, already mobilizing, our weapons deployed. The Hyadeans won't have fully worked-out plans for intervention, nor any presence here, as yet, in numbers. They have large problems of logistics to deal with and vast distances to cross. But once they set a goal, they pursue it relentlessly and effectively. Therefore, delay is to our detriment and their benefit."

Cade shook his head, alarmed now at what he was hearing. "You can't take those guys on in a straight slugging match. It isn't a question of numbers. You've all been around for the last twelve years. You can figure out what they're capable of."

Hudro, beside him, was equally disturbed. "I think you underestimate," he told the company. "These weapons you see in South America are just the small-scales. Experiments, yes? Nothing crosses ocean under orbiting bombs and beam platforms to land in South America. Saturation field turns air into fire, burns whole forest. Same forces that drive Hyadean starship bend space, pile desert into mountain, collapse city block like egg shell. I have seen in Querl wars. But Querl have defenses and understand."

Clewes, the Canadian, was looking worried— understandably: His country was next door to the developing battle zone, not six thousand miles away. Huia Xianem, the Chinese Air Force colonel, who had asked Hudro a lot of questions earlier, was nodding agreement solemnly. So not everyone was being carried away.

But the cautious were evidently not the ones calling the tune. "Indeed, that's the whole point," Mme. Deng answered. "To avoid such a direct conflict. Moving quickly now will eliminate the remnant of Terran power that depends on Hyadean support. By the time the Hyadeans are in a position to deploy significant force here, any reason to use it will have gone away."

"Is reinforcements arriving already from Chryse," Hudro started to point out, but Zhao brushed it aside.

"They still think in terms of the local-scale conflicts in South America to protect their elite in their palaces there," he said. "In taking things to a planetary scale, speed and surprise will be with us."

"Do you see Hyadeans intervening actively in your country, Mr. Cade?" Imarak asked, as if that made the point.

Maybe for the same reason that there weren't any Asians either, Cade thought to himself. Yet, anyway. Surely, the spectacle of Chinese troops landing in California to fight alongside Americans against other Americans was unthinkable. But similar enough things were written all through history.

"Is fine, maybe, while East Union army is in Texas and they still hope for help through Mexico," Hudro said. "But if Union gets in trouble, yes, you likely see Hyadeans fighting there then."

Zhao seemed unmoved. "You were in California how long ago, a few weeks?" he said to Cade. "CounterAction has been operating for two years there. Did you ever see any direct involvement of Hyadeans with the federal security forces?"

"They supplied equipment, advised on training . . ."

"But were they ever involved in *action*?"

Cade could only shake his head. "No." Zhao nodded, satisfied.

"And before they have time to get involved, Washington will have fallen," Mme. Deng said. "The Hyadeans' base of political collaboration will have ceased to exist. The only option open to them then will be to renegotiate their position here on new terms." She looked from Hudro to Cade. "Our terms."

Cade looked around at their faces. Clewes, and to a lesser degree Colonel Huia, were uneasy, but they weren't in control here. The rest were committed to their course and intractable. He'd thought that he and Hudro had been brought here for the benefit of their insight and experience. But it was clear that nothing they had to contribute was going to change anything. "What do you want from us?" he asked.

"Your face is known as the American in the movie," Zhao replied. "You and your former wife . . . What happened to her, by the way?"

"She's safe—back in California," Cade said.

"Oh, really? I'm glad." Zhao gestured at Hudro. "And here is the Hyadean whose story you told. We want to use you both in the same capacity here—at this crucial moment when we are about to launch our maximum effort. Talk to the people. Endorse our cause. Tell them that we are taking back our world from the aliens . . ." His gaze shifted to Hudro. "The human aliens as well as the ones who are propping up the Globalists."

So that was it. A public-relations campaign to promote the war. Cade sat back heavily in his chair. "You seem to disapprove, Mr. Cade," Mme. Deng commented. "Do you have some alternative strategy to suggest?"

Until the day before, Cade had thought he had. Especially after Cairns, he had entertained visions of sharing his new understanding of how both races were victims of exploitive minorities who together constituted the real common enemy; how the way to defeat them was not by taking on the Hyadean army but by winning over the mass of the Hyadean people. Why confront when they could undermine? Susan Gray had said.

Although dispirited by what he had heard, now that they were here, he had to try. He spoke with as much force as he could muster about the way Earth affected Hyadeans and how it awakened them to what they believed they could have been, and perhaps once had been. The way to defeat their economic imperialism lay in that direction, Cade said. Missiles and bombs could only bring disaster. Hudro followed, citing his own and Yassem's experience. Hyadeans didn't question, he pointed out. On the one hand that made their society easier to control; but it also meant that when they finally found out that they had been lied to, the effect would be incomparably more devastating than to any population on Earth—who pretty much took it for granted anyway. What had just happened to the U.S.A. could happen a hundred times more intensely across the whole of Chryse. "As Roland says, is the way you win here," he concluded. "Is not with bombs. That way, you, your cities—all goes is destroyed."

But it fell flat. Cade had told himself that surely the Chinese, if anybody, would respond to such a philosophy. Hadn't they themselves practically invented it? Or was the notion of fomenting a "people's" rebellion now part of a past that they considered themselves to have progressed beyond? But it was clear, even while Cade and Hudro were speaking, that the listeners who mattered were impervious. The leaders they served were already committed and were not going to be budged from their course. It was equally plain that Cade and Hudro would have no heart for the role that had been planned for them, and the matter was not pursued further. Thus, the meeting ended on a note of tacit withdrawal by both sides, each acknowledging that there was nothing further of mutual interest to be discussed.

Cade spoke briefly with Clewes in a corridor downstairs as they were leaving the building. "They're taking an awful gamble. I know you know it too. If Hudro's right, it's going to be a mess. Is there nothing that can be done?"

"Believe me, I've tried," Clewes told him. "But the high command back home are as bad. They've never had war in their country. It's something that happens in other places and in movies, or in exercises where nobody gets hurt. They're still academy kids playing a game. What they're letting themselves in for is beyond their comprehension."

What was really going on came to him only later that evening, when he was sitting morosely with Hudro in the hotel bar. China was using the Hyadean presence as a justification for uniting a power bloc to end to the West's domination of the world's affairs. The Beijing leadership was set on a path that seemed to guarantee the destruction of America as a world leader and the probable demise of Europe, which would lose the Hyadeans their economic leverage.

And then what, if a stable measure of autonomy from the Hyadeans was achieved? The AANS breaking up into rivalries—China and the Arab world, maybe; perhaps a fragmented China; a revitalized Russia—all emerging to take on each other? Would there ever be an end to it? Cade watched the other bar patrons and sipped his drink. He was starting to think like Marie.

The thought of her turned his mind back to the prospect of going home—he presumed there would be little further to detain him this side of the Pacific. "Tomorrow, it will be time to start making plans again," he said to Hudro. "I guess I go back to LA from here. Then I can make arrangements for Yassem to come over. What do you think you'll do? Go back to Cairns and wait there?"

Hudro seemed to have been thinking along the same lines. He answered without needing much time to consider. "Now, I am not sure what I do. Is not right that Yassem is there and I decide here where we go. Maybe I come back with you. Then Yassem and I make plans together about what we do."

"You're serious?"

"Yes, why not? Is better idea, yes?"

Cade reached over and gripped Hudro's arm. "I think it's a lot better," he said. "Things wouldn't be the same anymore without you around, Big Guy. I'll make arrangements with the office in the morning."

CHAPTER FORTY-SEVEN

Two days later, Cade and Hudro departed China on a Federation transport flight heading for California and carrying on its wings and fuselage the new, color-reversed insignia of a dark blue, five-pointed star on a white-circle ground. Due to uncertainties resulting from Union interceptors ranging out over the Pacific from bases in northwest Mexico, the flight was routed via Fairbanks, Alaska, and then down the coast of Canada. Washington had declared a war zone extending five hundred miles off the Federation's west coast, in which all aircraft and vessels were declared to be at risk of attack. This was drawn far enough north to affect the approaches to Vancouver, exacerbating the volatile situation with Canada, already threatening to fire on further intruders into its air space. Airborne units from several South American states had landed in southern Mexico to aid government troops embroiled in the

developing civil war, and an amphibious force was being
embarked at Caracas in Venezuela. With its southern
front stabilized, the Federation had gone over to the
offensive with air attacks on Union bases and crossing
points over the Mississippi.

The airfield at Fairbanks was busy with traffic and
showed recently added antiaircraft defenses and
dugouts, still being worked on in places. A tense but
purposeful atmosphere prevailed in the terminal
building during the four-hour stopover. There were
a lot of evacuees from the fighting areas in the con-
tinental states to the south, some dispersing in Alaska,
others en route to more distant destinations in Asia.
One family that Cade talked to were from Chicago,
which had become a scene of street-to-street fighting, with the Sears Tower and other high-rise observation points heavily damaged.

Communications were restricted, with military and
official use getting priority. Apparently, there had
been much attrition of Federation-controlled satellites. The Asians were rumored to be providing
additional capacity, but so far it wasn't making up
the difference. Cade was unable to put a call through
to Marie at the house, although he did leave a
message with Wyvex at the Hyadean mission saying
they were on their way. The mission seemed to be
functioning in some kind of autonomous role, independent of the official Hyadean presence in Washington. It seemed that Orzin was in charge, but Cade
couldn't quite figure out where he stood amid the
shifting politics.

The flight down the Canadian coast passed without incident. One of the crew told Cade that the
plane was fitted with "special" equipment to confuse
the Hyadean surveillance satellites. It implied a degree
of cooperation from at least some faction of the aliens.

Interesting, he and Hudro agreed between themselves. Hudro wasn't sure what to make of it.

They landed at March Air Force Base, thirty miles east of Los Angeles, at around the middle of the day following their departure from Beijing. It presented the same scene of recently initiated defenses and protective works that Cade had seen in Bolivia and Alaska. This time, however, he was startled to see evidence of actual attacks. The hulks of about a dozen burned-out aircraft had been bulldozed off the cratered apron area, which was still being cleared and repaired. Parts of the base facilities and hangars had been destroyed, with damage extending to surrounding buildings and houses. The regular control tower was demolished, and a temporary structure erected alongside the remains, while a dispersed annex of army tents and trailers kept other essential services functioning.

A bus painted Air Force gray took the arrivals to a section of the terminal buildings that had survived, where they went through the routine of presenting papers and answering questions for a clerk completing forms at a folding table. When it came to Cade and Hudro's turn, a tall woman with black hair piled high and tied in a band detached herself from the knot of people waiting in the background and came forward. It took Cade a moment to recognize her, in the slacks and unadorned zipper jacket that she was wearing over a military-style shirt, as Clara Norburn, once the fashion-conscious, upwardly mobile star of the former state governor's office. The last time Cade saw her, she had been talking about ways of marketing California's high-tech skills profitably on Chryse for the state's benefit. She nodded to an inquiring look from the clerk processing the papers and murmured,

"Yes, these are the ones. It's been taken care of," then looked at Cade while the clerk initialed boxes and appended stamps. "Welcome back, Roland. You've been getting around. Into some trouble too, I see." Cade still had marks on his face, a remaining light dressing, and patches of regrowing stubble from the injuries he'd received in Brazil. "How is it looking?"

Cade grinned. "It's rumored that I'll live. You people haven't been exactly idle here yourselves. I leave you alone for a few weeks and look at the trouble you've gotten yourselves into already." One of the men in the group at the back was with Clara. Cade introduced Hudro. "What happened to the socialite?" He waved at Clara's appearance. "You look as if you've taken up driving a truck."

"I guess personal aggrandizement got put on the back burner. We've all got a common cause now." They began walking toward a double door at the end of the room.

"So what are you doing, specifically?" Cade asked.

"Coordinating with the mission in Lakewood. They're still operating, but not tied to the Washington office anymore—obviously."

"I know—I talked to Wyvex."

The first person Cade saw among the groups waiting on the far side of the doors was Marie, looking something like the way she had when he first saw her in Chattanooga; a lightweight patterned sweater, loose slacks, and suede hook-lace boots. He approached warily. They stared at each other. Even now, after everything, each seemed unsure of exactly what reaction would be appropriate. Her face was blotchy, still carrying angry black and red marks from the crash. None looked as if they would scar permanently. She was looking at him, seemingly equally unsure. . . .

And then she was pressed against him clinging, and his arms enveloped her, pulling her close. He smelled her hair, felt the slenderness of her body through the sweater. It was the first intimate contact they had experienced since their reunion. To his surprise, she was trembling. "I thought it was all over . . . before anything began," she whispered, raising her face. "And then Luke told us. It was days after you called him."

"He had reasons," Cade murmured.

"Yes, I know."

Luke was there too, Cade saw—waiting patiently, a faint and rare smile on his lips. And Yassem—whom Cade had barely met during the ill-fated helicopter flight. And Vrel and Dee were there too, clustering around Yassem and Hudro, who were hugging ecstatically, Yassem weeping. Just for a brief moment, the war was far away and forgotten.

They went out to one of the mission's Hyadean flyers, parked at the rear of the building among an assortment of cars, trucks, and military vehicles, and within minutes were airborne over Riverside. The freeway traffic was thin compared to what used to be normal. Clara said the gasoline restrictions were having a big effect. Southern Californian oil installations had been hit, and a tanker from Asia had been sunk off Santa Rosa Island the previous day. Cade saw damage to some of the freeway intersections, in one case amounting to total demolition and causing a crush of diverted traffic in the surrounding streets. Aircraft flying sorties up the coast from Mexico had been trying to take out key nodes of the road system with offshore-launched missiles, but so far with limited success. Links through the Rockies were under constant attack, the southern I-10 route to Phoenix and El Paso being completely cut. It would get a lot worse if the carrier groups now moving north in the

Pacific got within striking range. There had been a lot of air combat over the Gulf.

For Cade, only just returned, it was all a new experience. Even with the tensions that had been mounting for years and the more recent instances of open domestic violence, he was unable to conceive jets carrying the insignia that had always meant USAF swooping in from the Pacific to attack targets in places like Anaheim or Pasadena, Bakersfield or San Diego. He looked down at the wreckage of an interchange that they were passing over. A swath of devastation extended through the nearby houses. "How can this be happening?" he asked Clara. "Isn't it obvious that there's been a corrupt administration on the other side for years? How can anyone there support it?"

"They're building a stronger America by allying with a superior power," she said. "We've been duped into becoming tools of the Asians. If we're not stopped, Chinese armies will be landing within a month and pouring through to make us a colony again."

Cade stared at her. "They believe that?"

"It's what they're being told. I'll run you some New York news clips and propaganda spiels when we get back."

"This *is* Roland I'm listening to?" Marie checked, still holding on to his arm.

From Luke and Vrel, Cade learned the story of Julia's untimely end. Marie had the grace not to say anything that might have sounded vengeful. Cade was dumbfounded. If he hadn't warned Luke, every one of those around him, Clara excepted, wouldn't have been there now.

Dee had moved out of travel agenting and was helping with school reorganization following separation from the federal system. It was only a small part,

she told him, but everything counted. A contrast to
the good-time-girl that he'd known, Cade reflected.
The new feeling of dedication to something that
mattered was affecting everybody.

Vrel asked about Krossig. Cade said he was fine
and described his situation. "And what about the
mission?" he asked. "Orzin's running things, right? So
what's the status of the place now? I couldn't quite
figure it out."

"I'm not exactly sure either," Vrel confessed.

"Do you still have the link to Chryse?"

"Not after Luodine tried to get her agency to put
out that documentary there. They ran straight to the
authorities. Xuchimbo cut us off in retaliation—and
to avoid any further risk." Cade remembered that the
gravity-wave converters in Earth orbit and the outer-
Solar-System relays were controlled from the Hyadean
General Embassy in Xuchimbo. Vrel shrugged. "Orzin
is with us, trying to find a way around the censor-
ship. If the real story got out on Chryse, it would
create havoc. That's what we should be doing."

"Hudro and I tried to tell them in Beijing, but the
hawks are in control there," Cade said. "What's the
line here? What will Jeye do?" He meant William
Jeye, who had become the FWA's president.

"He's under pressure to go along with the Chinese,"
Clara Norburn said. "You can see the argument:
Washington has the backing of technically superior
aliens. We're going to need as much of the world with
us as we can get." Cade listened gravely. Clara
sounded as if she almost bought it herself. She went
on: "And so far things are looking good. I can't see
the people in Sacramento throwing away the initiative here and expecting Chryse to cave in. Tanks and
bombs, they understand. But the psychology and
social dynamics of Hyadeans they've never met,

light-years away?" She shook her head. "You might as well ask them to put their trust in voodoo."

The flyer landed at the house first to drop off Cade, Marie, and Luke, and also to introduce Hudro to the rest of the household. Then Hudro departed with the remainder for the mission, where he would be staying. Cade would join them tomorrow after resting from the journey. He showered and changed while Henry put away the bags, clothes, and other things Cade had acquired in New Zealand, Australia, and China. Marie had been using one of the guest rooms, and without Julia's effects the master suite was strangely empty and bare. But the atmosphere was a lot lighter.

He joined Marie downstairs and took a stroll with her around the house and the outside to see if much had changed during his absence. Not a lot had. Henry had acted quickly before the rationing began to bite, so stocks of most things were good for the time being, apart from gas, which had been the first of the restrictions—although they wouldn't have to worry about running the Cadillac anymore. The neighborhood now had a siren to warn of incoming air attacks—in Newport Beach! External walls of sandbags had been put up around the garage and adjoining gym to make them into something of a blast shelter. Warren was worried about the vulnerability of the yacht, moored at the rear.

Despite the way they seemed to have found each other again, Cade was conscious of a vague uneasiness between himself and Marie when they sat down together for the evening meal. He had obtained this house since their splitting up, and he could tell that she was uncomfortable in the ostentatious surroundings. But there was more, also. It was as if there were something unseemly, almost, in the rapidity with which it had happened. Marie had been there at one time, and then gone; then there was Julia; and now Julia was gone and Marie back, it seemed virtually instantly. Thousands of miles away in South America, everything had been too different to matter. But here the change was too immediate. He would have felt more comfortable to have been alone for a while before Marie moved back into his life again. He sensed that Marie felt it too. But the mood didn't have time to take root. A string of old acquaintances began dropping by to say hi, having heard that Cade was back.

Anita Lloyd, from Norm Schnyder's law firm, had previously been an expert on reinvesting currency earned from cheap Hyadean imports in high-profit land deals. Now she was involved in rebuilding money, credit, and the trading system in conjunction with Asian markets, following the severance of ties to traditional East-Coast-based financial institutions and the issuing of its own currency by the Bank of California. Norman himself was away in Sacramento, working on emergency labor and housing allocation—to conserve fuel, thousands of people were being relocated closer to work. Anita joked that the firm was learning to do things that needed to be done, without worrying about billing. Her own personal million had been wiped out in the currency transition. To Cade's surprise, she didn't seem to care all that much. On reflection, she told him, she didn't really like that person that she used to be.

Damien Philps, the art dealer, had suspended business and volunteered his labor services. George Jansing, who used to sell rare Terran skills for high Hyadean profits, was involved in dispersing aircraft production. Homeowners were taking in refugees from the war zones. Whole new attitudes were being shaped. Despite the dangers and inconveniences, a lot of people said it gave life a purpose that had been lacking before. "Obsessive money grubbing and alienation," was how Jansing put it.

"Let's see how they sound when things start getting really tough," Luke commented to Cade dourly.

Later, the sirens wailed, and they all moved into the gym to be on the safe side; but nothing happened.

After the all-clear sounded and the visitors had gone, Cade helped Marie move her things out of the guest room. There was an interval of unspoken awkwardness, of fussing too long to arrange hangers in the closet, or dwelling pointlessly on snippets of the evening's talk and trivia dredged from the past. But closeness dissolved their misgivings. As Cade lay falling asleep, holding her, for the first time in all the turbulent years he could remember, he knew peace. Marie burrowed into the sheets and nuzzled her face against his chest.

"Cold nose," he mumbled drowsily.

"It's Mole Woman."

In rediscovering Marie, Cade had finally discovered himself.

CHAPTER FORTY-EIGHT

News the next morning was that Washington was threatening action against the Canadian supply routes. The rebellion in Mexico was spreading southward into the Central American states. Little was said of events on the Midwest and Southwest fronts. Wyvex sent one of the mission's flyers to collect Cade and Marie from the house. Again, damage was visible at several of the freeway interchanges and around LAX. Clara had said the previous evening that commercial flights over the Pacific had ceased for the time being. The Canada-Alaska route was being used for Asia.

On arriving, they found that a cordon of barriers and soldiers backed by military vehicles had been placed outside the mission's perimeter fence. Facing them were groups of demonstrators numbering maybe several hundred, displaying banners and placards. They were orderly as of the moment but seemed surly and restless. Cade couldn't pretend to be totally surprised.

Inside, they were greeted by Wyvex, still wearing his Navajo patch. He was pleased and intrigued to meet Marie at last. Vrel was out at UCLA with Mike Blair. They would be back later. "What's going on outside?" Cade asked as they walked through into the building.

"Some anti-Hyadean feeling is surfacing. The documentary you two sent from South America didn't help. Some Eastern units have been using Hyadean weapons in Arkansas. It makes us all the enemy to some people." Cade nodded. It was pretty much as he had guessed.

The elaborate security procedures at reception were gone—a sign of independence from the Hyadean Washington office, Cade presumed—and Wyvex conducted them straight through to the open-plan work areas with their cream-painted walls and dull metal furnishings. On the way, they talked about events that had taken place with both of them since Cade's departure for Atlanta, including another account of Julia's demise. Cade saw that many of the screens were shut down, and none of those that were functioning showed the kinds of scenes that he remembered from direct connections to Chryse and the other Hyadean worlds.

There were more people about than had been usual before—Hyadean and Terran. Seemingly, the mission had become a collecting center for stray Hyadeans left in the western half of the country after the secession. Also, to ease travel problems, a number of Terrans who worked here had moved in. They took an elevator to the top floor. Wyvex showed Cade and Marie into Orzin's office, and then left.

Orzin greeted them with smiles that made his

unusually rounded Hyadean features look rubbery. He had shed his tunic top for a tan, casual jacket which he wore open over a shirt with a low-tone colored design. But it was colored—the Hyadean equivalent of a Wall Street banker showing up at the office in a beach shirt. Of course, Orzin was delighted to meet Marie. They went over a summary of the same salient events that Wyvex had gone through.

"So what exactly is going on here, Orzin?" Cade asked when they had settled down. "It seems like you've taken over the mission. Where does it stand? Are you some kind of independent, one-building, Hyadean nation state now, or what?"

"We are Chryse," Orzin replied.

Cade shot Marie a puzzled look. She shook her head. "What do you mean?" he asked Orzin.

"We shall find again what Chryse once was. It will begin here." Orzin spread a pair of pudgy, blue, oversize hands. "Here in this mission. Not, as you say, a one-building nation-state. A one-building planet! When I first came here from Chryse, I saw only the things that confirmed what we had been told. Earth was disintegrating in chaos and disorder. We had come to save it by introducing our system of organization and discipline. Of course, there were stubborn elements of the old structure that would not give up their traditional powers so easily. But, with the cooperation of the more enlightened interests that you have termed the Globalist Coalition, they could be induced to come around." He held up a hand before either Cade or Marie could say anything.

"However, that wasn't the way things were. This system that Hyadeans have been conditioned to serve is a lie by which a layer of social parasites drains them of everything they produce. They do it by convincing them of the need to subjugate themselves to a higher authority that knows and represents the greater good of all. In doing so, they rob them not only of the right to think as individuals, but even of awareness of their ability to. And so they are made into expendables: sacrificial objects to enrich the lives of others.

"What I began to see on Earth after I had been here some time was not what I had been told to see. I saw a world of *individuals*, with different ideas and choices about how they wanted to live their lives. And yes, at times those differences caused disagreement and strife. But it was not a pathological world destroying itself in chaos; it was world of variety and vigor asserting its nature: the right to be *free*." Orzin showed his hands in a despairing gesture. "Yet in spite of all that, the same forces that enslaved Chryse are operating here. And *those* are the forces that we have been allying with. Other Hyadeans see it too. That is why Luodine and Nyarl are here. And Hudro and Yassem . . . and many others."

Cade frowned at the top of the desk with its several displays, rewritable paper pads with strings of Hyadean characters, and assortment of other objects, the function of all of which was not obvious. He feared that Orzin was oversimplifying. Earth's history showed a far less consistent and universal dedication to such values than the picture he was painting. . . . But if that was what he was seeing, Cade wasn't about to muddy the issue now.

Marie was all attention, looking as if she wanted to believe what she was hearing but just couldn't see it. "But you just told us, you're a one-building operation. Do you really think you can change anything?" she said.

"Us, no. But the people of Chryse can. The people

of all the Hyadeans worlds . . ." Orzin waved a hand
high, as if inviting them to visualize it.

"We were talking about that yesterday," Cade said.
"It's what Hudro and I tried to get across in Beijing."

Orzin nodded. "I know. Hudro told me. Hyadeans
don't question what they see and what they are told.
That was what made them exploitable on such a scale.
But that same fact means they won't tolerate deception. Luodine saw the same thing."

"But what can just a few of you *do*?" Marie asked
again.

Orzin gestured as if it should have been obvious.
"Show them the deception. Tell the real story to
Chryse. That's her business."

"But Xuchimbo controls all the channels," Cade
said.

"The official channels, yes," Orzin agreed. "But who
said we have to use those?" He turned one of the
flatscreen pads around on the desk and pushed it
across, at the same time uttering commands. An image
appeared that Cade and Marie had seen before in
New Zealand and China: themselves, narrating the
documentary recorded at Tevlak's house in Bolivia.
It took Cade a moment to register that there was
something different. The sound had been dubbed.
The voices he heard were speaking in Hyadean. He
looked up, nonplussed. "I don't understand. What's
going on?"

"That's you two," Orzin said needlessly. "You know
the item. This is a recording of a version of it that
went out *across Chryse* last night!" He looked from
one to the other, noted their incredulous looks with
evident satisfaction, and went on before they could
ask, "Luodine tried to get her agency to put it out,
but the people in charge there wouldn't do it. Too
obedient to the system. So Yassem decided that if

there was no way through the official net, she'd go around it. She used our facilities here to access the Xuchimbo system, and piggybacked a coded message on their outgoing trunk beam that the Querl intercepted. *They're* doing the broadcasting for us!"

Marie stared. "Querl? You mean the rebel worlds?"

"Yes! Amazing, isn't it! That was several days ago now. The Querl have positioned an arc of their own relays somewhere outside of Earth—they can't come as far in as orbit, since the Chryseans control near space. So we have our own link now. We lose contact for a little under ten hours each day."

Cade was having trouble taking it in. "Querl?" he repeated. "You mean they've showed up *here* . . . in our Solar System?"

"Well, they're out there somewhere, anyhow," Orzin replied, waving a hand vaguely. "And you can bet the Chryseans are out there looking for them too. But it's a lot of space to get lost in. And they have sophisticated ways of deploying decoys and switching the incoming return signals around to make it impossible to get a sure fix on where the relays are."

Cade and Marie looked at each other, stupefied. *They* were being broadcast around alien star systems light-years away . . . ?

"And you two aren't the only news that's going out. Luodine and Nyarl have been collecting material from all over." Orzin voiced more commands in Hyadean. The image on the screen changed to show Luodine speaking to the camera, and then soldiers and rescue workers pulling dazed and bleeding figures from wrecked vehicles scattered and upended all ways in front of a background of burning buildings. "A refugee column hit by an air strike near Minneapolis," Orzin commented. It was followed by an aircraft's gun-camera view of missiles flaming away and bursting among trucks halted on the approach to a pontoon bridge. Figures were jumping out, fleeing, falling. . . . "FWA fighter-bombers attacking one of the Mississippi crossing points." Then there was Luodine again, superposed on a desert scene littered with knocked-out armor. "Aftermath of a tank duel south of Odessa, Texas. There's lots more." Orzin looked across at Cade and Marie pointedly—as if this could have significance out of all proportion to appearances. "According to the first reports we're getting back from Querl sources, it's creating a sensation back home. This is the first time anyone has reported anything direct from the other side of what's been happening on Earth. We must be doing something right. Reactions from the Chrysean government are furious. Naturally, they're denouncing it all as Querl propaganda and fakery. But people on Chryse are taking notice. Luodine's face is familiar there. They know she talks straight." Orzin wagged a finger. "But that's not all. She doesn't want to just sit here passing on news that comes in. Her style has always been to go out herself and find it. She's persuaded the Air Force to provide her and Nyarl with a jet to turn into a mobile studio. You'd have to hear her enthusiasm to believe it. I think she has finally discovered what she really wants to do."

In an NBC news studio at the Rockefeller Center in New York, Casper Toddrel gazed somberly at the camera showing "live" and completed the address that he had prepared as part of a public relations effort being coordinated from the White House. "It will be a painful duty. It will not be a pleasant duty. But it is a necessary duty. For as long as it takes, we cannot speak of these places as belonging to America anymore. They have become an extension of foreign power into this continent. The next step will be a bridgehead for invasion. We, in the East at this hour, stand as the last bastion of defense for the values that America has always stood for. The people in California and Oregon, New Mexico and Montana are not our enemy. The enemy is the corrupt gang of traitors and opportunists who have turned Sacramento into a provincial capital of China. I ask you all to stand by us and our Hyadean allies to reverse this tragic aberration that had befallen us. We can, and we will, not only bring all of America back into the fold, but build out of it a stronger and more united America than has ever existed. A new United States, purged, reformed, revitalized, fit not only to assume again its rightful place as leader among the nations of this world, but to establish this world as a full and equal partner, enjoying all due rights and dignity, in the wider community of our newfound interstellar cousins." Toddrel paused to let his audience contemplate the vision, then nodded solemnly. "Thank you."

The red camera light went out. "Thanks, Mr. Toddrel," the set manager called from behind the lights. "That's was good. That's it. You're done."

Toddrel collected together the notes he had laid on the desk, got up, and headed for the door. Ibsan, his bodyguard, saw him through the glass wall of an adjacent monitor room and came out. "Mr. Toddrel. You'd better see this." Ibsan nodded back over his shoulder.

"What is it?"

"Flash just coming in from Bolivia. That Hyadean mining center at Uyali. Half their military base down there blew up. It's like it got nuked."

"*Jesus. . . .*"

Toddrel followed Ibsan into the room, which was

lined on one side with consoles and screens. Three of the operators were grouped in front of one showing a scene panning across the wreckage and carnage of whole blocks of peculiar Hyadean building-block architecture shattered and twisted into grotesque shapes, with a pall of smoke hanging over the background. Crews from emergency vehicles had started bringing out survivors, while more flyers and Terran-built helicopters descended into view from above. A voiceover was talking excitedly and breathlessly.

"About fifteen minutes ago," one of the operators commented, seeing that Toddrel had joined them. "The whole back end of the place just went up. From the accounts, it sounds as if it was the armory. It was loaded. A shipment of Hyadean ammo and stuff just arrived from orbit. They're counting the death toll in hundreds already." Toddrel watched grimly for a few minutes, but there was nothing of further significance to be learned. He caught Ibsan's eye and jerked his head curtly in the direction of the door as a sign for them to leave. They stopped by a door at the end of a corridor of offices.

"It had to be those new remote-detonatable munitions," Ibsan murmured. "Somehow the wrong people got access to the codes. I don't know what kind of a can of worms it opens up, but I figured you ought to know right away."

Toddrel nodded, still thinking frantically. "You did right, Earl."

He should never have agreed to letting Drisson look into it, he told himself. There were too many factions at large, too many conflicting interests. The opportunities for betrayal should have made the risks unthinkable. In normal circumstances he would never have condoned it. He had no idea who the perpetrators might have been. The Asians or one of their breakaway groups? Part of the guerrilla front? Some other lunatic sect? Drisson himself for some reason? Somebody Drisson was mixed up with, who had an agenda of their own? . . . But whatever, there was one person who was sure to be high on everybody's suspect list.

Roger Achim, the program's producer, came through from the set, accompanied by a couple of assistants. "Everything all right, Mr. Toddrel?"

"Yes, just fine," Toddrel responded mechanically.

"Good, good."

"Oh, one thing."

"Yes?"

"Is there somewhere private that I could use? I have to make a confidential call urgently."

"Sure. Susie, find Mr. Toddrel an empty office along there somewhere, would you?"

Minutes later, Toddrel was confronting the blue-purple features of Gazaghin, the Hyadean military commander in Washington. He had heard the news, and his mood was murderous.

"I just wanted to assure you personally that I had absolutely no knowledge of this appalling—"

Gazaghin interrupted. "Don't waste the breath, Toddrel. I don't believe for long time anything you say. It makes no difference now who does this, in any place. I warned you. Now it's not your war now."

"What do you mean?"

"Is too much. We trust to let Terrans in charge. Look what happens. Now there is protest risings and angry questions all over Chryse. We have orders from our government to put the stop. We control now."

"But it's not within their jurisdiction to," Toddrel objected. "You are still aliens within a sovereign territory. . . ."

Gazaghin slammed a hand down on the surface

where he was speaking. "When Hyadean dead are hundreds, it *is* our jurisdiction!" he bellowed. "When illegal propaganda pictures are flooding our world, it's our jurisdiction. Your President Ellis has just signed the order. This country's armed forces are now under my command."

CHAPTER FORTY-NINE

Cade decided that the luxurious Newport Beach mansion offended him. He instructed Henry to have the valuables and personal effects packed and put into storage, and the house made available to the authorities for housing evacuees. The influx would improve the tone of the neighborhood, he told Marie. As for the yacht, Warren was to place it at the disposal of the military for the coastal transportation fleet being hurriedly expanded. He and Marie would move into quarters at the mission. Luke elected to come too, retaining his position as Cade's right-hand man for the duration. Besides putting them close at hand for the work there, it would ease traveling. Marie preferred this arrangement.

Luodine planned to tour the front-line areas, rear bases, refugee centers, hard-hit zones, collecting original material that the mission would send back to Chryse along with whatever could be got from other sources—the fruition of the idea that had begun forming in her mind during her experiences in Segora. The plane that the Air Force provided turned out to be a C22-E twin turbofan military airlift VIP transport, normally carrying sixteen passengers, but in this instance fitted out as a flying communications post. It arrived with a pilot, copilot, and technical sergeant for support at Edwards Air Force Base in the high desert above Palmdale. The base had been hit by intermediate-range conventional missiles launched from over the Rockies but was still flying operations. Yassem flew out there with Hudro and Nyarl in one of the mission's flyers to meet the crew, brief them on the mission, and check over the equipment before tomorrow, when the team was due to depart. Since Hyadean flyers were few and in demand, after being dropped off at Edwards, they sent it on to Newport Beach to collect Cade, Marie, and Luke, and take them to the mission with the belongings they were bringing from the house.

Meanwhile, Luodine was organizing the mission's communications room as a clearing center for forwarding despatches to Chryse. A Colonel Nacey from FWA military intelligence, along with a small staff, was attached to the operation to ensure that sensitive information was not released prematurely. The main item that she had not mentioned in her outgoing reports—although the Union commanders who needed to know would be aware of it from their own sources in any case—was that a mixed AANS force under a Chinese flagship had sailed from Hawaii to intercept the carrier groups moving north, now approaching the equator west of the Galapágos Islands. The officers on Nacey's staff called the situation "Midway in reverse."

But it was becoming clear that the move from Hawaii was just part of a far larger and more audacious plan only now beginning reveal itself. Luodine sat, stunned, alongside Nacey, while on a screen in front of them a spokeswoman from Beijing summarized the action that had been taking place since early that morning. Confused reports had been coming in from various sources about air drops in Mexico and fighting along the Panama Canal Zone, but this was the first coherent account linking it all together. President Jeye himself had been notified officially only within the previous hour—although Nacey thought it likely that he and his military commanders had known privately before then.

"Scattered resistance only is being encountered at Acapulco. We have already commenced air operations farther to the south, supporting the landings north and south of the canal. The main Hyadean defenses were neutralized before they could come into effective operation. . . ."

"Wyv, you'd better get Orzin here," Nacey told Wyvex, who was hovering behind. "This is unbelievable." Wyvex tried calling Orzin on his communicator, failed to get a response, and left. Luodine thought of calling Nyarl at Edwards with the news, but then decided to let it ride. He would find out soon enough.

The Chinese had intervened in Central America with a series of long-range airborne landings and support strikes to secure air bases. So far, they were down at six locations in Mexico and two in Costa Rica, with planes refueling and flying missions from one of them already. In addition, forces had been dropped on both sides of the Panama Canal, clearly with the object of cutting the reinforcement and supply connection from the Caribbean to the Union carrier groups in the Pacific. In what sounded like an incredible series of blunders on the part of the defending Hyadeans, the attackers, moving fast and with sound jungle training, had achieved almost total surprise, in some instances overrunning opposition still flailing around, trying to get dressed. In others, the cumbersome and complicated Hyadean heavy weapons had been seized before they could be brought to bear, and spearheads had reached the shores of Gatun Lake, separating the two sections of the canal, in at least four places. With the defending airfields taken out preemptively by undetected sea-skimming cruise missiles, an entire Union supply squadron and battle group trapped between Colón and Balboa were shooting it out against shore-based missiles and guns that were becoming more effective by the hour, and which would soon be augmented by local air support.

Michael Blair hurried in, looking flustered, and came through between the Terrans and Hyadeans who were watching. "What's happening? I heard there was something big," he said. Luodine turned from the console and summarized. "Oh my God!" Blair breathed.

"Whoever dreamed this up isn't someone I'd want to play poker with," Nacey said. "They're stretched out to the limit— hanging on until the fleet from Hawaii gets within support range." He pointed at a situation display map on one of the walls. "Obviously, the aim is to get viable land-based air flying from Mexico to pincer those carriers that are coming up. If they pull it off . . ." He drew a breath, shook his head, and left it at that.

Wyvex reappeared with Orzin in tow. Luodine and Nacey repeated the story. By this time, the Chinese spokeswoman was reporting Mexican government troops protecting Union air bases changing sides and opening them to the rebels.

Luodine was excited. The entire Union position in the south seemed to be collapsing. Reports since yesterday had described them as all but halted in Texas, with armor and other units standing down or coming over to the Federation en masse. She stared at the wall screen showing the map and saw the Pacific Coast secure, Alaska a part of the Federation in all but declaration, Canada on the verge of allying formally. All that was propping the Union up now was their Hyadean backing. And she and the others at the mission were revealing its true nature to the people of Chryse already. Surely it couldn't last much longer now.

Only then did she become aware of a shrill tone emanating from one of the consoles across the room. Orzin turned his head sharply in alarm; at the same instant, an eerie wail started somewhere outside the building, rising in pitch and volume. A screen illuminated, showing a map of the Los Angeles coast with an inset of Hyadean symbols. On it was a line beginning from a point twenty miles or so out in the ocean and passing right over the mission's location on Carson Street. The line bore a red dot moving steadily inland. A Hyadean voice in public-address mode filled the room. "Alert! Alert! Submarine missile launch detected thirty-one kilometers, bearing two-twenty degrees. Three of them, heading directly at us. Estimated impact forty-two seconds. Evacuate immediately!" Wyvex translated for the Terrans, his voice cracking.

Luodine felt her mouth turn dry. Orzin turned a dazed face to the room. "Get out of the building as fast as you can. Keep it orderly. Use the stairs at both ends. . . ."

Even as he spoke, figures were sliding up out of chairs and converging toward the door, some forcing to get ahead, others refusing to yield as survival instincts took over; a few remained unmoving, transfixed in disbelief. Luodine found herself being drawn forward into the crush pressing to get through the door, conscious of a raw smell of fear all around, somehow being contained just short of panic. Somebody behind her was whimpering, shoving her in the back. Luodine jabbed back savagely with a elbow. There was an eternity of jostling, pushing, frightened voices, some blows. Then she was out in the corridor, running with the bodies around her, colliding with others coming out of doorways, running again, through onto crowded stairs . . . even though she knew already that they were never going to make it.

Luodine was still on the stairs between the third and second floors when the three missiles hit their target precisely at five-second intervals. Sending three had been insurance against possible defenses that had failed to materialize. Each of them carried a Hyadean catalyzed hydrogen warhead of power intermediate between high explosive and nuclear, and was capable of taking out a city block.

The flyer was over Seal Beach, when the synthetic voice of the vehicle's supervisory AI issued from the forward panel. "*Attention, please. Situation irregularity. We have lost our destination beacon and ground coordination transmission. Request instructions.*" Cade, startled, looked at Marie, then across at Luke. Luke shook his head to say he didn't know what they were supposed to do, either.

"Er . . . you'd better give us more detail," Cade said.

"Sys on," Luke hissed.

"Oh, right." Dialogues with the system needed to be prefixed. "System on. More detail," Cade said.

"*We were in contact with Hyadean traffic control located at the mission. Contact has been lost. Attempts to recontact the mission on other channels have failed. What do you want me to do?"*

Cade looked at Luke and Marie again, as if for inspiration. "What options do we have?"

"Continue under manual guidance to the same destination. Alternatively, go somewhere else."

"We don't know how to fly this," Cade said.

"I can fly and land it. You just supply voice directions."

"Okay, let's do that. . . . Continue to the mission."

"Acknowledged."

Marie was staring ahead through a view section of the nose. "Roland," she whispered, clutching his arm.

"What is it?"

"What is what?" the AI queried, still toggled to dialogue.

"System off," Cade said. There was no need to ask Marie again. Following her horrified gaze, he could already see the pall of smoke hanging over the skyline ahead. Although still five miles away, it had to be the mission.

"Oh, Jesus Christ," Luke breathed.

They stared, numbed and speechless, as the flyer closed over the houses and boulevards. In places below them, lines of cars could be seen pulling over, making way for police and emergency vehicles already speeding in the direction of whatever had happened. The phone in Cade's pocket emitted a call tone. He drew it out, still staring ahead woodenly. "Cade."

"Roland, you're okay!" It was Dee. "Thank heavens! We thought you might have been there already."

"It's Dee," Cade murmured to the others. Then, louder, "Almost. We're on our way, just a couple of miles south. What's happened?"

"I don't know. I'm at Anaheim, at work. Vrel's here too. He stopped by for lunch. There were these huge explosions toward the coast. We heard them from here. Nobody at the mission is contactable. Something terrible has happened there. . . ."

"Vrel's with her. Nobody's answering from the mission." There was no longer any wondering about why. The belt of demolished houses, shattered office towers, and streets choked with overturned cars, rubble, and debris was coming into view. Beyond, where the mission building had been, was just a crater partly visible through hanging dust and smoke. "Look, Dee, we're just coming in on our approach now."

"What can you see? Is it the mission?"

Cade had to swallow to prevent his voice from choking. "Bad news, Dee. Real bad. It's been taken out. I mean right out. There can't be any hope for anyone who was in there. Tell Vrel I'm sorry."

"Terrain doesn't match records," the flyer's AI reported. *"Unable to execute stored landing profile. Request instructions."*

"Dee, I have to go. We'll call you right back as soon as we know any more. You might want to call Hudro and the others out at Edwards. At least we know they're okay."

"Vrel's talking to them now. . . . Okay, Roland, we'll be waiting to hear from you."

Cade directed the flyer to a section of street where several police cars were parked haphazardly in a cluster, another visible from above, approaching a block away. Several uniformed figures were in a group, trying to take in the situation, while others ran to check a partly collapsed house alongside, and another directed an ambulance that was just drawing up. The surroundings looked as if they had been combed by a giant lawn rake. There had been a grotesque rain of bodies—probably the protestors who had been picketing the mission. The police in front of the cars

looked up as the flyer descended; two of them waved
it toward a clear area on one side. "Forward slow, two
o'clock," Cade instructed. "Lower. . . . Hold it here.
Take it straight down, vertically."

*"Confirm landing vicinity free of personnel and
obstructions?"* the AI requested.

"You're clear."

"Landing and terminating."

"System off."

It was worse outside the insulating confines of the
flyer's cabin. Stinging dust and fumes assailed Cade's
eyes and nostrils. Sirens whooped and howled from
the surrounding streets; police radios cackled. In the
lulls between, he could hear screams and terrified
shouting not far away.

There was little more to be learned at this junc-
ture. The officers had been among the first to arrive.
None of them knew what had happened. One speculated that something had come down from orbit. They
took details of the Hyadeans at Edwards and Anaheim and how they could be contacted, of Cade's
involvement with the mission, and relayed the information to headquarters. One reported to Cade that
Clara Norburn had just heard the news and was on
her way. Meanwhile, a helicopter had appeared and
was circling overhead; more ambulances, a string of
fire engines, and a truck filled with soldiers arrived.
A police mobile command post began setting up to
coordinate rescue and casualty-clearing operations
among the surrounding city blocks. But it was already
plain that nobody within the mission building itself
or its close vicinity could have survived.

Cade called for Hudro and Dee to get over and
gave the location. By the time they arrived in Dee's
car, the scene resembled a small war. Clara Norburn
appeared with staff and military liaison people in a

flotilla of cars and escorts; shortly afterward, a
National Guard helicopter touched down, bringing
Hudro, Yassem, and Nyarl from Edwards.

What they should do next was not obvious. Going
back to the house wouldn't address the immediate
issue of four Hyadeans who no longer belonged
anywhere. Clara arranged for them all, including
Cade, Marie, and Luke, to be taken to her department at the municipal offices near the Civic Center.
Vrel was still in shock and unable to communicate
much that was coherent. So far, just he and five others
who had been elsewhere for various reasons were all
that was left of the Hyadean West Coast Trade and
Cultural Mission.

CHAPTER FIFTY

They sat despondently around a staff room that had been put at their disposal until something could be worked out. Luke had gone to call Henry and tell him to put a hold on clearing the house in case they were about to receive some unexpected house guests. A meal had been brought in but nobody had touched very much of it. Only now were the Hyadeans recovering their faculties to a degree anywhere within sight of normality.

"Just when we had achieved what Luodine was working for," Nyarl said, staring at the carpet. "It was done to shut down the channel to Chryse. So we must have been having effect there. Now she will never know."

"She should have lived long enough to have known," Yassem agreed.

"Is Chryse that has problem, but missiles are from

Terran submarine," Hudro said. "So who commands this? These politics are all double faces."

Vrel just sat, holding Dee's hand. He had remarked several times that if he hadn't decided to stop at her office on the spur of the moment on his way back to the mission, he would have been there too.

Cade sat to one side, saying little. Marie was with Clara in Clara's office, following the reports coming in via Sacramento. For once, he didn't know what to say. Despite the time he had spent with Hyadeans, he didn't have any privileged insight into the inner workings of their the minds. And just at the moment, he was having enough trouble with the conflicting thoughts welling up from the deeper recesses of his own mind.

News that afternoon had been that the tide in Texas had turned, with Federation and turned-around Union tank columns reoccupying Forth Worth and Austin. The lines in front of Houston were declared open. Units defected from the Union cause were moving back toward the Mississippi, while growing agitation among the Southern states was rumored to be destabilizing the rear of the crumbling Union. Cade wondered if the Chinese in Beijing might have had it right all along when they insisted that the Union would cave in before the Hyadeans could intervene effectively. They had the professional military staffs, after all, and should know. Cade didn't. In that case, his fears based on the things he had seen had been wrong. Okay, he could live with that. And Hudro's convictions, based on his own direct experiences, were wrong too. With a slightly bigger push, Cade could accept that. But something still didn't feel right about it.

If the Washington regime's situation was really that precarious, then they would surely know it too. What didn't feel right was that they should choose such a moment for the strike against the mission, which didn't affect the military situation but could easily have the result of outraging the Hyadeans and dividing them to the degree that effective intervention became impossible, just when the East appeared to be in most need of it. It didn't make sense.

Or was he simply refusing to face that everything the Hyadeans he had come to know as friends had striven for, and finally achieved at the cost of today's tragedy, had been for nothing? For if the collapse of the Union was imminent with or without any action on the part of the population of Chryse, then all that Luodine, Orzin, Wyvex, and the others had hoped to bring about was happening anyway.

Cade's phone beeped. It was Marie. Her voice was low but tense. "Roland. I'm still with Clara. Something's come in that you ought to hear about. Can you get up here?"

"Sure." He cut the connection, hesitated, and then stood up. "They want me for something," he said to the Hyadeans. As he walked to the door, he was conscious of their stares following him. He had the strange feeling of abandoning them, as if they were his charges. It was ridiculous.

Clara's office was on the floor above. With the two women were Chester Di Milestro, a Los Angeles-based aide to President Jeye, and Major Gerofsky from the military liaison, both of whom Cade had met earlier. One of the screens on the wall next to Clara's desk showed the east central Pacific with colored lines plotting courses of naval units. Another held a frozen head-and-shoulders picture of an officer with lots of braid on his cap, addressing the camera. "It's big, Roland," Clara said without preamble. "Admiral Varney— commander of the lead carrier force. He's defected."

Cade looked from one to the other. "What do you mean?"

Di Milestro answered. "He issued a proclamation two hours ago, saying he took an oath to defend Americans, not attack them. If the other carrier groups continue on their present course, he will consider it his duty to oppose them with all the force at his disposal. It means he's with us."

Gerofsky waved a hand at the map. "Look—the red there. Varney has turned his force ninety degrees. He's steaming east, converging with the Asian fleet from Hawaii to head them off. With land-based air from Mexico, that sews it all up."

Marie came across and gripped Cade's arm. Her face was ecstatic. "Isn't it incredible news, Roland! You heard about Texas. Now they're expecting Canada to come in at any moment—close the northern edge all the way to the Atlantic. It would *have* to be all over then! We've won!"

"It's a bandwagon," Clara said. "And it's rolling."

Cade searched their faces. They were all intoxicated with the news. And they could be right, too. . . . But still he couldn't quite bring himself to share it. He sensed again the same relentless certainty and refusal to be deflected that he had seen in Beijing. Yet something kept telling him it felt wrong.

"What's the matter, Roland? I'd have expected to see a little more excitement," Marie said. Of course she was being swept along with it too. She was still the revolutionary. Everything which, for years, she had endured dangers and hardship for, seen her friends die for, was happening.

Cade wasn't sure what to say. He pictured again the four faces that he had just left in the room on the floor below. "I don't know. . . . I guess maybe because it's *our* bandwagon," he answered.

"I'm not sure I follow," Gerofsky said.

"Us. . . . Terrans." Cade made a motion with his head to indicate the direction he had come from. "What about those four downstairs? They put everything on the line too, and today they lost everything. It seems as if they're about to be left behind in the dust and forgotten, while we all go on a binge of self-congratulations." But even as he spoke, he knew it was just words to fill the space. It wasn't the reason.

Clara nodded, trying to be diplomatic. "I hear what you're saying, Roland. They did a heroic job—for us, because they decided it was right. And that won't be forgotten. But the part they wrote isn't in the final script. Nobody was to know it would work out this way."

"And it's cleaner," Di Milestro put in. "Fast. Surgical. Without depending on some other planet that nobody understands."

"They're in a nutcracker on both fronts," Gerofsky said. "In the Pacific, and on the mainland. They have to know it's over too. I'd bet even money we could get a peace offer from Washington before the end of today."

Which made it all the more incomprehensible that they should take out the Hyadean mission, Cade told himself. What was there for Washington to gain? Downstairs, the Hyadeans had been just as mystified. "These politics are all double faces," Hudro had said. Then his other words repeated again in Cade's mind: "So who commands this?"

Who commands?!

It hit Cade then what was wrong. Of *course* it made no sense for Washington to have ordered the mission strike. The only explanation, then, was that *Washington* hadn't ordered it. At least, not of their own initiation. *They were no longer in charge!*

"Oh, my God," Cade breathed. He licked his lips and looked quickly around the three faces watching him. "You're wrong," he told them. "All of you— Sacramento, Beijing. You're all wrong. It isn't over. It hasn't even started."

Clara gave the others a puzzled look. Marie alone seemed to have registered the graveness of Cade's expression. "What are you talking about, Roland?" Clara asked him.

He wiped a hand across his brow, still struggling to come to terms with the enormity of it. "The mission . . . that thing today. The Hyadean high command ordered it. It wasn't anybody in the Washington government. Don't you see what that means? They've taken over. And they've just cut the only independent link back to Chryse that could tell anyone there what happens next. What do you think *that* means?"

Gerofsky fingered his mustache and turned away to confront the shelves on the far wall. "No. . . . No, it can't be," he muttered.

"That's merely a speculation," Di Milestro said. "It's obviously something that's just occurred to you. You don't *know*." His tone accused Cade for even being capable of conceiving it.

"Then get the Hyadeans up here and see what they think," Cade said. "Hudro as good as said it already. Only he's still too shaken up to put together what it means." He looked around at them again. Di Milestro and Gerofsky were unsure, not wanting to believe him, yet unable to fault what he had said. Marie was persuaded but needed a moment to absorb it. Clara had been around long enough to know that Cade didn't let many things become serious enough to weigh down his life, and when he did, they were serious. But for now she had to consider her official position too.

"Suppose you're right, Roland," she said, standing behind her desk, her knuckles resting on the surface. "How can we change it? What are you suggesting we do? Just capitulate? Are you saying we should try to get Jeye to prevail on the Chinese to call it all off, then back down and accept whatever the Hyadeans choose to dictate?"

"Never!" Gerofsky wheeled back to face them. "And hand the world over as a colony state? I'd see it in flames from end to end first."

Just what they needed, Cade groaned inwardly. Yet this was would probably be the kind of reaction at every level. He realized that he wasn't sure himself exactly what he wanted them to do. Di Milestro talked direct to Jeye, but Cade didn't know him, and right at this moment he was acutely conscious of not commanding Di Milestro's confidence. Di Milestro confirmed it a moment later. "I think you're overreacting, Mr. Cade," he said. "Which is understandable. You've lost a lot of friends. But the way I see it, this attempt to set up a back-door PR link into Chryse was only a supplement to the military effort, anyway—in case we needed extra leverage." He shrugged. "It seems to me we're doing just fine without."

"Just fine? I'd say we're doing pretty damn great," Gerofsky said. "It looks like the Chinese are about to walk right over them in Panama. They don't need any link to Chryse."

Cade sighed and looked away. No, there wasn't a link from China to Chryse because the Hyadean Washington office controlled the channels, and right now they were permitting only approved traffic. That was why Yassem and Luodine had set up their illicit connection to the Querl. Cade blinked as the obvious finally struck him. He thought back to the things he had seen at Cairns: the scientific base and its easygoing independence; the local spirit of cooperation with the aliens and getting to know them. No, there wasn't another independent link. But there *could be*!

"We can still do it!" he said, turning back. "Luodine set the mission up as a collection center for items to go back to Chryse. But they've got the same kind of gear at Cairns, where we were with Krossig. We can set up another link to Chryse from *there*—from Australia!"

Gerofsky shook his head. "Throw away the initiative and get involved in alien psychology that we don't understand, when the things we do understand are working fine? What's the point? It goes against every rule in the book."

"How would these people in Australia know how to set their end up?" Di Milestro asked.

"I don't know," Cade retorted. "But the experts who set up the one at the mission are downstairs. We can still talk to Australia, can't we?"

"We don't need it," Gerofsky said again.

Cade stared from one to the other. Why were they hesitating, looking for reasons why not? "There's nothing to lose," he insisted. "If you're right and we take the board anyway, then it'll be a piece of insurance that costs nothing. If things turn sour, it could be the most important insurance we ever took." He pointed a finger in the direction of the floor. "And either way, it gives those four Hyadeans down there a chance to play a part. Are you going to deny them that, after what happened today?"

A deadlocked silence fell over the office. It was clear that neither Gerofsky nor Di Milestro wanted to be the person who was going to take this thing further; at the same time, they could find no refutation to what Cade had said. They looked as if they wished the whole thing would just go away. Before any resolution suggested itself, the terminal by Clara's desk sounded a priority tone. She answered at once, having blocked lower-level channels for privacy. Cade didn't recognize the face that appeared—a man in his fifties, white haired, professional looking, showing a jacket collar and necktie. "Clara, is Chester there?" he asked.

Clara moved aside as Di Milestro stepped forward. "It's Ed Flomer, from Sacramento," she said.

"Chester, the VP wants you on a conference call that he's setting up right away," Flomer said. His voice and expression were strained. "Can you get to a private line?"

"Sure. . . ." Di Milestro frowned inquiringly at the screen. "What's happening, Ed?"

Flomer shook his head. "I can't tell you. This is for a secure line only."

Di Milestro looked at Clara. "This way," she said, and led him out of the office. Cade and Gerofsky remained facing each other. After an awkward silence, Gerofsky moved over to the bookshelves to scan idly over the titles. Cade shook his head despairingly at Marie and began flipping mentally through his catalog of acquaintances for names that he might have to start recruiting to bring more weight to bear. Then Clara returned.

"Can't we have it referred to someone else?" she said, looking at Gerofsky. "Couldn't the commander at Edwards handle it? All you'd need to do is arrange an order from the top to authorize full cooperation, and then get on with your job. As Roland said, the cost is nothing. The payoff could be incalculable. There's no penalty clause. We can't lose."

"It would depend on what Sacramento has to say," Gerofsky replied. His manner was stiff, uncompromising. Clara studied him for a moment, then looked at Cade and Marie. "Why don't you go back down and update the others on what's been said?" she suggested to them. "I'll call you." Clearly, she wanted words with Gerofsky alone. Cade indicated the door with a nod, and he and Marie left.

Back in the staff room, Cade told the others the latest news, and then went on to relate his conclusion that the strike on the mission hadn't been ordered by Washington. It shook Hudro out of the stupor that had been gripping him. "Of course it wasn't Terrans who give order!" Hudro exclaimed. "How do I not see it? Hyadeans in charge now—maybe Gazaghin. Is not good."

Nyarl shook his head. "We had a channel working. . . ."

"And we can again—" Cade began. But before he could continue, the door opened and Clara came in with Di Milestro and Gerofsky. Di Milestro was pale. He faced the room while Clara closed the door. A hush fell. Something had changed very drastically in the last few minutes.

Di Milestro looked around. He had to take a long, shaky breath before speaking. "I'm breaking security on my own decision and telling you people what I've just learned because you might represent the only chance for averting a world-scale calamity." Cade caught Clara's eye with an incredulous, questioning look. But whatever this was about had apparently left her too numbed to respond. Di Milestro shifted his gaze to Cade. "Do you really think this thing you were telling us about could work?" he asked.

Cade nodded. "I believe it could work." What else was there to say?

"Run it by me again."

"Hyadeans see a different world here from what we see. Convince them that their government is about to destroy it and turn it into what they've got, and they'll pull out the rug." Cade flashed the Hyadeans a glance that let them know he was as mystified as they, then looked back. "What's happened?"

Di Milestro swallowed. "Admiral Varney's carrier group has been wiped out. A plane coming back off patrol shot the whole thing. I've just seen it upstairs. His flagship lit up like the Sun. There was nothing incoming on radar. The scientists are baffled."

"But Sacramento isn't budging," Gerofsky told the room. "Jeye says he would rather go out fighting than submit to a tyranny. If this other way of yours has a chance, we're going to have to do it ourselves."

CHAPTER FIFTY-ONE

The wall screen in the staff room showed a replay, wired from Sacramento at Di Milestro's request, of the carrier and its closer escorts disappearing in a gigantic ball of fire and vaporized ocean. The wall of foam surging outward capsized the more distant ships or scattered them like toys caught beneath a waterfall.

"Neutron beam from orbiting warship," Hudro pronounced. He explained that the flux would send critical any fission explosive not suitably shielded or designed to be resistant. Hence, it had detonated the carrier's nuclear weapons inventory. Since neutrons were uncharged, Hyadean gravitic technology was necessary to create and focus the beams.

A watered-down press release issued from Sacramento an hour later stated merely that Varney's task group had been "engaged" by hostile forces, implied to be the other two groups still with the Eastern Union. It was also announced that President Jeye would make a public address later that night. Di Milestro predicted it would be a rallying call for maximum effort and endurance side-by-side with the Asian allies now they were on the brink of success. Making the most of Gerofsky and his military credentials, Clara found working space in the communications section of the city administration's emergency headquarters, located beneath the Corry Building, containing more offices and a meeting center, situated along the next block. It was a dismal setting of concrete walls, fluorescent lights, fireproof doors guarding vaults of generators and the air-conditioning plant, and a disaster relief shelter. The people in the building above had long ago christened it "the Catacombs." Normally, nobody worked there, but since the Federation's secession, a caretaker staff had been installed to maintain a state of standby readiness.

The first thing was to open a connection to Krossig's group in Cairns. Yassem had kept a backup of the codes for linking to the Querl relays in a portable laptop-like device that she had taken with her to Edwards, so they were not lost. However, satellite communications were disrupted, and Gerofsky had to demand military priority before technicians established a land-line and cable connection through a Navy facility in San Francisco to Hawaii to Sydney, and from there to Cairns via the regular telecommunications system. Meanwhile, Di Milestro used his security clearances to get a line through to the Catacombs from an assistant in Sacramento who would keep him updated on developments. Cade and Luke got busy organizing contacts with wire services, news studios, military press officers, and other likely sources from Cade's numerous acquaintances, in order to recreate as far as possible the collection center that Luodine had set up at the mission. Australia would need to move into Earth's dark side before the link through Cairns, beaming outward toward the Querl relays, could be tested. This wouldn't happen until the early hours of the morning, California time. The crew of the C22-E waiting out at Edwards were notified that departure was on hold for the time being.

Nyarl was the obvious one to go in Luodine's place. Besides having the experience, he was resolved as a tribute to finish the work she had begun, in the way she would have finished it. He was already assembling further material to send. In addition to the sensational clips showing the annihilation of Varney's carrier group, he now had—obtained via Di Milestro's connection from Sacramento—a shot that a Marine flight had caught of the missiles actually going in at the Hyadean mission. Nyarl asked if Cade and Marie would go too—he seemed to think Cade possessed a proclivity for drawing the right people together to deal with any crisis. Yassem needed to remain in LA to guide the people setting up the link from Cairns. Who else would be flying, and who would form the rest of the base team at the Catacombs, was still to be decided.

President Jeye's message went out at nine o'clock and was along the lines that Di Milestro had anticipated. Jeye admitted that Varney's losses had been "more severe than we were initially led to believe" and included the admiral along with his flagship, but the full extent of the disaster remained undisclosed. But this was not a time to let one setback, however grievous, deter us from pressing home the victory that was already within grasp. The armies in Texas were moving up to leap across the Mississippi to where our Southern brothers and sisters were waiting to greet their liberators. Canada was opening a vast superhighway for supplies and reinforcements. Jeye concluded: "I don't pretend that this will be a pleasant task. The people of New York and Boston, Atlanta and Pittsburgh are not enemies. But the regime that they have been duped and coerced into serving has become an alien power standing for alien interests. We, in the Western Federation, must defend and preserve the values that have always been America. I call on each one of you to play your part and stand firm until our AANS allies sweep through in their millions to bring this sad episode in our history to a just and honorable close. Out of it will emerge a restored United States, prouder and stronger, ready to take its place alongside the other free nations of this world as a full partner in the planetary community that we are all now, irrevocably, a part of."

Forty minutes later, the AANS fleet steaming east-southeast from Hawaii suffered the same fate as Varney's force. It was deployed in several squadrons spread over a greater area, however, and a number of the capital ships presumably not carrying nuclear devices escaped destruction by the induced fission explosions. They were taken out during the next half hour by bombs sent down from orbit. Some of the lesser vessels survived to scatter away across the Pacific. In retaliation, the Chinese used tactical nuclear missiles against the naval force immobilized in the Panama Canal and Gatun Lake, including Hyadean defensive positions. By midnight, Union forces in Mexico were responding in kind against bases that the Chinese airborne units had seized earlier. Meanwhile, the two remaining carrier groups in the Pacific were continuing northward, now unopposed. Guesses were that their commanders had been threatened with similar treatment to the others if they failed to carry out their missions as ordered.

An exchange of nuclear weapons, even if relatively small ones, in Central America was hardly something that could be concealed from a world wrapped in communications networks. The early hours of the morning brought fear that the escalation would spread to the Midwest and Southern battle areas, and then engulf the whole continent. Emergency plans were set in motion to evacuate local populations from the vicinities of military installations and other likely targets. Indiscriminate destruction of cities was considered improbable, however, for the same reason that nobody in Sacramento felt any great urge to wipe out populaces wholesale in Pennsylvania or New Jersey— but with an imponderable alien element, who could be too sure? As a precaution, key government and military personnel began occupying their long-prepared emergency bunkers, while public announcements called for everyone else to keep calm, stay tuned, and heed the authorities. Even so, the night saw mass exoduses from major metropolitan areas from San Francisco to Minneapolis, burning up gasoline and precipitating clashes with police bent on imposing order before general panic could set in. No doubt similar scenes were occurring between the Mississippi and the East Coast too.

Staff called in on emergency shifts began arriving in the offices of the Corry Building, many of them bringing their families through fear of being separated in the event of sudden evacuation. The Catacombs below became a scene of increasing noise and activity as more functions were staffed and brought on-line, and personnel from above came down seeking space to move into, now at a premium.

A 2:00 A.M. news bulletin brought the surprise announcement that Louisiana, Arkansas, Oklahoma, and Kansas, no doubt following secret negotiations, had come over to the Federation, opening the way to the Mississippi. Virtually simultaneously, Federation aircraft and ground-based missiles opened a wave of attacks against Union positions on the far side. Gerofsky guessed that secretly prepared assault units for the crossing were already moving into position, while the armies in Texas raced forward in support. It all followed the policy that Jeye had committed to: going all-out now, before the odds against success got any less. And it seemed he was getting others to go along.

Then, at 3:35, Di Milestro's private channel from Sacramento brought the terse statement that McConnell Air Force Base near Wichita, one of the Federation's primary bases flying combat and support operations for the central sector of the front, and the air logistics center at Tinker, southeast of Oklahoma City, had been obliterated. Not simply "attacked," but "obliterated." Nine minutes later, it was the turn of the bomber and missile-support base at Grand Forks, North Dakota. They were being picked by something in polar orbit. The next sweep could be north-south through California. If so, Edwards would surely be a prime target.

Cade came around from the cubicle that Di Milestro and Gerofsky were using and into the cubbyhole where Hudro and Yassem were talking to a technician in Cairns. "Hudro, get onto the plane crew out at Edwards!" Cade exclaimed. "Tell them the hold's off. We're on our way *now*!"

Hudro looked startled. "What's happened?"

Vrel was nearby, looking across in alarm. Cade turned to him. "Vrel, bring the flyer here from the other building. We're loading up." On Vrel's other side, Nyarl was juggling data on one of the screens. "Time to wrap up," Cade told him. "That's Yassem's job now. Get the stuff sorted out now that you need to take." And then, finally answering Hudro's question, "We just got an answer to the air strikes. They're wiping out our main bases." Vrel nodded. There was no need to say anything. He hurried away. Luke finished a call he had been making. "Can you organize getting everything to be loaded up to the lobby?" Cade said to him, at the same time pulling out his phone. "See if you can get a cart from somewhere." He tried Clara's regular number. A voice told him calls were being switched to the answering system. He punched in Clara's priority code. "Where are Marie and Dee?"

"I'm here," Marie said from behind him. She had come over from the far side of the room to investigate the commotion. "Dee's upstairs talking supplies."

"Go find her. We're moving now."

"Why? What's happening?"

Clara's voice answered sleepily. "Tell you later. . . . Hi, Clara? It's Roland." Marie turned and disappeared toward the door.

"What time is it? I had to take a break."

"Sorry, but things have changed. We're leaving right away. Chester will give you the whole story. Briefly, they've started zapping air bases, and I don't want to wait for Edwards to be next. I guess you'll be the one keeping an eye on things at this end. We need to agreee who else you need to stay on here."

"Well, Luke, I guess. . . ." Clara and Luke had known each other for years. She was still having trouble surfacing.

"Yassem, we already decided," Cade said.

"Does that mean Hudro will be staying too?"

"I don't think we can let him. Neither of them knows anything about LA or anyone here. I'd rather it be Vrel. Besides, we'll need an on-board expert in Hyadean technical and military matters. That can only be Hudro. Dee can stay with Vrel."

"Fine." Clara sounded more herself now. "Do you want me to come over there? It would take me about thirty minutes."

"No, get some rest. We'll be in touch."

"Then . . . good luck. You take care, Roland. Of yourself and those others. Bring them all back in one piece."

"You too. 'Bye."

As Cade repocketed his phone, he realized that Gerofsky had joined him and had been listening. For a moment, the major seemed to have difficulty finding words. "Look, Cade . . . You were right, and we were wrong. I'd like to do more to help. Chester has to stay here as the contact man with Sacramento. But you don't know what you'll run into out there. You're going to need someone along who can deal with military people and situations. . . . Well, what I'm saying is . . ."

Cade managed a tired grin. "It's okay. You don't have to spell it out. And the answer's 'sure.' Welcome to the team."

It was a little after 4:15 A.M. when the flyer finally rose from the city and headed east of north for Palmdale. The night was clear with no moon. From above Pasadena, trains of lights showed on the darkened roads below, all heading northward to the desert. En route, Nyarl checked with the Catacombs. Yassem reported that the link from Cairns was sending, but so far there had been no response from the Querl. President Jeye wasn't backing down. The Federation had just launched IRBMs at Union air bases in Alabama and Ohio. Nobody aboard the flyer had much else to say.

Radio traffic indicated that flight operations were busy at Edwards. Ignoring ground control procedures, Hudro brought the flyer skimming in low over the perimeter fence to land at the hangars at the north end where the C22-E was waiting. The transfer of bodies, equipment, and bags still in the flyer from Cade's house that morning took place swiftly against a background of engine roars and black shapes lifting off into the night. The captain, Bob Powell, told them that operational aircraft were being dispersed to other fields and landing strips, with supply transports loading to follow later. He obviously didn't know about recent events and assumed it was a standard precaution. While they were stowing gear, Powell introduced Cade, Marie, and Gerofsky to his copilot, Lieutenant Koyne, and Technical Sergeant Davis, an aircraft engines and systems specialist. Nyarl and Hudro had met them previously.

"C22 Six Five Zero to Edwards control, we're ready to move out now and request immediate clearance," Powell said into his mike. As they ran up the engines, Koyne spotted lights approaching along the perimeter road and pointed. "Probably someone coming to check what came in over the fence," Powell grunted.

"We don't want to get bogged down now. Just pretend we haven't seen them," Cade said from behind.

Powell's face creased in the glow from the instrument panel. "Ground Control is gonna be sticky with all this traffic going out. I wouldn't want to upset them right now." He listened to something for a few seconds, then spoke into the mike again. "When? . . . We didn't see anything. . . . No, nothing to do with us. . . . Roger."

Meanwhile Nyarl, using headphones, was keeping contact with the Catacombs. He interrupted suddenly, "I'm talking to Chester. What's Travis?"

"I read you," Powell sang in the captain's seat. "Moving out now. How long is this queue gonna last?"

Koyne answered Nyarl, "Big air base up near San Francisco. Main transportation center for Pacific supply routes. Why?"

"It just got taken out."

"Never mind the queue! Get us out of here!" Cade snapped at Powell.

"You're talking court-martial offense here."

"Right now, that's the least of your worries."

"You'd better be sure about this." Powell sucked in a long breath, gunned the engines, and jerked the control column to take the plane around the shapes outlined ahead in the starlight, and across a connecting ramp to a shorter, auxiliary runway. Even from where he was sitting, Cade could hear indignant squawking in Powell's phones. Ahead, what looked like a bomber was turning to join the line lumbering toward the run-up point on the main runway. Another was waiting to mover forward. At the end of the base, several miles away in the other direction, a slim finger of peculiar violet radiance appeared suddenly, seemingly coming down from among the stars. Nyarl stared at it, speechless with sudden terror.

"Captain, go! Go now!" Hudro shouted.

His fear communicated itself. Powell opened the throttle, and the plane surged forward, even as the bomber began rolling onto the runway ahead. They squeezed through the gap accelerating flat-out. The runway seemed to flow by endlessly. Cade looked back and saw the beam of violet shift, as if registering. Nyarl seemed mesmerized by it. Finally, the plane lifted, banked, and turned away.

There was a lull, followed by several pulses of yellow light behind. A moment later, the desert lit up for miles around.

CHAPTER FIFTY-TWO

In the research center at Cairns, Krossig still hadn't recovered from the shock of learning that the Los Angeles mission, where he himself had been based until just recently, was no more. Orzin, Wyvex, Krossig's Terran colleague and friend, Mike Blair . . . all of them gone. What was happening to this world that had once been so wondrous?

The situation seemed to be deteriorating by the hour. Chinese news sources were revealing only parts of the story that he was getting from Yassem in Los Angeles—and not always accurately, at that. Further, it was only now becoming clear how much of the Terran satellite network—especially that operated by American and European concerns—the Hyadeans, by offering better technology for lower cost, had quietly replaced or come to assume control of over the years. With the remainder suddenly being subjected to jamming and neutralization following the widening hostilities, communications throughout the AANS states were drastically restricted. That meant that the connection through the precarious, politically sensitive patchwork of cables and submarine links between Cairns and Los Angeles could be broken at any time.

He sat with Ominzek, the resident Hyadean communications technician, in the gravcom room next to Freem's office in one of the timber-framed lab blocks, in front of several Terran conventional terminals and the array of gravitics gear. The center still had access to the official Chryse channel, although now subject to monitoring by the General Embassy in Xuchimbo. One of the Terran screens showed the room in Los Angeles, where Yassem reappeared intermittently to send further code patches or news input for the collection that Ominzek had ready, waiting to transmit. The Hyadean equipment showed readings from the outgoing beam control, probing regions of near-space to make contact with the Querl relays.

It was now night in Cairns. Communications with the LA mission had ceased abruptly in the early hours of the previous morning. Nobody at Cairns had been aware then of Orzin's plan to initiate an independent, uncensored channel to Chryse. The first reports that the mission had been hit by missiles came second-hand from Federation news sources. It had seemed so incongruous and devoid of rational motive that Freem had been skeptical, advising the staff not to accepting anything as final until reliable confirmation was received. The confirmation had come with the direct communication from Yassem later. Yassem was also able to confide information somehow extracted from privileged Federation sources, which so far neither side was telling the world at large.

Networks worldwide were blaring hysterically about the nuclear exchanges in Central America, which couldn't be concealed or played down. But Beijing was maintaining a blackout on the annihilation of the AANS fleet in the Pacific, and instead putting out strident appeals for solidarity and stressing the Federation's opening air offensive in the south. The retaliation against Federation air bases, carried out with direct Hyadean intervention, had not been publicized by Washington, Sacramento, or Beijing. The last thing heard from Yassem was that Cade had left in haste with Nyarl, Hudro, Marie, and a Terran officer to get their aircraft away from a base that Cade feared might be a target for further such strikes.

Freem and Susan Gray, the Terran biologist, came back in. "Anything yet?" Freem inquired.

Ominzek looked over the displays showing tables of beam-setting parameters and trial transmissions, and a graphical summary of the results so far. "Still scanning coordinates and spectra. The night's early yet."

Farther along, Krossig was watching a devastated Terran township, buildings flattened and in flames, with rescuers digging bodies and injured survivors from the ruins. The background was lost in an eerie glow, clearly radiating intense heat. "What these it show now time?" Susan asked, staring. She was one of the Terrans who attempted to learn Hyadean. The results were sometimes amusing, but Krossig and the others respected her effort.

"The latest from Yassem," Krossig replied. "Shots from McConnell. Just in over their wire from Sacramento."

"Who there provides them like this? Why?" Susan asked.

"Yassem didn't say."

An image of Nyarl appeared to one side, supplying a commentary. "The aftermath of a defenseless American habitat caught in the kill zone of one of our orbital bombardment masers." Nyarl was not actually present in LA when Yassem put the sequence together, of course; he had spoken from the flyer. "Its crime? Aircraft from the nearby McConnell base flew in defense of the newly proclaimed nation against armies sent by the Chryse-supported Washington regime. . . ."

Just then, a shrill tone sounded from the Hyadean equipment. Another display lit up with lines of data and code, while the system voice announced, *"Probe attempt Sector five six, scan three-nine, four-zero-three, five-five, Mode 7A-3, successful. Connection is to Querl deep-space monitor station, location undisclosed."*

Ominzek turned sharply and stabbed at control keys. "Gravcom Sys, Supervisor. Report link quality status."

"Resolution high at seven-two-zero. Submodal encoding. Recipient active and acknowledges."

"We're through!" Krossig whispered to Susan. "It's found one of the relays."

"Identify," Ominzek instructed.

"Nebula Two"—obviously a code name—*"Deputy commander, Querl long-range task group, nature of mission, undisclosed. Range and location coordinates suppressed. Identified as former contact established by Hetch Luodine from West Coast Trade and Cultural Mission."*

"Connect."

A relief display opened to show the figurine likeness of a lean, red-haired Hyadean in an officer-style

tunic, seated against a background tableau of panels
and bulkheads in what was evidently some kind of
control room. Nebula Two stared for a second or two,
looking at first uncertain, then suspicious. Finally, he
said, "I don't know you. We've been awaiting further
contact for over fifteen hours. What's happening? I
wish to speak with Luodine or Nyarl."

"There is unfortunate news here," Omnizek replied.
"The place Luodine was in has been destroyed. There
were no survivors. Nyarl was elsewhere and escaped.
I cannot specify our whereabouts, but we have established an alternate connection. I am a communications
technician. You can refer to me as *K*. The person who
has taken over Luodine's function is with me. His name
is *G*." Krossig moved closer to come within the viewing
angle of the unit that Omnizek was addressing.

"I must ask you to submit the agreed security
verification sequence," Nebula Two said.

"I can't. It was held in equipment that was also
destroyed," Ominzek said. "Everything was destroyed."
Codes of that kind would have been too sensitive for
Yassem to carry around as a copy. That was apparently how the technical information needed to recon-
struct the link had been preserved.

"Then how can I be sure you are who you say you
are?" Nebula Two asked.

The question had been expected. "Does it really
matter?" Krossig replied. "If we're sending you reports
that the Chrysean authorities would suppress if they
could, you can do nothing but help your own cause
by rebroadcasting them. Would impostors who were
working for the Chryseans do that?"

Nebula Two frowned as he considered the unexpected logic, but evidently couldn't fault it. He killed
the audio and disappeared from view, presumably to
consult with others.

"It isn't the time to count fishes," Susan said, attempting a Hyadean saying. It was the right sentiment but the wrong phrase. Krossig smiled tolerantly.

"How long it will take Xuchimbo to track down this equipment and silence it?" Freem muttered.

"I was wondering the same thing," Krossig said moodily. A movement caught his eye on the Terran screen connected to Los Angeles. He moved back to it. Yassem had reappeared. "We're through," he said before she had a chance to ask. "There's an authenticating problem, as we thought. I told them our answer. They're debating it now. . . ." He paused, seeing that the news wasn't having the effect he had anticipated. Yassem was looking dazed. Then Krossig realized she was in tears. "What is it?" he asked.

"They've just wiped out Edwards," she said, her voice choking. "Ten minutes after Hudro and the others arrived there." Krossig stared, horrified.

"Oh, no," Susan groaned behind him.

Nebula Two returned on the Hyadean display. "Very well," he said. "Send us what you have." Krossig nodded mutely to Ominzek.

"Gravcom Sys, Supervisor. Proceed with transfer of prepared file as previously specified," Ominzek instructed.

"*Executing.*"

Phones and terminals were beeping throughout the offices and work spaces in the vaults beneath the Corry Building. People tumbled in and out of doorways and scurried along the corridors. Everyone wanted details; city services everywhere were requesting updates and instructions. All that was known for sure was that Edwards Air Force Base had gone up in a fireball seen from Barstow to Bakersfield. There were no clear accounts of the extent of the damage, and anything could happen next.

Yassem was weeping freely, still looking at the image of Krossig in Cairns. Her tears were of relief. An adjacent screen showed Nyarl and Hudro, cramped together in the cabin of the Terran aircraft, now heading east. They had come through minutes after the news from Sacramento about Edwards. "You've got Roland to thank for it," Nyarl was saying. "If it hadn't been for him, we would never have gotten out in time."

"People seem to have a habit of surviving whenever he's around," Hudro commented, still seemingly having difficulty believing it himself.

"Marie always told me he lived a charmed life," Yassem said.

While the C22-E was setting course toward Arizona, it was early morning in New York State. It had been a night of panic in the city and continuous hysteria from the news. Drisson and Laura had moved for a couple of days to a lodge that he had rented some weeks previously away from town, up in the Catskills—as a precaution. Laura, wearing the short housecoat that she had slipped on, came back in from the kitchen, carrying two coffee cups. Drisson was sitting propped against the end of the bed. He accepted one and tasted the contents, all the time watching her contemplatively.

"Why the long, silent look?" she asked. "Don't tell me you're not satisfied. I'd never live it down."

"Oh, I'd say that's close to the last thing you have to worry about," he complimented.

"So what's such deep thought about at this time of the morning?"

Drisson took a moment to compose himself into

a more serious vein. "Things are a bit more complicated than I thought. Everybody's building walls.
Somebody like me can't go near Toddrel without
being logged and taped. If we end up having to do
this, it'll need to be from the inside. That means you
being point."

"You mean the one who actually does it? I thought
you were supposed to take care of that. I was only
an inside source. Information and access, remember?"

Drisson sighed in a way that conveyed both an
apology and weariness from considering alternatives.
"I know. But like I said, things have changed. Believe
me, I've been through all the angles. There isn't any
other way." Laura said nothing but didn't look happy
about it. He set his cup down and reached out to
grip her shoulder reassuringly. "If it comes to it, it'll
be worth it. Trust me. Then . . . it's whatever you want.
Choose a life. This outfit doesn't just deal in insurance, you know. With me you get the whole package." He eyed her for a moment. His voice took on
a coaxing tone. "Don't let me down on this, Laura.
We've both got too much at stake. He's dangerous.
You'd need it for yourself in any case, with or without me. . . . What do you say, eh? Are you made of
what I thought?"

"I'll need to think about it."

Drisson got up and went into the bathroom as if
that already decided the issue. His voice came back
through the open door. "What makes it different with
you is that you can get close and be invisible. I can't.
I figured the way would be to make it look like a
hooker or something—we all know about Casper's
kinky predilections. Totally anonymous. Nothing
anyone would want to be bothered putting any time
into—especially at times like this, with everything else
that's going on." The sound came of the shower being

turned on. Drisson's voice rose to carry above it. "So it just gets written off. We collect our retirement. Then it's away from the war to some sunny place in the world. Get the big picture, baby?"

"Oh yes." Laura murmured. "I get the picture."

CHAPTER FIFTY-THREE

Dawn greeted the C22-E, winging low over the mesas and canyons of Arizona. Cade pulled his blanket around his shoulders as he lay in the reclined seat, trying to force some sleep in the few hours that the flight would last. But he was apprehensive. The most recent news to be passed on by Yassem was of Asian missiles launched against Globalist satellites, along with orbiting Hyadean ships and other targets. Little seemed to have penetrated the Hyadean defenses, but it brought things to a new dimension of direct conflict between the AANS and the Hyadeans. Surely, there had already been clear warning of what further escalation could be expected to bring. Yet news of the setbacks was being withheld, and the Federation-AANS leaders still seemed committed to exhorting maximum effort for a swift victory, even though, as far as Cade could see, the gamble had already failed.

Marie was in the seat next to him—whether asleep or not, he couldn't tell. Copilot Koyne was flying the plane while Powell rested farther back, along with Hudro and Davis. Nyarl and Gerofsky were at consoles, editing and adding commentaries to items coming in from various sources and tagging them for transmission back to LA. The sequences included armor and supply columns moving forward to consolidate the Federation's positions between the Red River and the Mississippi, air cargo lifters delivering tanks to forward jump-off areas, and dramatic shots of the air attacks delivered during the night.

The current plan was to land and refuel near Russellville, Arkansas, in the southern Ozarks, at one of the secondary fields that the Federation's air strength was being dispersed to. There, they were to meet headquarters staff of an engineer brigade that Major Gerofsky had contacted via the military network, who would fill them in on the situation and look into further options for them to explore. In getting a connection to LA when the entire communications system was inundated, and finding contacts among the military commands in the area they were heading to, Gerofsky's contribution was already invaluable. Nyarl seemed possessed by fierce determination to carry through the task that Luodine had begun, which precluded rest and all other considerations.

As for the crew, in the little time he'd had to form any impression at all, Cade saw Powell as capable, easygoing, and sufficiently amenable to the unorthodox for an undertaking like this. Davis was taciturn, methodical, and, Cade guessed, solidly competent. Although Koyne hadn't said anything openly, Cade detected rancor at why they should be working with aliens when aliens were wiping out warships and bases, and a lot of people along with them. Cade had explained that Hudro and Nyarl were here to inform their home world of what was going on, not entertain it, and a lot of their colleagues had died, too, as a result of pursuing the same goal. Koyne seemed to accept it intellectually, but beneath, the resentment was still there. Cade hoped he would be able to just stick to his job and not let feelings become a problem.

Marie stirred, sighed drowsily, and pulled closer to his shoulder. He opened an eye momentarily. "Hi."

"Mmm. . . ."

"I thought you were asleep."

"Not really." A pause. "How do you sleep when you think the world might be about to be blown up?" A short silence passed while Marie blinked, yawned, then laid her head back, looking at him. Up front, Koyne was talking into his mike, identifying the flight in response to an interrogation from somewhere. Finally, Marie said, "Roland . . ."

"Hmm?"

"In case this whole thing doesn't . . . Well, if it all comes to the worst. I just want you to know that it could have worked again with us. There's a different side to you that I never saw until recent times."

"Maybe it didn't exist until recent times."

"It was always there. People are what they always were. It just sometimes takes new situations to bring other sides of them out."

It was meant as a genuine compliment. But Cade couldn't get lyrical at a time like this. "Well, you've sure got yourself a new situation," he said dryly.

Did Hyadeans really have a different side to them too, the way Cade thought, and Vrel, Luodine, Hudro, and others had said? If so, could it be brought out in time? Marie had told him why Luodine had believed things would happen quickly on Chryse.

Cade hoped Luodine was right. From what he could tell, everything hinged on it now.

By the time they cleared the Rockies, they were getting reports of the Union opening interdiction attacks on supply routes through Calgary, Saskatoon, Regina, and Winnipeg in answer to Canada's coming out openly for the AANS. The reason for the sudden activity in the northern theater quickly became clear. In keeping with the policy of going all-out for a quick win, the Federation was opening a second offensive, thrusting eastward between Chicago and Indianapolis, presumably to cut off the Michigan peninsula. Maybe taken by surprise, somebody in the Union command authorized the use of pocket nukes against armored spearheads that had broken through south of Indianapolis to secure a flank along the Ohio River. Sacramento ordered retaliation in kind, and a panic reaction set in on both sides to take out the other's launch sites before they could fire first, which spread rapidly. The Hyadeans in Washington decided that they weren't prepared to sit there, waiting to be nuked by squabbling Terrans, and before the C22-E reached Russellville they were intervening everywhere.

Powell was back in the skipper's seat. Everyone was awake. The airwaves were swamped with confusion on all bands as the plane descended above scrubby flats scarred by a winding creek bed, with dry hills rising on one side. There had been no response on the tower or emergency frequencies. Powell was making a visual approach based on map reading and using landmarks given by the on-board database. Ten miles out, they flew over the remains of a ground-attack intruder bearing Union markings, formerly

USAF, still burning. Black smoke rose into the sky where the airfield lay ahead.

Little of it was left. The airfield buildings and hangars were blown to pieces, the fuel storage area at one end ablaze, and the two major runways cratered and strewn with wrecked aircraft. Passing low, they could see figures moving about among scattered vehicles, many overturned or burning, more strung along the road serving the base. Some of the figures waved frantically, but it was impossible to make out what was meant. It didn't much matter, since landing was out of the question. Koyne managed to raise somebody local on radio, but what they were saying was incoherent. Nyarl got some telephoto shots.

They turned eastward to follow the Arkansas river downstream toward Little Rock. Koyne scanned frequencies for an alternative landing ground, finally making contact with the ground controller at a small airport for private planes that a Marine Corps unit had taken over in the mountainous country to the north. "C22 Six, Five Zero. We read you, Control, and are on our way in. What's the gas situation there? We're running on less than a quarter full."

"*I'll be watching for you. Every situation's a mess here. Right now we have stocks, but everyone and his brother is showing up. You may have to fight it out at the trough.*"

"Roger."

They were stacked in a pattern waiting to come in, which took them out over the flatter country around Conway and Greenbrier. Twisting plumes of smoke from downed planes and recently hit targets hung over the landscape like gigantic mutant trees. There was a lot of military activity below, with tanks and other vehicles deploying, artillery and missile positions being dug among the overlooking hills. The whole pattern of movement seemed to have reversed. In place of the confident pushes forward that had been reported all day, everything spoke of a sudden falling back on the defensive. Things were going wrong.

They had to make a slow circuit at the last moment while a crippled fighter limped in on one engine. Then, finally, they landed amid a confusion of aircraft loading and taking off, trucks and service vehicles jostling for space, and Marines digging in on the facing hillside. While Powell and Davis went to investigate the fuel situation, Cade, Gerofsky, and Hudro sought out a harassed adjutant officer who seemed to be the nearest there was to anyone knowing what was going on. It didn't amount to a lot. Orders were to get operable combat aircraft out to reserve strips farther back and clear the field for evacuation flights. Nobody was going anywhere across the Mississippi. The big buildup had been shattered by a storm of counterattacks unleashed from the other side, and what was left of it was in retreat all the way from St. Louis to the Gulf, apparently to try and form a line along the edge of the Ozark Plateau. Frantic efforts were being made to issue Nuclear, Biological and Chemical contamination suits, but preparations for such eventualities had been inadequate.

"Is wrong way," Hudro said, shaking his head. "Static lines no good against Hyadeans."

"What's the right way? Gerofsky asked.

"Move fast, all way back to Rockies, deploy new strategies, strike back unexpected. Need more air, orbit support than exists. There is no way. Terrans don't have mobility to fight Hyadean armies."

Reports coming in from elsewhere were garbled and contradictory. Even with Gerofsky's credentials linking him to the presidential staff, it proved impossible to get a connection to Yassem for the rest of the day. Amid the turmoil, Cade found a lieutenant in charge of a supply unit sending ammunition to positions being prepared farther forward. Cade explained their mission, and the lieutenant offered a ride out the next morning to see for themselves what was going on there. Cade put it to the others. They decided that Nyarl should go, naturally. Marie volunteered to assist. Since it would be a venture into a military operations area, they agreed that Gerofsky should go too. They spent the night with a Marine antiaircraft company on the edge of the airfield, sleeping in foxholes and listening to the distant drumming of artillery fire. Aircraft continued arriving and departing through the night.

After they had shared a dawn breakfast with the troops of sausage, beans, hash brown potatoes, and coffee, Hudro went to the tower with Davis to continue trying to contact Yassem. Cade remained with Powell and Koyne in the plane, preparing the new material for immediate transmission if a link was found. Marie, Nyarl, and Gerofsky hitched a ride to the supply unit, and an hour later drove out aboard an ammunition carrier going to a battery command post seven miles ahead. Nyarl carried the portable recording equipment. Gerofsky got himself and Marie issued with infantry submachine guns. She looked back in her element.

CHAPTER FIFTY-FOUR

Clara Norburn had told Major Gerofsky that Cade possessed an infectious charisma that turned people who started out as opponents into willing collaborators. That was how he had prospered in his unique business of trading commercial and political contacts. The South American TV documentary that had helped propel the Federation to secession had been the work of a mix of Terrans and Hyadeans that he, more than anyone, had brought together. And then Gerofsky had experienced it himself in the space of a few hours, when he found himself reversing his initial position to first endorse, and then join, the enterprise they were committed to now. Admittedly, Cade had failed to win any converts among the high command he had met in Beijing, but the fact that he had even gotten a hearing was in itself an accomplishment not to be belittled.

After hearing Hudro voicing his doubts, Gerofsky

was even more mindful now of Cade's warning that a head-on clash with the aliens could only lead to disaster. If the news they were getting of the Federation's offensive being hurled back all the way down the southern Mississippi front was correct— never mind what was happening farther north between St. Louis and Indianapolis—the war was not going to be won in a rapid pincers movement through Pittsburgh and up the east side of the Appalachians as had been intended. But the mood permeating from Sacramento was still to defy and fight, not look for ways of winding down. What disturbed Gerofsky most after hearing Hudro's pronouncement on mobility was the speed with which counter-thrusts seemed to have materialized out of nowhere, already this side of the river—in less than a day! It went against all the accepted norms and doctrines of what should have been possible. Conceivably for that very reason, the commanders were failing to grasp the implications and still preparing for defense against the kind of war they knew.

They drove past pits and emplacements being prepared among the low hills overlooking the plains extending away toward Stuttgart and the Mississippi valley: 125 mm howitzer batteries; 155 mm self-propelled howitzers being dug in hull-down; medium-range ground-to-ground missile launchers; mobile AA missile carriers and multibarrel antiaircraft cannon. Heavy-lift helicopters *whup-whupp*ed their way overhead, hauling dangling artillery pieces and crates of missiles to forward positions. Finally, the carrier bearing him and the others came to a false crest ahead of a ridge line, behind which the battery they were delivering to had been situated. The view over the lowlands ahead showed tanks spreading out and deploying behind cover; weapons emplaced along a creek bed; a command post undergoing camouflage and concealment. . . . All according to the book. But this was over a hundred miles from the Mississippi. If they were already facing a credible threat as far advanced as this, then what they were facing was from a totally different book.

Nyarl kept busy throughout, capturing anything that caught his interest. Since there was no quality connection back to the plane, he was storing the clips offline for delivery later. Some of the troops they passed reacted sourly to seeing a Hyadean, once or twice with open hostility, and Gerofsky had to defend Nyarl's presence repeatedly. He himself was having to work at accepting Marie—until so recently one of the enemy in the form of CounterAction. He studied her as she sat perched on one of the carrier's box sides, cradling her weapon, clearly awed by the extreme to which those efforts had finally contributed, yet also deeply apprehensive. She saw him from the corner of her eye and turned her head.

"It feels strange, us being on the same side." Gerofsky looked around. "A bit overwhelmed? Not what you expected?"

"We wanted to awaken the people," Marie answered. "Not all-out war. Somehow it all went out of control. Do you understand it?"

"I'm not sure anyone understands it. These things take on lives of their own."

The whoosh came of an outgoing missile launching distantly, followed by another. Marie gazed after them as they cleared the skyline. "And now we're trying to do the same thing again, only this time on Chryse."

"Is it possible to make it work there, when it didn't seem to here, do you think?" Gerofsky asked.

"Nyarl thinks so. He says minds work differently on Chryse."

Gerofsky stared across at him on the far side, panning the camera at a field radar being set up. "Let's hope he's right. It might be the only chance we've got."

As a precaution, Powell had moved the C22-E out to a corner of the field, away from the airport buildings and the crush of aircraft loading or maneuvering into a takeoff line to evacuate the field. That was probably what saved it when the attack came in.

Cade was in the cabin, keeping an open radio channel to Hudro and Davis in the tower; Powell was standing outside, taking in the general scene. Suddenly a shriek of warning sirens went up, and within moments, all over the airfield amid shouted orders and calls to stations, figures were jumping into slit trenches, running for cover, manning antiaircraft weapons. Short-range ground-to-air missiles were already flaming away all around like birds lifting in response to a spreading alarm call. Cade grabbed the helmet he had been given and tumbled out of the plane to join Powell in the ditch by the perimeter taxiway. The thudding of gunfire, felt as continuous jolting to the ears rather than heard, was already coming from the north. Then the harsher barking of fast-firing, smaller-caliber weapons joined in, getting nearer.

They came in low over the hilltops with a roar rising to a scream, a loose formation of maybe ten or twelve. Cade didn't know the type—they were just glimpses of bodies and wings outlined against the sky. One disintegrated as it cleared the ridge and fell on the slopes below in a cascade of flame. The lead group blanketed the ground defenses with rockets and fragmentation cluster. The rest went down into strafing runs to pour cannon fire and scatter low-yield bomblets across the field. One aircraft failed to lift with the others, hitting the ground and exploding somewhere beyond the far end of the field. Cade pushed himself up slowly from the ground, dazed by the suddenness and the violence of it. Slowly, he registered planes sagging and broken amid the smoke; figures picking themselves up, staggering among the wreckage, pulling others out; the cacophony impressing itself from all sides as his numbed ears recovered, of exploding ammunition, screams for help, voices shouting. Beside him, Powell straightened up, looking about. A transport on the main runway, one of its wings torn at the root and draped back over the fuselage, erupted into a fireball. Smoke billowed outward over the ground in a churning curtain, and then several figures ran out covered in blazing fuel. Somebody from a rescue tender doused them with foam while others grabbed them and tried to roll them on the ground. Another was trying to unfold a tarp. Cade could only stare, numbed by the horror of it. Then the sharp *crack* of something detonating overhead made him look up. It was like a Fourth of July star burst, except that the objects being ejected from the center were not incendiary submunitions but self-powered devices like birds that seemed to be dispersing. Another exploded above the far end of the field. Then another, off to one side. Still bewildered, Cade turned his head toward Powell. "What the hell are those?"

Powell shook his head. "It beats me. All I know is, I've never heard of anything like 'em before."

The side of the tower facing the field had been raked by cannon fire. In what was left of the day room on the ground floor, Hudro groped his way through the smoke and dust, lifting aside a steel locker that had been thrown at an angle against the wall. A body that had been pinned behind it slid down into a heap. Somebody was groaning and calling for aid in the direction of the stairs. A corpsman in a helmet bearing a red cross appeared from outside and went on through. Hudro came to the daylight but kept back within the frame of the doorway while he took in the situation. Sergeant Davis, his face bloody and covered in dust, stumbled up beside him.

Flocks of what looked like gliding, stubby-winged birds were spiraling down to settle all over the airfield. A plane that seemed to have escaped serious damage lurched its way out from behind a transport that was starting to burn and turned toward the main runway. A swarm of maybe a dozen small shapes, some rising from the surrounding ground, others not yet landed, converged upon it like dogs around a bear, each exploding on contact to leave the aircraft crippled and immobile. Two more homed on a staff car racing along the nearby verge, causing it to swerve and overturn. One came down off a hangar roof to explode among a group of figures running toward the fire shed. Another rose up from the sand to pursue a soldier who jumped up from a foxhole, getting close enough before detonating to blow off his upper body.

"What in the name of Christ are they?" Davis asked fearfully.

Hudro scanned the surrounding. Similar things were happening in every direction as panic took over. The sounds of intensifying battle were coming distantly but insistently from the east. "Smart drones," he replied. "Is way to deny use of base but not destroy. Means they plan to take over soon. Next attack will be with fragmentation—like rain of razors."

Davis gulped. "You mean we're supposed to just sit here, waiting to get blended?"

"Terrans don't have defenses."

"So what are we supposed to do?"

"Must first stop fear and movement. Need radio." Hudro led the way back inside, where they picked up a dazed tower crew operator in a blood-streaked shirt. "Find working radio," Hudro told him. "Local channels, all commanders you can talk with outside. Tell nobody to move. Stay still, is okay. Tell them pass message on."

A Marine private who had come down from the upper level overheard. "There was a Hummer out back. Its radio should be okay. It may have a loud hailer too." He thought about it. "Would that be safe?"

"Is good," Hudro said. "Drones don't use sound sensor. We go see."

While the tower officer started checking the equipment, Hudro, Davis, and the Marine made their way through to the rear of the building and looked out. A Hummer command car was parked along with several other vehicles, all looking unscathed. Hudro raised a warning hand as they were about to emerge. "Now must move very slow. Good chances. You see." They approached the Hummer like slow-motion mimes. Hudro indicated the driver's seat to Davis. "I never learn to drive Terran machines. Is yours."

Davis looked nervous. "With those things everywhere?"

"Must drive very careful. Move no more than one foot in two seconds. Can do, yes?"

They climbed in. Davis started the motor, and with his knuckles white on the wheel, negotiated the Hummer foot by foot around the building until they could see out over the field again, then stopped. The Marine located the loud hailer and began addressing the general area. "HEAR THIS.

HEAR THIS. GENERAL ALERT. BE AWARE OF MOTION DETECTION. MAKE NO RAPID MOVEMENT. REPEAT, DO NOT MAKE RAPID MOVEMENTS. . . ."

Hudro, meanwhile, toyed with the vehicle's radio and raised the operator they had left inside the tower. "We've managed to contact some of the units out there," the operator reported. "Still trying more." Sure enough, the panic seemed to be abating, giving way to a strained, nervous paralysis spreading across the field.

"Maybe there is way to get out," Hudro said finally.

"What?" Davis asked.

Hudro squinted, peering through the intervening smoke in the direction of a large, four-turbofan freighter that he had spotted earlier, stopped at the far end of the runway. It had been about to turn for its takeoff run when the attack came in. Its tail was in tatters, but it seemed otherwise intact. "What kind of aircraft is this?" he asked Davis.

"Which?"

Hudro pointed. "Far away distance. Other end of runway. Tail in pieces."

"Looks like a C-17."

Hudro talked to the operator in the tower. "This airfield. It has electronics for take-off blind, yes?'

"Yes sir. The Marines set up mobile ILS system that would do that. Don't know if it's still functioning, though."

"So we have to risk. Is C-17 plane at other end runway. Can speak with captain?"

"Let me try." The operator did, and got a connection.

"Tell him this," Hudro instructed. "Turn plane very, very slow so that engine fans blow down along field, yes. Contact officer who commands unit that end. Must get together tires, spare wheels from trucks . . . whatever. Cover with gasoline and set fire. C-17 must blow across field. Thick rubber smoke confuses drone sensors. Is even better if they add magnesium flare or white phosphorus from smoke rounds. Set plenty fire to grass."

"You think it could really work?" Davis asked dubiously.

"You want wait for blender instead?"

While the instructions were being relayed to the far end of the field, Hudro told Davis to begin heading back to where the C22-E was parked. The Marine private opted to stay with them. They inched their way agonizingly toward the edge of the field, Hudro remaining outwardly impassive, the Marine white-faced and rigid. Davis had to stop three times to calm his nerves. They had about fifty yards to go, when a desperate voice called out to them. Davis stopped. They looked around. "There," the Marine said, pointing.

It was Koyne, lying in the grass behind a mound of sand where he had taken cover—presumably on his way back from the workshops, where he had gone to check for some parts. "Are you hurt?" Davis called over. Koyne shook his head in a short, jerky motion, then inclined it to indicate a spot to the side of him. A drone was lying there, just a yard or two away. It was yellow with black markings, about the size of a crow, but at close range looking more like a malevolent giant insect.

"Oh shit. . . ." Davis hissed.

"Is okay if you move slow," Hudro called over, striving to keep his voice calm. "But careful." In a lowered tone he muttered to the other two, "More close, gets riskier."

But Koyne just shook his head again. "I can't."

Clearly, he was petrified. He must have been pinned there for over thirty minutes.

Hudro looked around. There was a fire extinguisher behind the seat on the Hummer's passenger side. "Give that," he said to the Marine, motioning with his head. The Marine moved warily, as if he were picking up Koyne's terror, unclamped the extinguisher and passed it forward. Hudro took it, removed the pin, and clasped the activating lever in readiness. Then, moving in carefully controlled slow motion, he straightened up from the passenger seat to place one foot outside the vehicle, following it slowly with the other.

Davis, the Marine, and Koyne watched barely daring to breath as the alien took what must have been five seconds to complete one step, then did the same again with the other foot as if approaching a coiled cobra. Koyne looked up, rivers of perspiration running down his face, while Hudro drew nearer until he was standing immediately over the drone. Keeping his movement just as slow, he raised the nozzle of the extinguisher and covered the drone in foam.

"Is safe now," he told Koyne.

It took Koyne a few seconds more to move. He rose slowly and backed away toward the Hummer, unable to take his eyes off the drone. Hudro gave it another blast of foam and then followed.

"You okay?" Davis asked Koyne as he climbed shakily into the seat behind.

Koyne licked his lips and nodded. He looked disbelievingly at Hudro as Hudro got back in up front. "I guess those people were right. . . . Some of you guys are okay. That took a lot of guts. Thanks."

"Is we Hyadeans who make drone and bring here. What else I can do?" Hudro replied.

✧   ✧   ✧

They were in the form of immense, flattened pyramids, five times as wide across the base as they were tall, glinting a peculiar bronzelike luster between black ribbing and casement structures in the light of the late afternoon sun. Armor-piercing shells skidded harmlessly off their angled faces. Proximity-bursting missiles seemed to have no effect. They advanced in a line several hundred feet above the ground, generating a zone of boiling light and fire beneath that progressed like a wall. Nothing stood up to it. Gerofsky had watched tanks, armored personnel carriers, gun emplacements, consumed like paper balls thrown into a furnace. A wing of the newest supersonic F-19s that went in against them had been picked off like ducks by beams of some kind directed from unseen sources above.

In the positions among the crests of the overlooking slopes, order was starting to break down, with troops getting jumpy, some already falling back, commanders frantically talking into field radios and pleading for orders. Gerofsky could feel himself verging on panic. Yet Nyarl was actually standing, his face expressionless, training his camera, catching everything. The task had become an obsession with him. Suddenly, he looked at Marie, crouched behind the edge of the trench they were occupying ahead of the battery, clutching her useless submachine gun. "Come out and stand up," he called to her. "I want you in the foreground. A Terran woman facing Chrysean war engines that are destroying her world." Marie stared at him, as if checking that his sanity hadn't snapped. He gestured and smiled humorlessly. "I know the psychology of Hyadeans. . . . No, don't put the gun down. Keep it in your hand. Defiant to the last, eh? They'll love it." Gerofsky watched as Marie climbed out from the trench and complied. "The world that invented

painting and music, philosophy and dreams," Nyarl
went on as he lined up the camera. "Einstein and
Mozart. Both crafters of realities that captivate the
imagination but could never be."

Surely, Gerofsky thought, if Nyarl could get this
one shot back to Chryse, it would be enough to stop
this. It was obscenity, not war. For the first time in
his career, he found himself wondering if there had
ever been a difference.

Bolts of plasma began coming down from the sky
and exploding among weapons positions, defense lines,
supply dumps. There was nothing for the targeting
radars to register on, nothing to be done if they could.
The troops entrenched along the crests began falling back; then the support units. Soon, everything
became a scramble to get away to the rear. Gerofsky
halted the ammunition carrier that they had ridden
out on, now jammed with troops, just as it was pulling
out and bundled Marie and Nyarl aboard. A half mile
down the road it became bogged down in a jam
tailing back from some kind of obstruction ahead. It
would be a death trap when the next attack came in.
Gerofsky ordered the other two out. Hauling a radio
after him, he stumbled with them across the slopes
toward a dirt track rising to follow a ridge. It was
bumpy and not all that wide; but it ran straight.
Before very much longer there wouldn't be any other
chance.

The smoke swirled by outside as an opaque fog.
From behind Powell, Cade watched the lights of the
transport ahead vanish as if they had been switched
off. Powell counted off fifteen seconds and then
gunned the C22-E's engines. The plane headed into
a black wall hurtling by at increasing speed. Cade felt
his hands and back going clammy, wishing he could

share the faith in technology of the two seated in front
of him. Powell concentrated on the ILS readouts,
while Koyne read off the instruments. Cade didn't
want to think about the consequences if something
had screwed up invisibly ahead of them. There could
be no ground control. Visibility from the tower was
zero. Finally, they were at liftoff speed. Powell hauled
back the stick, and moments later they emerged into
evening. Leveling out low, he banked into a broad
right turn that would take them over the hills toward
the east, where ominous black clouds towered over
the skyline.

They had waited while the evacuation proceeded,
following Hudro's crazy plan. With an attack expected
at any time, Powell had set a time limit, after which
the safety of the aircraft would have to come first.
They would leave and endeavor to make contact with
the others again later, somehow. Despite his sickening visions of being parted from Marie yet again, Cade
had been unable to argue. Gerofsky reached them on
radio minutes before the deadline was up. Now, all
they had to do was find him.

"Okay, we're airborne, turning your way," Powell
said into his mike. "Keeping it down, just above
stalling. Let us know when you have visual."

"Jesus, it's a mess down there," Koyne said, cran-
ing on the other side of the cockpit. "Whatever
happened up front? They're streaming back everywhere." Cade stared down. How could the confidence
that had been everywhere this morning have degenerated to this in one day? Hudro looked out sadly,
shook his head, and said nothing.

They took a slow, winding course, banking to sweep
left and right. Suddenly, Powell announced, "They've
got us!" Then, into his mike, "Roger, Major. I read
you. Turning as directed. . . . Yes, I see a ridge with

a track. Okay, got it. . . . I'm going to have to go around again and line up. . . ."

It was a bone-shaking landing, but they made it. Nyarl climbed in first, still with his camera. Marie followed, and then Gerofsky. With them were three young, frightened soldiers they had run into on the way. Powell took them aboard.

Marie collapsed into Cade's arms before the plane had even commenced its run. She was pale and gaunt, with a look in her eyes that Cade had never seen before—the kind of look that might never completely go away. He looked at her and shook his head uncomprehendingly, not sure what to say. She leaned her head against his shoulder for what seemed a long time. "Oh God, Roland," she managed finally. "It was horrible. I thought I was tougher than this by now. . . . This has become insane."

"Was always insane," Hudro said neutrally from his seat farther back.

Cade pulled her close and pressed her head against him. "We don't split up again," he told her. "Through whatever happens, wherever it leads. We're together until the end now."

CHAPTER FIFTY-FIVE

They flew west into the night, heading north of Tulsa toward what had seemed to be a major staging area. Koyne reported air activity in the vicinity and registered numerous radar contacts. There were many fires along the route: some isolated and confined, suggesting burning vehicles or downed planes; others covering whole areas. In one place a sizable town looked to be ablaze from end to end. With the navigation aids disrupted, it was difficult to say exactly where it was.

The snippets coming in over the radio were garbled and panicky. A Union spearhead was already halfway between St. Louis and Kansas City, with another thrusting north along the Mississippi valley and threatening a massive left hook at Chicago, which would cut off the Federation armies that had advanced into Indiana and Illinois—assuming they hadn't been annihilated already. To the south they were reported to be near Shreveport, and the Dallas area was under attack. Gerofsky shook his head in bewilderment as Nyarl read off the details. "How is it possible? Under combat conditions? Nothing could move that fast."

"I tell you, you don't have mobility," Hudro said. "They don't move like you think. Hyadeans unroll carpet from sky." Twenty minutes later, Nyarl proved it with a shot he had received from somewhere along the Missouri valley, of Union armor emerging from huge, lumpy, gray vessels, looking like wedge-shaped landing craft, that had descended from the sky. "They're the size of battleships!" a commentator's terrified voice jabbered. "The defense is just coming apart! We've got a total rout on our hands here."

There were some heroics to record. West of St. Louis, a Federation Ranger force drew a detachment of Hyadean ground troops that had been landed on a flank into a classic ambush with pre-targeted mortars and prepared mines, and wiped them out. A pair of aging F-15s destroyed one of the flying pyramid-fortresses at Texarkana and Nyarl got a clip of it. But the overall picture was grim. But still there seemed to be no word from Sacramento to call it off. Gerofsky's guess was that events had happened so quickly, and communications were in such chaos, that nobody there had grasped the enormity of what was going on.

"Darn it, look at that!" Powell exclaimed suddenly, at the same time banking the plane sharply to port.

"What is it?" Gerofsky called from behind Cade.

Koyne half turned his head, keeping his eyes on the outside. "Tracer coming up. Friendly fire."

"I guess there must be a lot of trigger-happy people down there tonight," Powell growled.

"Let's hope they're nervous enough not to shoot straight," Marie said. Even as she spoke, a series of flak bursts lit up ahead.

Powell throttled up and went into a tight, diving, starboard turn. "This is getting serious," he muttered. Moments later, there was an explosion outside close enough to light up the inside of the cabin, and the plane shuddered under a hail of impacting fragments. Wind whipped through the cabin from a rent in the skin somewhere. Powell straightened out but held the dive, shedding altitude for ground cover. Something was beeping up front. From where he was sitting, Cade could see alarm indicators flashing and lighting up all over the instrument panel. Powell and Koyne went into an emergency check routine. "Losing fuel on one engine," Powell called. "We're going down. Be ready for fire." Behind him, Davis broke out an extinguisher from a bulkhead rack. Marie found another at the rear of the cabin. Powell switched to emergency band and began sending out Mayday messages for a landing ground.

They found haven at a airstrip that was being used for night operations. A young Officer of the Watch who met them informed them they were twenty miles southeast of Wichita. The strip's combat aircraft were being evacuated before dawn; then it would be handling ambulance flights for as long as possible. Apart from that, he didn't know too much except that things seemed to be a mess everywhere. He sounded as if he was from New York.

The three soldiers that the C22-E had picked up left to find a unit to attach themselves to. While Powell and Davis began checking over the damage to the airplane, the others shared a beef stew supper with a maintenance crew in an Air Force trailer. Afterward, Gerofsky and Hudro borrowed a jeep and drove off in the direction of Wichita to seek news at the headquarters of an armored corps stationed in the area. A little over an hour later, a corporal from the signals unit serving the airstrip telephoned the trailer to report that he had Gerofsky on another channel with a data connection open, and could Nyarl get over with the material to be transmitted? Cade and Marie went with Nyarl to the sandbagged dugout that the CO's staff and signals unit were occupying, close to the airstrip's few buildings. Gerofsky had a landline connection to the Southern California Military Command in Los Angeles, and from there had succeeded in getting through to the Catacombs. So, finally, they were able to send through the recordings that had been accumulating. Yassem and Vrel were at the other end. Having spoken with Hudro and Gerofsky already, they had recovered by now from their anxiety at hearing nothing for two days.

They still had the link to Cairns, but it would be six or seven hours before Cairns would be able to link with the Querl. The unpublicized news from Beijing, obtained via Di Milestro's line from Sacramento, was even more alarming than what had happened in the previous forty-eight hours in the Midwest. A Chinese nuclear antisatellite missile had knocked out a major Hyadean vessel in orbit, and the Hyadeans were retaliating against military targets on the Asian mainland. Nothing of the kind had been heard in Australia. The entire global situation was unstable. Collapse into universal catastrophe seemed only a matter of time.

"I don't understand it," Cade said to Yassem and Vrel. "Why isn't Jeye doing anything to restrain them—after what's happened here? He must know it's all over."

"But that's the problem," Yassem said. "I don't think they *do* know. It's as Major Gerofsky feared. They're still talking about a decisive struggle going on along the Mississippi valley—as if they still think they really can be in Washington in days. None of the advisers there understands how fast Hyadeans can move. They've lost touch with the real world."

"Get Chester to find someone up there that he can talk sense into," Cade pleaded. "We may have to be out of here by morning. I'm not even sure the plane will be able to fly."

They slept, exhausted, in an adjacent trailer serving as a billet. As Cade was dropping off, he heard the first of the helicopters coming in, bringing wounded to the ambulance planes. Nyarl was still over in the signals dugout, sorting through clips that Gerofsky and Hudro had sent via the data line and adding his own histories and commentaries for the benefit of the Chryseans. Sounds of gunfire and explosions came continuously from the direction of Wichita like dull, intermittent thunder.

Cade regained consciousness sluggishly to the feeling that something was strange. A reflex inside him didn't want to know what. It wanted to retreat back into sleep and not face any more of reality. But a more responsible part of himself still in control forced him back to wakefulness.

The distant booming was still going on, but he had already learned to tune that out. Nearer, everything was too quiet. There were no sounds of helicopter rotors or the roars of planes taking off. He sat up in the bunk and looked around the trailer. Marie was still fast asleep. So was Nyarl—for once—and Hudro, who must have returned with Gerofsky sometime in the middle of the night. Voices sounded nearby outside, followed by a truck motor starting up. Cade felt a mind-deadening weariness. It was as if the adrenaline charge that had kept him going through the previous few days had finally worn off, letting him sink to rock bottom. He had no recollection of the names of the officer who had received them or the signals corporal. They were just faces in a daily pageant that unrolled, and beyond the immediate object of staying alive, was ceasing to mean anything. And right now, he admitted to himself, he was scared. He didn't care that much about the Federation, what happened on Chryse, or great plans for how things would be a hundred years from now. What mattered was getting through until next week.

He swung his legs down to the floor and pulled on his boots. His face, when he rubbed it, felt stubbly and greasy. He went through to the washroom at the end of the trailer and ran water into the metal basin. The water was cold. The only towel was wet. He dried himself with tissue, came back to put on his shirt and jacket, and went outside.

The scene in daylight was the kind of litter that only the military in wartime can produce. Cartons, cases, drums, and debris were everywhere, with scatterings of dead cartridge cases, oddments of ammunition, tangles of wire, emptied food cans and rations packs, remnants of clothing. All that was left of the air traffic were several disabled planes and a helicopter, which a demolition crew was wiring with charges. A huge pall of smoke hung in the sky to the northwest. The remainder of the detachment that hadn't already left was congregating around a mix of cars, trucks, a couple of tankers, and other vehicles in the final stages of loading. Some civilians had appeared in a gaggle of heavily loaded cars and pickup trucks standing along the road at the end of the strip. Evidently, they were pulling out but had decided it would be safer to stay with the soldiers. Several men were rummaging among the piles of discarded supplies. Gerofsky and the C22-E's crew were conferring by the aircraft, parked fifty yards or so away. They saw Cade emerge. Gerofsky and Powell came over.

"We've got a problem with one of the pumps," Powell informed him. "Davis has rigged a temporary fix, but it needs a part we don't have. If it fails, I wouldn't trust the other engine alone to keep us up. We can risk it, but we might not be so lucky finding a place to get down next time. The alternative is to go with these guys in one of the trucks."

Cade didn't like the thought of leaving all that equipment while it might still have some use. He looked at Gerofsky. "What do you think, Major?"

"I say we risk it. Look at the jam we ran into yesterday—and that was up among hills. Everything's going to be squeezing through Wichita." A series of cracking sounds rippled from the north. They looked and saw the smoke of air bursts a mile or two off, that had come in several seconds previously. "And that's going to get worse," Gerofsky added.

"Where do we head for?" Cade asked.

"Anywhere. Union troops are already in Kansas City. Let's just get out of here."

"That's good enough for me," Cade said. He nodded to Powell. "Okay, let's have her loaded and ready. I'll get the others up."

Wichita had become a bottleneck of retreating infantry, armor, and support columns, and streams of refugees converging northward from Oklahoma City and Tulsa, and west from the region south of Kansas City toward routes west through Dodge City and Pueblo. The area had been under attack through the night, and by the time the C22-E skirted low over the city on the southern side, presented a virtually unbroken spectacle of burning and devastation. Connecting the camera directly to one of the cabin displays, Nyarl brought telescopic views of knocked-out tanks, cratered malls and highways, streets ablaze, strewn with bodies and overturned vehicles. In one place, an overpass had fallen on a line of army trucks and yellow schoolbuses. A suburban airfield was covered with the wreckage of dozens of planes caught on the ground. Stranded vehicles were everywhere, their occupants sitting outside waiting for direction, besieging dressing stations and aid posts, or simply taking what they could and joining a tide of stragglers heading onward toward the west on foot, or at least just getting clear of the city.

Radio traffic was primarily local and concerned with emergencies: a hospital somewhere was on fire and being evacuated; a supply battalion was out of reserves of gasoline; a plane was in trouble and needed a directional fix. From an armchair up in the sky, it was easy to let it all feel unreal and detached. But just looking at Marie's face as they listened to the snatches of people in fear, people dying, calling for help, others just trying to do their jobs, forced Cade to be mindful that every one was a tragedy happening to somebody right now, each representative of a hundred others that they didn't know about, and very probably no one ever would know about. The pointlessness and the waste of it all came to him then in a way as never before. The inexhaustible potential of human creativity, and what it could produce, the limitless resource of young, educated minds to turn worlds into gardens, tame the power that drove stars, bring life and consciousness to the cosmos. And instead of what could have been, how much of it was squandered on death-dealing and destruction? The Hyadeans had created a whole legend out of what Earth could have been—what they described as the world of dreams. Was it to end as a nightmare?

As they came around onto a course heading for Denver, the skyline behind erupted in a series of black fountains from another salvo of missiles descending on the stricken city.

Nyarl made contact with an airborne command post flying somewhere above Colorado. The latest they had heard was that the attacks on China were now public news and intensifying. Houston was in Union hands, San Antonio was threatened, and Chicago encircled. Ellis in Washington was demanding unconditional surrender, but Jeye, following Beijing, had vowed to fight on and was escalating the use of battlefield nuclear devices. Nyarl sent off his latest package.

They covered a further four hundred miles, most of it over a flat, checkerboard Kansas landscape of straight roads and rectangular fields before the pump that Davis had jury-rigged failed. Soon afterward, the other engine began misbehaving under the added load, and Powell decided it would be better to land now, while they still had power at all. They were past the Colorado border, above dry prairie grasslands beginning to give way to desert. Powell found a road carrying military traffic widely spaced against air attack, mixed with clusters of civilian vehicles, all heading west, and put down on a stretch of sandy flat close by. The nose wheel collapsed, probably from a combination of plowing into the soft ground and the rough landing on the ridge the previous day, and they came to a spectacular skidding, grinding halt, shaken but otherwise unharmed.

Nyarl selected a minimum of equipment to be carried, while the others sorted out personal kit, tools, maps and documents, and supplies from the plane's galley. Davis broke out a cache of weapons that he had acquired and distributed them in addition to the ones that Marie and Gerofsky were already carrying, giving Cade an automatic rifle. Cade had never fired a gun. Marie promised him an improvised lesson.

Hudro refused. "No," he said. "I see too much. I no longer carry weapons."

CHAPTER FIFTY-SIX

A staff car stopped in response to Gerofsky's flagging. It was carrying the acting commanding officer of a motorized infantry regiment pulling back to a redoubt that was being formed south of Denver. Apparently, the armies of the central front were attempting to consolidate a line along the eastern edge of the Rockies. The vehicles were already crammed with wounded and stragglers picked up along the way, and the group from the downed plane had to be spread out among several to find room. Gerofsky squeezed into the staff car with the officers. Koyne insisted on accompanying Hudro in an armored personnel carrier to make it clear to any objectors that "this guy is okay." Nyarl went with Powell and Davis in a supply truck. Cade and Marie found space in an open truck carrying a field-gun crew with their artillery piece hauled behind. Cade felt as if he were back in Brazil after the helicopter crash. But this wasn't happening in

Brazil; it was the middle of what used to be the U.S.A. At least, whatever lay ahead this time, he and Marie would face it together.

The air attacks came in at intervals ranging from twenty or thirty minutes to an hour or more. Sometimes they took the form of jets screaming in low to strafe and walk bombs and rockets along the column; at others, air-bursting missiles launched from several miles away. These were Terran weapons systems, not Hyadean, and Cade saw a number of the attacking aircraft brought down. Existence degenerated into a dull, stomach-churning, constant awareness of vulnerability and feeling helpless. The shouts of *"Cover! Air incoming!"*; the sour taste of fear, face pressed to the sand while the ground shuddered and white-hot metal hissed overhead; climbing wearily back into the truck, blurred into a routine that he found himself acting out mechanically with deadened senses. A few images remained etched in his memory: a soldier staggering from a truck that had been hit, one arm and one side of his face a blackened mass; a limbless torso in a ditch; a civilian bus with corpses hanging out of the shattered windows. And he began to understand how it was possible for people to see others killed, maimed, burned, blown apart, and no longer be capable of feeling anything. When survival became the driving consideration, something primitive and protective took over, shrinking one's focus to a narrow world of self and the few who qualified for the time being as one's "own."

Changing drivers in shifts, the depleted column carried on through the night through Pueblo, the terrain becoming more broken and craggy. Flashes and lights continued to light up the horizon all around, but the immediate attacks slackened to a few intermittent missiles coming in just often enough to make rest impossible when physical and nervous exhaustion craved relief into sleep. Cade sat hunched by Marie, his body aching and protesting more as with every mile the truck's metal-and-fabric seats seemed to get harder and grow new sharp corners. If life ever returned to normal, and if they survived to enjoy it, he would never complain about airlines again, he told himself.

Daybreak brought a scene of dry gulches, mesas, and rocky bluffs rising among broken, dusty mountains of brown and gray ahead. This seemed to be the outer edge of the defensive line, with forward positions being prepared and activity visible away into the distance on both sides. The commander called a halt to regroup the regiment's scattered vehicles, give the stragglers time to catch up, and assess losses. Two trucks were missing, which was not as bad as the attrition that some units had suffered. One of them, however, was the one that Nyarl, Powell, and Davis had been riding in. Radio calls for it to report in brought no response. Hudro and Koyne were the most shaken by the news—understandably.

Heroic and desperate, maybe, but it all seemed an invitation for a repeat of the carnage that had happened yesterday. Cade and the others made themselves as useful as they could, all the time waiting apprehensively; but as the morning drew on, the skies remained strangely quiet. Subtly but significantly, something had changed. Everyone could sense it, but nobody was quite able to say what.

Cade watched a tank crew carrying out repairs under camouflage netting to something in the engine compartment of their machine, which they had opened up. None of them could have been more than in their early twenties, except maybe the captain, who could have been brushing twenty-five. They worked calmly and competently, despite the stress and fatigue they had to have suffered over the past few days. Cade had never had much of a head for machinery or technicalities—his talents lay more with human foibles—but he had always respected and marveled at the mentalities that could conceive and construct generating plants, jet planes, automobiles, and telephone networks, and generally bring into being the world of material productivity that enabled his world to exist comfortably and prosperously. He marveled at it now, seeing the exposed, precisely machined gears, tangles of piping, bundles of color-coded cables snaking like vines to reach mysterious cylinders and inscrutable metal boxes. What had it taken in human worth and ingenuity, education, training, dedication to make possible the display of skill that he was witnessing now? And by how much more would that need to be multiplied to take into account everything else that was going on across the continent right now? And then add the factories that had produced it all, and behind them all the mining, drilling, rolling, forging, refining, processing that sustained them. For what? The price in expended human value was incalculable.

Though awesome in its image of menace and power, the tank was ugly and utilitarian. Cade took in the squat lines of the turret carrying its long-barreled cannon; the impersonal lethality of the grenade throwers and machine guns protruding from invisible stations within; the hatch lids open, revealing the armor thickness that its crew would depend on when they became the stakes in a duel pitting the abilities of rival teams of designers. Two armorers were loading ammunition from a field tractor:

different shapes and casings, some with dull black bodies, others yellow, another kind white. Gerofsky had described a standard type of armor-piercing round which punched a hole through the hull and blasted a jet of white-hot molten metal into the interior.

He looked at the crew again: each life potentially priceless by the measures of the economy of Chryse, dedicated to the sole purpose of killing and maiming indistinguishable others who had played the same games, had the same kinds of kid brothers and older sisters, parents, lovers, guys on the street in the same kinds of neighborhoods of the same kinds of homes. In Australia, Krossig had described the new insight that he and Mike Blair had found, which made all of physical reality an environment contrived—implicitly by some as-yet incomprehensible intelligence?—for the purpose of enabling consciousnesses to make choices. If so, then surely the choices being made by the consciousnesses dominating this particular part of that reality qualified it as the lunatic asylum of the cosmos. Or was it as bad everywhere? Cade wondered.

"Guys! Look!" A shout from Marie pulled his attention away. He turned to where she had been managing a stove and dispensing hot water for washing, shaving, and coffee to the troops, and found her standing, pointing toward the road. Hudro and Koyne climbed up from a slit trench that they had been digging. A dust-covered flatbed carrying two large-caliber howitzers, and with disheveled passengers taking up every spare foot of space, had stopped to let several figures dismount. Most were in regular combat dress, carrying packs and weapons, but two stood out immediately. One was of pinkish countenance beneath streaks of dirt and a field dressing on one cheek, with a wide brow, and wearing a

bedraggled Air Force flying suit; the other was big and wide although youthful in looks—and blue-skinned. It was Nyarl and Davis. They both managed tired grins as they traipsed across the rocky shoulder of the road to where the regiment's vehicles were clustered. Gerofsky appeared as the others went forward to greet them.

"We'd given you up," Koyne told Davis, clapping him on the back. "What happened to the truck? They've been trying to raise you on radio."

Hudro clasped both Nyarl's hands and said something in Hyadean that sounded very emotional and happy. Cade took the camera and shoulder bag of ancillary equipment, which Nyarl still had with him.

"A stick of bombs went through us while we were taking cover," Davis said. "The truck was totaled, and some of the guys didn't make it. We thought we might end up walking all the way, but that transporter picked us up."

The news was not all happy, however. Powell was among those who hadn't made it. Something like that had been expected eventually, of course. Nevertheless, it dulled what spirit they had been managing to summon back together that morning.

Shortly afterward, Gerofsky revealed what perhaps was the reason for the absence of hostile activity all morning. The Hyadean conveyor had unrolled around and behind them. Denver to the north and Albuquerque to the south were already occupied. A blocking force had landed in the pass this side of Grand Junction. There was no way open to the west.

Presumably, the lull was an invitation to give it up in the face of a hopeless situation. But no surrender appeared to be forthcoming. Jeye—assuming orders were still coming from Sacramento—was sticking to his word. The brigade that the regiment belonged to received orders to move on deeper into the mountains to a position in what was evidently being prepared as a last stronghold for the Federation forces fleeing westward along the central front. Cade and the others stayed with them. What else was there to do?

That night, they found themselves preparing to bed down with one of the sections dug in on a forward slope ahead of brigade headquarters. The air was calm, bringing the creaking of tanks moving among the light of arc lamps in the darkness below. Still, the respite was continuing. It was generally interpreted as a last lull before the storm that would unleash with the morning: a final chance to reconsider. Apparently, there had been heavy air attacks in California, but once again, it proved impossible to get a communications link to the group in Los Angeles to find out more.

It was going to be a chilly night, spent in holes scraped in the ground, huddling in blankets or whatever else could be improvised. Cade and Marie sat sharing a mess tin of soup in the pit that they occupied with Nyarl, separated by a parapet from Hudro, Koyne, and Davis. Gerofsky was away, conferring with the brigade staff in the tents and trailers farther back below the ridge line. Soldiers were talking, brewing coffee, and sharing cigarettes in sandbagged positions dimly visible on the far side.

"I don't like it," Marie said, dunking a piece of biscuit and nibbling on it. "It feels too much like where we were in Oklahoma—before the big attack came in. Everything's going to hit in the morning. I can feel it."

Cade stared at the rocky hillside, formless in the starlight, while he searched for an encouraging response. There wasn't one. "Well, if you're right, at least we go out together," he offered finally. "We made it in time to do that."

Nyarl shook his head. "Fighting to the end when there is no hope. Again this is part of the Terran mystery. Hyadeans would never understand it."

"So how would it affect them on Chryse . . . if they knew?" Marie asked.

"It's part of the mystery," Nyarl said again. "Or is it mystique? They wouldn't let you do it."

"Then maybe Jeye's doing the right thing without realizing it," Marie said. She turned her head toward Cade. "I thought I was a born fighter. You know—one of those deluded self-images that you carry around in your head. And in the games I got mixed up in these last five years. Because that's what they were, games. . . . But all this in the last few days—the real thing. I never knew the insanity of it. Whatever problem this is supposed to solve, it could have been solved for a fraction of what it all costs. And it doesn't even solve anything. It only makes it worse for next time."

"I was thinking the same earlier," Cade said. He shifted to ease a cramped foot. "I used to think that what made people worth getting to know was who they networked with, what favors they could do—what you could get out of them. Now I've seen the qualities that make people truly valuable. And often it's in the same people . . . like Clara, maybe, or George, or Anita, Neville Baxter . . . even Dee."

"Dee was always okay."

"Yeah, well. . . . But you know what I'm saying. Why does it have to take something like this to bring that side of people out? Why couldn't they be what they're capable of from the beginning?"

"I hope they're okay back there," Marie mused. "Dee and Vrel, Luke, Henry . . . all of them."

"It's the same with us too," Cade went on. "Don't you get the feeling it's a bit late to find out now who you really are? Especially since it seems there's not going to be a lot we'll be able to do with the knowledge."

Marie could only shrug. "Maybe better late than never, all the same."

"Unless those things that Krossig and Michael Blair used to get excited about turn out to be close after all," Nyarl suggested.

"What things?" Cade asked.

"Personalities in this reality being incarnations of souls to help them develop. The things Hudro wants to discover. As do many Hyadeans."

"If it's true, then I must be working some enormous piece of karma off the debit side," Cade said resignedly.

"If?" Nyarl repeated. "Now you're sounding as if you don't believe it yourself."

Cade looked at him, the dark-hued face all but invisible against the jacket hood pulled around in the darkness. "It was a legend that you wanted to hear, and we played at being. It was how I got rich, and my friends got rich."

"You're making you and them sound responsible," Nyarl objected. "But you just used the situation that you found. You didn't create it. It resulted from the worst elements of both our worlds working in collusion."

"That's my point," Cade said. "If Earth had really been the legend that you thought, none if this could have happened. The best elements of both worlds would have . . ." He sighed and shook his head. "I don't know what." The strange thing was, he found himself almost believing that it could have been different. But even those who he'd thought might bring about something better had ended up going for the throat when they thought everything was in their favor. He leaned back and looked up at the stars. "Maybe one day it will all be told differently as stories change," he said to the others. "Another legend of an Earth that never happened."

CHAPTER FIFTY-SEVEN

Cade awoke chilled and stiff. He freed his arms from the blanket and stretched sluggishly. Marie was gone; Nyarl, still asleep, was wrapped in blankets and a greatcoat. He stood up, brushing frost from the predawn cold of the mountains off his jacket and beating his arms across his chest, while his breath steamed in white clouds. A thin film clung to the tops of the sandbagged parapets and the boulders, adding extra bleakness to the scene of daybreak creeping into the landscape like the light being slowly turned up on a stage setting. He saw Marie now, with Hudro, Koyne, and some soldiers, huddled around a stove under the awning covering the field kitchen a hundred yards or so back in a gully.

The scarp they were on faced east, overlooking an expanse of sand and broken rock that lay flat for a mile or two before rising to a line of craggy uplands. They were about twenty miles behind the forward positions that they had seen being prepared yesterday, looking down over rearward missile and gun emplacements, antitank defenses, and staging areas for reserve armor. Over the ridge behind them would be the long-range artillery, antiaircraft positions, command bunkers. Cade was getting to know the pattern already.

Footsteps crunched on the gravel behind. Cade turned to find Gerofsky in a combat jacket and helmet, accompanied by a couple of troopers, coming down from the ridge, where he had gone to learn the latest at brigade HQ. The troopers went off toward their own unit. Gerofsky came to the edge of the parapet and stepped down to join Cade. He looked grim.

"Forget any ideas of a breakout west from the Rockies. They've as good as closed the ring. This is the last act, right here. Or something has to change pretty drastically somewhere."

"Nothing from Sacramento?" Cade asked.

Gerofsky shook his head. "Not much from the West Coast at all. I'm not sure what it's supposed to mean. Orders are to hold out with maximum effort. I don't know what with, though. Our air support is practically nonexistent. They still have satellite cover. We're like ducks in a barrel."

Cade didn't reply. Nyarl, stirred by the talking, sat up, rubbed his eyes, mumbled something incomprehensible, and began removing frosty wrappings from his equipment. Behind him, Marie was coming across from the kitchen, carrying a metal lid as a tray for steaming coffee mugs. Slowly, the scene around them was coming to life. Troops began appearing out of the ground to congregate around spots dispensing heat and breakfast. Some tanks away to the right were moving out from their parking area. A jeep scuttled by busily below, raising a train of dust. But beneath the appearances of calm ran an undercurrent of tension everywhere, waiting for the first shocks and rolls of thunder that would signal the opening assault at the front. Or would it begin as a sudden saturation from the sky by some unknown form of destruction?

Marie arrived and passed the coffees around, setting one down by Nyarl. Davis joined them from the far side of the dividing parapet. Gerofsky repeated for their benefit what little news there was.

"Nothing on what's happening in China?" Davis inquired.

"I'm not even sure there still is a China," Gerofsky said.

Davis watched Nyarl laying out components and checking them into pockets in his various carrying cases. "What's the point, Nyarl?" he asked. "Whatever you get, who's ever going to see it? LA might not be there."

"I'll see it through to the end. It's what Luodine would have wished." Nyarl thought, then added, "Terran sentiment. I thought you'd understand."

The sound of jets flying low came from far away to the left. Heads turned, but the aircraft were out of sight. A lot of birds were aloft and making agitated noises, disturbed by all the unfamiliar activity. A loud hailer somewhere back over the hill was reciting something in a monotone unintelligible at the distance. As Cade watched, a field radar sited near the top of the rise to command the forward approaches tilted to maximum elevation, probing directly above.

Marie moved closer to Cade as he stood, warming his hands around the mug. "You finally look the part—a soldier," she told him. "There was a time when I'd never have believed it."

Cade glanced at the automatic rifle he'd been given, standing propped against the parapet next to where he had slept. Marie and Gerofsky had shown him what the various knobs and catches were for, but he had never gotten around to actually firing it. Some soldier!

He gazed back out over the terrain. "You know, now and again you find yourself wondering how it will be in the end . . . when it's checkout time. You hope that when it happens it won't be too drawn-out and messy. I never imagined anything like this: stuck on some mountainside in Colorado, in a place I've never heard of." He shrugged. "You'd have thought that after the life I've lived, I could have managed something with a bit more style, wouldn't you? You know, lots of friends at the funeral, big speeches. . . ."

"I thought all that really mattered was that we were together," Marie reminded him.

He turned, and looked at her, checking himself. Then he put an arm around her and drew her close. "Yes. A pity we won't be able to do a hell of a lot with it. . . . But I'm glad it worked out in the end. Do you always do things in such roundabout ways?"

"Why just me? You got here via China too, as I recall."

Cade pulled a face, couldn't argue, nodded, and conceded the point. "And Australia," he said, as if that somehow made a difference. He stared moodily for a while, content with the feel of Marie pressing against him. "It was a shame about Mike Blair. He shouldn't have put off going over there to work with Krossig. They were getting into such great ideas on what life ought to be about trying to understand. . . ." Cade motioned briefly with the hand holding the coffee mug, indicating nothing in particular. "Instead of whatever it is we're blowing each other up over. As if any of it mattered . . ."

Cade's voice trailed off as he registered alarmed voices around them. Faces were turning skyward. He looked up, and at the same instant felt Marie tense. An object that looked like a blunt, black arrowhead had appeared overhead, silhouetted against the brightening sky. It appeared about the size of a dime held at arm's length, hanging practically stationary but getting perceptibly larger—evidently descending. A second became visible behind and to the side, smaller but also enlarging. Then a third. More . . . They were unlike anything that had ever emerged from assembly shops on Earth. Cade felt his mouth turning dry, a knot tightening in his stomach as the realization came that the rest of his life might be measured in minutes or less.

Klaxons and alarm sirens were sounding in all directions. Across the slopes below, figures scattered to take cover in foxholes and trenches. In the gun pits and antiaircraft emplacements, barrels and missile racks were swinging to near vertical. Nyarl was already unslinging his camera, resolved to see it through to the last, whatever the futility. "Looks like they've decided to save Washington's ground forces the trouble," Davis commented dryly. Beside him, Gerofsky just stood staring upward incredulously, at a loss for coherent words.

Still the shapes were enlarging, now taking on a sinister aspect, with rows of bulges, nacelles, studs and rodlike protuberances becoming discernible along the dull black of their undersides. As finer levels of detail continued to resolve themselves, awareness came over Cade slowly that these structures were *huge*. He had thought of them as aircraft and unconsciously assigned them a comparable scale. But although just covered by the palm of his hand now, they were still high up. "Large warship" might have been a better comparison; or even small town. A dull pulsing, hinting of immense power being contained and ready to unleash, throbbed in his ears and seemed to permeate his body through his legs from the ground, as if the entire basin to the far wall of mountains were resonating. A second formation was becoming visible above and beyond the first, diamond-shaped this time.

A series of *whoosh*es sounded from somewhere along the ridge to the left. Cade jerked his head away to see a salvo of missiles streaking upward from some hidden battery. Then more came from immediately behind. They were antimissile types, with fearsome acceleration; even so, seconds passed by with the flaming tails dwindling as they climbed toward the shapes looming above, telling of the distance that still intervened. The first salvo exploded in a string of crimson bursts like a fireworks display. Cade watched, looking for some sign of damage inflicted; then he realized that they had never gotten close but been destroyed by some kind of shield or defensive beam. The second salvo fared no better, nor the others that followed. The shapes were impregnable: self-contained battle units built for combat of a different kind, on a scale that was incomprehensible.

A flight of aircraft appeared from the rear. Nyarl turned to catch them releasing their missiles and breaking away, and then followed the missiles toward their targets until they exploded harmlessly like the rest. He moved his face away from the eyepiece of the camera to look up at the craft directly for a few seconds. He seemed puzzled. Then he peered through the sighting lens again. Finally, he looked away toward Hudro, still at the field kitchen, and shouted something in Hyadean. Cade saw then that Hudro had been looking up with the same bemused

expression. Nyarl called again. Hudro looked toward
him, seeming to hear for the first time, and called
something back. There was a brief exchange in
Hyadean. Nyarl saw Cade looking at him. "The
markings on those craft. They're not of any Chrysean
military units, Roland. They're Querl!"

Only then did what should have been obvious
become clear: The ships weren't engaging in any acts
that were hostile. Everything they had done was
defensive. Gerofsky was the first to snap out of the
trance that had gripped all of them. Not saying
anything, as if unwilling to come to any premature
conclusion as to what it might mean, he climbed the
parapet out of the entrenchment and set off almost
at a run back up the ridge toward the brigade headquarters. Hudro and Koyne were already heading
across the slope to meet him higher up. Cade and
Marie followed Gerofsky. Davis grabbed Nyarl's carrying case as they brought up the rear.

They arrived at the brigade communications post,
sandbagggged under a camouflage net awning. Radios
were chattering, operators calling reports from consoles and battlefield displays, figures rushing excitedly among the tents and trailers. On one of the
screens, Cade saw a flotilla of daughter vessels
descending from one of the mother ships toward the
basin that they had just been overlooking. Another
screen showed the head and shoulders of a Hyadean
in a military-style tunic. Gerofsky, breathless, was with
two staff officers. He turned toward Cade and Marie
as they approached.

"Word from the front is that all Union forces are
standing down! Washington has called a truce!" he
told them. The look in his eyes was still disbeliev-
ing. "The government on Chryse has collapsed. Their
military here have disengaged. It's over!"

CHAPTER FIFTY-EIGHT

A Querl landing craft, looking something like the personal flyers but larger and sleeker, brought a deputation of officers from the command ship down to brigade headquarters after preliminary landings had ascertained its location. Since Querl were not accustomed to dealing with Terrans and had little experience of English, Nyarl acted as interpreter. It turned out that the news clips sent by the brigade's communications unit to Los Angeles the previous evening had made it through Cairns and been received by the Querl relays. Querl intelligence located the military unit that the two Hyadeans shown in the recordings—Nyarl and Hudro—said they were attached to, and the Querl leaders directed the initial landing to the area where it was operating.

There was something more dynamic about the Querl compared to what Cade had come to accept as typical of Hyadeans. Their manner was more expressive; they walked with more bounce; their uniforms had more style. These were the bad guys? It dawned on him how much he and probably just about all Terrans had been influenced by the Chrysean propaganda image—practically as much as any unquestioning, xenophobic Chrysean. The commanding general of the Federation forces in the central area was being rushed by helicopter from divisional headquarters some miles to the rear. In the meantime, Nyarl summarized events to Cade and the others, along with a mix of weary, red-eyed staff officers, many still struggling to grasp that a last-minute reprieve had been granted them. Behind them, the Querl war craft hung like geometrically fashioned islands in the sky, while life began showing itself again across the hills and the plain below as news spread that the war was over.

"After the AANS attacks on Chrysean craft in orbit, the Chryseans began launching punitive strikes against China and elsewhere. It was a panic, overreaction, and ill-judged in the light of the other things that had been going on back at Chryse." Nyarl paused to check something in Hyadean with a couple of the Querl officers. "We don't have all the details yet, since these people have been here in your Solar System for the last week, but unrest has been sweeping over Chryse since the Querl started broadcasting what has been taking place on Earth." He looked across to Cade and the rest of the group to address them specifically. His voice caught. "She did it! It worked the way Luodine planned—the way we carried on. It bypassed the controls that had always operated in the past. The Chrysean population learned the truth." Nyarl indicated the Querl deputation. "Until just now, even these people didn't know where the reports were originating from. But they caused an upheaval on

Chryse that was unprecedented. The whole Chrysean system has fallen. The people are calling for the Querl to take over. Their ships are moving in there now, even while I'm speaking. A standoff between Querl and Chrysean military forces has been going on around Earth, the Moon, and as far out as the orbit of Mars, for several days now. But without political legitimization from Chryse, the Chrysean military here has ceased operations," Nyarl finished with a helpless gesture that said he was having trouble enough absorbing so much in so little time, too. "And the same seems to be happening here. Deprived of its Chrysean backing, the Globalist Coalition is in disarray everywhere. Washington is on stand-down, waiting for terms from Sacramento. Europe is in chaos. Nobody has any idea where it might all lead."

And for the time being—probably for a while to come after that too—that was about as much as could be said. The general arrived shortly afterward and went into conference with the Querl deputation. All around, as the morning wore on, the winding down and disbanding commenced of the elaborate orchestration of men and machines that had come together to make a last stand. The group found transport to an air supply base in the rear, where Koyne and Davis bade their farewells and departed to report to Air Force administration. Two hours later, Cade and his remaining companions boarded an airlift flight bound for the Los Angeles area. On the way, they restored contact with the Catacombs via one of the temporary satellite links that the Querl were setting up. Yassem, Vrel, Dee, Luke, and Di Milestro had stories of their own to tell, but they were all fine. Los Angeles was going to need some rebuilding in places. But perhaps that wasn't such a bad thing, either.

CHAPTER FIFTY-NINE

Cars by the thousands, along with trucks, buses, and planes were pouring back into Washington, D.C., reversing the exodus that had cleared the city of eighty percent of its population. Compared to what had gone on in other places, however, damage in the east was light. Hyadean orbital weapons had dealt effectively with the long-range missiles lobbed from submarines and the easternmost parts of Asia, while conventional interceptors and antiaircraft ground systems had stopped most of the bombers and cruise missiles on their way from Federation territory or from Canada. The ones that got through had not brought the all-out nuclear annihilation of cities that the panic had been about. Now, Ellis's administration had been toppled by rebellious military chiefs, following the Chrysean pull-out, and what might happen next was anybody's guess. One sure thing was that the shakeup would be worldwide.

The news going around the Hill didn't exactly speak of loyal camaraderie and trusty friends staying true to the end. With protectors and patrons tumbling by the hour, and the power holders of yesterday rushing to denounce each other while displaying their own clean hands, distinct risks could attend knowing too much about those with dangerous rivals. Acting as Toddrel's dirty-work specialist had paid off and brought its benefits; but that same history also meant that Toddrel had much on Drisson that could be bargained or turned around to sanitize his own image. In short, it was time to claim on the insurance.

Drisson pushed a package wrapped in a plastic bag across the table to Laura as they sat in a secluded corner of a cocktail lounge called the Fairway, on the west side of the city toward Georgetown. "Untraceable. All identifying marks removed," he murmured. He had established long ago that she could use a gun. Making sure of detail was another part of his business. Toddrel was in town, staying at a hotel called the Grantham that he often used, a couple of blocks off Rhode Island Avenue.

Laura took the package and put it in her purse on the chair beside her, zipping the top closed. "You're really sure you want to trust an amateur with this?" She made it sound mildly playful, as if complimenting his own professionalism.

Drisson smiled. "We both know it has to be this way. You're sure you have the routine? You call him to say you're in town and need to talk to him. Turn on the charm once you're over there. Then do the job after you've serviced him. Throw a few things around the room, fingernail scratches on the body. . . . Use your creativity. So when they find him, it's a simple, open-shut case of Casper getting some relaxation after all the tension, ending up in a fight, and things went too far. Anonymous hooker. No political implications. Clean."

Laura swirled her drink while she considered, then took a sip. "Isn't it being a bit overfinicky?" she queried. "From what I hear, political cleanups are likely to be the fashion around here. Is anybody going to be caring about one more, one less?"

"Why risk anything needlessly?" Drisson watched as she thought it through, still looking for the flaws, her gaze darting now across the items on the table, then to the far side of the room. His hand gripped her wrist reassuringly. "Just this one thing, and we'll be in the clear," he told her. "Then we break out the stash, make a big transfer to Australia, south of France, Argentina—wherever you want. A year or two of yachts, classy people, sunshine, and beaches while the heat here dies down."

Laura stared for several seconds at the almost-emptied glass of bourbon in front of him, then raised her eyes to meet his. For a moment, Drisson thought she was about to decline or start debating the issue. But she nodded finally and said, simply, "Okay."

Drisson smiled, relieved. "I knew you had it in you. Call me immediately to confirm, before you leave. That's important. I need the timing right to make sure Ibsan isn't around when you leave. Afterward, I'll meet you back here at say . . . eleven, unless we agree something different. Any more questions?" Laura shook her head. Drisson raised his glass, emptied it, and brushed his mustache with a knuckle. "Okay. Then we probably shouldn't walk out together. I'll see you here later." He rose and squeezed her shoulder. "Don't let me down, eh, baby?"

Actually, Drisson had arranged a quiet meeting between Ibsan and a confidential informant from the Pentagon concerning private matters that evening, so

Ibsan wouldn't be anywhere around. But the timing was still important. Drisson had other plans.

"No, no! I don't want to talk to them. Just say you couldn't find me. . . . I *said* I'd take care of it." In his room at the Grantham, Toddrel cut off the phone. Everything was closing in. The Hyadeans were looking for blood over what had gone wrong in South America. Police detectives were already rounding up victims for the war crimes show-trial circus that would be staged eventually to allay the public's already emerging thirst for revenge and justice. His name would surely be on a dozen lists. He wiped his brow. The clean shirt he had put on after getting back was already sodden. Had to control his nerves. He reached for the printout he had taken of the progress being made in restoring travel services. As he did so, his eye caught the shot being presented on the room's view screen of Cade, Cade's former wife, and the two Hyadeans talking to a news reporter on their arrival in California. *Cade!* . . . Toddrel's fingers crumpled the paper involuntarily. Ever since their interference in Chattanooga, vanishing and subsequent reappearance in South America, and then the screening of that disastrous TV documentary, it seemed they had been at the center of everything connected with the reversal of Toddrel's fortunes. Arcadia, the agent in California, was supposed to settle the score; only, Arcadia turned out to be the one who was blown up instead. Toddrel still hadn't heard a satisfactory explanation of how that could have happened. Cade hadn't even been there, in any case. So Cade had to be dead—killed in South America somewhere, Toddrel had been told—until intelligence reported him turning up again, alive and well in Beijing with the Hyadean. And finally bringing the whole house down, Cade and his woman were there in the broadcasts coming back from Chryse itself!—which had resulted in a whole planet erupting in turmoil there and the final ruin of everything here. Now all Toddrel had left was his neck, and that was on the line.

The phone beeped again before his anger boiled over. Even though it was his private channel tone, he kept it on audio. "Yes?"

"Casper, it's Laura. I was in town. With everything that's going on I thought you might be here."

Toddrel keyed the screen on to reveal Laura. "I . . . I am rather busy just now." He didn't sound especially pleased.

"Staying low? I hear it's a witch hunt out there. The long knives are coming out everywhere."

"That's friends for you. It's what you get to expect."

"Can I come over there?"

"I'm hardly in a mood for romantic distractions right now."

"Nothing like that. I'm scared, Casper. I need to talk to you. A lot's going on that I don't understand." Her gaze from the screen was insistent.

Toddrel gazed at her sourly, seemed about to refuse, then thought better of it. "Very well," he said curtly. "I'll order dinner in the room at, say, eight. We can talk then. Would that suit you?"

"That would suit fine. I'll be there shortly just. Which room is it? The desk wouldn't tell me."

"Six fifty-one. I'll tell them to give you a key."

Laura called Drisson immediately afterward. "It's arranged," she said. "He's having dinner in the room. I'll be arriving there at seven."

"Don't forget to call me as soon as it's done," Drisson said.

She entered the main door of the Grantham Hotel shortly before seven, walked to the desk, and collected a magnetically coded key to room 651. Then she paused, looking in her purse, until there was a knot of people waiting at the elevators before crossing the lobby to join them. As she did so, she had the strange, prickly sensation of being certain that unseen eyes were watching her. A car arrived. She got in with several others, made sure that the sixth floor button was pressed, but went all the way up to the penthouse bar and found a booth far from the door, where she ordered a coffee. She stayed there almost an hour. Ten minutes before eight, she took the elevator back down to the mezzanine terrace, from where she was able to observe the lobby floor below from behind a screen of ornamental ferns and a rubber-tree plant. She had stopped by earlier, after leaving the Fairway lounge, to check over the hotel layout. Laura believed in getting the details right too.

She called Drisson's number from there, making her voice shaky and a little breathless. "Okay . . . it's done. I'm on my way out."

Drisson appeared from a corner of the lobby below, talking into his phone. "No, don't. We've got an unexpected problem. Ibsan is around in the building. Stay where you are. I'm coming there to get you out a safe way."

"How long will you be?"

"On my way now. Just a couple of minutes."

Laura watched him cross to the elevators and push the call button. One of the sets of doors opened. He disappeared inside. She nodded faintly to herself. It was the way she had guessed. She raised the phone again and called Toddrel's private number. He answered almost at once. "I'm on my way up now," she told him. "There was a crowd around the desk.

I'll get the key later." Unzipping the top of her purse, she made her way back across the terrace to the mezzanine-level elevator doors and pressed the "up" button.

Drisson would arrive at the room any moment now. He would knock, thinking Laura was there, waiting. Toddrel would open the door, expecting Laura; or even if he checked through the spyglass first, seeing it was Drisson, he would let him in. Finding Toddrel alone and unharmed, Drisson, being Drisson, would immediately conclude a double cross and have seconds to decide his move. Laura thought she knew what the outcome would be.

She came out of the elevator and followed the corridor to 651, holding the key in one gloved hand, the other resting lightly inside the top of her purse. She looked quickly left, then right. The corridor was empty. Producing the gun, she slid the key softly into the slot until she heard the lock disengage, then pushed the door open and stepped quickly inside. Toddrel's body was crumpled on the floor, crimson spreading across his shirt and oozing onto the carpet. Drisson was between it and the door, already turning at the sound of its opening, the gun still in his hand. Laura shot him before his mouth had framed the first word. Then she eased the door shut and stood motionless with her back pressed against it, feeling her chest pounding while she listened for any reaction to the shot. Everything outside seemed quiet. She looked apprehensively at Drisson, dreading that he might make some sound or move, and if so, wondering if she would be able to bring herself to finish the thing. But he remained inert. Laura could detect no sign of breathing. She forced herself to be calm.

The line about making it look like a hooker had

been for Laura's benefit. She was supposed to have been next. Drisson's real intent had been to set up a scene that would look like a fatal quarrel between Toddrel and his high-class mistress. Being the only other person who would have known about Drisson's insurance to protect himself hadn't seemed like the surest way of getting to see much sunshine or many beaches.

Laura walked past Drisson to where Toddrel was lying, stooped to press his hand around the gun that she had used, and then tossed it on the floor in the middle of the room. Then she dug deeper into her purse, took out a plastic bag stuffed with napkins, and from them carefully extracted the glass Drisson had been drinking from in the Fairway lounge earlier. She looked around, and after a moment set it on the countertop above the room's mini refrigerator, along with a half bottle of bourbon which she had partly emptied. She had no idea, really, what the police would make of it; but she had every confidence in their ability to come up with something ingenious and satisfying.

The final thing that caught her eye as she checked over the room was a picture frozen on the viewscreen of two people facing the camera in front of a background of planes releasing missiles at targets on what looked like the outskirts of a city. It was the man called Cade, from California, who seemed to have been involved wherever trouble broke out during the past few weeks. The woman with him was his former wife, who had been with the CounterAction terrorists. Casper had developed some kind of an obsession about them.

As Laura walked away along the corridor, she reflected that curiously it was those same two who, in a way, had been instrumental in bringing about the events that had just transpired in Room 651. Ever since the first documentary they had appeared in, which a few renegade Hyadeans made in South America, Laura had found herself seized by a growing feeling of revulsion at the pictures of burning villages, maimed children, pain, suffering, terror on the faces of defenseless people—the real price that had been paid to make possible the life she had enjoyed. Now, somehow, she felt cleansed of it, as if, to some degree at least, she had atoned.

Had Toddrel had some kind of premonition that they would be a cause of this? she wondered as she waited for the elevator. She had never really had much time for things like that. By some accounts that she'd read, Hyadeans found such possibilities intriguing. And they seemed pretty smart. Maybe it would be something to look into.

A feeling of relief enveloped her as she came out into the night air without incident. Getting away from Washington and the East Coast in general for a while seemed like a wise move in any case, she decided. As she walked away along the street, the thought occurred to her that maybe the kind of work she heard was going on in California could use some help: putting the U.S.A. back together again along the lines that had been intended—or maybe along new lines that were even better; learning to work with the Hyadeans in ways that would benefit everybody; discovering the other sides to life there were besides just making money. Maybe she would even get a chance there to meet this mysterious Mr. Cade and his ex—Marie, was it?—in person there. Now *that* sounded interesting and different.

She came to an intersection, managed to stop one of the few cabs that were back on the streets, and gave the address of the hotel across town that Drisson had checked her into.

Something challenging, creative, and useful to people. A way, maybe, to make up to some degree for a life that so far hadn't had a lot going for it that she felt particularly good about or proud of. Yes, Laura decided as she settled herself back in the rear seat of the cab. That was the kind of change she wanted.

EPILOGUE

Cade had seen pictures of the Hyadean launch complex at Xuchimbo in western Brazil, which gave him a general idea of what to expect. But none of them had quite prepared him for the scale of the engineering—even "grandeur" would not have been an inappropriate word, despite the characteristically dull and utilitarian flavor of all things Hyadean. The optimists and visionaries on both worlds were saying that would all change very quickly now in the years ahead.

He stared out at it from a medium-size Hyadean passenger transport completing its flight from Denver. The pointed gray, white, and silver spires of the landers stood amid immense service gantries towering above the pad and associated constructions like a metallic castle from some giants' fairyland dominating the surrounding landscape of forested hills and steep-sided valleys. On the near side, several miles from the launch complex, was the landing area for conventional craft toward which they were descending, attended by a conglomeration of base facilities, roadways, bridges, pipe systems, and conveyor lines. One of the Querl officers in the party picked out a tall shape of pale gray, flaring at the tail into cruciform deltas set between a booster cluster. Cade studied it, intrigued. That was the ferry that would carry them up tomorrow morning to join the orbiting Querl mother ship due to depart for Chryse.

Marie was with Cade, looking for once the part of a presentable, urbane Western woman instead of a desperado, in a cream jacket-skirt set with chocolate blouse and trim. Vrel was there too, insistent on being their self-appointed tour guide and general attendant on Chryse. And Dee was with Vrel too, of course. And finally, making up their group, was Nyarl, going home by popular demand to meet millions for whom his face had become a phenomenon on display screens, and receive a public honor decreed by the provisional administration that the Querl had installed to take stock of the Chrysean condition.

A month had gone by since the people of Earth— bewildered and frightened; resolute and defiant— had emerged from foxholes, come out onto streets, listened to announcements in refugee centers, turned on radios and TV screens, to learn that the war which yesterday had seemed about to explode into ever greater levels of ferocity and consume the whole planet, was over. It didn't mean that the world's problems or the future of Terran-Hyadean dealings was solved, or that anyone had clear ideas as yet of how to solve them. Nobody knew what form the reconstruction of what had been the United States was to assume, based on what formulation

Constitution. It was not even agreed where the capital would be, which was why negotiations were taking place in Denver: as effectively neutral as anywhere, and the nearest principal city to the Querl's first landing. But what it did signify was something akin to a collective version of the shaking up experienced after an automobile accident that could have killed everyone. If all the pain, grief, and loss of those three weeks of mass insanity—and it had been substantial—had been for anything, it was the imperative now acknowledged across both worlds that the fundamental values that life should be seeking were in drastic need of reexamination. And the people who needed to make the judgment were not the ones who so far had been allowed to be in charge.

Representatives from various Terran nations, organizations, institutions, other interests, had been invited to Chryse to begin a joint exploring of which way to go next. The other passengers on the flight from Denver were some of them. More had arrived the day before. And to Cade and Marie's amazement, they had been invited too. Nyarl, it seemed, wasn't the only one to have become an instant celebrity among the Chrysean worlds. The Terran couple who had appeared with him and symbolized their world's defiance and determination to fight through in the face of impossible odds, facing Hyadean war engines, speaking against backgrounds of burning cities, were equally famous. The Chryseans wanted to meet them too.

The transport landed among rows of cavernous cargo-carrying hulls looking vaguely like monstrous, flattened guppy fish; single-stage space-planes that could make orbit, maneuver for hours, and return; assorted special-purpose craft whose nature could only be guessed. From ground level, the peculiar alien structures rising in the background were as imposing as the launch complex had appeared from the air. Cade had the feeling of practically being on a small piece of Chryse already. The transport's cabin section detached from the airframe as a unit and slid onto a conveyor rail alongside. Moments later, it was being carried toward an opening into the terminal complex.

Hudro and Yassem were installed in Cade's place at Newport Beach, which was where Vrel would be returning. The area had escaped damage, although the house itself had shown the wear and tear of being used as a shelter for displaced children from the war areas by the time Cade came back to it. Cade wasn't quite sure what he wanted to do with the house. It struck him as gaudy and extravagant now, somehow. Luke had suggested making it an open house for visiting Hyadeans. Whatever the outcome, Cade couldn't see the kind of life being resurrected that he had come to know over the years. It wasn't so much that the rewards seemed shallow now in comparison to the cost—which was true enough—so much as life having so much more to offer that was too intriguing to ignore. Trying to understand some of the questions that Krossig and Blair had raised, for example; or seeing people in terms of more than just gains to be assessed and realized. And in any case, the prospects, contacts, hangers-on, around whom that life had revolved and depended weren't going to be around anymore—at least, not in those roles. They all seemed to have changed too in some fundamental ways, just as he had.

As, indeed, had the world. For what else did all the fumbling and reexamination to find a new direction mean than the dawning, finally, of a new perception that sought more than could be captured by Terran monetarist bookkeeping or the Hyadean calculus of efficiency as the sole measure of the worth of a life or the purpose of existence? Maybe now, together, the two races could build the legend the Hyadeans had created of what Earth could have been. If so, then perhaps the war had not been in vain.

The cabin came to a halt beside a platform in a roomy concourse of service desks and seating areas laid out beneath bright panel lights set amid a typically functional configuration of tie beams and roof supports. The arrivals disembarked to a throng of Hyadean officials and agents waiting to receive them. The Hyadean who had accompanied Cade and his companions from Denver conducted them to the two Hyadeans, a male and a female, who had been assigned to look after them. Waiting with them was a familiar purple-and-crimson-haired figure, dressed glaringly in an embroidered Bolivian shawl, straw hat with a band of wildy colored design, and bright green gaucho pants. It was Tevlak, going back on the same ship to spread Terran art on Chryse.

"So how things have changed since we were together," he said, shaking hands vigorously with Vrel, Cade, and Marie. "Then, the security people invaded us. Now they no longer exist." He put a hand on Nyarl's shoulder. "So sorry about Luodine. She should have been here today to see this."

"It was still as much her doing as anyone's," Nyarl told him. The guide from Denver performed the remaining introductions.

"You know, this routine at airports is getting to be kind of old," Cade said to Marie as they began walking toward a ramp leading though to another space.

"I guess we're just going to have to get used to being famous for a while," Marie replied.

"Without the gun, I could get used to it," Cade said. He snorted. "I never even got to shoot it. I told you I was never cut out for that kind of stuff."

"So we complement each other. That's supposed to be a good thing."

Dee was looking around and up at the utilitarian drabness of what passed for decor, and raw engineering of the architecture. "Is it all going to be like this?" she asked Vrel. "If they're catching on to our ways there, there has to be a whole load of openings for interior designers."

"I think there are going to be some big changes very soon," Vrel said. "We can't import the Andes valleys or the Amazon forest. So what we lack naturally, we'll make up with through ingenuity."

"Ten years from now, Terran tourists will be flocking to sample the exotica of Chryse," Tevlak assured them.

"That soon, eh?" Dee sounded skeptical.

"It isn't going to be just enthusiasts like me—just one person on his own," Tevlak said. "Bringing Earth to Chryse will involve everybody. Lots to do for lots of people."

Cade glanced at them and thought for a few seconds. "You reckon so, eh? I think I know a few people who could be a big help. Maybe we could sound out a few leads for them as part of the agenda while we're there."

Marie nudged him pointedly. "I thought we said that all that's over. You were going to find a new meaning in life."

"But hey, people still need to talk to each other. A lot of them are still going to be too busy to know all the options. . . . And besides, I *like* meeting people."

"What happened to the celebrity?"

"Oh, by next month they'll have found another one to put on the screens everywhere. That's the way it works. But with real friends you don't get forgotten." His voice warmed to the thought as a lot of aspects he really hadn't considered before started clicking into place. "In fact, it could even be a lot *better* now, considering what we know. Take those people in Australia that I told you about, for instance. They're already doing it right, but only in a small way that suits their own needs. You know what scientists are like. Now if a few more of the right people on Chryse knew more about that . . ."

They came out into a glass annex with a walkway leading down to an outside door. Through the wall they could see the landing area with its assembly of Hyadean aircraft, and across a stretch of terrain beyond, the distant silhouettes and towering shapes of the launch complex. Cade stopped to stare again at the Querl vessel that would ferry them up to the mother ship tomorrow. Even after all that had happened, he still found it unreal to think that in the morning they would be leaving Earth itself, and in a matter of days be at a different star system. What changes the rest of his life might have in store beyond that, he was unable to imagine. But he would make certain that it was all for worthwhile things. He thought of people like Rocco and Miguel and the things he had learned from them; Mike Blair and Bob Powell, who wouldn't be seeing Chryse, ever; Wyvex and Luodine, who wouldn't be going back there. All so that something better might come out of it. He resolved to himself that he wouldn't let them down.

He felt a tug at his sleeve. It was Marie. "Come on. We'll be there soon enough." The rest of the party were disappearing through the door at the bottom of the walkway.

Cade grinned and took her arm. They followed down after the others, through a ramp to a Hyadean ground vehicle that would take them to the accommodation arranged for the night.